FIVE NOVELS

Ronald Firbank
(*from a drawing by Augustus John*)

FIVE NOVELS

RONALD FIRBANK

THE FLOWER BENEATH THE FOOT

PRANCING NIGGER

VALMOUTH

THE ARTIFICIAL PRINCESS

CONCERNING THE ECCENTRICITIES
OF CARDINAL PIRELLI

With an introduction by
OSBERT SITWELL

A NEW DIRECTIONS BOOK

Manufactured in the United States of America
First published clothbound by New Directions in 1949 and as
New Directions Paperbook 518 in 1981
Published simultaneously in Canada by Penguian Books Canada Ltd.
New Directions books are printed on acid-free paper
Library of Congress Cataloging in Publication Data

Firbank, Arthur Annesley Ronald, 1886-1926

    Five novels. With an introd. by Osbert Sitwell
    (A New Directions Book)
    CONTENTS.—Valmouth.—The flower beneath the foot.—Prancing nigger.—Concerning the eccentricitie [sic] of Cardinal Pirelli.—The artificial Princess
    PZ3.F514Fi   49-48966*
    ISBN-13: 978-0-811-20799-7 (pbk)

New Directions Books are published for James Laughlin
by New Directions Publishing Corporation
80 Eighth Avenue, New York 10011

SEVENTH PRINTING

Contents

‥◦‥━━▶▸●◂◀━━‥◦‥

INTRODUCTION

By OSBERT SITWELL

RONALD FIRBANK! The name immediately conjures up, to those who know his work, the titles of his various novels. How enticingly, how ably they beckon to one: *Vainglory, Valmouth, The Flower Beneath the Foot, Caprice, Santal,* and *Prancing Nigger!* ... But I must leave them in order to attempt to pin down upon a sheet of paper that unrivalled butterfly, their author—a butterfly, indeed, which perhaps he alone of authors could have tackled successfully—and to record a little of him before it is forgotten; a little of a shy, charming, sad, comic and altogether unusual personality.

It was, as I have related in *Great Morning,* during the early months of 1912 that I found myself in the Army attached to a cavalry regiment in Aldershot. Even when I was allowed to take refuge for a few hours in London, the black cloud of Aldershot hung ever over me like the spectre of the Judgment Day over the evil-doer. In consequence, I strove to make the most of every minute, luxuriating in the new magic of *L'Oiseau de Feu,* and other ballets and Russian operas, in the kaleidoscopic inconsequence of the Futurist Exhibition at Sackville Galleries, or in the new vista of strangeness and epochal beauty to be divined in the second Post-Impressionist Show in Grafton Street. No detail of these pleasures, or of the appearance of the other members of the audience whom I saw, escaped me, with the keen, sensitive edge of my nineteen years. And always I noticed in gallery, opera-house, or theatre—so that afterwards, when back at Aldershot, pondering over those few though vivid, now intolerably distant hours of happiness, his image would come back to me and set me wondering—the lonely, stooping, rather absurd figure of a man some ten years older than myself. With a thin frame, long head, and a large aquiline, somewhat chinless face, the cheekbones prominent and rather highly coloured, showing that he was ill, he had something of the air, if one can imagine such a combination, of a witty and decadent Red Indian. And on to this stock had been grafted, too, a touch of priest, and even of curate. I have never seen anyone who in the least resembled him in looks, except, as I have mentioned, the late Alban Berg. This stranger haunted the background of my favourite scenes for me, just as those of Greco's pictures are frequented by a gaunt and spectral saint. The eyes of my phantom, I noticed, were full of wit, though he spoke never a word, being always alone. In the intervals he would stand at the bar, occasionally gulping down a drink, as though with difficulty, nervous and ill at ease, his long hands clutching the lapels of his coat, examining the correctness of his tie, smoothing his hair, or fluttering round him apprehensively. Rather ill and unhealthy, one judged him to be; but certainly, I decided, his silence differed in kind from that of my brother officers. Often I would wonder who he might be, and why so much alone; for it was before I began myself to understand all the cruel and humiliating mysteries of the nervous system.

Times changed, and with them my regiment; now I was stationed in London. And always, whenever I went, let us say, to the first performance of Scriabin's *Prometheus*, to a concert of Fauré's music conducted by the old composer himself, or to the first night of the *Rosenkavalier*, invariably would I see at it this curious figure. But never could I discover his identity.

Then the war came, with for me two winters in

the trenches, and the diminutive spiritual paradise of books, music, and conversation into which I had recently found my way (in spite of constant drill and dull bouts of Pirbright, Purfleet, and such places) was utterly smashed and broken. Thus one did not see him for several years: for there were no longer many concerts in London at which—even if one could be present at them—to see this silent spectre. Indeed, music was under suspicion as a German agent and even someone so civilized and cultivated as Ethel Smyth, in a bout of patriotism, said to my friend Violet Gordon Woodhouse: "Don't play Bach . . . It's playing the German game."

One Sunday towards the end of the "Great" War, my sister opened a weekly review and read a short criticism by Gerald Gould of a novel called *Vainglory*. The critic owned manfully that he could make nothing of it, but fortunately quoted a short passage in which a mother describes a quarrel with her child's nurse. This passage so greatly amused Edith that she read it aloud to me, and to this day the quotation remains in my memory, almost word for word. Enchanted, we bought the book and all else that issued from the same pointed, absurd, yet indeed magic pen.

Here was to be found a new if minute world, which existed by its own pulse of time and exhibited its own standards of behaviour. Strange, fresh tides of rhythm played and lapped round its breathless shores, on which figures that, however etiolate, were sufficiently substantial for the reader never to be able to forget them, moved to their own measure and were left striking the most unexpected attitudes against the mauve and lime-green horizon. Each book, as it appeared, was a new revelation of style, and of a wit that rippled the surface of every page without ever breaking it. The virtuosity of the author was able to net any situation, however crazy or occasionally even obscene, and let it loose in the realms of a harmless reality. Just as in the autumn the silver cobwebs lightly cover the trees with a thin mist of impalpable beauty, so a similar highly stylised but intangible loveliness hung over every page, while wit ran in, round, and underneath each word. But the chief claim that is to be advanced for the author, I think, is his startling technical achievement. His dialogues are quicker and less weighty than had hitherto been designed for a novel. He altered the pace of the dialogue for the novel, and already his influence can be detected in writers of more content than himself, and indeed, in the most unlikely quarters.

This novel that we read of Firbank's, then, filled us with curiosity about its author. Who was he, where did he live? we wondered. But for a while our search went unrewarded. The first information that reached us was through an old friend of ours who had known him since boyhood. She told us that Arthur Annesley Ronald Firbank, to give him his full name, was the son of the late Sir Thomas Firbank, a noted railway magnate, and of Lady Firbank, a charming and beautiful woman, who was at this time still alive. Ronald had spent his childhood at St. Julian's, near Newport, a fine house that had formerly been part of the Welsh estates of my great-uncle, the eighth Duke of Beaufort. Both the boy's parents were conventional enough, it seemed, so that the education of their son had been planned on the ordinary school—university model. But, when travelling in Egypt as a small child, he had been struck down with sunstroke and proved in consequence to be too delicate to remain at a public school for more than one " half." (Incidentally, it was the sunstroke which later saved him from the necessity of military service, for he showed my brother the certificate of his exemption.) At the age of eighteen

or nineteen he had, however, been strong enough to
fulfil parental ambitions by going up to Cambridge.
There he became an esthete, and was particularly
interested in every society connected with the drama.
He had already published a first book* and it was at
the time understood that he was engaged on an absolute
masterpiece of a second, for, after the manner of all
intelligent and self-respecting undergraduates, he held
very strongly the opinion that a man was finished at
twenty-five. In due course he left Cambridge. Years
fled by—years spent in drifting round Spain, Italy,
North Africa and the Near East—but nothing more
was heard of a second book until, some ten years later,
suddenly, now unexpectedly even, it swung into the
literary firmament, with, for a new writer, an extraordinary mastery, within its scope, of words and technique, and with its own quaint but unbiased view of
a mad world. His long sojourns and travels abroad
he broke, she told us, by visits to London. Here he
would usually take furnished rooms in the neighbourhood of Piccadilly. Since the war he was living
in the country, in England, but she was not sure
where.

The next accurate information we obtained was
from C. R. W. Nevinson, who had met him at luncheon
with Grant Richards, Firbank's publisher. Nevinson
had once divined in him an amusing character. He
described his appearance to us, I remember, and re-

* Firbank often in later years talked to me about his work,
but never for one moment did he mention this book. He had
always given me to understand that *Vainglory* was his first
published volume. The title is *Odette d'Antrevernes* and it was
issued in 1905 by Elkin Mathews. It contains also *A Study in
Temperament*—and though the name of the author is given as
Arthur Firbank, this tale is said to be prophetic in style of the
Ronald Firbank who was to come.

† Grant Richards later republished *Odette*, but without including in it *A Study in Temperament*.

lated how after the meal Firbank, rising willowly to
his feet, observed, " Now I must go to the Bank."
" But they are all shut. You won't be able to get in!"
objected Richards; to which Firbank, displaying his
long, unmuscular arms and thin fingers, replied
anxiously, " What? Not even with my *crowbar?*"

Soon we heard that Firbank was living at Oxford,
and when, in the February after the war, I went there to
see my brother, we decided to call on him. Only now
was it that I realised who he was, this silent, nervous,
absurd figure of theatre, concert-hall and gallery, only
now did I discover the identity of him upon whom I
had so often pondered at Aldershot. And his past
phantomhood strengthened my feeling of friendliness
for him. Moreover, this hitherto soundless spectre
proved to be possessed of his own voice and accents,
sharp and clear, with very much his own interpreta-
tion of the world he haunted: though the voice was,
indeed, more practised and incisive on paper than in
conversation. For at the time we first met him in
Oxford, Ronald Firbank had, during two whole years,
spoken to no one there except his charwoman and a
guard on the train to London (upon this line he was,
as we shall notice later, a well-known figure).   He
felt himself totally out of place in a khaki-clad, war-
mad world, where there was no music, no gaiety, and
in which one could no longer travel except about the
business of death. He failed to summon up any enthusiasm whatever over the current war, protesting that
for his part he had always found the Germans " most
polite." In fact " that awful persecution " was the
phrase which it was most often his wont to use in
alluding in after years to the first World War. It had
driven him to become more than ever a recluse; it had
deprived him of all outside interests, until finally *ennui*
forced him to write the book of which he had talked
for so long. These volumes were, therefore, far more

truly than any others in the English language, the product of the war. He was in the best, the least boring, sense a " war writer."

Very seldom, then, would he go out, except occasionally, and rather unexpectedly, for a bicycle ride. Or again, he might journey up to London to call on his publisher or solicitor. . . . Firbank occupied charming rooms opposite Magdalen Tower, and we were to view there now for the first time that small collection of *objets d'art* from which he was never parted, and which we were to see so often, in so many different settings. With these few chosen belongings, he standardised each temporary home, whether it was a tent in the desert, a palace in Portugal*, a furnished flat in London, an old house in Constantinople or rooms at Oxford. In every country, they provided a sufficiently personal setting for him and spread over his dwelling-place an indefinable but luxurious atmosphere. Chief among these objects, were two drawings by Downman, a bronze bull (would it be Greek or Renaissance?), a Felicien Rops drawing, a pencil portrait of Firbank by Albert Rutherston, a little green-bronze Egyptian figure of some bearded god or pharaoh, standing rigidly above a miniature marble pedestal, all the latest novels, a number of the silliest illustrated weekly papers (which provided him with a constant source of amusement), several of his own published books and manuscripts bound in white vellum, a photograph of his mother wearing Court Dress, mounted in a large silver frame, elaborate inkpots, coloured quill-pens, a vast tortoiseshell crucifix, and cubes of those large, blue, rectangular postcards upon which it was his habit to write. To this collection he subsequently added a fine drawing by Augustus John. There was always, too, a palm-tree near him, and in some way

* One year he rented the palace at Cintra, in which William Beckford once lived; a house I have often seen.

the author's personality was able to translate it back
into a tropical and interesting plant, so that here it
lacked that withered, 1880-boarding-house air which
usually it assumes in England. On this occasion, moreover, he had provided for our reception a veritable
beacon of a fire and a profusion of orchids and peaches,
gay cornucopia that banished the dim February light
creeping in through the grey windows. It was, then,
in this Oxford version of his habitual setting, which
staged him so appropriately, that we first heard those
delightful fits of deep, hoarse, helpless and ceaseless
laughter, in such contrast to the perpetual struggle of
his speech. For so nervous was he, that the effort
required to produce his words shook his whole frame,
and his voice, when at last it issued forth, was slow,
muffled and low, but never perfectly in control. Most
of his sentences in conversation he left unfinished—so
that it was evocative, elusive, full of implication and
allusion, more than factual. It was nearly always a
little absurd, but the first ten minutes—only the first
ten minutes—were an enchantment. He suffered, I
believe, from a nervous affection of the throat which
prevented him swallowing food easily. To this misfortune was due the fact that he drank so much more
than the little he ate. On one occasion, for example,
he went to dine with a friend of ours, who in his
honour had ordered a magnificent dinner, and refused
to eat anything except one green pea.

As for his laughter, to which we have just referred,
it would often descend on him just as he was beginning
work. Usually he wrote his novels upon those huge
blue postcards, which we noticed piled up on his
desk, writing on each wide oblong side of them,
though each blank face only gave room enough for
a few—perhaps ten—words, so much space did his
large regular handwriting take up. Thus at the moment
when he would be starting to inscribe laboriously

one more word on the card in front of him, the essential ludicrousness of the situation that he was with such care elaborating would overcome him, and he would be obliged to quit work till the next day.

It was during this first acquaintance with him in a frosty and snowbound February at Oxford that Siegfried Sassoon and my brother and I gave a dinner-party in Ronald Firbank's honour. Typically, our chief guest himself declined to attend the meal—no doubt because he ate so little, more than because he was so greatly afflicted by his nerves—but he agreed to come in with the dessert, and even consented to read us a chapter from his new novel, as yet unfinished. The scene of our feast was the dining-room of the Golden Cross Inn, and the memory of that unusual evening must, I think, always hover with a peculiar glow and with a luculence all its own in the minds of those who were present. Apart from Sassoon, Gabriel Atkin, my brother and myself, they were mostly selected from under-graduate poets, and the guests numbered Wilfred Childe, V. de Sola Pinto, and Thomas Earp—now the art-critic of *The Daily Telegraph*—among them. It was their introduction—I think in every case—to Ronald and his works: but they were prepared to be enthusiastic, and by the time the guest of honour arrived, he was given a rousing reception. The evident goodwill of his audience, however, by no whit lessened his agitation, which he sought to clothe with a semblance of debonair indifference. He sauntered towards our large table by the window, now shuttered, and past the curious faces of the other smaller groups of people, as if he were going for a stroll or had come in by chance, walking slowly, and looking from side to side, but never at the human beings in the room. He swung one arm, while under the other was his manuscript, type-written, in a cover. He seldom frequented restaurants, except the Café Royal, or the Eiffel Tower in Percy Street, and here in the Golden Cross, the background of low rooms, sanded floors, oak beams, roast pork and tobacco smoke—so different from the scene he provided for himself—must have made him feel still less at home in his surroundings. Moreover it must have been the sole occasion, I believe, on which he read aloud to a gathering—though admittedly a small one, nine persons in all. Eventually, he reached our table safely, and we persuaded him to sit down and drink some port. By now, the other occupants of the dining-room were beginning to leave, and soon we had the place to ourselves.

Firbank sat on a chair, sideways to the audience, and at last began to read in a voice which contained in it the strangled notes of a curate's first sermon, but was warmed, from time to time—indeed, fairly frequently —by fits of genial, deep chuckling. He continued throughout to pluck wildly at his tie and feverishly to avoid the gaze of those watching him and concentrating on his words. The book, not yet named, from which he read, was *Valmouth:* and it was so individual, so highly stylised, that in spite of his bad reading, in spite of a certain lack of consequence (indeed its exquisite inconsequence was one of its great merits) it held our rapturous attention from beginning to end —though I recall that subsequently the author complained to me about one of his own difficulties with it:

" You have no idea how difficult it is to keep up one's interest, when writing of a heroine who is over one hundred and twenty years of age—not that the other characters are meant to be any younger!"

I was able subsequently to arrange for the printing of the chapter he had read, then entitled *Fantasia in A Sharp Minor*, in *Art and Letters*, a periodical of which I was then one of the three editors. The publication of this fragment, I reflect, helped to bring Firbank's

work to the notice of a discriminating audience—
though in the interests of truth it must be admitted
that many of the people who now constitute his greatest admirers were at the time enraged by it beyond
measure!

During the summers that were to follow in London,
and during certain winters and springs (as, for example,
during that April and May when he was living in a
villa that had formerly belonged to the Swiss painter
Böcklin, situated outside Florence, and when we
would so often meet him in the Via Tornabuoni,
staggering under the load of flowers he had bought,
and craning round in a wild and helpless way for a
cab to carry him home), we saw much of Firbank.
Looking back over those years, let us face the truth;
for the strange being of whom we write is interesting
enough both as writer and man to deserve such
treatment. Let us admit, then, that there was about
him something a little ridiculous, which blinded
fools to his other remarkable and much more characteristic qualities, and which since his death, as during
his lifetime, has made him an easy butt. As a talker
he was most unequal; and if we are bound to say
how extremely amusing he was for the first ten minutes
of any meeting with him (always a deliriously funny
period), we are also bound to add that, after a time,
conversation became difficult. Also he could be peculiarly irritating, though he himself always seemed
surprised at the result of these moods, and when on
occasion he had annoyed my brother and me, he
would remark in a dazed manner, " Sachie is glaring
at me like an *angry lion*!" But if, for some minutes
he contrived to provoke his friends, it would not be
long before he would again convulse them with laughter. Moreover, one was always surprised in talking
with him, so vague and almost incoherent did he
seem, at his love and knowledge of beautiful things.

He was not, I think, a deeply read man, but his reading was very different from the rather blowsy pastures so well cropped by the ordinary " literary man." French novels, French poetry and eighteenth-century memoirs of every European country composed the bulk of it, and in these matters he was excessively well-informed; yet often in his books there flashes out an allusion to some subject or another on which one would not have expected him to be an author-ity, but which this reference proved him to have mastered.

In addition, there is surely to be traced in all his books a marked love and understanding of the stage and its personalities. Just as virtuosity and style were for him the chief merits of literature, so he demanded in his favourites of the footlights, absolute control, manner and, above all, established fame; for the effect of celebrity, through a decade or so, upon the tempera-mental nature essential to the executant artist, delighted him; and thus among those he most adored in the theatre were to be numbered Pavlova, Isadora Duncan, and Mrs. Patrick Campbell.

If it was his reading, as much as his own experience, which made the general sense of his books so cos-mopolitan, yet it must be remembered that he had not only travelled, but had lived in various cities of South-ern Europe and Northern Africa for quite considerable periods. He had spent nearly a year, for example, in Madrid, and asseverated that there he had become a mighty horseman. Moreover he always accused a then promising young diplomat (now a well-known author) of having stolen his charger out of jealousy of his prowess; an unlikely, indeed mythical, theft, but one which caused him to harbour the greatest resentment, and accounts for the rather unflattering portraits of young diplomats in general in *The Flower Beneath the Foot*. But Firbank was not given to feuds and treasured hardly a single hatred, though he was apt, he said, to be " disappointed " in his friends.

Occasionally, though, he would be angry, as, for instance, when he suddenly announced to everyone that I had said that the Firbank fortune had been founded on boot-buttons—a remark of which I had never been guilty. He was enraged about this, and would sit in the Café Royal for hours, practising what he was going to say in court, during the libel action which he intended to bring against me. The great moment in it, he had determined, was to be when he lifted up his hands, which were beautifully shaped, and of which he was very proud, and would say to the Judge, " Look at my hands, my lord! How could my father have made boot-buttons? Never! He made the most *wonderful* railways." . . . But within three weeks we were the best of friends again.

The first impression of him in conversation must always have been surprise that so frail, vague, and extraordinary a creature could have arranged—let alone have created—a book. But there it was; he was a born, as opposed to a self-made, writer. This is, perhaps, the greatest gift that can descend upon authors, so many of whom will write because they are intelligent or clever, and want to—not because they must—write. It was obvious as well, even at first sight, that Firbank's health was far from strong. But this delicacy at least was possessed of one advantage. It prevented him from being forced to waste his time in the Army. The constant callings-up and medical examinations had, though, further shattered his health, just as he, in his turn, must have somewhat shattered the health of the various military authorities with whom he came in contact. He related to us, for example, that when, after a dozen or so examinations, the War Office rejected him as totally unfit for service (which anyone else could have told at a glance), and then, in their usual muddled way, immediately called him up again, he replied to them through his lawyer with the threat of libel action. The War Office, at a time when it governed the world, was so startled by this simple piece of individual initiative that it at once sent back to him a humble apology.

Wonderful as it was that a man, with apparently so tenuous a hold on life and its business, should be able to write novels, it was even more astonishing that so vague, delicate, and careless a person—one, in addition, who ate almost nothing and usually drank a good deal—should survive travelling by himself in wild and distant countries. One would have taken him, the moment one saw him, as plainly destined to be defrauded or, if necessary, murdered, so weak and helpless did he appear, so obvious a victim for guile and violence. But his resistance towards the world was of an order more subtle than that of the average person, and it may be that swindler and murderer desisted because they felt the latent strength of his personality. Moreover, not only did his apparent helplessness fail to injure, it actually tended to protect him, both from danger and from boredom, for he was always able, by dint of it, to compel others to carry out for him the tedious things of life. Far from feeling it a moral duty, as we had been taught, to do something unpleasant every day, he conceived that it was his moral duty to find others who would on every occasion perform it by proxy. Thus, for example, there was his visit to Augustus John. It was related that, torn between his desire for a drawing by that artist and his nervousness at having to meet him and express it, he drove round to John's studio in a taxi-cab, and decided, on the way, that the taxi-driver should introduce him to the great man and explain his business. The poor driver, therefore, was forced to act the rôle of St. John the Baptist, to take the strain of the ultimate emergence of Ronald upon himself. After a time our novelist appeared, much quieted, from the cab, and everything was arranged.

Here I should like to acknowledge my debt to Mr. Augustus John for his great kindness Remembering this story, and knowing of Firbank's tremendous admiration for him, I wrote to him, and received in reply a most interesting letter, some of which I quote below, while other anecdotes contained in it I have, for the sake of context, incorporated elsewhere in this study.

" Ronald Firbank," he wrote, " came to me to have his portrait drawn some while before the publication of *Vainglory*. As you have heard, he sent his taxi-man in to prepare the way, himself sitting in the taxi with averted face, the very picture of exquisite confusion.

" He came frequently afterwards, although always with the utmost diffidence, and I made various studies of him. When the strain of confronting me became unbearable, he would seek refuge in the lavatory, there to wash his hands, This manœuvre occurred several times at each sitting.

" His mother once called and lamented the solitary life he led—a dear old lady, to whom Ronald was, I think, quite attached. Upon her death he for a moment, in my presence, hesitated on the brink of some almost Dickensian sentiment, but corrected himself just in time . . . It's amazing how sometimes he struck, amidst his excellent persiflage, a chord of deep and heart-rending sentiment."

All those who knew Firbank best, agree that under cover of this seeming futility in matters of the world he was a shrewd and capable man of affairs. " He had," writes John, " in spite of appearances a practical side to his nature, carrying always in his trunk, as he did, a few good big blocks of Welsh anthracite." And in accordance with this theory I must record that he was certainly always coming to me to request that I would witness wills, deeds, sales of land and the like; which suggests that there must have been a quite extensive business undercurrent to his life. One document, I remember, concerned his sale of a cemetery to a Welsh town, and seemed all that it could be of a morbid bargain... On another occasion, I recollect his arriving at my house in a taxi, somewhat perturbed. But all he could say was, over and over again, "It's time Una learnt about life!" Then, averting his face, at an angle of 45 degrees, he stopped speaking. Eventually he fled back to the shelter of his cab.

His ability as a traveller was not less marked, or more to be expected, than his talent for the affairs of life. On meeting him for the first time one would without doubt have pronounced against his journeying alone, even for such a short distance as that from London to Oxford; but here, again, he had found someone to be responsible for him. It was his custom, during the two years he lived at Oxford, to travel back on the " milk train," but owing to the lateness of the hour, the difficult machinery of buying, and the unpleasantness of handling, tickets for himself, he had arranged a running account with the guard. This score he settled once every two months. And then, at the worst, his longer voyages, and those on which his helplessness found no answer to its appeal, at least led to the unexpected—and it was precisely in the unexpected that he most revelled. Moreover, his seeming incompetence furthered as much as it hindered his travelling. Thus, as a very young man he went to France with some Cambridge friends. Their arrival in Rheims happened to coincide with the local " Wine Week," in which celebration they all joined with the due earnestness and enthusiasm of their years. Ronald remembered little that took place after dinner—and woke up to find himself in Venice! It appeared that in those peaceful days a train touched Rheims once a fortnight, on its way to Venice, and that he had contrived to wander into the station and, with little money and no ticket, to catch this *rara avis* and remain undisturbed in it until his safe arrival at his distant but unintended destination the following day.

Rheims, however, is hardly dangerous for a visitor except in a bacchic sense, but Ronald Firbank even managed to make a considerable stay in the negro republic of Hayti (which, however incorrect the impression may be, does, nevertheless, sound wild and far to ordinary English ears) without any untoward incident occurring. The announcement of his intention to go there was very typical. Usually he would correspond with me, in his large, regular hand, on a whole series of these enormous blue postcards, already mentioned, upon which he also wrote his novels. He would write on both sides of these postcards, using them instead of letters, and would then place them in a large blue envelope, and post them. This was his normal method. But on this occasion he sent us a simple postcard, simply posted, on which were the words: " Tomorrow I go to Hayti. They say the President is a *Perfect Dear!*"

There were occasions, nevertheless, on which surprising events occurred, events that were so like those that take place in his novels that they could only have happened to him. We have already suggested that there was something of the ecclesiastic in his appearance. After the war he spent a good deal of time in Rome; and we remember his being much alarmed because he declared that the priests had tried to kidnap him. He descended the steps of his hotel one evening, and had asked the concierge to call him a cab. A smart, black-painted brougham drove up immediately and he had stepped into it. The door was

closed at once, and it drove off at a quick trot, before
he had time even to tread on the toes of its occupants,
for he found, to his bewilderment, that it was occupied by two priests, who quickly pulled him down
between them, saying, "You are one of us, aren't
you!" Eventually, however, Ronald managed to
escape.

After the war he had resumed his old method of
life, the travelling and the returning to London for
the season. But flying had recently come to his rescue,
and now he often flew from London to Rome or Constantinople. While, in another respect, his life had
altered, for in these later days he would always solemnly announce his arrival in London through the
social columns of *The Times* or *Morning Post*. By this
time he had found many admirers of his writings
among painters and authors, though among the more
purely intellectual of these there was to be found,
joined to their admiration, a sort of contempt, wholly
undeserved. This was caused, I think, by the perfection
of Firbank's novels, and by their lack of striving
earnestness in a time when nearly every author was
setting out to air his inward struggles to an unwilling
but awed public. His assured income may also have
been a reason for envy, since it spared him the worries
of forced journalism; while he, for his part, conscious
of the income which separated him from most of
the world, felt that many people were only nice for
the sake of the meals and drinks which they could
expect from him. He would reply by treating them
with an almost childish hauteur, as though he were
a Tsar among authors, in itself an amusing feat from
so amiable and delicate a man. Nobody who understood him could be offended, for this affectation of
proud eccentricity was only equalled by the genuine
kindness he displayed at other times.

During these years just after the war he was once

again constantly to be seen. No theatrical or musical performance of note passed without his attending it. Now we usually found him lunching, dining or having supper at the Eiffel Tower, though formerly he had frequented one of the " Junior " political clubs, where his appearance and manner must have formed a strange contrast to that of the musty, bearded elders sitting all round him. It was always related that in his early days there, at luncheon, he had taken fright at sight of the head waiter, and had hidden himself under the table!

The genial and talented proprietor of the Eiffel Tower Restaurant, Stulik, an Austrian by birth, used to take a deep interest in Firbank's welfare. He was, nevertheless, somewhat grieved at the smallness of this customer's appetite, and I remember once, when Firbank had just arrived from Rome by air, Stulik saying: " Mr. Firbank is much better. He is vonderful. Vhat an appetite he has got now! Yesterday for dinner he ate a whole slice of toast with his caviare . . . How I lofe my customers!" Augustus John gives the ensuing graphic account of a typical afternoon spent with Ronald, starting at this restaurant. " I once presented him to the Marchesa C—— at the Eiffel Tower; and we lunched together, all three. He then proposed that we should go to his rooms in Brook Street, but on the way deposited us at Claridge's and on some vague pretext disappeared himself. The Marchesa and I were becoming rather bored (it was ' between hours '), when Ronald reappeared with an enormous bundle, which he unfolded in his rooms, displaying a magnificent bunch of highly exotic lilies which he offered with many apologies to the lady. He also showed her, but did not give her, a complete edition of his works, luxuriously bound. Naturally she was enchanted, and proposed we should all go to America together without wasting a moment. The plan was agreed to, but somehow or other never came to pass."

Often, too, Ronald was to be found at the old Café Royal, observing the odd life that centred there, the bookmakers in their bowler hats, the celebrities, the art-dealers, the painters, touts, financiers, and sculptors. Indeed, it inspired several passages in his novels, notably that one in *Caprice*, where the daughter of a rural dean enters the Café for the first time. And it was the situation of it, as much as its habituals, that entertained him, since he was always impressed by the moral of the tombstone-shop opposite; for just across the road there was a large plate-glass window, in which the white marble spectres of all the Christian emblems, weeping females, and modest, plain head-pieces gleamed all ghostly under the primrose light of arc-lamps. Dark inscriptions could be read on them, expressive of morbid hopes or fears, while, after any riot at the Café, when one or two people had been forcibly requested by the giant in charge of such procedure to leave the premises, they could be seen ricochetting across the road towards these graveyard paraphernalia, or standing swearing in return at his uniformed figure against this ominous and inevitable background. " It ought to be a warning to us all!" Ronald would remark as he watched such scenes.

Yet whenever one saw him, whether it was here, at the opera, in a concert room or theatre, he seemed to be alone. This is not to say that very often he was not the centre of an appreciative crowd of friends; but even then he appeared to be solitary and by him-self; a figure who, however kind and amusing, was hedged off from his fellows by his temperament, and must live in a world of his own seeing, different from that of others. Even his longing for friendship, which was strong in him, could seldom surmount the barriers of his own intense nervousness. It seemed to him that he must ever seek the affection of others to a greater extent than they sought his friendship. There was a pathetic instance of this unhappy outlook one day at luncheon time in the Café Royal. Firbank entered and walked up to one of his friends, Gabriel Atkin, a young painter who was sitting at a table with a glass of sherry in front of him, and asked him to give him luncheon. The young man replied that he could not do so for he had no money; upon which Firbank took a pound-note out of his pocket, pressed it into the hand of his friend and, sinking at the same time into the seat opposite, exclaimed, " How wonderful to be a guest!"

Yet his summer visits to London were really a delight to all his friends and acquaintances, for he never disappointed them. First there would be the solemn heralding of his arrival in *The Times* or *Morning Post*, and then some fresh piece of grotesque fantasy was sure to mark each occasion. One year he rented a small flat in Sloane Square, and there set out the few objects that were the assertion and extension of himself, raising aloft once more the standard of his palm-tree. Accordingly, he arranged with a flower shop in the Square to send in a gardener twice a day to water and attend to it properly. Ronald was much pleased with this man, for he wore a green baize apron, and had a rustic way of speaking, so that it was " just like being in the country." When, therefore, after a fortnight, he decided to move to an apartment in Piccadilly, he insisted that, no matter what the cost, the same gardener should come twice a day to water the palm-tree. Further, he laid down, as a condition of his employment, that the man must walk the whole way—except in wet weather—from Sloane Square to Piccadilly and back again, and must wear his green baize apron and carry a miniature watering-can, painted green to match it. The proprietor of the shop made no objection, for by this time he knew his customer, money rained in on him for orchids, and the gardener found him " very nice-spoken," while, from Firbank's point of view, it was worth it, for the peripatetic gardener added a touch of rural pageantry to the grey streets of London. We can still recall the joy it used to give us, as we sailed down the ugly desert of Sloane Street on the top of a then open motor omnibus, to see this solemn rather self-conscious procession of one, and to realise that a familiar, fantastic sense of humour was again at play among us.

Towards the end of his life he was as much pleased with the select appreciation of his books as he was disappointed at the small range of it. He had been simple enough, perhaps, to expect for his work as large and wide an audience as that obtained by Miss Ethel M. Dell or some such book of the period as *Beau Tarzan*. He was especially gratified by the enthusiastic tone of Mr. Carl van Vechten, and would carry about his letters, in bulging pockets, together with various laudatory notices of his writings that had appeared recently in the American Press. He was also very elated at a letter sent to him by some transatlantic cinema magnate, asking for the film-rights of *Caprice*, the novel in which the heroine—the daughter, as I have said, of a rural dean—sets up in theatrical management, herself playing the chief part, but, after an enthusiastic first-night, being still too poor to rent a bedroom, has to sleep on the stage and finally meets her death by falling into a mouse-trap that she had not observed in the darkness!

At this period Ronald undoubtedly looked very ill. He knew how delicate he was, and as he sat there at the Café Royal showing one these documents, or as he lay, rather than sat, in the front row of the stalls at a theatre, the sable angel of death ever hung over him. Moreover, he was much given to fortune-tellers, crystal-gazers, and givers of Egyptian amulets, and the soothsayers, seeing him, prophesied evil. It may be that it was his intense relish and understanding of the silly and absurd side of modern life that made him consult them. But he was in many ways, I think, so near the things he so beautifully skimmed and parodied that perhaps he was genuinely superstitious. Be that as it may, however, at the end of each summer for five or six years it was his habit to drive round in state to say good-bye to my brother and myself, at the same time telling us that he knew there were but a few months more for him to live. These doleful tidings had invariably been conveyed to him either by a Syrian magician or by some wretched drunkard at the Café Royal. Whilst talking with us of it, he would keep his taxi-cab waiting outside, ominously ticking out the pence and minutes, and would then leave us in order to drive on and bid farewell to his other friends. So many times did these final scenes occur that when in truth he came to us for the last good-bye in our house, it conveyed little, being merely part of a regular and ordinary routine. But actually my final meeting with him was in the Café Royal, then undergoing at the same moment the dual, and apparently contradictory, process of being pulled down and rebuilt. And upon that occasion, owing to a sudden impulse, I had the pleasure of telling him how exquisite a writer I judged him to be, and how much, how infinitely, better than most of his contemporaries, many of whom were more highly esteemed. For Ronald suffered rather than gained from the fact that he was a true, born artist, with no propagandist axe to grind.

That winter he spent in Egypt, and then came back to Rome, where he had taken an apartment in the Palazzo Orsini for a term of years. But the change of climate from Cairo to Rome gave him a severe chill, which turned to pneumonia, and he died within a few days.

It was odd how slowly the news of his death travelled and it was several weeks before most of his friends heard of it. It was barely recorded in the press, and, at that, three weeks after it had taken place, while little or no mention was made of his books. The only friend of his who was in Rome at the time of his demise was Lord Berners. The latter saw him a day or two before the end, when he was already ill, and tells me that Firbank entertained no suspicion that he was dying. The doctor, too, appears at first to have treated the matter lightly, as an ordinary chill. So little did the dying man himself expect the end that only a few hours before it, feeling very much better, he discharged his nurse.

He died at the age of thirty-nine. He never saw forty, the thought of which he so much disliked. Growing older pained him, and would have pained him more, though he held, with one of the characters he created, that " I suppose when there's no more room for another crow's-foot, one attains a sort of peace."

In any case, his death could not have been long averted, even if he had not contracted that fatal chill. Apparently he had been examined by a doctor before leaving England, and though he did not inform his patient of it, lungs and heart were already then in such a bad state that it was obvious that any illness must finish fatally for him.

Through a strange error, typical of much that was paradoxical in his life, the Catholic Firbank was laid to rest near the pyramid of Gaius Sestius—not far from, of all people, Keats and Shelley—in the Protestant Cemetery. When, however, in the spring of 1933, I went there to visit the grave, all sign of it had vanished! Subsequently it was explained to me by a sexton that the mistake had been discovered and rectified, and that the body had been moved to a Catholic burial-ground. Thus about his first resting-place, itself, there was an inconsequential no less than a tragic element; but then, one could always, even in his lifetime, see a miniature legend in attendance upon him, hovering round him, waiting like a bird of prey to batten on his dead body: and still, today, some persons say—and write—that Firbank never in fact died; that he is alive, wandering round and observing in remote countries. And we, who knew him, are left to wish that this myth were the reality, and that again we might see that jaunty, sad, and unique figure, or hear once more those sudden gusts of deep, silly laughter which so convulsed and shook his frame, or those few unexpected remarks, wrenched out of himself with so much seeming effort; that we might again receive a sheaf of ridiculous postcards, with his large handwriting on them; and, above all, that we might have the joy of reading a new book from his pen, a book that would be so deliciously unlike any others in the world save his own.

OSBERT SITWELL.

The Flower Beneath the Foot

The Flower Beneath the Foot

NEITHER her Gaudiness the Mistress of the Robes nor her Dreaminess the Queen were feeling quite themselves. In the Palace all was speculation. Would they be able to attend the *Fêtes* in honour of King Jotifa, and Queen Thleeanouhee of the Land of Dates?—Court opinion seemed largely divided. Countess Medusa Rappa, a woman easily disturbable, was prepared to wager what the Countess of Tolga 'liked' (she knew), that another week would find the Court shivering beneath the vaulted domes of the Summer Palace.

'I fear I've no time (or desire) now, Medusa,' the Countess answered, moving towards the Royal apartments, 'for making bets'; though, turning before the ante-room door, she nodded: 'Done!'

She found her sovereign supine on a couch piled with long Tunisian cushions, while a maid of honour sat reading to her aloud:

'*Live with an aim, and let that aim be high!*' the girl was saying as the Countess approached.

'Is that you, Violet?' her Dreaminess enquired without looking round.

'How is your condition, Madam?' the Countess anxiously murmured.

'Tell me, do, of a place that soothes and lulls one . . .'

The Countess of Tolga considered.

'Paris,' she hazarded.

'Ah! Impossible.'

'The Summer Palace, then,' the Countess ejaculated, examining her long slender fingers that were like the tendrils of a plant.

'Dr. Cuncliffe Babcock flatly forbids it,' the Royal woman declared, starting slightly at the sound of a gun. 'That must be *the Dates!*' she said. And in effect, a vague reverberation, as of individuals cheering, resounded fitfully from afar. 'Give me my diamond anemones,' the Queen commanded, and motioning to her Maid: 'Pray conclude, mademoiselle, those lofty lines.'

With a slight sigh, the lectress took up the posture of a Dying Intellectual.

1

'*Live with an aim, and let that aim be high!*' she reiterated in tones tinged perceptibly with emotion.

'But not *too* high, remember, Mademoiselle de Nazianzi . . .'

There was a short pause. And then——

'Ah, Madam! What a dearest he is!'

'I think you forget yourself,' the Queen murmured with a quelling glance. 'You had better withdraw.'

'He has such strength! One could niche an idol in his dear, dinted chin.'

'Enough!'

And a moment later the enflamed girl left the room warbling softly: *Depuis le Jour.*

'Holy Virgin,' the Countess said, addressing herself to the ceiling. 'Should his Weariness, the Prince, yield himself to this caprice . . .'

The Queen shifted a diamond bangle from one of her arms to the other.

'She reads at such a pace,' she complained, 'and when I asked her *where* she had learnt to read so quickly she replied "On the screens at Cinemas." '

'I do not consider her at all distinguished,' the Countess commented, turning her eyes away towards the room.

It was a carved-ceiled and rather lofty room, connected by tall glass doors with other rooms beyond. Peering into one of these the Countess could see reflected the 'throne,' and a little piece of broken Chippendale brought from England, that served as a stand for a telephone, wrought in ormolu and rock-crystal, which the sun's rays at present were causing to emit a thousand playful sparks. Tapestry panels depicting the Loves of *Mejnoun and Leileh* half concealed the silver *boiseries* of the walls, while far down the room, across old rugs from Shirvan that were a marvellous wonder, showed fortuitous jardinières filled with every kind of flowering plant. Between the windows were canopied recesses, denuded of their statues by the Queen's desire, 'in order that they might appear suggestive,' while through the windows themselves the Countess could catch, across the forecourt of the castle, a panorama of the town below, with the State Theatre and the Garrisons, and the Houses of Parliament, and the Hospital, and the low white dome, crowned by turquoise-tinted tiles, of the Cathedral, which was known to all churchgoers as *the Blue Jesus.*

'It would be a fatal connexion,' the Queen continued, 'and it must never, never be!'

By way of response the Countess exchanged with her sovereign a glance that was known in Court circles as her *tortured-animal* look. 'Their Oriental majesties,' she observed, 'to judge from the din, appear to have already endeared themselves with the mob!'

The Queen stirred slightly amid her cushions.

'For the aggrandisement of the country's trade, an alliance with Dateland is by no means to be depreciated,' she replied, closing her eyes as though in some way or other this bullion to the State would allow her to gratify her own wildest whims, the dearest, perhaps, of which was to form a party to excavate (for objects of art) among the ruins of Chedorlahomor, a *faubourg* of Sodom.

'Am I right, Madam, in assuming it's Bananas? . . . ' the Countess queried.

But at that moment the door opened, and his Weariness the Prince entered the room in all his tinted Orders.

Handsome to tears, his face, even when he had been a child, lacked innocence. His was of that *magnolia* order of colouring, set off by pleasantly untamed eyes, and teeth like flawless pearls.

'You've seen them? What are they like . . . ? Tell Mother, darling!' the Queen exclaimed.

'They're merely dreadful,' his Weariness, who had been to the railway-station to welcome the Royal travellers, murmured in a voice extinct with boredom.

'They're in European dress, dear?' his mother questioned.

'The King had on a frock coat and a cap. . . .'

'And she?'

'A tartan skirt, and checked wool stockings.'

'She has great individuality, so I hear, marm,' the Countess ventured.

'Individuality be——! No one can doubt she's a terrible woman.'

The Queen gently groaned.

'I see life to-day,' she declared, 'in the colour of mould.'

The Prince protruded a shade the purple violet of his tongue.

'Well, it's depressing,' he said, 'for us all, with the Castle full of blacks.'

'That is the least of my worries,' the Queen observed. 'Oh, Yousef, Yousef,' she added, 'do you wish to break my heart?'

The young man protruded some few degrees further his tongue.

'I gather you're alluding to Laura!' he remarked.

'But what can you *see* in her?' his mother mourned.

'She suits my feelings,' the Prince simply said.

'Peuh!'

'She meets my needs.'

'She's so housemaid. . . . I hardly know . . . !' The Queen raised beautiful hands, bewildered.

'Très gutter, ma'am,' the Countess murmured, dropping her voice to a half-whisper.

'She saves us from *cliché*,' the Prince indignantly said.

'She saves us from nothing,' his mother returned. 'Oh, Yousef, Yousef. And what *cerné* eyes, my son. I suppose you were gambling all night at the Château des Fleurs!'

'Just hark to the crowds!' the Prince evasively said. And never too weary to receive an ovation, he skipped across the room towards the nearest window, where he began blowing kisses to the throng.

'Give them the Smile Extending, darling,' his mother beseeched.

'Won't you rise and place your arm about him, Madam?' the Countess suggested.

'I'm not feeling at all up to the mark,' her Dreaminess demurred, passing her fingers over her hair.

'There is sunshine, ma'am . . . and you have your *anemones* on . . .' the Countess cajoled, 'and to please the people, you ought indeed to squeeze him.' And she was begging and persuading the Queen to rise as the King entered the room preceded by a shapely page (of sixteen) with cheeks fresher than milk.

'Go to the window, Willie,' the Queen exhorted her Consort, fixing an eye on the last trouser button that adorned his long, straggling legs.

The King, who had the air of a tired pastry-cook, sat down.

'We feel,' he said, 'to-day, we've had our fill of stares!'

'One little bow, Willie,' the Queen entreated, 'that wouldn't kill you.'

'We'd give perfect worlds,' the King went on, 'to go, by Ourselves, to bed.'

'Get rid of the noise for me. *Quiet them*. Or I'll be too ill,' the Queen declared, 'to leave my room to-night!'

'Should I summon Whisky, Marm?' the Countess asked, but before there was time to reply the Court physician, Dr. Cuncliffe Babcock, was announced.

4

'I feel I've had a relapse, doctor,' her Dreaminess declared.

Dr. Babcock beamed: he had one blind eye—though this did not prevent him at all from seeing all that was going on with the other.

'Leave it to me, Madam!' he assured, 'and I shall pick you up in *no* time!'

'Not Johnnie, doctor?' the Queen murmured with a grimace. For a glass of *Johnnie Walker* at bedtime was the great doctor's favourite receipt.

'No; something a little stronger, I think.'

'We need expert attention, too,' the King intervened.

'You certainly are somewhat pale, sir.'

'Whenever I go out,' the King complained, 'I get an impression of raised hats.'

It was seldom King William of Pisuerga spoke in the singular tense, and Doctor Babcock looked perturbed.

'Raised hats, sir?' he murmured in impressive tones.

'Nude heads, doctor.'

The Queen commenced to fidget. She disliked that the King should appear more interesting than herself.

'These earrings tire me,' she said, 'take them out.'

But the Prince, who seemed to be thoroughly enjoying the success of his appearance with the crowd, had already begun tossing the contents of the flower vases into the street.

'Willie . . . prevent him! Yousef . . . I forbid you!' her Dreaminess faintly shrieked. And to stay her son's despoiling hand she skimmed towards him, when the populace, catching sight of her, redoubled their cheers.

Meanwhile Mademoiselle de Nazianzi had regained her composure. As a niece of her Gaudiness the Mistress of the Robes (the Duchess of Cavaljos), she had made her recent début at Court under the brightest conceivable of conditions.

Laura Lita Carmen Etoile de Nazianzi was more piquant perhaps then pretty. A dozen tiny moles were scattered about her face, while on either side of her delicate nose a large grey eye surveyed the world with a pensive critical glance.

'Scenes like that make one sob with laughter,' she reflected, turning into the corridor where two of the Maids of Honour, like strutting idols, were passing up and down.

'Is she really very ill? Is she *really* dying?' they breathlessly enquired.

5

Mademoiselle de Nazianzi disengaged herself from their solicit-ously entwining arms.

'She is not!' she answered, in a voice full of eloquent inflections.

But beguiled by the sound of marching feet, one of the girls had darted forward towards a window.

'Oh, Blanche, Blanche, Blanchie love!' she exclaimed, 'I could dance to the click of your brother's spurs.'

'You'd not be the first to, dear darling!' Mademoiselle de Lambèse replied, adjusting her short shock of hair before a glass.

Mademoiselle de Lambèse believed herself to be a very valuable piece of goods, and seemed to think she had only to smile to stir up an ocean of passion.

'Poor Ann-Jules,' she said: 'I fear he's in the clutches of that awful woman.'

'Kalpurnia?'

'Every night he's at the Opera.'

'I hear she wears the costume of a shoeblack in the new ballet,' Mademoiselle de Nazianzi said, 'and is too strangely extraordinary!'

'Have you decided, Rara,* yet, what you'll wear for the ball?'

'A black gown and three blue flowers on my tummy.'

'After a shrimp-tea with the Archduchess, I feel I *want* no dinner,' Mademoiselle Olga Blumenghast, a girl with slightly hunched shoulders, said, returning from the window.

'Oh? Had she a party?'

'A curé or two, and the Countess Yvorra.'

'Her black-bordered envelopes make one shiver!'

'I thought I should have died it was so dull,' Mademoiselle Olga Blumenghast averred, standing aside to allow his Naughtiness Prince Olaf (a little boy racked by all the troubles of spring) and Mrs. Montgomery, the Royal Governess, to pass. They had been out evidently among the crowd, and both were laughing heartily at the asides they had overheard.

' 'Ow can you be so frivolous, your royal 'ighness?' Mrs. Montgomery was expostulating: 'for shame, wicked boy! For shame!' And her cheery British laugh echoed gaily down the corri-dors.

'Well, *I* took tea at the Ritz,' Mademoiselle de Lambèse related.

'Anybody?'

'Quite a few!'

* The name by which the future saint was sometimes called among her friends.

'There's a rumour that Prince Yousef is entertaining there to-night.'

Mademoiselle Blumenghast tittered.

'Did you hear what he called the lanterns for the *Fête*?' she asked.

'No.'

'A lot of "bloody bladders"!'

'What, what a dearest!' Mademoiselle de Nazianzi sighed beneath her breath. And all along the almost countless corridors as far as her bedroom door she repeated again and again: 'What, *what* a dearest!'

⁕ *II* ⁕

BENEATH a wide golden ceiling people were dancing. A capricious concert waltz, drowsy, intricate, caressing, reached fitfully the supper-room, where a few privileged guests were already assembled to meet King Jotifa and Queen Thleeanouhee of the Land of Dates.

It was one of the regulations of the Court that those commanded to the King's board should assemble some few minutes earlier than the Sovereigns themselves, and the guests at present were mostly leaning stiffly upon the chair-backs, staring vacuously at the olives and salted almonds upon the table-cloth before them. Several of the ladies indeed had taken the liberty to seat themselves, and were beguiling the time by studying the menu or disarranging the smilax, while one dame went as far as to take, and even to nibble, a salted almond. A conversation of a non-private kind (carried on between the thin, authoritative legs of a Court Chamberlain) by Countess Medusa Rappa and the English Ambassadress was being listened to by some with mingled signs of interest.

'Ah! How clever Shakespeare!' the Countess was saying. 'How gorgeous! How glowing! I once knew a speech from "Julia Sees Her!..." perhaps his greatest *œuvre* of all. Yes! "Julia *Sees* Her" is what I like best of that great, great master.'

The English Ambassadress plied her fan.

'Friends, Comrades, Countrymen,' she murmured, 'I used to know it myself!'

But the lady nibbling almonds was exciting a certain amount of

7

comment. This was the Duchess of Varna, voted by many to be one of the handsomest women of the Court. Living in economical obscurity nearly half the year round, her appearances at the palace were becoming more and more infrequent.

'I knew the Varnas were very hard up, but I did not know they were *starving*,' the Countess Yvorra, a woman with a would-be indulgent face that was something less hard than rock, remarked to her neighbour the Count of Tolga, and dropping her glance from the Count's weak chin she threw a fleeting smile towards his wife, who was looking 'Eastern' swathed in the skin of a blue panther.

'Yes, their affairs it seems are almost desperate,' the Count returned, directing his gaze towards the Duchess.

Well-favoured beyond measure she certainly was, with her immense placid eyes, and bundles of loose, blonde hair. She had a gown the green of Nile water, that enhanced to perfection the swan-like fairness of her throat and arms.

'I'm thinking of building myself a Villa in the Land of Dates!' she was confiding to the British Ambassador, who was standing beside her on her right. 'Ah, yes! I shall end my days in a country strewn with flowers.'

'You would find it I should say too hot, Duchess.'

'My soul has need of the sun, Sir Somebody!' the Duchess replied, opening with equanimity a great black ostrich fan, and smiling up at him through the sticks.

Sir Somebody Something was a person whose nationality was written all over him. Nevertheless, he had, despite a bluff and some-what rugged manner, a certain degree of feminine sensitiveness, and any reference to the *soul* at all (outside the Embassy Chapel) invari-ably made him fidget.

'In moderation, Duchess,' he murmured, fixing his eyes upon the golden head of a champagne bottle.

'They say it is a land of love!' the Duchess related, raising indolently an almond to her sinuously chiselled lips.

'And even, so it's said, too,' his Excellency returned, 'of licence!' when just at this turn of things the Royal cortège entered the supper-room to the exhilarating strains of King Goahead's War-March.

Those who had witnessed the arrival of King Jotifa and his Queen earlier in the afternoon were amazed at the alteration of their aspect now. Both had discarded their European attire for the loosely-flowing vestments of their native land, and for a brief while there was

8

some slight confusion among those present as to which was the gentleman and which the lady of the two. The King's beard, long and blonde, should have determined the matter outright, but on the other hand the Queen's necklet of reeds and plumes was so very misleading. . . . Nobody in Pisuerga had seen anything to compare with it before. 'Marvellous, though terrifying,' the Court passed verdict.

Attended by their various suites, the Royal party gained their places amid the usual manifestation of loyal respect.

But one of the Royal ladies, as it soon became evident, was not yet come.

'Where's Lizzie, Lois?' King William asked, riveting the Archduchess's empty chair.

'We'd better begin without her, Willie,' the Queen exclaimed, 'you know she never minds.'

And hardly had the company seated themselves when, dogged by a lady-in-waiting and a maid-of-honour, the Archduchess Elizabeth of Pisuerga rustled in.

Very old and very bent, and (even) very beautiful, she was looking, as the grammar-books say, 'meet' to be robbed, beneath a formidable tiara, and wearing a dozen long strands of pearls.

'Forgive me, Willie,' she murmured, with a little high, shrill, tinkling laugh: 'but it was so fine that, after tea, I and a Lady went paddling in the Basin of the Nymphs.'

'How was the water?' the King enquired.

The Archduchess repressed a sneeze. 'Fresh,' she replied, 'but not too . . .'

'After sunset beware, dear Aunt, of chills.'

'But for a frog I believe nothing would have got me out!' the august lady confessed as she fluttered bird-like to her chair.

Forbidden in youth by parents and tutors alike the joys of paddling under pain of chastisement, the Archduchess Elizabeth appeared to find a zest in doing so now. Attended by a chosen lady-in-waiting (as a rule the dowager Marchioness of Lallah Miranda), she liked to slip off to one of the numerous basins or natural grottos in the castle gardens, where she would pass whole hours in wading blissfully about. Whilst paddling, it was her wont to run over those refrains from the vaudevilles and operas (with their many shakes and rippling *cadenze*) in favour in her day, interspersed at intervals by such cries as: 'Pull up your skirt, Marquise, it's dragging a little,

my friend, below the knees . . .' or, 'A shark, a shark!' which was
her way of designating anything that had fins, from a carp to a
minnow.

'I fear our Archduchess has contracted a slight catarrh,' the Mistress of the Robes, a woman like a sleepy cow, observed, addressing
herself to the Duke of Varna upon her left.

'Unless she is more careful, she'll go paddling once too often,'
the Duke replied, contemplating with interest, above the moonlight-
coloured daffodils upon the table board, one of the button-nosed
belles of Queen Thleeanouhee's suite. The young creature, referred
to cryptically among the subordinates of the castle as 'Tropical
Molly,' was finding fault already, it seemed, with the food.

'Take it away,' she was protesting in animated tones: 'I'd as soon
touch a foot-squashed mango!'

'No *mayonnaise*, miss?' a court-official asked, dropping his face
prevailingly to within an inch of her own.

'Take it right away . . . And if you should *dare*, sir, to come any
closer . . . !'

The Mistress of the Robes fingered nervously the various Orders
of Merit on her sumptuous bosom.

'I trust there will be no contretemps,' she murmured, glancing
uneasily towards the Queen of the Land of Dates, who seemed to be
lost in admiration of the Royal dinner-service of scarlet plates, that
looked like pools of blood upon the cloth.

'What pleases me in your land,' she was expansively telling her
host, 'is less your food than the china you serve it on; for with us
you know there's none. And now,' she added, marvellously wafting
a fork, 'I'm for ever spoilt for shells.'

King William was incredulous.

'With you no china?' he gasped.

'None, sir, none!'

'I could not be more astonished,' the King declared, 'if you told
me there were fleas at the Ritz,' a part of which assertion Lady
Something, who was blandly listening, imperfectly chanced to
hear.

'Who would credit it!' she breathed, turning to an attaché, a
young man all white and penseroso, at her elbow.

'Credit what?'

'Did you not hear what the dear King said?'

'No.'

'It's almost *too* appalling . . .' Lady Something replied, passing a small, nerveless hand across her brow.

'Won't you tell me though?' the young man murmured gently, with his nose in his plate.

Lady Something raised a glass of frozen lemonade to her lips.

'Fleas,' she murmured, 'have been found at the Ritz.'

'. . . . . . ! . . . . ? . . . ! !'

'Oh and *poor* Lady Bertha! And poor good old Mrs. Hunter!' And Lady Something looked away in the direction of Sir Somebody, as though anxious to catch his eye.

But the British Ambassador and the Duchess of Varna were weighing the chances of a Grant being allowed by Parliament for the excavation of Chedorlahomor.

'Dear little Chedor,' the Duchess kept on saying, 'I'm sure one would find the most enthralling things there. Aren't *you*, Sir Somebody?'

And they were still absorbed in their colloquy when the King gave the signal to rise.

Although King William had bidden several distinguished Divas from the Opera House to give an account of themselves for the entertainment of his guests, both King Jotifa and Queen Thleeanouhee with disarming candour declared that, to their ears, the music of the West was hardly to be borne.

'Well, I'm not very fond of it either,' her Dreaminess admitted, surrendering her skirts to a couple of rosy boys, and leading the way with airy grace towards an adjacent salon, 'although,' she wistfully added across her shoulder to a high dignitary of the Church, 'I'm trying, it's true, to coax the dear Archbishop to give the first act of *La Tosca* in the Blue Jesus. . . . Such a perfect setting, and with Desiré Erlinger and Maggie Mellon . . . !'

And as the Court now pressed after her the rules of etiquette became considerably relaxed. Mingling freely with his guests, King William had a hand-squeeze and a fleeting word for each.

'In England,' he paused to enquire of Lady Something, who was warning a dowager, with impressive earnestness, against the Ritz, 'have you ever seen two cooks in a kitchen-garden?'

'No, never, sir!' Lady Something simpered.

'Neither,' the King replied, moving on, 'have *we*.'

The Ambassadress beamed.

'My dear,' she told Sir Somebody, a moment afterwards, 'my

dear, the King was simply charming. Really I may say he was more than gracious! He asked me if I had ever seen two cooks in a kitchen-garden, and I said no, never! And he said that neither, either, had he! And oh isn't it so strange how few of us ever have?'

But in the salon one of Queen Thleeanouhee's ladies had been desired by her Dreaminess to sing.

'It seems so long,' she declared, 'since I heard an Eastern voice, and it would be such a relief.'

'By all means,' Queen Thleeanouhee said, 'and let a *darbouka* or two be brought! For what charms the heart more, what touches it more,' she asked, considering meditatively her babouched feet, 'than a *darbouka*?'

It was told that, in the past, her life had been a gallant one, although her adventures, it was believed, had been mostly with men. Those, however, who had observed her conduct closely had not failed to remark how often her eyes had been attracted in the course of the evening towards the dimpled cheeks of the British Ambassadress.

Perceiving her ample form not far away, Queen Thleeanouhee signalled to her amiably to approach.

Née Rosa Bark (and a daughter of the Poet) Lady Something was perhaps not sufficiently tactful to meet all the difficulties of the rôle in which it had pleased life to call her. But still, she tried, and did do her best, which often went far to retrieve her lack of *savoir faire*. 'Life is like that dear,' she would sometimes say to Sir Somebody, but she would never say what it was that life was like; '*That*,' it seemed. . . .

'I was just looking for my daughter,' she declared.

'And is she as sympathetic,' Queen Thleeanouhee softly asked, 'as her mamma?'

'She's shy—of the Violet persuasion, but that's not a bad thing in a young girl.'

'Where *I* reign shyness is a quality which is entirely un-known . . . !'

'It must be astonishing, ma'am,' Lady Something replied, caressing a parure of false jewels, intended, indeed, to deceive no one, 'to be a Queen of a sun-steeped country like yours.'

Queen Thleeanouhee fetched a sigh.

'Dateland—my dear, it's a scorch!' she averred.

'I conclude, ma'am, it's what *we* should call "conservatory"
scenery?' Lady Something murmured.

'It is the land of the jessamine-flower, the little amorous jessamine-
flower,' the Queen gently cooed, with a sidelong smiling glance,
'that twines itself sometimes to the right hand, at others to the left,
just according to its caprices!'

'It sounds, I fear, to be unhealthy, ma'am.'

'And it is the land, also, of romance, my dear, where *shyness* is a
quality which is entirely unknown,' the Queen broke off, as one of
her ladies, bearing a *darbouka*, advanced with an air of purposefulness
towards her.

The hum of voices which filled the room might well have tended
to dismay a vocalist of modest powers, but the young matron
known to the Court as 'Tropical Molly,' and whom her mistress
addressed as Timzra, soon showed herself to be equal to the
occasion.

> 'Under the blue gum-tree
> I am sitting waiting,
> Under the blue gum-tree
> I am waiting all alone!'

Her voice reached the ears of the fresh-faced ensigns and the
beardless subalterns in the Guard Room far beyond, and startled the
pages in the distant dormitories, as they lay smoking on their beds.

And then, the theme changing, and with an ever-increasing
passion, fervour and force:

> 'I heard a watch-dog in the night . . .
> Wailing, wailing . . .
> Why is the watch-dog wailing?
> He is wailing for the Moon!'

'That is one of the very saddest songs,' the King remarked, 'that
I have ever heard. "Why is the watch-dog wailing? He is wailing
for the Moon!" ' And the ambitions and mortifications of kingship
for a moment weighed visibly upon him.

'Something merrier, Timzra!' Queen Thleeanouhee said.

And throwing back her long love-lilac sleeves, Timzra sang:

> 'A negress with a margaret once lolled frousting in the sun
> Thinking of all the little things that she had left undone . . .
> With a hey, hey, hey, hey, hi, hey ho!'

'She has the air of a cannibal!' the Archduchess murmured behind her fan to his Weariness, who had scarcely opened his lips except to yawn throughout the whole of the evening.

'She has the air of a ——' he replied laconically turning away.

Since the conversation with his mother earlier in the day his thoughts had revolved incessantly around Laura. What had they been saying to the poor wee witch, and whereabouts was she to be found?

Leaving the salon, in the wake of a pair of venerable politicians, who were helping each other along with little touches and pats, he made his way towards the ball-room, where a new dance known as the Pisgah Pas was causing some excitement, and gaining a post of vantage, it was not long before he caught a glimpse of the agile, boyish figure of his betrothed. She passed him, without apparently noticing he was there, in a whirlwind of black tulle, her little hand pressed to the breast of a man like a sulky eagle; and he could not help rejoicing inwardly that, *once* his wife, it would no longer be possible for her to enjoy herself exactly with whom she pleased. As she swept by again he succeeded in capturing her attention, and, nodding meaningly towards a deserted picture-gallery, wandered away towards it. It was but seldom he set foot there, and he amused himself by examining some of the pictures to be seen upon the walls. An old shrew with a rose . . . a drawing of a man alone in the last extremes . . . a pink-robed Christ . . . a seascape, painted probably in winter, with cold, hard colouring . . .

'Yousef?'

'Rara!'

'Let us go outside, dear.'

A night so absolutely soft and calm was delicious after the glare and noise within.

'With whom,' he asked, 'sweetheart, were you last dancing?'

'Only the brother of one of the Queen's Maids, dear,' Mademoiselle de Nazianzi replied. 'After dinner, though', she tittered, 'when he gets Arabian-Nighty, it's apt to annoy one a scrap!'

'*Arabian-Nighty*?'

'Oh, never mind!'

'But (pardon me, dear) I do.'

'Don't be tiresome, Yousef! The night is too fine,' she murmured, glancing absently away towards the hardly moving trees, from whose

branches a thousand drooping necklets of silver lamps palely
burned.

Were *those* the 'bladders' then?

Strolling on down hoops of white wistaria in the moon they came
to the pillared circle of a rustic temple, commanding a prospect
on the town.

'There,' she murmured, smiling elfishly and designating something, far below them, through the moon mist, with her fan, 'is
the column of Justice and,' she laughed a little, 'of *Liberty*!'

'And there,' he pointed inconsequently, 'is *the Automobile
Club*!'

'And beyond it . . . the Convent of the Flaming-Hood. . . .'

'And those blue revolving lights; can you see them, Rara?'

'Yes, dear . . . what are *they*, Yousef?'

'Those,' he told her, contemplating her beautiful white face
against the dusky gloom, 'are the lights of the Café Cleopatra!'

'And what,' she questioned, as they sauntered on, pursued by all
the sweet perfumes of the night, 'are those berried-shrubs that smell
so passionately?'

'I don't know,' he said. 'Kiss me, Rara!'

'No, no.'

'Why not?'

'Not now!'

'Put your arm about me, dear.'

'What a boy he is!' she murmured, gazing up into the starry
clearness.

Overhead a full moon, a moon of circumstance, rode high in the
sky, defining phantasmally, far off, the violet-farded hills beyond
the town.

'To be out there among the silver bean-fields!' he said.

'Yes, Yousef,' she sighed, starting at a Triton's face among the
trailing ivy on the castle wall. Beneath it, half concealed by water-
flags, lay a miniature lake: as a rule, nobody now went near the
lake at all, since the Queen had called it '*appallingly smelly*,' so that
for rendezvous it was quite ideal.

'Tell me, Yousef,' she presently said, pausing to admire the
beautiful shadow of an orange-tree on the path before them: 'tell
me, dear, when Life goes like that to one—what does one do?'

He shrugged. 'Usually nothing,' he replied, the tip of his tongue
(like the point of a blade) peeping out between his teeth.

15

'Ah, but isn't that being strong?' she said half audibly, fixing her eyes as though fascinated upon his lips.

'Why,' he demanded, with an engaging smile that brought half-moons to his hollow cheeks, 'what has the world been doing to Rara?'

'At this instant, Yousef,' she declared, 'it brings her nothing but Joy!'

'You're happy, my sweet, with me?'

'No one knows, dearest, how much I love you.'

'Kiss me, Rara,' he said again.

'Bend, then,' she answered, as the four quarters of the twelve strokes of midnight rang out leisurely from the castle clock.

'I've to go to the Ritz!' he announced.

'And *I* should be going in.'

Retracing reluctantly their steps they were soon in earshot of the ball, and their close farewells were made accompanied by selections from *The Blue Banana*.

She remained a few moments gazing as though entranced at his retreating figure, and would have, perhaps, run after him with some little capricious message, when she became aware of someone watching her from beneath the shadow of a garden vase.

Advancing steadily and with an air of nonchalance, she recognised the delicate, sexless silhouette and slightly hunched shoulders of Olga Blumenghast, whose exotic attraction had aroused not a few heart-burnings (and even feuds) among several of the grandes dames about the court.

Poised flatly against the vase's sculptured plinth, she would have scarcely been discernible but for the silver glitter of her gown.

'Olga? Are you faint?'

'No; only my slippers are *torture*.'

'I'd advise you to change them, then!'

'It's not altogether my feet, dear, that ache. . . .'

'Ah, I see,' Mademoiselle de Nazianzi said, stooping enough to scan the stormy, soul-tossed eyes of her friend: 'you're suffering, I suppose, on account of Ann-Jules?'

'He's such a gold-fish, Rara . . . any fingers that will throw him bread. . . .'

'And there's no doubt, I'm afraid, that lots do!' Mademoiselle de Nazianzi answered lucidly, sinking down by her side.

'I would give all my soul to him, Rara . . . my chances of heaven!'

16

'Your chances, Olga——' Mademoiselle de Nazianzi murmured, avoiding some bird-droppings with her skirt.

'How I envy *the men*, Rara, in his platoon!'

'Take away his uniform, Olga, and what does he become?'

'Ah *what*——!'

'No.... Believe me, my dear, he's not worth the trouble!'

Mademoiselle Blumenghast clasped her hands brilliantly across the nape of her neck.

'I want to possess him at dawn, at dawn,' she broke out: 'beneath a sky striped with green....'

'Oh, Olga!'

'And I shall never rest,' she declared, turning away on a languid heel, 'until I *do*.'

Meditating upon the fever of love, Mademoiselle de Nazianzi directed her course slowly towards her room. She lodged in that part of the palace known as 'The Bachelors' Wing,' where she had a delicious little suite just below the roof.

'If she loved him absolutely,' she told herself, as she turned the handle of her door, 'she would not care about the colour of the sky; even if it snowed or hailed!'

Depositing her fan upon the lid of an old wedding-chest that formed a couch, she smiled contentedly about her. It would be a wrench abandoning this little apartment that she had identified already with herself, when the day should come to leave it for others more spacious in the Keep. Although scarcely the size of a ship's cabin, it was amazing how many people one could receive together at a time merely by pushing the piano back against the wall and wheeling the wedding-chest on to the stairs; and once no fewer than seventeen persons had sat down to a birthday *fête* without being made too much to feel like herrings. In the so-called salon, divided from her bedroom by a folding lacquer screen, hung a few studies in oils executed by herself, which, except to the initi-ated, or the naturally instinctive, looked sufficiently enigmatic against a wall-paper with a stealthy design.

Yes, it would be a wrench to quit the little place, she reflected, as she began setting about her toilet for the night. It was agreeable going to bed late without anybody's aid, when one could pirouette interestingly before the mirror in the last stages of déshabillé, and do a thousand (and one) things besides* that one might otherwise

---

* Always a humiliating recollection with her in after years. *Vide* 'Confessions.'

lack the courage for. But this evening, being in no frivolous mood, she changed her ball dress swiftly for a robe-de-chambre bordered deeply with ermines, that made her feel nearer somehow to Yousef, and helped her to realise her position in its various facets as future Queen.

'Queen!' she breathed, trailing her fur flounces towards the window.

Already the blue revolving lights of the Café Cleopatra were growing paler with the dawn, and the moon had veered a little towards the Convent of the Flaming-Hood. Ah . . . how often as a lay boarder there had she gazed up towards the palace wondering half-shrinkingly what life 'in the world' was like; for there had been a period, indeed, when the impulse to take the veil had been strong with her—more, perhaps, to be near one of the nuns whom she had *idolised* than from any more immediate vocation.

She remained immersed in thoughts, her introspectiveness fanned insensibly by the floating zephyrs that spring with morning. The slight sway-sway of the trees, the awakening birds in the castle eaves, the green-veined bougainvillæas that fringed her sill—these thrilled her heart with joy. All virginal in the early dawn what magic the world possessed! Slow speeding clouds like knots of pink roses came blowing across the sky, sailing away in titanic bouquets above the town.

Just such a morning should be their wedding-day! she mused, beginning lightly to apply the contents of a jar of milk of almonds to her breast and arms. Ah, before that Spina Christi lost its leaves, or that swallow should migrate . . . that historic day would come! Troops . . . hysteria . . . throngs. . . . The Blue Jesus packed to suffocation. . . . She could envisage it all.

And there would be a whole holiday in the Convent, she reflected, falling drowsily at her bedside to her knees.

'Oh! help me, heaven,' she prayed, 'to be decorative and to do right! Let me always look young, never more than sixteen or seventeen—at the *very* outside, and let Yousef love me—as much as I do him. And I thank you for creating such a darling, God (for he's a perfect dear), and I can't tell you how much I love him; especially when he wags it! I mean his tongue. . . . Bless all the sisters at the Flaming-Hood—above all Sister Ursula . . . and be sweet, besides, to old Jane. . . . Show me the straight path! And keep me ever free from the malicious scandal of the Court. Amen.'

And her orisons (ending in a brief self-examination) over,
Mademoiselle de Nazianzi climbed into bed.

⁂ *III* ⁂

IN the Salle de Prince or Cabinet d'Antoine, above the Café
Cleopatra, Madame Wetme, the wife of the proprietor, sat perusing the Court gazettes.

It was not often that a *cabinet particulier* like Antoine was disengaged at luncheon time, being as a rule reserved many days in advance, but it had been a 'funny' season, as the saying went, and there was the possibility that a party of late-risers might look in yet (officers, or artistes from the Halls), who had been passing a night 'on the tiles.' But Madame Wetme trusted not. It was pleasant to escape every now and again from her lugubrious back-drawing-room that only faced a wall, or to peruse the early newspapers without having first to wait for them. And to-day precisely was the day for the hebdomadal *causerie* in the *Jaw-Waw's Journal* on matters appertaining to society, signed by that ever popular diarist 'Eva Schnerb.'

'Never,' Madame Wetme read, 'was a gathering more brilliant than that which I witnessed last night! I stood in a corner of the Great ball-room and literally *gasped* at the wealth of jewels. . . . Beauty and bravery abounded, but no one, *I* thought, looked better than our most gracious Queen, etc. . . . Among the supper-guests I saw their Excellencies Prince and Princess Paul de Pismiche—the Princess impressed me as being *just* a trifle pale: she is by no means strong, and unhappily our nefarious climate does not agree with everybody!—their Excellencies Sir Somebody and Lady Somebody (Miss Ivy Something charming in cornflower *charmeuse* danced indefatigably all the evening, as did also one of the de Lambèse girls); the Count and Countess of Tolga—she all in blue furs and literally *ablaze* with gorgeous gems (I hear on excellent authority she is shortly relinquishing her post of Woman of the Bedchamber which she finds is really too arduous for her); the Duchess of Varna, looking veritably radiant (by the way where has she been?) in the palest of pistachio-green mashlaks, which are all the rage at present.

'*Have you a Mashlak?*

19

'Owing to the visit of King Jotifa and Queen Thleeanouhee, the Eastern mashlak is being worn by many of the smart women about the Court. I saw an example at the Opera the other night in silver and gold *lamé* that I thought too——' Madame Wetme broke off to look up, as a waiter entered the room.

'Did Madame ring?'

'No!...'

'Then it must have been "Ptolemy"!' the young man murmured, bustling out.

'I dare say. When will you know your bells?' Madame Wetme retorted, returning with a headshake to the gazette: her beloved Eva was full of information this week and breathlessly she read on:

'I saw Minnie, Lady Violetrock (whose daughter Sonia is being educated here), at the garden *fête* the other day at the Château des Fleurs, looking chic as she *always* does, in a combination of petunia and purple ninon raffling a donkey.

'I hear on the best authority that before the Court goes to the Summer Palace later on there will be at least *one* more Drawing-room. Applications, from those entitled to attend, should be made to the Lord Chamberlain as *soon* as possible.'

One more Drawing-room—! The journal fell from Madame Wetme's hand.

'I'm getting on now,' she reflected, 'and if I'm not presented soon I never will be....'

She raised imploring eyes to the mural imagery—to the 'Cleopatra couchant,' to the 'Arrival of Anthony,' to the 'Sphinx,' to the 'Temple of Ra,' as though seeking inspiration. 'Ah my God!' she groaned.

But Madame Wetme's religion, her cruel God, was the *Chic*: the God Chic.

The sound of music from below reached her faintly. There was not a better orchestra (even at the Palace) than that which discoursed at the Café Cleopatra—and they played, the thought had sometimes pleased her, the same identical tunes!

'Does it say when?' she murmured, re-opening the gazette. No: but it would be 'before the Court left.' ... And when would that be?

'I have good grounds for believing,' she continued to read, 'that in order to meet his creditors the Duke of Varna is selling a large portion of his country estate.'

If it were true . . . Madame Wetme's eyes rested in speculation on the oleanders in the great flower-tubs before the Café; if it were true, why the Varnas must be desperate, and the Duchess ready to do anything. 'Anything—for remuneration,' she murmured, rising and going towards a table usually used for correspondence. And seating herself with a look of decision, she opened a leather writing-pad, full of crab-coloured, ink-marked blotting-paper.

In the fan-shaped mirror above the writing-table she could see herself in fancy, all veils and aigrettes, as she would be on 'the day' when coiffed by Ernst.

'Among a bevy of charming débutantes, no one looked more striking than Madame Wetme, who was presented by the Duchess of Varna.' Being a client of the house (with an unpaid bill) she could *dictate* to Eva. . . . But first, of course, she must secure the Duchess. And taking up her pen she wrote: 'Madame Wetme would give the Duchess of Varna fifty thousand crowns to introduce her at Court.' A trifle terse perhaps? Madame Wetme considered. How if the Duchess should take offence. . . . It was just conceivable! And besides, by specifying no fixed sum, she might be got for less.

'Something more mysterious, more delicate in style . . .' Madame Wetme murmured with a sigh, beginning the letter anew:

'If the Duchess of Varna will call on Madame Wetme this afternoon, about five, and partake of a cup of tea, she will hear of something *to her advantage.*'

Madame Wetme smiled. 'That should get her!' she reflected, and selecting an envelope, she directed it boldly to the Ritz. 'Being hard up, she is sure to be there!' she reasoned, as she left the room in quest of a page.

The French maid of the Duchess of Varna was just putting on her mistress's shoes, in a private sitting-room at the Ritz, when Madame Wetme's letter arrived.

The pleasure of being in the capital once more, after a long spell of the country, had given her an appetite for her lunch and she was feeling braced after an excellent meal.

'I shall not be back, I expect, till late, Louison,' she said to her maid, 'and should anyone enquire where I am, I shall either be at the Palace, or at the Skating Rink.'

'Madame la Duchesse will not be going to her corsetier's?'

'It depends if there's time. What did I do with my shopping-list?' the Duchess replied, gathering up abstractedly a large, becoroneted vanity-case and a parasol. She had a gown of khaki and daffodil and a black tricorne hat trimmed with green. 'Give me my other sunshade, the jade—and don't forget—On me trouvera, soit au Palais Royal, soit au Palais de Glace!' she enjoined, sailing quickly out.

Leaving the Ritz by a side door, she found herself in a quiet shady street bordering the Regina Gardens. Above, a sky so blue, so clear, so luminous seemed to cry out: 'Nothing matters! Why worry? Be sanguine! Amuse yourself!! Nothing matters!'

Traversing the gardens, her mind preoccupied by Madame Wetme's note, the Duchess branched off into a busy thoroughfare leading towards the Opera, in whose vicinity lay the city's principal shops. To learn of anything to one's advantage was, of course, always welcome, but there were various other claims upon her besides that afternoon, which she was unable, or loath, to ignore— the palace, a *thé dansant* or two, and then her favourite rink ... although the unfortunate part was that most of the rink instructors were still unpaid, and on the last occasion she had hired one to waltz with her he had taken advantage of the fact by pressing her waist with greater freedom than she felt he need have done.

Turning into the Opera Square with its fine arcades, she paused, half furtively, before a florist's shop. Only her solicitors and a few in the secret were aware that the premises known as *Haboubet of Egypt* were her own; for, fearful lest they might be occupied one day by sheriffs' officers, she had kept the little business venture the closest mystery. Lilies 'from Karnak,' Roses 'from the Land of Punt' (all grown in the gardens of her country house, in the purlieus of the capital) found immediate and daily favour among amateurs of the choice. Indeed, as her gardener frequently said, the demand for Roses from the Land of Punt was more than he could possibly cope with without an extra man.

'I may as well run in and take whatever there's in the till,' she reflected—'not that, I fear, there's much. . . .'

The superintendent, a slim Tunisian boy, was crouching pitcher-posture upon the floor, chanting languidly to himself, his head supported by an osier pannier lately arrived from 'Punt.'

'Up, Bachir!' the Duchess upbraided. 'Remember the fresh consignments perish while you dream there and sing.'

The young Tunisian smiled.

He worshipped the Duchess, and the song he was improvising

as she entered had been inspired by her. In it (had she known) he had led her by devious tender stages to his father's fonduk at Tifilalet 'on the blue Lake of Fetzara,' where he was about to present her to the Sheik and the whole assembled village as his chosen bride.

The Duchess considered him. He had a beautiful face spoiled by a bad complexion, which doubtless (the period of puberty passed) he would outgrow.

'Consignment him come not two minute,' the youth replied.

'Ah, Bachir? Bachir!'

'By the glorious Koran, I will swear it.'

'Be careful not to shake those *Alexandrian Balls*,' the Duchess peremptorily enjoined, pointing towards some Guelder-roses—'or they'll fall before they're sold!'

'No matter at all. They sold already! An American lady this morning she purchase all my Alexandrian-balls; two heavy bunch.'

'Let me see your takings. . . .'

With a smile of triumph, Bachir turned towards the till. He had the welfare of the establishment at heart as well as his own, and of an evening often he would flit, garbed in his long gandourah, through the chief Cafés and Dancings of the city, a vast pannier upon his head heaped high with flowers, which he would dispose of to dazzled clients for an often exorbitant sum. But for these excursions of his (which ended on occasion in adventure) he had received no authority at all.

'Not so bad,' the Duchess commented. 'And, as there's to be a Court again soon, many orders for bouquets are sure to come in!'

'I call in outside hands to assist me: I summon Ouardi! He an Armenian boy. Sympathetic. My friend. More attached to him am I than a branch of jessamine is about a vine.'

'I suppose he's capable?' the Duchess murmured, pinning a green-ribbed orchid to her dress.

'The garlands of Ouardi would make even a jackal look bewitching!'

'Ah: he has taste?'

'I engage my friend. Much work always in the month of Redjeb!'

'Engage nobody,' the Duchess answered as she left the shop, 'until I come again.'

Hailing in the square one of the little shuttered cabs of the city, she directed the driver to drop her at the palace gates, and pursued by an obstreperous newsboy with an evening paper, yelling 'Chedorlahomor! Sodom! Extra Special!' the cab clattered off at a languid trot. Under the plane-trees, near the Houses of Parliament, she was overtaken by the large easy-stepping horses of the Ambassadress of England and acknowledged with a winning movement of the wrist Lady Something's passing accueil. It was not yet quite the correct hour for the Promenade, where beneath the great acacias Society liked best to ride or drive, but, notwithstanding, that zealous reporter of social deeds, the irrepressible Eva Schnerb, was already on the prowl and able with satisfaction to note: 'I saw the Duchess of Varna early driving in the Park, all alone in a little one-horse shay, that really looked more elegant than any Delaunay-Belleville!'

Arriving before the palace gates, the Duchess perceived an array of empty carriages waiting in the drive, which made her apprehensive of a function. She had anticipated an intimate chat with the Queen alone, but this it seemed was not to be.

Following a youthful page with a *resigned* face down a long black rug woven with green and violet flowers, who left her with a sigh (as if disappointed of a tip) in charge of a couple of giggling colleagues, who, in turn, propelled her towards a band of sophisticated-looking footmen and grim officials, she was shown at last into a vast white drawing-room whose ceiling formed a dome.

Knowing the Queen's interest in the Chedorlahomor Excavation Bill, a number of representative folk, such as the wives of certain Politicians or Diplomats, as well as a few of her own more immediate circle, had called to felicitate her upon its success. Parliament had declared itself willing to do the unlimited graceful by all those concerned, and this in a great measure was due to the brilliant wire-pulling of the Queen.

She was looking singularly French in a gold helmet and a violet Vortniansky gown, and wore a rope of faultless pearls, clasped very high beneath the chin.

'I hope the Archbishop will bless the excavators' tools!' she was saying to the wife of the Premier as the Duchess entered. 'The *picks* at any rate. . . .'

That lady made no reply. In presence of Royalty she would usually sit and smile at her knees, raising her eyes from time to time to throw, beneath her lashes, an ineffable expiring glance.

'God speed them safe home again!' the Archduchess Elizabeth, who was busy knitting, said. An ardent philanthropist, she had begun already making 'comforts' for the men, as the nights in the East are cold. The most philanthropic perhaps of all the Royal Family, her hobby was designing, for the use of the public, sanitary, but artistic, places of necessity on a novel system of ventilation. The King had consented to open (and it was expected appropriately) one of these in course of construction in the Opera Square.

'Amen,' the Queen answered, signalling amiably to the Duchess of Varna, whose infrequent visits to court disposed her always to make a fuss of her.

But no fuss the Queen could make of the Duchess of Varna could exceed that being made by Queen Thleeanouhee, in a far-off corner, of her Excellency Lady Something. The sympathy, the *entente* indeed that had arisen between these two ladies, was exercising considerably the minds of certain members of the diplomatic corps, although, had anyone wished to eavesdrop, their conversation upon the whole must have been found to be anything but esoteric.

'What I want,' Queen Thleeanouhee was saying, resting her hand confidentially on her Excellency's knee, 'what I want is an English maid with Frenchified fingers—— Is there such a thing to be had?'

'But surely——' Lady Something smiled: for the servant-topic was one she felt at home on.

'In Dateland, my dear, servant girls are nothing but sluts.'

'Life is like *that*, ma'am, I regret, indeed, to have to say: I once had a housemaid who had lived with Sarah Bernhardt, and oh, wasn't she a terror!' Lady Something declared, warding off a little black bat-eared dog who was endeavouring to scramble on to her lap.

'Teddywegs, Teddywegs!' the Archduchess exclaimed, jumping up and advancing to capture her pet. 'He arrived from London not later than this morning,' she said; 'from the Princess Elsie of England.'

'He looks like some special litter,' Lady Something remarked.

'How the dear girl loves animals!'

'The rumour of her betrothal it seems is quite without foundation?'

'To my nephew: ah alas. . . .'

'Prince Yousef and she are of an equal age!'

'She is interested in Yousef I'm inclined to believe; but the worst of life is, nearly everyone marches to a different tune,' the Archduchess replied.

'One hears of her nothing that isn't agreeable.'

'Like her good mother, Queen Glory,' the Archduchess said, 'one feels, of course, she's all she should be.'

Lady Something sighed.

'Yes . . . and even *more*!' she murmured, letting fall a curtsey to King William who had entered. He had been lunching at the Headquarters of the Girl Guides and wore the uniform of a general.

'What is the acme of nastiness?' he paused of the English Ambassadress to enquire.

Lady Something turned paler than the white candytuft that is found on ruins. 'Oh *la*, sir,' she stammered, 'how should I know!'

The King looked the shrinking matron slowly up and down. 'The supreme disgust——'

'Oh *la*, sir!' Lady Something stammered again.

But the King took pity on her evident confusion. 'Tepid potatoes,' he answered, 'on a stone-cold plate.'

The Ambassadress beamed.

'I trust the warmth of the girls, sir, compensated you for the coldness of the plates?' she ventured.

'The inspection, in the main, was satisfactory! Although I noticed that one or two of the guides seemed inclined to lead astray,' the King replied, regarding Teddywegs, who was inquisitively sniffing his spurs.

'He's strange yet to everything,' the Archduchess commented.

'What's this—a new dog?'

'From Princess Elsie. . . .'

'They say she's stupid, but I do not know that intellect is always a blessing!' the King declared, drooping his eyes to his abdomen with an air of pensive modesty.

'Poor child, she writes she is tied to the shore, so that I suppose she is unable to leave dear England.'

'Tied to it?'

'And bound till goodness knows.'

'As was Andromeda!' the King sententiously exclaimed. . . . 'She would have little, or maybe nothing, to wear,' he clairvoyantly went on. 'I see her standing shivering, waiting for Yousef. . . . Chained by the leg, perhaps, exposed to the howling winds.'*

* *Winds*, pronounced as we're told 'in poetry.'

26

'Nonsense. She means to say she can't get away yet on account of her engagements; that's all.'

'After Cowes-week,' Lady Something put in, 'she is due to pay a round of visits before joining her parents in the North.'

'How I envy her ' the Archduchess sighed, 'amid that entrancing scene. . . .'

Lady Something looked *attendrie*.

'Your Royal Highness is attached to England?' she asked.

'I fear I was never there. . . . But I shall always remember I put my hair up when I was twelve years old because of the Prince of Wales.'

'Oh? And . . . which of the Georges?' Lady Something gasped.

'It's so long ago now that I really forget.'

'And pray, ma'am, what was the point of it?'

The Archduchess chuckled.

'Why, so as to look eligible of course!' she replied, returning to her knitting.

Amid the general flutter following the King's appearance it was easy enough for the Duchess of Varna to slip away. Knowing the palace inside out it was unnecessary to make any fuss. Passing through a long room, where a hundred holland-covered chairs stood grouped, Congresswise, around a vast table, she attained the Orangery, that gave access to the drive. The mellay of vehicles had considerably increased, and the Duchess paused a moment to consider which she should borrow when, recollecting she wished to question one of the royal gardeners on a little matter of mixing manure, she decided to return through the castle grounds instead. Taking a path that descended between rhododendrons and grim old cannons towards the town, she was comparing the capriciousness of certain bulbs to that of certain people when she heard her name called from behind and, glancing round, perceived the charming silhouette of the Countess of Tolga.

'I couldn't stand it inside. Could you?'

'My *dear*, what a honeymoon hat!'

'It was made by me!'

'Oh, Violet . . .' the Duchess murmured, her face taking on a look of wonder.

'Don't forget, dear, Sunday.'

'Is it a party?'

'I've asked Grim-lips and Ladybird, Hairy and Fluffy, Hardylegs and Bluewings, Spindleshanks and Our Lady of Furs.'

'Not Nanny-goat?'

'Luckily . . .' the Countess replied, raising to her nose the heliotropes in her hand.

'Is he no better?'

'You little know, dear, what it is to be all alone with him chez soi when he thinks and sneers into the woodwork.'

'*Into the woodwork?*'

'He addresses the ceiling, the walls, the floor—me never!'

'Dear dove.'

'All I can I'm plastic.'

'Can one be plastic ever enough, dear?'

'Often but for Olga . . .' the Countess murmured, considering a little rosy ladybird on her arm.

'I consider her ever so compelling, ever so wistful——' the Duchess of Varna averred.

'Sweet girl—! She's just my consolation.'

'She reminds me, does she you? of that *Miss Hobart* in de Grammont's *Memoirs.*'

'C'est une âme exquise!'

'Well, au revoir, dear: we shall meet again at the Princess Leucippe's later on,' the Duchess said, detecting her gardener in the offing.

By the time she had obtained her recipe and cajoled a few special shoots from various exotic plants, the sun had begun to decline. Emerging from the palace by a postern-gate, where lounged a sentry, she found herself almost directly beneath the great acacias on the Promenade. Under the lofty leafage of the trees, as usual towards this hour, society in its varying grades had congregated to be gazed upon. Mounted on an eager-headed little horse, his Weariness (who loved being seen) was plying up and down, while in his wake a '*screen artiste*,' on an Arabian mare with powdered withers and eyes made up with kohl, was creating a sensation. Every time she used her whip the powder rose in clouds. Wending her way through the throng the duchess recognised the rose-harnessed horses of Countess Medusa Rappa—the Countess bolt upright, her head carried stiffly, staring with a pathetic expression of dead *joie-de-vie* between her coachman's and footman's waists. But the intention of calling at the Café Cleopatra caused the duchess to hasten. The possibility of learning something beneficial to herself was a lure not to be resisted. Pausing to allow the marvellous blue automobile of Count Ann-Jules to pass (with the dancer Kalpurnia inside), she crossed the Avenue, where there seemed, on the whole, to be fewer people. Here she remarked a little ahead of her the masculine form of the Countess Yvorra, taking a quiet stroll before *Salut* in the company of her Confessor. In the street she usually walked with her hands clasped behind her back, huddled up like a statesman. '*Des choses abominables! . . . Des choses hors nature!*' she was saying, in tones of evident relish, as the duchess passed.

Meanwhile Madame Wetme was seated anxiously by the samovar in her drawing-room. To receive the duchess, she had assumed a mashlak à la mode, whitened her face and rouged her ears, and set a small but costly aigrette at an insinuating angle in the edifice of her hair. As the hour of Angelus approached the tension of waiting grew more and more acute, and beneath the strain of expectation even the little iced sugar cakes upon the tea-table looked green with worry.

Suppose, after all, she shouldn't come? Suppose she had already left? Suppose she were in prison? Only the other day a woman of the highest fashion, a leader of 'society' with an *A*, had served six months as a consequence of her extravagance. . . .

In agitation Madame Wetme helped herself to a small glassful of *Cointreau* (her favourite liqueur), when, feeling calmer for the consommation, she was moved to take a peep out of Antoine.

But nobody chic at all met her eye.

Between the oleanders upon the kerb, that rose up darkly against a flame-pink sky, two young men dressed 'as poets' were arguing and gesticulating freely over a bottle of beer. Near them, a sailor with a blue drooping collar and dusty boots (had he walked, poor wretch, to see his mother?) was gazing stupidly at the large evening gnats that revolved like things bewitched about the café lamps, while below the window a lean soul in glasses, evidently an impresario, was loudly exclaiming: 'London has robbed me of my throat, sir! ! It has deprived me of my voice.'

No, an 'off' night certainly!

Through a slow, sun-flower of a door (that kept on revolving long after it had been pushed) a few military men bent on a game of billiards, or an early *fille de joie* (only the discreetest *des filles 'serieuses'* were supposed to be admitted), came and went.

'To-night they're fit for church,' Madame Wetme complacently smiled as the door swung round again. 'Navy-blue and silver-fox looks the goods,' she reflected, 'upon any occasion! It suggests something sly—like a nurse's uniform.'

'A lady in the drawing-room, Madame, desires to speak to you,' a chasseur tunefully announced, and fingering nervously her aigrette Madame Wetme followed.

The Duchess of Varna was inspecting a portrait with her back to the door as her hostess entered.

'I see you're looking at my Murillo!' Madame Wetme began.

'Oh. . . . Is it o-ri-gi-nal?' the Duchess drawled.

'No.'

'I *thought* not.'

'To judge by the bankruptcy-sales of late (and it's curious how many there've been . . .), it would seem, from the indifferent figure he makes, that he is no longer accounted chic,' Madame Wetme observed as she drew towards the Duchess a chair.

'I consider the chic to be such a very false religion! . . .' the Duchess said, accepting the seat which was offered her.

'Well, I come of an old Huguenot family myself!'

'—— . . . ?'

'Ah, my early home. . . . Now, I hear, it's nothing but a weed-crowned ruin.'

The Duchess considered the ivory cat handle of her parasol. 'You wrote to me?' she asked.

'Yes: about the coming court.'

'About it?'

'Every woman has her dream, Duchess! And mine's to be presented.'

'The odd ambition!' the Duchess crooned.

'I admit we live in the valley. Although *I* have a great sense of the hills!' Madame Wetme declared demurely.

'Indeed?'

'My husband, you see . . .'

'. . . . .'

'Ah! well!'

'Of course.'

'If I'm not asked this time, I shall die of grief.'

'Have you made the request before?'

'I have attempted!'

'Well?'

'When the Lord Chamberlain refused me, I shed tears of blood,' Madame Wetme wanly retailed.

'It would have been easier, no doubt, in the late king's time!' Madame Wetme took a long sighing breath.

'I only once saw him in my life,' she said, 'and then he was standing against a tree, in an attitude offensive to modesty.'

'Tell me . . . as a public man, what has your husband done——'

'His money helped to avert, I always contend, the noisy misery of a War!'

'He's open-handed?'

'Ah . . . as you would find. . . .'

The Duchess considered. 'I *might*,' she said, 'get you cards for a State concert. . . .'

'A State concert, Duchess? That's no good to me!'

'A drawing-room you know is a very dull affair.'

'I will liven it!'

'Or an invitation perhaps to begin with to one of the Embassies— the English for instance might lead. . . .'

'Nowhere . . . ! You can't depend on that: people have asked me to lunch, and left me to pay for them . . . ! There is so much trickery in Society. . . .' Madame Wetme laughed.

The Duchess smiled quizzically. 'I forget if you know the Tolgas,' she said.

'By "name"!'

'The Countess is more about the throne at present than I.'

'Possibly—but oh *you* who do *everything,* Duchess?' Madame Wetme entreated.

'I suppose there are things still one wouldn't do however——!' the Duchess took offence.

'The Tolgas are so hard.'

'You want a misfortune and they're sweet to you. Successful persons they're positively hateful to!'

'These women of the bedchamber are all alike so glorified. You would never credit they were chambermaids at all! I often smile to myself when I see one of them at a *première* at the Opera, gorged with pickings, and think that, most likely, but an hour before she was stumbling along a corridor with a pailful of slops!'

'You're fond of music, Madame?' the Duchess asked.

'It's my joy: I could go again and again to *The Blue Banana*!'

'I've not been.'

'Pom-pom, pompity-pom! We might go one night, perhaps, together.'

'...'

'Doudja Degdeg is always a draw, although naturally now she is getting on!'

'And I fear so must I'—the Duchess rose remarking.

'So soon?'

'I'm only sorry I can't stay longer——!'

'Then it's all decided,' Madame Wetme murmured archly as she pressed the bell.

'Oh, I'd not say that.'

'If I'm not asked, remember, this time, I shall die with grief.'

'To-night the duke and I are dining with the Leucippes, and possibly ...' the Duchess broke off to listen to the orchestra in the café below, which was playing the waltz-air from *Der Rosenkavalier*.

'They play well!' she commented.

'People often tell me so.'

'It must make one restless, dissatisfied, that yearning, yearning music continually at the door!'

Madame Wetme sighed.

'It makes you often long,' she said, 'to begin your life again!'

'Again?'

'Really it's queer I came to yoke myself with a man so little fine. . . .'

'Still——! If he's open-handed,' the Duchess murmured as she left the room.

<hr/>

✿✿✿ *IV* ✿✿✿

ONE grey, unsettled morning (it was the first of June) the English Colony of Kairoulla* awoke in arms. It usually did when the Embassy entertained. But the omissions of the Ambassador were, as old Mr. Ladboyson, the longest-established member of the colony, declared, 'not to be fathomed,' and many of those overlooked declared they should go all the same. Why should Mrs. Montgomery (who, when all was said and done, was nothing but a governess) be

* The Capital of Pisuerga.

invited and not Mrs. Barleymoon who was 'nothing' (in the most distinguished sense of the word) at all? Mrs. Barleymoon's position, as a captain's widow with means, unquestionably came before Mrs. Montgomery's, who drew a salary and hadn't often an h.

Miss Grizel Hopkins, too—the cousin of an Earl, and Mrs. Bedley, the 'Mother' of the English Colony, both had been ignored. It was true Ann Bedley kept a circulating library and a tea-room combined and gave 'Information' to tourists as well (a thing she had done these forty years), but was that a sufficient reason why she should be totally taboo? *No*; in old Lord Clanlubber's time all had been made welcome and there had been none of these heartburnings at all. Even the Irish coachman of the Archduchess was known to have been received—although it had been outside of course upon the lawn. Only gross carelessness, it was felt, on the part of those attachés could account for the extraordinary present neglect.

'I don't myself mind much,' Mrs. Bedley said, who was seated over a glass of morning milk and 'a plate of fingers' in the *Circulating* end of the shop: 'going out at night upsets me. And the last time Dr. Babcock was in he warned me not.'

'What is the Embassy there for but to be hospitable?' Mrs. Barleymoon demanded from the summit of a ladder, where she was choosing herself a book.

'You're showing your petticoat, dear—excuse me telling you,' Mrs. Bedley observed.

'When will you have something new, Mrs. Bedley?'

'Soon, dear . . . soon.'

'It's always "soon," ' Mrs. Barleymoon complained.

'Are you looking for anything, Bessie, in particular?' a girl, with loose blue eyes that did not seem quite firm in her head, and a literary face, enquired.

'No, only something,' Mrs. Barleymoon replied, 'I've not had before and before and before.'

'By the way, Miss Hopkins,' Mrs. Bedley said, 'I've to fine you for pouring tea over *My Stormy Past.*'

'It was coffee, Mrs. Bedley—not tea.'

'Never mind, dear, what it was, the charge for a stain is the same as you know,' Mrs. Bedley remarked, turning to attend to Mrs. Montgomery who, with his Naughtiness, Prince Olaf, had entered the Library.

'Is it in?' Mrs. Montgomery mysteriously asked.

The Flower Beneath the Foot

Mrs. Bedley assumed her glasses.

'*Mmnops*,' she replied, peering with an air of secretiveness in her private drawer where she would sometimes reserve or 'hold back' a volume for a subscriber who happened to be in her special good graces.

'I've often said,' Mrs. Barleymoon from her ladder sarcastically let fall, 'that Mrs. Bedley has her pets!'

'You are all my pets, my dear,' Mrs. Bedley softly cooed.

'Have you read *Men—My Delight*, Bessie?' Miss Hopkins asked, 'by Cora Velasquez.'

'No!'

'It's not perhaps a very . . . It's about two dark, and three fair, men,' she added vaguely.

'Most women's novels seem to run off the rails before they reach the end, and I'm not very fond of them,' Mrs. Barleymoon said.

'And anyway, dear, it's out,' Mrs. Bedley asserted.

'*The Passing of Rose* I read the other day,' Mrs. Montgomery said, 'and *so* enjoyed it.'

'Isn't that one of Ronald Firbank's books?'

'No, dear, I don't think it is. But I never remember an author's name and I don't think it matters!'

'I suppose I'm getting squeamish! But this Ronald Firbank I can't take to at all. *Valmouth!* Was there ever a novel more coarse? I assure you I hadn't gone very far when I had to put it down.'

'It's *out*,' Mrs. Bedley suavely said, 'as well,' she added, 'as the rest of them.'

'I once met him,' Miss Hopkins said, dilating slightly the *retinae* of her eyes. 'He told me writing books was by no means easy!'

Mrs. Barleymoon shrugged.

'Have you nothing more enthralling, Mrs. Bedley,' she persuasively asked, 'tucked away?'

'Try *The Call of the Stage*, dear,' Mrs. Bedley suggested.

'You forget, Mrs. Bedley,' Mrs. Barleymoon replied, regarding solemnly her *crêpe*.

'Or *Mary of the Manse*, dear.'

'I've read *Mary of the Manse* twice, Mrs. Bedley—and I don't propose to read it again.'

'. . . . . ?'

'. . . . . !'

Mrs. Bedley became abstruse.

34

'It's dreadful how many poets take to drink,' she reflected.

A sentiment to which her subscribers unanimously assented.

'I'm taking *Men are Animals*, by the Hon. Mrs. Victor Smythe, and *What Every Soldier Ought to Know*, Mrs. Bedley,' Miss Hopkins breathed.

'And I *The East is Whispering*,' Mrs. Barleymoon in hopeless tones affirmed.

'Robert Hitchinson! He's a good author.'

'Do you think so? I feel his books are all written in hotels with the bed unmade at the back of the chair.'

'And I dare say you're right, my dear.'

'Well, Mrs. Bedley, I must go—if I want to walk to my husband's grave,' Mrs. Barleymoon declared.

'Poor Bessie Barleymoon,' Mrs. Bedley sighed, after Mrs. Barleymoon and Miss Hopkins had gone: 'I fear she frets!'

'We all have our trials, Mrs. Bedley.'

'And some more than others.'

'Court life, Mrs. Bedley, it's a funny thing.'

'It looks as though we may have an English Queen, Mrs. Montgomery.'

'I don't believe it!'

'Most of the daily prints I see are devoting leaders to the little dog the Princess Elsie sent out the other day.'

'Odious, ill-mannered, horrid little beast. . . .'

'It seems, dear, he ran from room to room looking for her until he came to the prince's door, where he just lay down and whined.'

'And what does that prove, Mrs. Bedley?'

'I really don't know, Mrs. Montgomery. But the press seemed to find it "significant," ' Mrs. Bedley replied as a Nun of the Flaming-Hood with a jolly face all gold with freckles entered the shop.

'Have you *Valmouth* by Ronald Firbank or *Inclinations* by the same author?' she asked.

'Neither, I'm sorry—both are out!'

'Maladetta ✠ ✠✠ ✠ ! But I'll be passing soon again,' the Sister answered as she twinklingly withdrew.

'You'd not think now by the look of her she had been at Girton!' Mrs. Bedley remarked.

'Once a Girton girl always a Girton girl, Mrs. Bedley.'

'It seems a curate drove her to it. . . .'

35

The Flower Beneath the Foot

'I'm scarcely astonished. Looking back, I remember the average curate at home as something between a eunuch and a snigger.'

'Still, dear, I could never renounce my religion. As I said to the dear Chaplain only the other day (while he was having some tea), Oh, if only I were a man, I said! Wouldn't I like to *denounce* the disgraceful goings-on every Sabbath down the street at the church of the Blue Jesus.'

'And I assure you it's positively *nothing,* Mrs. Bedley, at the Jesus, to what it is at the church of St. Mary the Fair! I was at the wedding of one of the equerries lately, and never saw anything like it.'

'It's about time there was an English wedding, in *my* opinion, Mrs. Montgomery!'

'There's not been one in the Colony indeed for some time.'

Mrs. Bedley smiled undaunted.

'I trust I may be spared to dance before long at Dr. and Mrs. Babcock's!' she exclaimed.

'Kindly leave Cunnie out of it, Mrs. Bedley,' Mrs. Montgomery begged.

'So it's Cunnie already you call him!'

'Dr. Cuncliffe and I scarcely meet.'

'People talk of the immense sameness of marriage, Mrs. Montgomery; but all the same, my dear, a widow's not much to be envied.'

'There are times, it's true, Mrs. Bedley, when a woman feels she needs fostering; but it's a feeling she should try to fight against.'

'Ah, my dear, I never could resist *a mon!*' Mrs. Bedley exclaimed.

Mrs. Montgomery sighed.

'Once,' she murmured meditatively, 'men (those procurers of delights) engaged me utterly. . . . I was their *slave.* . . . Now . . . One does not burn one's fingers twice, Mrs. Bedley.'

Mrs. Bedley grew introspective.

'My poor husband sometimes would be a little frightening, a little fierce . . . at night, my dear, especially. Yet how often now I miss him!'

'You're better off as you are, Mrs. Bedley, believe me,' Mrs. Montgomery declared, looking round for his Naughtiness, who was amusing himself on the library-steps.

'You must find him a handful to educate, my dear.'

'It will be a relief *indeed*, Mrs. Bedley, when he goes to Eton!'

'I'm told so long as a boy is grounded . . .'

'His English accent is excellent, Mrs. Bedley, and he shows quite a talent for languages,' Mrs. Montgomery assured.

'I'm delighted, I'm sure, to hear it!'

'Well, Mrs. Bedley. I mustn't stand dawdling: I've to 'ave my 'air shampooed and waved for the Embassy party to-night you know!' And taking his Naughtiness by the hand, the royal governess withdrew.

V

AMONG those attached to the Chedorlahomor expedition was a young—if thirty-five be young—eccentric Englishman from Wales, the Hon. 'Eddy' Monteith, a son of Lord Intriguer. Attached first to one thing and then another, without ever being attached to any, his life had been a gentle series of attachments all along. But this new attachment was surely something better than a temporary secretaryship to a minister, or 'aiding' an ungrateful general, or waiting in through draughts (so affecting to the constitution) in the ante-rooms of hard-worked royalty, in the purlieus of Pall Mall. Secured by the courtesy of his ex-chief, Sir Somebody Something, an old varsity friend of his father, the billet of 'surveyor and occasional help' to the Chedorlahomorian excavation party had been waywardly accepted by the Hon. 'Eddy' just as he had been upon the point of attaching himself, to the terror of his relatives and the amusement of his friends, to a monastery of the Jesuit Order as a likely candidate for the cowl.

Indeed he had already gone so far as to sit to an artist for his portrait in the habit of a monk, gazing ardently at what looked to be the Escurial itself, but in reality was nothing other than an 'impression' from the kitchen garden of Intriguer Park. And now this sudden change, this call to the East instead. There had been no time, unfortunately, before setting out to sit again in the picturesque 'sombrero' of an explorer, but a ready camera had performed miracles, and the relatives of the Hon. 'Eddy' were relieved to behold his smiling countenance in the illustrated weeklies, pick in hand, or with one foot resting on his spade while examining a broken jar, with just below the various editors' comments: *To join the Expedition to Chedorlahomor—the Hon. 'Eddy' Monteith, only son of Lord Intriguer*; or, *Off to Chedorlahomor!* or, *Bon Voyage . . . !*

Yes, the temptation of the expedition was not to be withstood, and for vows and renunciations there was always time! . . . And now leaning idly on his window ledge in a spare room of the Embassy, while his man unpacked, he felt, as he surveyed the distant dome of the Blue Jesus above the dwarf-palm trees before the house, half-way to the East already. He was suffering a little in his dignity from the contretemps of his reception; for, having arrived at the Embassy among a jobbed troop of serfs engaged for the night, he had at first been mistaken by Lady Something for one of them. 'The cloak-room will be in the smoking-room!' she had said, and in spite of her laughing excuses and ample apologies he could not easily forget it. What was there in his appearance that could conceivably recall a cloak-room attendant—? *He* who had been assured he had the profile of a 'Rameses' ! And going to a mirror he scanned, with less perhaps than his habitual contentment, the light, liver-tinted hair, grey narrow eyes, hollow cheeks, and pale mouth like a broken moon. He was looking just a little fatigued, he fancied, from his journey, and, really, it was all his hostess deserved, if he didn't go down.

'I have a headache, Mario,' he told his man (a Neapolitan who had been attached to almost as many professions as his master). 'I shall not leave my room! Give me a kimono: I will take a bath.'

Undressing slowly, he felt, as the garments dropped away, he was acting properly in refraining from attending the soirée, and only hoped the lesson would not be 'lost' on Lady Something, who, he feared, must be incurably dense. ·

Lying amid the dissolving bath crystals while his man-servant deftly bathed him, he fell into a sort of coma, sweet as a religious trance. Beneath the rhythmic sponge, perfumed with *Kiki*, he was St. Sebastian, and as the water became cloudier, and the crystals evaporated amid the steam, he was Teresa . . . and he would have been, most likely, the Blessed Virgin herself but that the bath grew gradually cold.

'You're looking a little pale, sir, about the gills!' the valet, solicitously observed, as he gently dried him.

The Hon. 'Eddy' winced. 'I forbid you ever to employ the word gill, Mario,' he exclaimed. 'It is inharmonious, and in English it jars; whatever it may do in Italian.'

'Overtired, sir, was what I meant to say.'

'Basta!' his master replied, with all the brilliant glibness of the Berlitz-school.

Swathed in towels, it was delicious to relax his powder-blanched limbs upon a comfy couch, while Mario went for dinner: 'I don't care what it is! So long as it isn't—' (naming several dishes that he particularly abhorred, or might be 'better,' perhaps, without)—'And be sure, fool, not to come back without champagne.'

He could not choose but pray that the Ambassadress had nothing whatever to do with the Embassy cellar, for from what he had seen of her already he had only a slight opinion of her discernment.

Really he might have been excused had he taken her to be the cook instead of the social representative of the Court of St. James, and he was unable to repress a caustic smile on recollecting her appearance that afternoon, with her hat awry, crammed with *Maréchal Niel* roses, hot, and decoiffed, flourishing a pair of garden-gauntlets, as she issued her commands. What a contrast to his own Mamma—'so different,' . . . and his thoughts, returned to Intriguer —'dear Intriguer, . . .' that, if only to vex his father's ghost, he would one day turn into a Jesuit college! The Confessional should be fitted in the paternal study, and engravings of the Inquisition, or the sweet faces of Lippi and Fra Angelico, replace the Agrarian certificates and tiresome trophies of the chase; while the crack of the discipline in Lent would echo throughout the house! How 'useful' his friend Robbie Renard would have been. But alas poor Robbie; he had passed through life at a rapid canter, having died at nineteen. . . .

Musingly he lit a cigarette. Through the open window a bee droned in on the blue air of evening. Closing his eyes he fell to considering whether the bee of one country would understand the remarks of that of another. The effect of the soil of a nation, had it consequences upon its flora? Were plants influenced at their roots? People sometimes spoke (and especially ladies) of the language of flowers . . . the pollen therefore of an English rose would probably vary, not inconsiderably, from that of a French, and a bee born and bred at home (at *Intriguer,* for instance) would be at a loss to understand (it clearly followed) the conversation of one born and bred, here, abroad. A bee's idiom varied then, as did man's! And he wondered, this being proved the case, where the best bees' accents were generally acquired. . . .

Opening his eyes, he perceived his former school chum, Lionel

Limpness—Lord Tiredstock's third (and perhaps most gifted) son, who was an honorary attaché at the Embassy—standing over him, his spare figure already arrayed in an evening suit.

'Sorry to hear you're off colour, Old Dear!' he exclaimed, sinking down upon the couch beside his friend.

'I'm only a little shaken, Lionel . . . : have a cigarette.'

'And so you're off to Chedorlahomor, Old Darling?' Lord Tiredstock's third son said.

'I suppose so . . .' the only son of Lord Intriguer replied.

'Well, I wish I was going too!'

'It would be charming, Lionel, of course to have you: but they might appoint you Vice-Consul at Sodom, or something?'

'Why *Vice*? Besides . . . ! There's no consulate there yet,' Lord Tiredstock's third son said, examining the objects upon the portable altar, draped in prelatial purple, of his friend.

'Turn over, Old Dear, while I chastise you!' he exclaimed, waving what looked to be a tortoiseshell lorgnon to which had been attached three threads of 'cerulean' floss silk.

'Put it down, Lionel, and don't be absurd.'

'Over we go. Come on.'

'Really, Lionel.'

'Penitence! To thy knees, Sir!'

And just as it seemed that the only son of Lord Intriguer was to be deprived of all his towels, the Ambassadress mercifully entered.

'*Poor* Mr. Monteith!' she exclaimed in tones of concern, bustling forward with a tablespoon and a bottle containing physic, '*so* unfortunate. . . . Taken ill at the moment you arrive! But Life is like that!'

Clad in the flowing circumstance of an oyster satin ball-dress, and all a-glitter like a Christmas tree (with jewels), her arrival perhaps saved her guest a 'whipping.'

'Had I known, Lady Something, I was going to be ill, I would have gone to the Ritz!' the Hon. 'Eddy' gasped.

'And you'd have been bitten all over!' Lady Something replied.

'Bitten all over?'

'The other evening we were dining at the Palace, and I heard the dear King say—but I oughtn't to talk and excite you——'

'By the way, Lady Something,' Lord Tiredstock's third son asked: 'what is the etiquette for the Queen of Dateland's eunuch?'

'It's all according; but you had better ask Sir Somebody, Mr.

40

Limpness,' Lady Something replied, glancing with interest at the portable altar.

'I've done so, and he declared he'd be jiggered!'

'I recollect in Pera when we occupied the Porte, they seemed (those of the old Grand Vizier—oh what a good-looking man he was—! such eyes—! and such a *way* with him—! *Despot! !*) only too thankful to crouch in corners.'

'Attention with that castor-oil . . . !'

'It's not castor-oil; it's a little decoction of my own,—aloes, gregory, a dash of liquorice. And the rest is buckthorn!'

'Euh!'

'It's not so bad, though it mayn't be very nice. . . . Toss it off like a brave man, Mr. Monteith (nip his nostrils, Mr. Limpness), and while he takes it, I'll offer a silent prayer for him at that duck of an altar,' and, as good as her word, the Ambassadress made towards it.

'You're altogether too kind,' the Hon. 'Eddy' murmured, seeking refuge in a book—a volume of *Juvenilia* published for him by 'Blackwood of Oxford,' and becoming absorbed in its contents: 'Ah Doris'—'Lines to Doris'—'Lines to Doris: written under the influence of wine, sun and fever'—'Ode to Swinburne'—'Sad Tamarisks'—'Rejection'—'Doigts Obscènes'—'They Call me *Lily* !!' —'Land of Titian! Land of Verdi! O Italy!'—'I Heard the Clock:

> 'I heard the clock strike seven,
> Seven strokes I heard it strike!
> His Lordship's gone to London
> And won't be back to-night.'

He had written it at Intriguer, after a poignant domestic disagreement; his Papa,—the 'his lordship' of the poem—had stayed away, however, considerably longer. . . . And here was a sweet thing suggested by an old Nursery Rhyme, 'Loves, have you Heard?'

> 'Loves, have you heard about the rabbits? ?
> They have such odd fantastic habits. . . .
> Oh, Children . . . ! I daren't disclose to You
> The licentious things *some* rabbits do.'

It had 'come to him' quite suddenly out ferreting one day with the footman. . . .

But a loud crash as the portable altar collapsed beneath the weight of the Ambassadress roused him unpleasantly from his thoughts.

'Horrid dangerous thing!' she exclaimed as Lord Tiredstock's third son assisted her to rise from her 'Silent' prayer: 'I had no idea it wasn't solid! But Life is like that . . .' she added somewhat wildly.

'Pity O my God! Deliver me!' the Hon. 'Eddy' breathed, but the hour of *deliverance* it seemed was not just yet; for at that instant the Hon. Mrs. Chilleywater, the 'literary' wife of the first attaché, thrust her head in at the door.

'How are you?' she asked, 'I thought perhaps I might find *Harold.* . . .'

'He's with Sir Somebody.'

'Such mysteries!' Lady Something said.

'This betrothal of Princess Elsie's is simply wearing him out,' Mrs. Chilleywater declared, sweeping the room with half-closed, expressionless eyes.

'It's a pity you can't pull the strings for us,' Lady Something ventured: 'I was saying so lately to Sir Somebody.'

'I wish I could, dear Lady Something: I wouldn't mind wagering I'd soon bring it off!'

'Have you fixed up Grace Gillstow yet, Mrs. Chilleywater?' Lord Tiredstock's third son asked.

'She shall marry Baldwin: but not before she has been seduced first by Barnaby. . . .'

'What are you talking about?' the Hon. 'Eddy' queried.

'Of Mrs. Chilleywater's forthcoming book.'

'Why should Barnaby get Grace—? Why not Tex?'

But Mrs. Chilleywater refused to enter into reasons.

'She is looking for cowslips,' she said, 'and oh I've such a wonderful description of a field of cowslips. . . . They make quite a darling setting for a powerful scene of lust.'

'So Grace loses her virtue!' Lord Tiredstock's third son exclaimed.

'Even so she's far too good for Baldwin; after the underhand shabby way he behaved to Charlotte, Kate, and Millicent!'

'Life is like that, dear,' the Ambassadress blandly observed.

'It ought not to be, Lady Something!' Mrs. Chilleywater looked vindictive.

Née Victoria Gellybore-Frinton, and the sole heir of Lord Seafairer of Sevenelms, Kent, Mrs. Harold Chilleywater, since her marriage 'for Love,' had developed a disconcerting taste for fiction

—a taste that was regarded at the Foreign Office with disapproving forbearance. . . . So far her efforts (written under her maiden name in full with her husband's as well appended) had been confined to lurid studies of low life (of which she knew nothing at all); but the Hon. Harold Chilleywater had been gently warned that if he was not to remain at Kairoulla until the close of his career the style of his wife must really grow less *virile*.

'I agree with V. G. F.,' the Hon. Lionel Limpness murmured, fondling meditatively his 'Charlie Chaplin' moustache—'Life ought not to be.'

'It's a mistake to bother oneself over matters that can't be remedied.'

Mrs. Chilleywater acquiesced. 'You're right indeed, Lady Something,' she said, 'but I'm so sensitive. . . . I seem to *know* when I talk to a man the colour of his braces . . . I I say to myself: "Yours are violet. . . ." "Yours are blue. . . ." "His are red. . . ." '

'I'll bet you anything, Mrs. Chilleywater, you like, you won't guess what mine are,' the Hon. Lionel Limpness said.

'I should say, Mr. Limpness, that they were *multi-hued*—like Jacob's,' Mrs. Chilleywater replied, as she withdrew her head.

The Ambassadress prepared to follow.

'Come, Mr. Limpness,' she exclaimed, 'we've exhausted the poor fellow quite enough—and besides, here comes his dinner.'

'Open the champagne, Mario,' his master commanded immediately they were alone.

' "Small " beer is all the butler would allow, sir.'

'Damn the b . . . butler!'

'What he calls a *demi-brune*, sir. In Naples we say *spumanti*!'

'To —— with it.'

'Non è tanto amaro, sir, it's more sharp, as you'd say, than bitter. . . .'

' . . . . . . ! ! ! ! ! ! '

And language *unmonastic* far into the night reigned supreme.

Standing beneath the portraits of King Geo and Queen Glory, Lady Something, behind a large sheaf of mauve malmaisons, was growing stiff. Already, for the most part, the guests were welcomed, and it was only the Archduchess now, who as usual was late, that kept their Excellencies lingering at the head of the stairs. Her Majesty Queen Thleeanouhee of the Land of Dates had just arrived, but seemed loath to leave the stairs, while her hostess, whom she addressed affectionately as her *dear gazelle*, remained upon them—

'Let us go away by and by, my dear gazelle,' she exclaimed with a primitive smile, 'and remove our corsets and talk.'

'Unhappily Pisuerga is not the East, ma'am!' Lady Something replied.

'Never mind, my dear; we will introduce this innovation. . . .'

But the arrival of the Archduchess Elizabeth spared the Ambassadress from what might too easily have become an 'incident.'

In the beautiful chandeliered apartments several young couples were pirouetting to the inevitable waltz from the Blue Banana, but most of the guests seemed to prefer exploring the conservatories and winter garden, or elbowing their way into a little room where a new portrait of Princess Elsie had been discreetly placed. . . .

'One feels, of course, there *was* a sitting—; but still, it isn't like her!' those that had seen her said.

'The artist has attributed to her at least the pale spent eyes of her father!' the Duchess of Cavaljos remarked to her niece, who was standing quite silent against a rose-red curtain.

Mademoiselle de Nazianzi made no reply. Attaching not the faintest importance to the rumours afloat, still, she could not but feel, at times, a little heart-shaken. . . .

The duchess plied her fan.

'She will become florid in time like her mother!' she cheerfully predicted, turning away just as the Archduchess herself approached to inspect the painting.

Swathed in furs, on account of a troublesome cough contracted paddling, she seemed nevertheless in charming spirits.

'Have you been to my new *Pipi*?' she asked.

'Not yet——'

'Oh but you must!'

'I'm told it's even finer than the one at the railway station. Ah, from musing too long on that Hellenic frieze, how often I've missed my train!' the Duchess of Cavaljos murmured, with a little fat deep laugh.

'I have a heavenly idea for another—yellow tiles with thistles. . . .'

'Your Royal Highness never repeats herself!'

'Nothing will satisfy me this time,' the Archduchess declared, 'but files of state-documents in all the dear little boxes: in secret, secrets!' she added archly, fixing her eyes on the assembly.

'It's positively pitiable,' the Duchess of Cavaljos commented,

'how the Countess of Tolga is losing her good looks; she has the
air to-night of a tired business-woman!'

'She looks at other women as though she would inhale them,' the
Archduchess answered, throwing back her furs with a gesture
of superb grace, in order to allow her robe to be admired by a lady
who was scribbling busily away behind a door, with little nervous
lifts of the head. For *noblesse oblige*, and the correspondent of the
Jaw-Waw, the illustrious Eva Schnerb, was not to be denied.

'Among the many balls of a brilliant season,' the diarist, with her
accustomed fluency wrote, 'none surpassed that which I witnessed
at the English Embassy last night. I sat in a corner of the Winter
Garden and literally gorged myself upon the display of dazzling
uniforms and jewels. The Ambassadress Lady Something was
looking really regal in dawn-white draperies, holding a bouquet
of the new mauve malmaisons (which are all the vogue just now),
but no one, *I* thought, looked better than the *Archduchess, etc. . . .*
Helping the hostess, I noticed Mrs. Harold Chilleywater, in an
"æsthetic" gown of flame-hued Kanitra silk edged with Armousky
fur (to possess a dear woolly Armousk as a pet as considered *chic*
this season), while over her brain—an intellectual caprice, I wonder?—I saw a tinsel bow. . . . She is a daughter of the fortieth
Lord Seafairer of Sevenelms Park (so famous for its treasures)
and is very artistic and literary, having written several novels of
English life under her maiden name of Victoria Gellybore-Frinton:
—she inherits considerable cleverness *also* from her Mother. Dancing
indefatigably (as she always does!), Miss Ivy Something seemed
to be thoroughly enjoying her Father's ball: I hear on *excellent
authority* there is no foundation in the story of her engagement to a
certain young Englishman, said to be bound ere long for the ruins of
Sodom and Gomorrah. Among the late arrivals were the Duke
and Duchess of Varna—*she* all in golden tissues: they came together
with Madame Wetme, who is one of the new hostesses of the season,
you know, and they say has bought the Duke of Varna's palatial
town-house in Samaden Square——'

'There,' the Archduchess murmured, drawing her wraps about
her with a sneeze: 'she has said quite enough now I think about
my *toilette*!'

But the illustrious Eva was in unusual fettle, and only closed
her notebook towards Dawn, when the nib of her pen caught fire.

⟨⟩ VI ⟨⟩

AND suddenly the Angel of Death passed by and the brilliant season waned. In the Archduchess's bed-chamber, watching the antics of priests and doctors, he sat there unmoved. Propped high by many bolsters, in a vast blue canopied bed, the Archduchess lay staring laconically at a diminutive model of a flight of steps, leading to what appeared to be intended, perhaps, as a hall of Attent, off which opened quite a lot of little doors, most of which bore the word: 'Engaged.' A doll, with ruddy face, in charge, smiled indolently as she sat feigning knitting, suggesting vague 'fleshly thoughts,' whenever he looked up, in the Archduchess's spiritual adviser.

And the mind of the sinking woman, as her thoughts wandered, appeared to be tinged with 'matter' too: 'I recollect the first time I heard the *Blue Danube* played!' she broke out: 'it was at Schönbrunn—schönes Schönbrunn—My cousin Ludwig of Bavaria came—I wore—the Emperor said——'

'If your imperial highness would swallow this!' Dr. Cuncliffe Babcock started forward with a glass.

'Trinquons, trinquons et vive l'amour! Schneider sang that——'

'If your imperial highness——'

'Ah my dear Vienna. Where's Teddywegs?'

At the Archduchess's little escritoire at the foot of the bed her Dreaminess was making ready a few private telegrams, breaking without undue harshness the melancholy news, 'Poor Lizzie has ceased articulating,' she did not think she could improve on that, and indeed had written it several times in her most temperamental hand, when the Archduchess had started suddenly cackling about Vienna.

'*Ssssh*, Lizzie—I never can write when people talk!'

'I want Teddywegs.'

'The Countess Yvorra took him for a run round the courtyard.'

'I think I must undertake a convenience next for dogs. . . . It is disgraceful they have not got one already, poor creatures,' the Archduchess crooned, accepting the proffered glass.

'Yes, yes, dear,' the Queen exclaimed, rising and crossing to the window.

The bitter odour of the oleander flowers outside oppressed the breathless air and filled the room as with a faint funereal music. So still a day. Tending the drooping sun-saturated flowers, a gardener with long ivory arms alone seemed animate.

'Pull up your skirt, Marquise! Pull it up. . . . It's dragging, a little, in the water.'

'*Judica me, Deus,*' in imperious tones the priest by the bedside besought: '*et discerne causam meam de gente non sancta. Parce, Domine. Parce populo tuo. Ne in aeternum irasceris nobis.*'

'A whale! A whale!'

'*Sustinuit anima mea in verbo ejus, speravit anima mea in Domino.*'

'Elsie?' A look of wondrous happiness overspread the Archduchess's face—She was wading—wading again among the irises and rushes; wading, her hand in Princess Elsie's hand, through a glittering golden sea, towards the wide horizon.

The plangent cry of a peacock rose disquietingly from the garden.

'I'm nothing but nerves, doctor,' her Dreaminess lamented, fidgeting with the crucifix that dangled at her neck upon a chain. *Ultra* feminine, she disliked that another—even *in extremis*—should absorb *all* the limelight.

'A change of scene, ma'am, would be probably beneficial,' Dr. Cuncliffe Babcock replied, eyeing askance the Countess of Tolga who unobtrusively entered.

'The couturiers attend your pleasure, ma'am,' in impassive undertones she said, 'to fit your mourning.'

'Oh, tell them the Queen is too tired to try on now,' her Dreaminess answered, repairing in agitation towards a glass.

'They would come here, ma'am,' the Countess said, pointing persuasively to the little ante-room of the Archduchess, where two nuns of the Flaming-Hood were industriously telling their beads.

'—— I don't know why, but this glass refuses to flatter me!'

'*Benedicamus Domino! Ostende nobis Domine misericordiam tuam. Et salutare tuum da nobis!*'

'Well, just a toque,' the Queen sadly assented.

'*Indulgentiam absolutionem et remissionem peccatorum nostrorum tribuat nobis omnipotens et misericors Dominus.*'

'Guess who is at the Ritz, ma'am, this week!' the Countess demurely murmured.

'Who is at the Ritz this week, I can't,' the Queen replied.

'*Nobody!*'

'Why, how so?'

'The Ambassadress of England, it seems, has alarmed the world away. I gather they mean to prosecute!'

The Archduchess sighed.

'I want mauve sweet-peas,' she listlessly said.

'Her spirit soars; her thoughts are in the *Champs-Elysées*,' the Countess exclaimed, withdrawing noiselessly to warn the milliners.

'Or in the garden,' the Queen reflected, returning to the window. And she was standing there, her eyes fixed half wistfully upon the long ivory arms of the kneeling gardener, when the Angel of Death (who had sat unmoved throughout the day) arose.

It was decided to fix a period of mourning of fourteen days for the late Archduchess.

VII

SWANS and sunlight. A little fishing-boat with coral sails. A lake all grey and green. Beatitude intense. Consummate calm. It was nice to be at the Summer Palace after all.

'The way the air will catch your cheek and make a rose of it,' the Countess of Tolga breathed. And as none of the company heeded her: 'How sweetly the air takes one's cheek,' she sighed again.

The post-prandial exercise of the members of the Court through the palace grounds was almost an institution.

The first half of the mourning prescribed had as yet not run its course, but the tongues of the Queen's ladies had long since made an end of it.

'I hate dancing with a fat man,' Mademoiselle de Nazianzi was saying: 'for if you dance at all near him, his stomach hits you, while if you pull away, you catch either the scent of his breath or the hair of his beard.'

'But, you innocent baby, *all* big men haven't beards,' Countess Medusa Rappa remarked.

'Haven't they? Never mind. Everything's so beautiful,' the young girl inconsequently exclaimed. 'Look at that Thistle! and that Bee! Oh, you darling!'

'Ah, how one's face unbends in gardens!' the Countess of Tolga said, regarding the scene before her with a far-away pensive glance.

Along the lake's shore, sheltered from the winds by a ring of wooded hills, showed many a proud retreat, mirroring its marble terraces to the waveless waters of the lake.

Beneath a twin-peaked crag (known locally as the White Mountain, whose slopes frequently would burst forth into patches of garlic that from the valley resembled snow) nestled the Villa Clement, rented each season by the Ambassador of the Court of St. James, while half screened by conifers and rhododendrons, and in the lake itself, was St. Helena—the home and place of retirement of a 'fallen' minister of the Crown.

Countess Medusa Rappa cocked her sunshade. 'Whose boat is that,' she asked, 'with the azure oars?'

'It looks nothing but a pea-pod!' the Countess of Tolga declared.

'It belongs to a darling, with delicious lips and eyes like brown chestnuts,' Mademoiselle de Lambèse informed.

'Ah!... Ah!... Ah!... Ah!...' her colleagues crooned.

'A sailor?'

The Queen's maid nodded. 'There's a partner, though,' she added, 'a blue-eyed, gashed-cheeked angel. . . .'

Mademoiselle de Nazianzi looked away.

'I love the lake with the white wandering ships,' she sentimentally stated, descrying in the distance the prince.

It was usually towards this time, the hour of the siesta, that the lovers would meet and taste their happiness, but to-day it seemed ordained otherwise.

Before the heir apparent had determined whether to advance or retreat, his father and mother were upon him, attended by two dowagers newly launched.

'The song of the pilgrim women, how it haunts me,' one of the dowagers was holding forth: 'I could never tire of that beautiful, beautiful music! Never tire of it. Ne-ver. . . .'

'Ta, ta, ta, ta, ' the Queen vociferated girlishly, slipping her arm affectionately through that of her son.

'How spent you look, my boy. . . . Those eyes. . . .'

His Weariness grimaced.

'They've just been rubbing in Elsie!' he said.

'Who?'

' "Vaseline" and "Nanny-goat"!'

'Well?'

'Nothing will shake me.'

'What are your objections?'

49

'She's so extraordinarily uninteresting!'

'Oh, Yousef!' his mother faltered: '*do you wish to break my heart?*'

'We had always thought you too lacking in initiative,' King William said (tucking a few long hairs back into his nose), 'to marry against our wishes.'

'They say she walks too wonderfully,' the Queen courageously pursued.

'What? Well?'

'Yes.'

'Thank God for it.'

'And can handle a horse as few others can!'

Prince Yousef closed his eyes.

He had not forgotten how as an undergraduate in England he had come upon the princess once while out with the hounds. And it was only by a consummate effort that he was able to efface the sinister impression she had made—her lank hair falling beneath a man's felt-hat, her habit skirt torn to tatters, her full cheeks smeared in blood—the blood, so it seemed, of her 'first' fox.

A shudder seized him.

'No, nothing can possibly shake me,' he murmured again.

With a detached, cold face, the Queen paused to inhale a rose.

(Oh, you gardens of Palaces . . . ! How often have you witnessed agitation and disappointment? You smooth, adorned paths . . . ! How often have you known the extremes of care . . . ?)

'It would be better to do away I think next year with that bed of cinerarias altogether,' the Queen of Pisuerga remarked, 'since persons won't go round it.'

Traversing the flower plat now, with the air of a black-beetle with a purpose, was the Countess Yvorra.

'We had supposed you higher-principled, Countess,' her sovereign admonished.

The Countess slightly flushed.

'I'm looking for groundsel for my birds, Sire,' she said—'for my little dickies!'

'We understand your boudoir is a sort of menagerie,' His Majesty affirmed.

The Countess tittered.

'Animals love me,' she archly professed. 'Birds perch on my breast if only I wave. . . . The other day a sweet red robin came and stayed for hours . . . !'

'The Court looks to you to set a high example,' the Queen declared, focusing quizzically a marble shape of Leda green with moss, for whose time-corroded plinth the late Archduchess's toy-terrier was just then showing a certain contempt.

The Countess's long, slightly pulpy fingers strayed nervously towards the rosary at her thigh.

'With your majesty's consent,' she said, 'I propose a campaign to the Island.'

'What? And beard the Count?'

'The salvation of one so fallen, in my estimation should be worth hereafter (at the present rate of exchange, but the values vary) . . . a Plenary perpetual-indulgence: I therefore,' the Countess said, with an upward fleeting glance (and doubtless guileless of intention of irony), 'feel it my *duty* to do what I can.'

'I trust you will take a bodyguard when you go to St. Helena?'

'And pray tell Count Cabinet from us,' the King looked implacable, 'we forbid him to serenade the Court this year! or to throw himself into the Lake again or to make himself a nuisance!'

'He was over early this morning, Willie,' the Queen retailed: 'I saw him from a window. Fishing, or feigning to! And with white kid gloves, and a red carnation.'

'Let us catch him stepping ashore!' The King displayed displeasure.

'And as usual the same mignon youth had charge of the tiller.'

'I could tell a singular story of that young man,' the Countess said: 'for he was once a choir-boy at the Blue Jesus. But perhaps I would do better to spare your ears. . . .'

'You would do better, a good deal, to spare my cinerarias,' her Dreaminess murmured, sauntering slowly on.

Sun so bright, trees so green, it was a perfect day. Through the glittering fronds of the palms shone the lake like a floor of silver glass strewn with white sails.

'It's odd,' the King observed, giving the dog Teddywegs a sly prod with his cane, 'how he follows Yousef.'

'He seems to know!' the Queen replied.

A remark which so annoyed the Prince that he curtly left the garden.

VIII

B UT this melancholy period of *crêpe,* a time of idle secrets and unbosomings, was to prove fatal to the happiness of Mademoiselle de Nazianzi. She now heard she was not the first in the Prince's life, and that most of the Queen's maids, indeed, had had identical experiences with her own. She furthermore learned, amid ripples of laughter, of her lover's relations with the Marquesa Pizzi-Parma and of his light dealings with the dancer April Flowers, a negress (to what depths??), at a time when he was enjoying the waxen favours of the wife of his Magnificence the Master of the Horse.

Chilled to the point of numbness, the mortified girl had scarcely winced, and when, on repairing to her room a little later, she had found his Weariness wandering in the corridor on the chance of a surreptitious kiss, she had bolted past him without look or word and sharply closed her door.

The Court had returned to colours when she opened it again, and such had been the trend of her meditations that her initial steps were directed, with deliberate austerity, towards the basilica of the Palace.

Except for the Countess Yvorra, with an *écharpe de décence* drawn over her hair, there was no one in it.

'I thank Thee God for this *escape,*' she murmured, falling to her knees before the silver branches of a cross. 'It is terrible; for I did so love him. . . . .
. . . .
. . . .
. . . . .and oh how could he ever, with *a negress?* . . . .
. . . .
. . . . Pho . . . .
. . . . I fear this complete upset has considerably aged me. . . . .
. . . . .But to Thee I cling . . . .
. . . .
. . . .
Preserve me at all times from the toils of the wicked, and forgive him, as *I* hope to forgive him soon.' Then kindling several candles,

with a lingering hand, she shaped her course towards the Kennels, called Teddywegs to her, and started, with an aching heart, for a walk.

It was a day of heavy somnolence. Skirting the Rosery, where gardeners with their slowly moving rakes were tending the sandy paths, she chose a neglected footway that descended towards the lake. Indifferent to the vivacity of Teddywegs, who would race on a little before her, then wait with leonine accouchments of head until she had almost reached him, when he would prick an ear and spring forward with a yap of exhortation, she proceeded leisurely and with many a pause, wrapped in her own mournful thoughts.

Alack! Among the court circle there was no one to whom in her disillusion she could look for solace, and her spirit yearned for Sister Ursula and the Convent of the Flaming-Hood.

Wending her way amid the tall trees, she felt she had never cared for Yousef as she had for Ursula . . . and broodingly, in order to ease her heart, she began comparing the two together as she walked along.

After all, what had he ever said that was not either commonplace or foolish? Whereas Sister Ursula's talk was invariably pointed, and often indeed so delicately that words seemed almost too crude a medium to convey her ethereal meanings, and she would move her evocative hands, and flash her aura, and it was no fault of hers if you hadn't a peep of the beyond. And the infinite tenderness of her last caress! Yousef's lips had seldom conveyed to hers the spell of Ursula's; and once indeed lately, when he had kissed her, there had been an unsavoury aroma of tobacco and *charcuterie*, which, to deal with, had required both tact and courage. . . . Ah dear Hood! What harmony life had held within. Unscrupulous and deceiving men might lurk around its doors (they often did) coveting the chaste, but Old Jane, the porteress, would open to no man beyond the merest crack. And how right were the nuns in their mistrust of man! Sister Ursula one day had declared, in uplifted mood, that 'marriage was obscene.' Was it—? . . . ? ? . . . Perhaps it might be—! How appalling if it was!

She had reached the lake.

Beneath a sky as white as platinum it lay, pearly, dove-like, scintillating capriciously where a heat-shrouded sun kindled its torpid waters into fleeting diamonds. A convulsive breeze strayed gratefully from the opposite shore, descending from the hills that rose up all veiled, and without detail, against the brilliant whiteness of the morning.

Sinking down upon the shingle by an upturned boat, she heaved a brief sigh, and drawing from her vanity-case the last epistles of the Prince, began methodically to arrange them in their proper sequence.

(1) 'What is the matter with my Dearest Girl?'
(2) 'My own tender little Lita, I do not understand—'
(3) 'Darling, what's this—?'
(4) 'Beloved one, I swear—'
(5) 'Your cruel silence—'

If published in a dainty brochure format about the time of his Coronation they ought to realise no contemptible sum and the proceeds might go to charity, she reflected, thrusting them back again carefully into the bag.

Then, finding the shingle too hard through her thin gown to remain seated long, she got up, and ran a mournful race with Teddywegs along the shore.

Not far along the lake was the 'village,' with the Hôtel d'Angleterre et du Lac, its stucco, belettered walls professing: 'Garages, Afternoon Tea, Modern Comfort!' Flitting by this and the unpretentious pier (where long, blonde fishing-nets lay drying in the sun), it was a relief to reach the remoter plage beyond.

Along the banks stretched vast brown carpets of corn and rye, broken by an occasional olive-garth, beneath whose sparse shade the heavy-eyed oxen blinked and whisked their tails, under the attacks of the water-gnats that were swarming around.

Musing on Negresses—and Can-Can dancers in particular—she strolled along a strand all littered with shells and little jewel-like stones.

The sun shone down more fiercely now, and soon, for freshness sake, she was obliged to take to the fields.

Passing among the silver drooping olives, relieved here and there by a stone-pine, or slender cypress-tree eternally green, she sauntered on, often lured aside to pluck the radiant wild-flowers by the way. On the banks the pinkest cyclamens were in bloom, and cornflowers of the hue of paradise, and fine-stemmed poppies flecked with pink.

'Pho! A Negress . . .' she murmured, following the flight of some waterfowl towards the opposite shore.

The mists had fallen from the hills, revealing old woods wrapped in the blue doom of summer.

Beyond those glowing heights, towards this hour, the nuns, each in her cool, shuttered cell, would be immersed in noontide prayer.

'Ursula—for thee!' she sighed, proffering her bouquet in the direction of the town.

A loud splash . . . the sight of a pair of delicate legs (mocking the Law's requirements under the Modesty Act as relating to bathers). . . . Mademoiselle de Nazianzi turned and fled. She had recognised *the Prince*.*

❧ IX ❧

AND in this difficult time of spiritual distress, made more trying perhaps because of the blazing midsummer days and long, pent feverish nights, Mademoiselle de Nazianzi turned in her tribulation towards religion.

The Ecclesiastical set at Court, composed of some six, or so, ex-Circes, under the command of the Countess Yvorra, were only too ready to welcome her, and invitations to meet Monsignor this or 'Father' that, who constantly were being *coaxed* from their musty sacristies and wan-faced acolytes in the capital, in order that they might officiate at Masses, Confessions and Breakfast-parties *à la fourchette*, were lavished daily upon the bewildered girl.

Messages, and hasty informal lightly-pencilled notes, too, would frequently reach her; such as: 'I shall be pouring out cocoa after dinner in bed. Bring your biscuits and join me!' . . . or a rat-a-tat from a round-eyed page and: 'The Countess's comp'ts and she'd take it a Favour if you can make a "Station" with her in chapel later on,' or: 'The Marchioness will be birched to-morrow, and *not* to-day.'

Oh, the charm, the flavour of the religious world! Where match it for interest or variety!

An emotion approaching sympathy had arisen, perhaps a trifle incongruously, between the injured girl and the Countess Yvorra, and before long, to the amusement of the sceptical element of the Court, the Countess and her Confessor, Father Nostradamus, might often be observed in her society.

* The recollection of this was never quite forgotten.

'I need a cage-companion, Father, for my little bird,' the Countess one evening said, as they were ambling, all the three of them, before Office up and down the perfectly tended paths: 'ought it to be of the same species and sex, or does it matter? For as I said to myself just now (while listening to a thrush), *All* birds are His creatures.'

The priest discreetly coughed.

'Your question requires reflection,' he said. 'What is the bird?'

'A hen canary!—and with a voice, Father! Talk of soul! !'

'H—m . . . a thrush and a canary, I would not myself advise.'

Mademoiselle de Nazianzi tittered.

'Why not let it go?' she asked, turning her eyes towards the window-panes of the palace, that glanced like rows of beaten-gold in the evening sun.

'A hawk might peck it!' the Countess returned, looking up as if for one into a sky as imaginative and as dazzling as Shell͵,'s poetry.

'Even the Court,' Father Nostradamus ejaculated wryly, 'will peck at times.'

The Countess's shoulder-blades stiffened.

'After over thirty years,' she said, 'I find Court-life *pathetic*. . . .'

'Pathetic?'

'Tragically pathetic. . . .'

Mademoiselle de Nazianzi considered wistfully the wayward outline of the hills.

'I would like to escape from it all for a while,' she said, 'and travel.'

'I must hunt you out a pamphlet, by and by, dear child, on the "Dangers of Wanderlust." '

'The Great Wall of China and the Bay of Naples! It seems so frightful never to have seen them!'

'I have never seen the Great Wall, either,' the Countess said, 'and I don't suppose, my dear, I ever shall; though I once did spend a fortnight in Italy.'

'Tell me about it.'

The Countess became reminiscent.

'In Venice,' she said, 'the indecent movements of the gondolieri quite affected my health, and, in consequence, I fell a prey to a sharp nervous fever. My temperature rose and it rose, ah, yes . . . until I became quite ill. At last I said to my maid (she was an English girl from Wales, and almost equally as sensitive as me): "Pack. . . . Away!" And we left in haste for Florence. Ah, and Florence, too, I regret to say I found very far from what it ought to have been! ! ! I had a window giving on the Arno, and so I could *observe*. . . . I used to see some curious sights! I would not care to scathe your ears, my Innocent, by an inventory of one half of the wantonness that went on; enough to say the tone of the place forced me to fly to Rome, where beneath the shadow of dear St. Peter's I grew gradually less distressed.'

'Still, I should like, all the same, to travel!' Mademoiselle de Nazianzi exclaimed, with a sad little snatch of a smile.

'We will ask the opinion of Father Geordie Picpus when he comes again.'

'It would be more fitting,' Father Nostradamus murmured (professional rivalry leaping to his eye), 'if Father Picpus kept himself free of the limelight a trifle more!'

'Often I fear our committees would be corvés without him. . . .'

'Tchut.'

'He is very popular . . . too popular, perhaps . . .' the Countess admitted. 'I remember on one occasion, in the Blue Jesus, witnessing the Duchess of Quaranta and Madame Ferdinand Fishbacher fight like wild cats as to which should gain his ear—(any girl might envy Father Geordie his ear)—at Confession next. The odds seemed fairly equal until the Duchess gave the Fishbacher-woman such a violent push—(well down from behind, in the crick of the joints)—that she overturned the confessional box, with Father Picpus within: and when we scared ladies, standing by, had succeeded in dragging him out, he was too shaken, naturally as you can gather, to absolve anyone else *that* day.'

'He has been the object of so many unseemly incidents that one can scarcely recall them all,' Father Nostradamus exclaimed, stooping to pick up a dropped pocket-handkerchief with 'remembrance' knots tied to three of the corners.

'Alas. . . . Court life is not uplifting,' the Countess said again, contemplating her muff of *self-made* lace, with a half-vexed forehead. What that muff contained was a constant problem for conjecture; but it was believed by more than one of the maids-in-waiting to harbour 'goody' books and martyrs' bones.

'By generous deeds and Brotherly love,' Father Nostradamus exclaimed, 'we should endeavour to rise above it!'

With the deftness of a virtuoso, the Countess seized, and crushed with her muff, a pale-winged passing gnat.

'Before Life,' she murmured, 'that saddest thing of all, was thrust upon us, I believe I was an angel. . . .'

Father Nostradamus passed a musing hand across his brow.

'It may be,' he replied; 'and it very well may be,' he went on, 'that our ante-nativity was a little more brilliant, a little more *h—m* . . .; and there is nothing unorthodox in thinking so.'

'Oh what did I do then to lose my wings? ? What did I ever say to Them? ! Father, Father. How did I annoy God? Why did He put me here?'

'My dear child, you ask me things I do not know; but it may be you were the instrument appointed above to lead back to Him our neighbour yonder,' Father Nostradamus answered, pointing with his breviary in the direction of St. Helena.

'Never speak to me of that wretched old man.'

For despite the ablest tactics, the most diplomatic angling, Count Cabinet had refused to rally.

'We followed the sails of your skiff to-day,' Mademoiselle de Nazianzi sighed, 'until the hazes hid them!'

'I had a lilac passage.'

'You delivered the books?'

The Countess shrugged.

'I shall never forget this afternoon,' she said. 'He was sitting in the window over a decanter of wine when I floated down upon him; but no sooner did he see me than he gave a sound like a bleat of a goat, and disappeared: I was determined however to call! There is no bell to the villa, but two bronze door-knockers, well out of reach, are attached to the front-door. These with the ferrule of my parasol I tossed and I rattled, until an adolescent, with bougainvillæa at his ear, came and looked out with an insolent grin, and I recognised Peter Passer from the Blue Jesus grown quite fat.'

'Eh mon Dieu!' Father Nostradamus half audibly sighed.

'Eh mon Dieu . . .' Mademoiselle de Nazianzi echoed, her gaze roving over the palace, whose long window-panes in the setting sun gleamed like sumptuous tissues.

'So that,' the Countess added, 'I hardly propose to venture again.'

'What a site for a Calvary!' Father Nostradamus replied, indicating with a detached and pensive air the cleft in the White Mountain's distant peaks.

'I adore the light the hills take on when the sun drops down,' Mademoiselle de Nazianzi declared.

'It must be close on *Salut.* . . .'

It was beneath the dark colonnades by the Court Chapel door that they received the news from the lips of a pair of vivacious dowagers that the Prince was to leave the Summer Palace on the morrow to attend 'the Manœuvres,' after which it was expected his Royal Highness would proceed '*to England.*'

⇛ X ⇝

AND meanwhile the representatives of the Court of St. James were enjoying the revivifying country air and outdoor life of the Villa Clement. It was almost exquisite how rapidly the casual mode of existence adopted during the summer villeggiatura by their Excellencies drew themselves and their personnel together, until soon they were as united and as *sans gêne* as the proverbial family party. No mother, in the 'acclimatisation' period, could have dosed her offspring more assiduously than did her Excellency the attachés in her charge; flavouring her little inventions frequently with rum or gin until they resembled cocktails. But it was Sir Somebody himself if anyone that required a tonic. Lady Something's pending litigation, involving as it did the crown, was fretting the Ambassador more than he cared to admit, and the Hon. Mrs. Chilleywater, ever alert, told 'Harold' that the injudicious chatter of the Ambassadress (who even now, notwithstanding her writ, would say to every other visitor that came to the villa: 'Have you heard about the Ritz? The other night we were dining at the Palace, and I heard the King,' *etc.*) was wearing their old Chief out.

And so through the agreeable vacation life there twitched the grim vein of tension.

Disturbed one day by her daughter's persistent trilling of the latest coster song *When I sees 'im I topple giddy,* Lady Something gathered up her morning letters and stepped out upon the lawn.

Oh so formal, oh so slender towered the cypress-trees against the rose-farded hills and diamantine waters of the lake. The first hint of autumn was in the air; and over the gravel paths, and in the basins of the fountains, a few shed leaves lay hectically strewn already.

The Flower Beneath the Foot

Besides an under-stamped missive, with a foreign postmark, from Her Majesty the Queen of the Land of Dates beginning 'My dear Gazel,' there was a line from the eloquent and moderately victorious young barrister, engaged in the approaching suit with the Ritz: He had spared himself no pains, he assured his client, in preparing the defence, which was, he said, to be *the respectability of Claridge's*.

'Why bring in Claridge's? . . . ?' the Ambassadress murmured, prodding with the tip of her shoe a decaying tortoiseshell leaf; 'but anyway,' she reflected, 'I'm glad the proceedings fall in winter, as I always look well in furs.'

And mentally she was wrapped in leopard-skins and gazing round the crowded court saluting with a bunch of violets an acquaintance here and there, when her eyes fell on Mrs. Chilleywater seated in the act of composition beneath a cedar-tree.

Mrs. Chilleywater extended a painful smile of welcome which revealed her pointed teeth and pale-hued gums, repressing, simultaneously, an almost irresistible inclination to murder.

'What! . . . Another writ?' she suavely asked.

'No, dear; but these legal men *will* write. . . .'

'I love your defender. He has an air of d'Alembert, sympathetic soul.'

'He proposes pleading Claridge's.'

'Claridge's?'

'Its respectability.'

'Are hotels ever respectable?—I ask you. Though, possibly, the horridest are.'

'Aren't they all horrid!'

'*Natürlich:* but do you know those cheap hotels where the guests are treated like naughty children?'

'No. I must confess I don't,' the Ambassadress laughed.

'Ah, there you are. . . .'

Lady Something considered a moment a distant gardener employed in tying chrysanthemum blooms to little sticks.

'I'm bothered about a cook,' she said.

'And I, about a maid! I dismissed ffoliott this morning—well I simply *had* to—for a figure salient.'

'So awkward out here to replace anyone; I'm sure I don't know . . .' the Ambassadress replied, her eyes hovering tragically over the pantaloons strained to splitting point of the stooping gardener.

'It's a pretty prospect. . . .'

'Life is a compound!' Lady Something defined it at last.

Mrs. Chilleywater turned surprised. 'Not even Socrates,' she declared, 'said anything truer than that.'

'A compound!' Lady Something twittered again.

'I should like to put that into the lips of Delitsiosa.'

'Who's Delitsiosa?' the Ambassadress asked as a smothered laugh broke out beside her.

Mrs. Chilleywater looked up.

'I'd forgotten you were there. Strange thing among the cedar-boughs,' she said.

The Hon. Lionel Limpness tossed a slippered foot flexibly from his hammock.

'You may well ask "who's Delitsiosa"!' he exclaimed.

'She is my new heroine,' Mrs. Chilleywater replied, after a few quick little clutches at her hair.

'I trust you won't treat her, dear, quite so shamefully as your last.'

The Authoress tittered.

'Delitsiosa is the wife of Marsden Didcote,' she said, 'the manager of a pawnshop in the district of Maida Vale, and in the novel he seduces an innocent seamstress, Iris Drummond, who comes in one day to redeem her petticoat (and really I don't know how I did succeed in drawing the portrait of a little fool!) . . . and when Delitsiosa, her suspicions aroused, can no longer doubt or ignore her husband's intimacy with Iris, already engaged to a lusty young farmer in Kent (some boy)—she decides to yield herself to the entreaties of her brother-in-law Percy, a junior partner in the firm, which brings about the great tussle between the two brothers on the edge of the Kentish cliffs. Iris and Delitsiosa—Iris is anticipating a babelet soon—are watching them from a cornfield, where they're boiling a kettle for afternoon tea; and oh, I've such a darling description of a cornfield. I make you *feel* England!'

'No, really, my dear,' Lady Something exclaimed.

'Harold pretends it would be wonderful arranged as an Opera . . . with duos and things and a *Liebestod* for Delitzi towards the close.'

'No, no,' Mr. Limpness protested. 'What would become of our modern fiction at all if Victoria Gellybore-Frinton gave herself up to the stage?'

'That's quite true, strange thing among the cedar-boughs,' Mrs.

Chilleywater returned, fingering the floating strings of the bandelette at her brow. 'It's lamentable; yet who is there doing anything at present for English Letters . . . ? Who among us to-day,' she went on, peering up at him, 'is carrying on the tradition of Fielding? Who really cares? I know *I* do what I can . . . and there's Madam Adrian Bloater, of course. But I can think of no one else;—we two.'

Mr. Limpness rocked, critically.

'I can't bear Bloater's books,' he demurred.

'To be frank, neither can I. I'm very fond of Lilian Bloater, I adore her *weltbürgerliche* nature, but I feel like you about her books; I *cannot* read them. If only she would forget Adrian; but she will thrust him headlong into all her work. Have *I* ever drawn Harold? No. (Although many of the public seem to think so!) And please heaven, however *great* my provocation at times may be, I never shall!'

'And there I think you're right,' the Ambassadress answered, frowning a little as the refrain that her daughter was singing caught her ear.

'And when I sees 'im
My heart goes boom! . . .
And I topple over;
I topple over, over, over,
All for Love!'

'I dreamt last night my child was on the Halls.'
'There's no doubt she'd dearly like to be.'
'Her Father would never hear of it!'

'And when she sees me,
Oh when she sees me—
(*The voice slightly false was Harold's*)
Her heart goes boom! . . .
And she topples over;
She topples over, over, over,
All for Love!'

'There; they've routed Sir Somebody. . . .'
'And when anything vexes him,' Lady Something murmured, appraising the Ambassador's approaching form with a glassy eye, 'he always, you know, blames me!'

Shorn of the sombre, betailed attire, so indispensable for the town-duties of a functionary, Sir Somebody, while rusticating, usually wore a white twill jacket and black multi-pleated pantaloons; while for headgear he would favour a Mexican sugar-loaf, or green-draped puggaree. 'He looks half-Irish,' Lady Something would sometimes say.

'Infernal Bedlam,' he broke out: 'the house is sheer pandemonium.'

'I found it so too, dear,' Lady Something agreed; 'and so,' she added, removing a fallen tree-bug tranquilly from her hair, 'I've been digesting my letters out here upon the lawn.'

'And no doubt,' Sir Somebody murmured, fixing the placid person of his wife with a keen psychological glance, 'you succeed my dear, in digesting them?'

'Why shouldn't I?'

'...' the Ambassador displayed discretion.

'We're asked to a Lion hunt in the Land of Dates; quite an *entreating* invitation from the dear Queen,—really most pressing and affectionate,—but Princess Elsie's nuptial negotiations and this pending Procès with the Ritz may tie us here for some time.'

'Ah, Rosa.'

'Why these constant moans?...? A clairvoyant once told me I'd "the bump of Litigation"—a *cause célèbre* unmistakably defined; so it's as well, on the whole, to have it over.'

'And quite probably; had your statement been correct——'

The Ambassadress gently glowed.

'I'm told it's simply swarming!' she impenitently said.

'Oh, Rosa, Rosa....'

'And if you doubt it at all, here is an account direct from the Ritz itself,' her Excellency replied, singling out a letter from among the rest. 'It is from dear old General Sir Trotter-Stormer. He says: "I am the only guest here. I must say, however, the attendance is beyond all praise, more *soigné* and better than I've ever known it to be, but after what you told me, dear friend, I feel *distinctly uncomfortable* when the hour for bye-bye comes!" '

'Pish; what evidence, pray, is that?'

'I regard it as of the very first importance! Sir Trotter admits—a distinguished soldier admits, his uneasiness; and who knows—he is so brave about concealing his woes—his two wives left him!—what he may not have patiently and stoically endured?'

'Less I am sure, my dear, than I of late in listening sometimes
to you.'

'I will write, I think, and press him for a more detailed report. . . .'
The Ambassador turned away.

'She should no more be trusted with ink than a child with fire-
arms!' he declared, addressing himself with studious indirectness
to a garden-snail.

Lady Something blinked.

'Life is a compound,' she murmured again.

'Particularly with women!' the Authoress agreed.

'Ah, well,' the Ambassadress majestically rose, 'I must be off
and issue household orders; although I derive hardly my usual
amount of enjoyment at present, I regret to say, from my morning
consultations with the cook. . . .'

⟨❊⟩ XI ⟨❊⟩

IT had been once the whim and was now the felicitous habit of the
Countess of Tolga to present Count Cabinet annually with a
bouquet of flowers. It was as if Venus Anadyomene herself, standing*
on a shell and wafted by all the piquant whispers of the town and
court, would intrude upon the flattered exile (with her well-wired
orchids, and malicious, soulless laughter), to awaken delicate, pagan
images of a trecento, Tuscan Greece.

But upon this occasion desirous of introducing some few features,
the Countess decided on presenting the fallen senator with a pannier
of well-grown, early pears, a small 'heath' and the Erotic Poems,
bound in half calf with tasteful tooling, of a Schoolboy Poet, cherish-
able chiefly perhaps for the vignette frontispiece of the author.
Moreover, acting on an impulse she was never able afterwards to
explain, she had invited Mademoiselle Olga Blumenghast to
accompany her.

Never had summer shown a day more propitiously clement than
the afternoon in mid-autumn they prepared to set out.

Fond of a compliment, when not too frankly racy,† and knowing

---

* *Vide* Botticelli.

† In Pisuerga compliments are apt to rival in this respect those of the
ardent South.

how susceptible the exile was to clothes, the Countess had arrayed herself in a winter gown of kingfisher-tinted silk turning to turquoise, and stencilled in purple at the arms and neck with a crisp Greek-key design; while a voluminous violet veil, depending behind her to a point, half concealed a tricorne turquoise toque from which arose a shaded lilac aigrette branching several ways.

'I shall probably die with heat, and of course it's most unsuitable; but poor old man, he likes to recall the Capital!' the Countess panted, as, nursing heath, poems and pears, she followed Mademoiselle Olga Blumenghast blindly towards the shore.

Oars, and swaying drying nets, a skyline lost in sun, a few moored craft beneath the little rickety wooden pier awaiting choice:—'The boatmen, to-day, darling, seem all so ugly; let's take a sailing-boat and go alone!'

'I suppose there's no danger, darling?' the Countess replied, and scarcely had she time to make any slight objection when the owner of a steady wide-bottomed boat—the *Calypso*—was helping them to embark.

The Island of St. Helena, situated towards the lake's bourne, lay distant some two miles or more, and within a short way of the open sea.

With sails distended to a languid breeze the shore eventually was left behind; and the demoiselle cranes, in mid-lake, were able to observe there were two court dames among them.

'Although he's dark, Vi,' Mademoiselle Olga Blumenghast presently exclaimed, dropping her cheek to a frail hand upon the tiller, 'although he's dark, it's odd how he gives one the impression somehow of perfect fairness!'

'Who's that, darling?' the Countess murmured, appraising with fine eyes, faintly weary, the orchid-like style of beauty of her friend.

'Ann-Jules, of course.'

'I begin to wish, do you know, I'd brought pomegranates, and worn something else!'

'What are those big burley-worleys?'

'Pears. . . .'

'Give me one.'

'Catch, then.'

'Not that I could bear to be married; especially like *you*, Vi!'

'A marriage like ours, dear, was so utterly unworthwhile. . . .'

'I'm not sure, dear, that I comprehend altogether?'

'Seagulls' wings as they fan one's face. . . .'

'It's vile and wrong to shoot them: but oh! how I wish your happiness depended, even ever so little, on me.'

The Countess averted her eyes.

Waterfowl, like sadness passing, hovered and soared overhead, casting their dark, fleeting shadows to the white, drowned clouds, in the receptive waters of the lake.

'I begin to wish I'd brought grapes,' she breathed.

'Heavy stodgy pears. So do I.'

'Or a few special peaches,' the Countess murmured, taking up the volume of verse beside her, with a little, mirthless, half-hysterical laugh.

To a Faithless Friend.

To V.O.I. and S.C.P.

For Stephen.

When the Dormitory Lamp burns Low.

Her gaze travelled over the Index.

'Read something, dear,' Mademoiselle Blumenghast begged, toying with the red-shaded flower in her burnished curls.

'Gladly; but oh, Olga!' the Countess crooned.

'What!'

'Where's the wind?'

It had gone.

'We must row.'

There was nothing for it.

To gain the long, white breakwater, with the immemorial willow-tree at its end, that was the most salient feature of the island's approach, required, nevertheless, resolution.

'It's so far, dear,' the Countess kept on saying. 'I had no idea how far it was! Had you any conception at all it was so far?'

'Let us await the wind, then. It's bound to rally.'

But no air swelled the sun-bleached sails, or disturbed the pearly patine of the paralysed waters.

'I shall never get this peace, I only realise it *exists* . . .' the Countess murmured with dream-glazed eyes.

'It's astonishing . . . the stillness,' Mademoiselle Blumenghast murmured, with a faint tremor, peering round towards the shore.

On the banks young censia-trees raised their boughs like strong white whips towards the mountains, upon whose loftier heights lay, here and there, a little stray patch of snow.

'Come hither, ye winds, come hither!' she softly called.

'Oh, Olga! Do we really want it?' the Countess in agitation asked, discarding her hat and veil with a long, sighing breath.

'I don't know, dear; no; not, not much.'

'Nor I,—at all.'

'Let us be patient then.'

'It's all so beautiful it makes one want to cry.'

'Yes; it makes one want to cry,' Mademoiselle Blumenghast murmured, with a laugh that in brilliance vied with the October sun.

'Olga!'

'So,' as the *Calypso* lurched: 'lend me your hanky, dearest.'

'*Olga*— ?— ? Thou fragile, and exquisite thing!'

Meanwhile Count Cabinet was seated with rod-and-line at an open window, idly ogling a swan. Owing to the reluctance of tradespeople to call for orders, the banished statesman was often obliged to supplement the larder himself. But hardly had he been angling ten minutes to-day when lo! a distinguished mauvish fish with vivid scarlet spots. Pondering on the mysteries of the deep, and of the subtle variety there is in Nature, the veteran ex-minister lit a cigar. Among the more orthodox types that stocked the lake, such as carp, cod, tench, eels, sprats, shrimps, etc., this exceptional fish must have known its trials and persecutions, its hours of superior difficulty . . . and the Count with a stoic smile recalled his own. Musing on the advantages and disadvantages of personality, of 'party' viewpoints, and of morals in general, the Count was soon too self-absorbed to observe the approach of his 'useful' secretary and amanuensis, Peter Passer.

More valet perhaps than secretary, and more errand-boy than either, the former chorister of the Blue Jesus had followed the fallen statesman into exile at a moment when the Authorities of Pisuerga were making minute enquiries for sundry missing articles,* from the *Trésor* of the Cathedral, and since the strain of constant choir-practice is apt to be injurious for a youngster suffering from a delicate chest, the adolescent had been willing enough to accept, for a time at least, a situation in the country.

---

* The missing articles were:

   5 chasubles.
   A relic-casket in lapis and diamonds, containing the Tongue of St. Thelma.
   4¾ yards of black lace, said to have 'belonged to' the Madonna.

'Oh, sir,' he exclaimed, and almost in his excitement forgetting altogether the insidious, lisping tones he preferred as a rule to employ: 'oh, sir, here comes that old piece of rubbish again with a fresh pack of tracts.'

'Collect yourself, Peter, pray do: what, lose our heads for a visit?' the Count said, getting up and going to a glass.

'I've noticed, sir, it's impossible to live on an island long without feeling its effects; you *can't* escape being insular!'

'Or insolent.'

'Insular, sir!'

'No matter much, but if it's the Countess Yvorra you might show her round the garden this time, perhaps, for a change,' the Count replied, adjusting a demure-looking fly, of indeterminate sex, to his line.

And brooding on life and baits, and what *A* will come for while *B* won't, the Count's thoughts grew almost humorous as the afternoon wore on.

Evening was approaching when, weary of the airs of a common carp, he drew in, at length, his tackle.

Like a shawl of turquoise silk the lake seemed to vie, in serenity and radiance, with the bluest day in June, and it was no surprise, on descending presently for a restricted ramble—(the island, in all, amounted to scarcely one acre)—to descry the invaluable Peter enjoying a pleasant swim.

When not boating or reading or feeding his swans, to watch Peter's fancy-diving off the terrace end was perhaps the favourite pastime of the veteran *viveur*: to behold the lad trip along the riven breakwater, as naked as a statue, shoot out his arms and spring, the *Flying-head-leap* or the *Backsadilla*, was a beautiful sight, looking up now and again—but more often now—from a volume of old Greek verse; while to hear him warbling in the water with his clear alto voice—of Kyries and Anthems he knew no end—would often stir the old man to the point of tears. Frequently the swans themselves would paddle up to listen, expressing by the charmed or rapturous motions of their necks (recalling to the exile the ecstasies of certain musical or 'artistic' dames at Concert-halls, or the Opera House, long ago) their mute appreciation, their touched delight. . . .

'Old goody Two-shoes never came, sir,' Peter archly lisped, admiring his adventurous shadow upon the breakwater wall.

'How is that?'

'Becalmed, sir,' Peter answered, culling languidly a small, nodding rose that was clinging to the wall.

> 'Oh becalmed is my soul,
> I rejoice in the Lord!'

At one extremity of the garden stood the Observatory, and after duly appraising various of Peter's neatest feats the Count strolled away towards it. But before he could reach the Observatory he had first to pass his swans.

They lived, with an ancient water-wheel, beneath a cupola of sun-glazed tiles, sheltered, partially, from the lake by a hedge of towering red geraniums, and the Count seldom wearied of watching these strangely gorgeous creatures as they sailed out and in through the sanguine-hued flowers. A few, with their heads sunk back beneath their wings, had retired for the night already; nevertheless, the Count paused to shake a finger at one somnolent bird, in disfavour for pecking Peter. 'Jealous, doubtless of the lad's grace,' he mused, fumbling with the key of the Observatory door.

The unrivalled instrument that the Observatory contained, whose intricate lenses were capable of drawing even the remote Summer Palace to within an appreciable range, was, like most instruments of merit, sensitive to the manner of its manipulation; and fearing lest the inexpert tampering of a homesick housekeeper (her native village was visible in clear weather, with the aid of a glass) should break or injure the delicate lenses, the Count kept the Observatory usually under key.

But the inclination to focus the mundane and embittered features of the fanatic Countess, as she lectured her boatmen for forgetting their oars, or, being considerably superstitious, to count the moles on their united faces as an esoteric clue to the Autumn Lottery, waned a little before the mystery of the descending night.

Beneath a changing tide of deepening shadow, the lifeless valleys were mirroring to the lake the sombreness of dusk. Across the blue forlornness of the water, a swan, here and there, appeared quite violet, while coiffed in swift, clinging, golden clouds the loftiest hills alone retained the sun.

A faint nocturnal breeze, arising simultaneously with the Angelus-bell, seemed likely to relieve, at the moon's advent, the trials to her patience of the Countess Yvorra: 'who must be cursing,' the Count reflected, turning the telescope about with a sigh, to suit her sail.

Ah poignant moments when the heart stops still! Not since the hour of his exile had the Count's been so arrested.

From the garden Peter's voice rose questingly; but the Count was too wonderstruck, far, to heed it.

Caught in the scarlet radiance of the afterglow, the becalmed boat, for one brief and most memorable second, was his to gaze on.

In certain lands with what diplomacy falls the night, and how discreetly is the daylight gone. Those dimmer-and-dimmer, darker-and-lighter twilights of the North, so disconcerting in their playfulness, were unknown altogether in Pisuerga. There, Night pursued Day as though she meant it. No lingering or arctic sentiment! No concertina-ishness. . . . Hard on the sun's heels pressed Night. And the wherefore of her haste; Sun-attraction? Impatience to inherit? An answer to such riddles as these may doubtless be found by turning to the scientist's theories on Time and Relativity.

Effaced in the blue air of evening became everything, and with the darkness returned the wind.

'Sir, sir? . . . Ho, Hi, hiiiiiiiiiiiii!!' Peter's voice came again.

But transfixed, and loath just then for company, the Count made no reply.

A green-lanterned barge passed slowly, coming from the sea, and on the mountain-side a village light winked wanly here and there.

'Oh, why was I not *sooner*?' he murmured distractedly aloud.

'Oh, Olga!'
'Oh, Vi!'
' . . . I hope you've enough money for the boat, dear? . . . ?'
' . . . ! ! ?'
'Tell me, Olga: Is my hat all sideways?'
' . . . .'
The long windows of the Summer Palace were staring white to the moon as the Countess of Tolga, hugging still her heath, her aigrettes casting *heroic* shadows, re-entered the Court's precincts on the arm of her friend.

◈ *XII* ◈

ONE evening, as Mrs. Montgomery was reading *Vanity Fair* for the fifteenth time, there came a tap at the door. It was not the first interruption since opening the cherished green-bound book, and Mrs. Montgomery seemed disinclined to stir. With the Court about to return to winter quarters, and the Summer Palace upside down, the royal governess was still able to command her habitual British phlegm. It had been decided, moreover, that she should remain behind in the forsaken palace with his Naughtiness, the better to 'prepare' him for his forthcoming Eton exam.

Still, with disputes as to the precedence of trunks and dress-baskets simmering in the corridors without, it was easier to enjoy the barley-sugar stick in one's mouth than the novel in one's hand.

'Thank God I'm not touchy!' Mrs. Montgomery reflected, rolling her eyes lazily about the little white-wainscoted room.

It was as if something of her native land had crept in through the doorway with her, so successfully had she inculcated its tendencies, or spiritual Ideals, upon everything around.

A solitary teapot, on a bracket, above the door, two *Jubilee* plates, some peacocks' feathers, an image of a little fisher-boy in bathing-drawers with a broken hand,—'a work of delicate beauty!' —a mezzotint, *The Coiffing of Maria*—these were some of the treasures which the room contained.

'A blessing to be sure when the Court has gone!' she reflected, half rising to drop a curtsey to Prince Olaf who had entered.

'Word from your country,' sententiously he broke out. 'My brother's betrothed! So need I go on with my preparation?'

'Put your tie straight! And just look at your socks all tumbling down. Such great jambons of knees! . . . What will become of you, I ask myself, when you're a lower boy at Eton.'

'How can I be a lower boy when I'm a Prince?'

'Probably the Rev. Ruggles-White, when you enter his House, will be able to explain.'

'I won't be a lower boy! I will *not*!'

'Cs, Cs.'

'Damn the democracy.'

'Fie, sir.'

'Down with it.'

71

'For shame.'

'Revenge.'

'That will do: and now, let me hear your lessons: I should like,' Mrs. Montgomery murmured, her eyes set in detachment upon the floor, 'the present-indicative tense of the Verb *To be*! Adding the words, Political h-Hostess;—more for the sake of the pronunciation than for anything else.'

And after considerable persuasion, prompting, and 'bribing' with various sorts of sweets:

> 'I am a Political Hostess,
> Thou art a Political Hostess,
> He is a Political Hostess,
> We are Political Hostesses,
> Ye are Political Hostesses,
> They are Political Hostesses.'

'Very good, dear, and only one mistake. *He* is a Political h-Hostess: can you correct yourself? The error is so slight. . . . '

But alas the Prince was in no mood for study; and Mrs. Montgomery very soon afterwards was obliged to let him go.

Moving a little anxiously about the room, her meditations turned upon the future.

With the advent of Elsie a new régime would be established: increasing Britishers would wish to visit Pisuerga; and it seemed a propitious moment to abandon teaching, and to inaugurate in Kairoulla an English hotel.

'I have no more rooms. I am quite full up!' she smiled, addressing the silver andirons in the grate.

And what a deliverance to have done with instructing unruly children, she reflected, going towards the glass mail-box attached to her vestibule door. Sometimes about this hour there would be a letter in it, but this evening, there was only a picture postcard of a field mouse in a bonnet, from her old friend Mrs. Bedley.

'We have *Valmouth* at last,' she read, 'and was it you, my dear, who asked for *The Beard Throughout the Ages*? It is in much demand, but I am keeping it back anticipating a *reply*. Several of the plates are missing I see, among them those of the late King Edward and of Assur Bani Pal; I only mention it that you may know I shan't blame you! We are having wonderful weather, and I am keeping pretty

72

well, although poor Mrs. Barleymoon, I fear, will not see through
another winter. Trusting you are benefiting by the beautiful country
air: your obedient servant to command,   ANN BEDLEY.

'P.S.—*Man, and All About Him,* is rebinding. Ready I expect
soon.'

'Ah! Cunnie, Cunnie . . . ?' Mrs. Montgomery murmured, laying
the card down near a photograph of the Court-physician with a
sigh. 'Ah! Arthur Amos Cuncliffe Babcock . . . ?' she invoked
his name dulcetly in full: and, as though in telepathic response,
there came a tap at the door, and the doctor himself looked in.

He had been attending, it seemed, the young wife of the Comp-
troller of the Household at the extremity of the corridor, a creature
who, after two brief weeks of marriage, imagined herself to be in
an interesting state. '*I believe baby's coming!*' she would cry out every
few hours.

'Do I intrude?' he demanded, in his forceful, virile voice, that
ladies knew and liked: 'pray say so if I do.'

'Does he intrude!' Mrs. Montgomery flashed an arch glance
towards the cornice.

'Well, and how are you keeping?' the doctor asked, dropping
on to a rep causeuse that stood before the fire.

'I'm only semi-well, doctor, thanks!'

'Why, what's the trouble?'

'You know my organism is not a very strong one, Dr. Cuncliffe . . .' Mrs. Montgomery replied, drawing up a chair, and
settling a cushion with a sigh of resignation at her back.

'Imagination!'

'If only it were!'

'Imagination,' he repeated, fixing a steady eye on the short train
of her black brocaded robe that all but brushed his feet.

'If that's your explanation for continuous broken sleep . . .' she
gently snapped.

'Try mescal.'

'I'm trying Dr. Fritz Millar's treatment,' the lady stated, desiring
to deal a slight *scratch* to his masculine *amour propre*.

'Millar's an Ass.'

'I don't agree at all!' she incisively returned, smiling covertly
at his touch of pique.

'What is it?'

73

'Oh it's horrid. You first of all lie down; and then you drink cold water in the sun.'

'Cold what? I never *heard* of such a thing: it's enough to kill you.' Mrs. Montgomery took a deep-drawn breath of languor.

'And would you care, doctor, so *very* much if it did?' she asked, as a page made his appearance wth an ice-bucket and champagne.

'To toast our young Princess!'

'Oh, oh, Dr. Cuncliffe? What a wicked man you are.' And for a solemn moment their thoughts went out in unison to the sea-girt land of their birth—Barkers', Selfridge's, Brighton Pier, the Zoological Gardens on a Sunday afternoon.

'Here's to the good old country!' the doctor quaffed.

'The Bride, and,' Mrs. Montgomery raised her glass, 'the Old Folks at h-home.'

'The Old Folks at home!' he vaguely echoed.

'Bollinger, you naughty man,' the lady murmured, amiably seating herself on the causeuse at his side.

'You'll find it dull here all alone after the Court has gone,' he observed, smiling down, a little despotically, on to her bright, abundant hair.

Mrs. Montgomery sipped her wine.

'When the wind goes whistling up and down under the colonnades: oh, then!' she shivered.

'You'll wish for a fine, bold Pisuergian husband; shan't you?' he answered, his foot drawing closer to hers.

'Often of an evening I feel I need fostering,' she owned, glancing up yearningly into his face.

'Fostering, eh?' he chuckled, refilling with exuberance her glass.

'Why is it that wine always makes me feel *so good*?'

'Probably because it fills you with affection for your neighbour!'

'It's true; I feel I could be very affectionate: I'm what they call an "amoureuse" I suppose, and there it is. . . .'

There fell a busy silence between them.

'It's almost too warm for a fire,' she murmured, repairing towards the window; 'but I like to hear the crackle!'

'Company, eh?' he returned, following her (a trifle unsteadily) across the room.

'The night is so clear the moon looks to be almost transparent,' she languorously observed, with a long tugging sigh.

'And so it does,' he absently agreed.

'I adore the pigeons in my wee court towards night, when they sink down like living sapphires upon the stones,' she sentimentally said, sighing languorously again.

'Ours,' he assured her; 'since the surgery looks on to it, too. . . .'

'Did you ever see anything so ducky-wucky, so completely twee!' she inconsequently chirruped.

'Allow me to fill this empty glass.'

'I want to go out on all that gold floating water!' she murmured listlessly, pointing towards the lake.

'Alone?'

'Drive me towards the sweet seaside,' she begged, taking appealingly his hand.

'Aggie?'

'Arthur—Arthur, for God's sake!' she shrilled, as with something between a snarl and a roar he impulsively whipped out the light.

'H-Help! Oh, Arth——'

Thus did they celebrate the 'Royal engagement.'

XIII

BEHIND the heavy moucharaby in the little dark shop of Habou-bet of Egypt all was song, *fête* and preparation. Additional work had brought additional hands, and be-tarbouched boys, in burn-ouses, and baskets of blossoms lay strewn all over the floor.

'Sweet is the musk-rose of the Land of Punt!
Sweet are the dates from Khorassân . . .
But bring *me* (O wandering Djinns) the English rose,
    the English apple!
O sweet is the land of the Princess Elsie,
Sweet indeed is England——'

Bachir's voice soared, in improvisation, to a long-drawn, strident wail.

'Pass me the scissors, O Bachir bed Ahmed, for the love of Allah,' a young man with large lucent eyes and an untroubled face, like a flower, exclaimed, extending a slender, keef-stained hand.

'Sidi took them,' the superintendent of the Duchess of Varna replied, turning towards an olive-skinned Armenian youth, who, seated on an empty hamper, was reading to a small, rapt group the *Kairoulla Intelligence* aloud.

' "Attended by Lady Canon-on-Noon and by Lady Bertha Chamberlayne (she is a daughter of Lord Frollo's*) the Princess was seen to alight from her saloon, in a *chic* toque of primrose paille, stabbed with the quill of a nasturtium-coloured bird, and, darting forward, like the Bird of Paradise that she *is,* embraced her future parents-in-law with considerable affection. . . ." '

'Scissors, for the love of Allah!'

' "And soon I heard the roll of drums! And saw the bobbing plumes in the jangling browbands of the horses: it was a moment I shall never forget. She passed . . . and as our Future Sovereign turned smiling to bow her acknowledgments to the crowd I saw a happy tear . . . !'

'Ah Allah.'

'Pass me two purple pinks.'

' "Visibly gratified at the cordial ovation to her Virgin Daughter was Queen Glory, a striking and impressive figure, all a-glitter in a splendid dark dress of nacre and nigger tissue, her many Orders of Merit almost bearing her down." '

'Thy scissors, O Sidi, for the love of Muhammed!'

' "It seemed as if Kairoulla had gone wild with joy. Led by the first Life-Guards and a corps of ladies of great fashion disguised as peasants, the cortège proceeded amid the whole-hearted plaudits of the people towards Constitutional Square, where, with the sweetest of smiles and thanks, the Princess received an exquisite sheaf of Deflas (they are the hybrids of slipper-orchids crossed with maidens-rue, and are all the mode at present), tendered her by little Paula Exelmans, the Lord Mayor's tiny daughter. Driving on, amid showers of confetti, the procession passed up the Chausée, which presented a scene of rare animation: boys and even quite elderly dames swarming up the trees to obtain a better view of their new Princess. But it was not until Lilianthal Street and the Cathedral Square were reached that the climax reached its height! Here a short standstill was called and, after an appropriate address from the Archbishop of Pisuerga, the stirring strains of the National Anthem, superbly rendered by Madame Marguerite Astorra of the State Theatre (she

* Although the account of Princess Elsie's arrival in Kairoulla is signed 'Green Jersey,' it seems not unlikely that 'Eva Schnerb' herself was the reporter on this eventful occasion.

is in perfect voice this season), arose on the air. At that moment a black cat and its kitties rushed across the road, and I saw the Princess smile." '

'Thy scissors, O Sidi, in the Name of the Prophet!'

' "A touching incident," ' Sidi with equanimity pursued, ' "was just before the English Tea Rooms, where the English Colony had mustered together in force. . . ." '

But alack for those interested. Owing to the clamour about him much of the recital was lost: ' "Cheers and tears. . . . Life's benison . . . Honiton lace. . . . If I live to be *forty*, it was a moment I shall never forget. . . . Panic . . . congestion. . . . Police." '

But it was scarcely needful to peruse the paper, when on the boulevards outside the festivities were everywhere in full swing. The arrival of the princess for her wedding had brought to Kairoulla unprecedented crowds from all parts of the kingdom, as much eager to see the princess as to catch a glimpse of the fine pack of beagles that it was said had been brought over with her, and which had taken an half-eerie hold of the public mind. Gilderoy, Beausire, Audrey, many of the hounds' names were known pleasantly to the crowd already; and anecdotes of Audrey, picture-postcards of Audrey, were sold as rapidly almost as those even of the princess. Indeed mothers among the people had begun to threaten their disobedient offspring with Audrey, whose silky, thickset frame was supported, it appeared, daily on troublesome little boys and tiresome little girls. . . .

'Erri, erri, get on with thy bouquet, oh Lazari Demitraki!' Bachir exclaimed in plaintive tones, addressing a blond boy with a skin of amber, who was 'charming' an earwig with a reed of grass.

'She dance the *Boussadilla* just like in the street of Halfaouine in Gardaïa, my town, any Ouled Naïl!' he rapturously gurgled.

'Get on with thy work, oh Lazari Demitraki,' Bachir besought him, 'and leave the earwigs alone for the clients to find.'

'What with the heat, the smell of the flowers, the noise of you boys, and with filthy earwigs Boussadillaing all over one, I feel I could *swoon*.' The voice, cracked yet cloying, was Peter Passer's.

He had come to Kairoulla for the 'celebrations,' and also, perhaps, aspiring to advance his fortunes, in ways known best to himself. With Bachir his connection dated from long ago, when as a Cathedral choir-boy it had been his habit to pin a shoulder- or bosom-blossom to his surplice, destroying it with coquettish, ring-laden fingers in the course of an anthem, and scattering the petals from the choir-loft, leaf by leaf, on to the grey heads of the monsignori below.

'Itchiata wa?' Bachir grumbled, playing his e̱ es distractedly around the shop. And it might have been better for the numerous orders there were to attend to had he called fewer of his acquaintance to assist him. Sunk in torpor, a cigarette smouldering at his ear, a Levantine Greek, known as 'Effendi darling' was listening to a dark-cheeked Tunisian engaged at the Count of Tolga's private Hammam Baths—a young man, who, as he spoke, would make mazy gestures of the hands as though his master's ribs, or those of some illustrious guest, lay under him. But by no means all of those assembled in the little shop bore the seal of Islam. An American, who had grown too splendid for the copper 'Ganymede' or Soda-fountain of a Café bar and had taken to teaching the hectic dance-steps of his native land in the night-halls where Bachir sold, was achieving wonders with some wires and Eucharist lilies, while discussing with a shy-mannered youth the many difficulties that beset the foreigner in Kairoulla.

'Young chaps that come out here don't know what they're coming to,' he sapiently remarked, using his incomparable teeth in place of scissors. 'Gosh! Talk of advancement,' he growled.

'There's few can mix as I can, yet I don't never get no rise!' the shy youth exclaimed, producing a card that was engraved: *Harry Cummings, Salad-Dresser to the King*. 'I expect I've arrived,' he murmured, turning to hide a modest blush towards a pale young man who looked on life through heavy horn glasses.

'Salad dressing? I'd sooner it was hair! You do get tips there anyway,' the Yankee reasoned.

'I wish *I* were—arrived,' the young man with the glasses, by name Guy Thin, declared. He had come out but recently from England to establish a 'British Grocery,' and was the owner of what is sometimes called an expensive voice, his sedulously clear articulation missing out no syllable or letter of anything he might happen to be saying, as though he were tasting each word, like the Pure tea, or the Pure marmalade, or any other of the so very Pure goods he proposed so exclusively to sell.

'If Allah wish it then you arrive,' Lazari Demitraki assured him with a dazzling smile, catching his hand in order to construe the lines.

78

'Finish thy bouquet, O Lazari Demitraki,' Bachir faintly moaned.

'It finished—arranged: it with Abou!' he announced, pointing to an aged negro with haunted sin-sick eyes who appeared to be making strange grimaces at the wall. A straw hat of splendid dimensions was on his head, flaunting bravely the insignia of the Firm.

But the old man seemed resolved to run no more errands:

'Nsa, nsa,' he mumbled. 'Me walk enough for one day! Me no go out any more. Old Abou too tired to take another single step! as soon would me cross the street again dis night as the Sahara! . . .'

And it was only after the promise of a small gift of Opium that he consented to leave a débutante's bouquet at the Théâtre Diana.*

'In future,' Bachir rose, remarking, 'I only employ the women; I keep only girls,' he repeated, for the benefit of 'Effendi darling' who appeared to be attaining Nirvana.

'And next I suppose you keep a Harem?' 'Effendi darling' somnolently returned.

Most of the city shops had closed their shutters for the day when Bachir, shouldering a pannier bright with blooms, stepped with his companions forth into the street.

Along the Boulevards thousands were pressing towards the Regina Gardens to view the Fireworks, all agog to witness the pack of beagles wrought in brilliant lights due to course a stag across the sky, and which would change, if newspaper reports might be believed, at the critical moment, into ' something of the nature of a surprise. '

Pausing before a plate-glass window that adjoined the shop to adjust the flowing folds of his gandourah, and to hoist his flower tray to his small scornful head, Bachir allowed his auxiliaries to drift, mostly two by two, away among the crowd. Only the royal saladdresser, Harry Cummings, expressed a demure inclination (when the pushing young grocer caressed his arm) to 'be alone'; but Guy Thin, who had private designs upon him, was loath to hear of it! He wished to persuade him to buy a bottle of Vinegar from his Store, when he would print on his paper-bags *As supplied to his Majesty the King.*

'Grant us, O Allah, each good Fortunes,' Bachir beseeched, looking up through his eyelashes towards the moon, that drooped like a silver amulet in the firmament above: in the blue nocturnal

* The Théâtre Diana: a Music Hall dedicated to Spanish Zarzuelas and Operettes. It enjoyed a somewhat doubtful reputation.

air he looked like a purple poppy. 'A toute à l'heure mes amis!' he murmured as he moved away.

And in the little closed shop behind the heavy moucharaby now that they had all gone, the exhalations of the *flowers* arose; pungent, concerted odours, expressive of natural antipathies and feuds, suave alliances, suffering, pride, and joy. . . . Only the shining moon through the moucharaby, illumining here a lily, there a leaf, may have guessed what they were saying:

'My wires are hurting me: my wires are hurting me.'

'I have no water. I cannot reach the water.'

'They have pushed me head down into the bottom of the bowl.'

'I'm glad I'm in a Basket! No one will hurl *me* from a window to be bruised underfoot by the callous crowd.'

'It's uncomfy, isn't it, without one's roots?'

'You Weed you! You, you, you . . . *buttercup*! How dare you to *an Orchid*!'

'I shouldn't object to sharing the same water with him, dear . . . ordinary as he is! If *only* he wouldn't smell. . . .'

'She's nothing but a piece of common grass and so I tell her!'

Upon the tense pent atmosphere surged a breath of cooler air, and through the street-door slipped the Duchess of Varna.

Overturning a jar of great heavy-headed gladioli with a crash, she sailed, with a purposeful step, towards the till.

Garbed in black and sleepy citrons, she seemed, indeed, to be equipped for a long, long Voyage, and was clutching, in her arms, a pet Poodle dog, and a levant-covered case, in which, doubtless, reposed her jewels.

Since her rupture with Madame Wetme (both the King and Queen had refused to receive her), the money *ennuis* of the Duchess had become increasingly acute. Tormented by tradespeople, dunned and bullied by creditors, menaced, mortified, insulted—an offer to 'star' in the *rôle* of *A Society Thief* for the cinematograph had particularly shocked her—the inevitable hour to quit the Court, so long foreseen, had come. And now with her departure definitely determined upon, the Duchess experienced an insouciance of heart unknown to her assuredly for many a year. Replenishing her reticule with quite a welcome sheaf of the elegant little bank-notes of Pisuerga, one thing only remained to do, and taking pen and paper she addressed to the Editor of the *Intelligence* the supreme announcement:—'*The Duchess of Varna has left for Dateland.*'

Eight light words! But enough to set *tout* Kairoulla in a rustle.

'I only regret I didn't go sooner,' she murmured to herself aloud, breaking herself a rose to match her gown from an arrangement in the window.

Many of the flowers had been newly christened, 'Elsie,' 'Audrey,' 'London-Madonnas' (black Arums these), while the roses from the 'Land of Punt' had been renamed 'Mrs. Lloyd George'—and priced accordingly. A basket of odontoglossums eked out with gypsophila seemed to anticipate the end, when supplies from Punt must necessarily cease. However, bright boys, like Bachir, seldom lacked patrons, and the duchess recalled glimpsing him one evening, from her private sitting-room at the Ritz Hotel, seated on a garden bench in the Regina Gardens beside the Prime Minister himself; both, to all seeming, on the most cordial terms, and having reached a perfect understanding as regards the Eastern Question. Ah, the Eastern Question! It was said that, in the Land of Dates, one might study it well. In Djezira, the chief town, beneath the great golden sun, people, they said, might grow wise. In the simoon that scatters the silver sand, in the words of the nomads, in the fairy mornings beneath the palms, society with its foolish *cliché* . . . the duchess smiled.

'But for that poisonous woman, I should have gone last year,' she told herself, interrupted in her cogitations by the appearance of her maid.

'The train, your Grace, we shall miss it. . . .'

'Nonsense!' the duchess answered, following, leaving the flowers alone again to their subtle exhalations.

'I'm glad *I'm* in a Basket!'

'I have no water. I cannot reach the water.'

'Life's bound to be uncertain when you haven't got your roots!'

◦◦◦ XIV ◦◦◦

ON a long-chair, with tired, closed eyes, lay the Queen. Although spared from henceforth the anxiety of her son's morganatic marriage, yet, now that his destiny was sealed, she could not help feeling perhaps he might have done better. The bride's lineage was nothing to boast of—of her great-great-grandparents, indeed, in the year 17—, it were gentler to draw a veil—while, for the rest, disingenuous, undistinguished, more at home in the stables than in a drawing-room, the Queen much feared that she and her future daughter-in-law would scarcely get on.

Yes, the little princess was none too engaging, she reflected, and her poor sacrificed child if not actually trapped . . .

The silken swish of a fan, breaking the silence, induced the Queen to look up.

In waiting at present was the Countess Olivia d'Omptyda, a person of both excellent principles and birth, if lacking, somewhat, in social boldness. Whenever she entered the royal presence she would begin visibly to tremble, which considerably flattered the Queen. Her father, Count 'Freddie' d'Omptyda, an infantile and charming old man, appointed in a moment of unusual vagary Pisuergan Ambassador to the Court of St. James', had lately married a child wife scarcely turned thirteen, whose frivolity and numerous pranks on the high dames of London were already the scandal of the *Corps Diplomatique.*

'Sssh! Noise is the last vulgarity,' the Queen commented, raising a cushion embroidered with raging lions and white uncanny unicorns behind her head.

Unstrung from the numerous *fêtes,* she had retired to a distant boudoir to relax, and, having partly disrobed, was feeling remotely Venus of Miloey with her arms half hidden in a plain white cape.

The Countess d'Omptyda furled her fan.

'In this Age of push and shriek . . .' she said and sighed.

'It seems that neither King Geo, nor Queen Glory, *ever* lie down of a day!' her Dreaminess declared.

'Since his last appointment, neither does Papa.'

'The affair of your step-mother, and Lady Diana Duff Semour,' the Queen remarked, 'appears to be assuming the proportions of an Incident!'

The Countess dismally smiled. The subject of her step-mother, mistaken frequently for her grand-daughter, was a painful one. 'I hear she's like a colt broke loose!' she murmured, dropping her eyes fearfully to her costume.

She was wearing an apron of Parma-violets, and the Order of the Holy Ghost.

'It's a little a pity she can't be more sensible,' the Queen returned, fingering listlessly some papers at her side. Among them was the

Archæological Society's initial report relating to the recent finds among the Ruins of Sodom and Gomorrah. From Chedorlahomor came the good news that an *amphora* had been found, from which it seemed that men, in those days, rode sideways, and women straddle-legs, with their heads to the horses' tails, while a dainty cup, ravished from a rock-tomb in the Vale of Akko, ornamented with naked boys and goblets of flowers, encouraged a yet more extensive research.

'You may advance, Countess, with the Archæologists' report,' the Queen commanded. 'Omitting (skipping, I say) the death of the son of Lord Intriguer.'*

' "It was in the Vale of Akko, about two miles from Saada," ' the Countess tremblingly began, ' "that we laid bare a superb tear-bottle, a unique specimen in *grisaille,* severely adorned with a matron's head. From the inscription there can be no doubt whatever that we have here an authentic portrait of Lot's disobedient, though unfortunate, wife. Ample and statuesque (as the salten image she was afterwards to become), the shawl-draped, masklike features are by no means beautiful. It is a face that you may often see to-day, in down-town 'Dancings,' or in the bars of the dockyards or wharves of our own modern cities—Tilbury, 'Frisco, Vera Cruz—a sodden, gin-soaked face that helps to vindicate, if not, perhaps, excuse, the conduct of Lot. . . . With this highly interesting example of the Potters' Art was found a novel object, of an unknown nature, likely to arouse, in scientific circles, considerable controversy. . . ." '

And just as the lectrice was growing hesitant and embarrassed, the Countess of Tolga, who had the *entrée,* unobtrusively entered the room.

She was looking particularly well in one of the new standing-out skirts ruched with rosebuds, and was showing more of her stockings than she usually did.

'You bring the sun with you!' the Queen graciously exclaimed.

'Indeed,' the Countess answered, 'I ought to apologise for the interruption, but the *poor little thing* is leaving now.'

'What? has the Abbess come?'

'She has sent Sister Irene of the Incarnation instead. . . .'

'I had forgotten it was to-day.'

* The Hon. 'Eddy' Monteith had succumbed: the shock received by meeting a jackal while composing a sonnet had been too much for him. His tomb is in the Vale of Akko, beside the River Dis. Alas, for the *triste* obscurity of his end!

With an innate aversion for all farewells, yet the Queen was accustomed to perform a score of irksome acts daily that she cordially disliked, and when, shortly afterwards, Mademoiselle de Nazianzi accompanied by a Sister from the Flaming-Hood were announced, they found her quite prepared.

Touched, and reassured at the ex-maid's appearance, the Queen judged, at last, it was safe to unbend. Already very remote and unworldly in her novice's dress, she had ceased, indeed, to be a being there was need any more to either circumvent, humour, or suppress; and now that the threatened danger was gone, her Majesty glanced, half-lachrymosely, about among her personal belongings for some slight token of 'esteem' or *souvenir*. Skimming from cabinet to cabinet, in a sort of hectic dance, she began to fear, as she passed her bibelots in review, that beyond a Chinese Buddha that she believed to be ill-omened, and which for a nun seemed hardly suitable, she could spare nothing about her after all, and in some dilemma she raised her eyes, as though for a crucifix, towards the wall. Above the long-chair a sombre study of a strangled negress in a ditch by Gauguin conjured up to-day with poignant force a vivid vision of the Tropics.

'The poor Duchess!' she involuntarily sighed, going off into a train of speculation of her own.

Too tongue-tied, or, perhaps, too discreet, to inform the Queen that anything she might select would immediately be confiscated by the Abbess, Sister Irene, while professing her rosary, appraised her surroundings with furtive eyes, crossing herself frequently with a speed and facility due to practice, whenever her glance chanced to alight on some nude shape in stone. Keen, meagre, and perhaps slightly malicious, hers was a curiously pinched face—like a cold violet.

'The Abbess is still in retreat; but sends her duty,' she ventured as the Queen approached a guéridon near which she was standing.

'Indeed? How I envy her,' the Queen wistfully said, selecting as suited to the requirements of the occasion, a little volume of a mystic trend, the *Cries of Love* of Father Surin,* bound in grey velvet, which she pressed upon the reluctant novice, with a brief, but cordial, kiss of farewell.

'She looked quite pretty!' she exclaimed, sinking to the long-chair as soon as the nuns had gone.

* Author of *In the Dusk of the Dawn*.

'So like the Cimabue in the long corridor...' the Countess of Tolga murmured chillily. It was her present policy that her adored ally, Olga Blumenghast, should benefit by Mademoiselle de Nazianzi's retirement from Court, by becoming nearer to the Queen, when they would work all the wires between them.

'I'd have willingly followed her,' the Queen weariedly declared, 'at any rate, until after the wedding.'

'It seems that I and Lord Derbyfield are to share the same closed carriage in the wake of the bridal coach,' the Countess of Tolga said, considering with a supercilious air her rose *suède* slipper on the dark carpet.

'He's like some great Bull. What do you suppose he talks about?'

The Countess d'Omptyda repressed a giggle.

'They tell me Don Juan was nothing *nothing* to him. . . . He cannot see, he cannot be, oh every hour. It seems he can't help it, and that he simply *has* to!'

'Fortunately Lady Lavinia Lee-Strange will be in the landau as well!'

The Queen laid her cheeks to her hands.

'I all but died, dear Violet,' she crooned, 'listening to an account of her Ancestor, who fell, fighting Scotland, at the battle of Pinkie Cleugh.'

'These well-bred, but detestably insular women, how they bore one.'

'They are not to be appraised by any ordinary standards. Crossing the state saloon while coming here what should I see, ma'am, but Lady Canon of Noon on her hands and knees (all fours!) peeping below the loose-covers of the chairs in order to examine the Gobelins-tapestries beneath. . . .'

'Oh——'

'"Absolutely authentic," I said, as I passed on, leaving her looking like a pickpocket caught in the act.'

'I suppose she was told to make a quiet survey. . . .'

'Like their beagles and deer-hounds, that their Landseer so loved to paint, I fear the British character is, at bottom, *nothing* if not rapacious!'

'It's said, I believe, that to behold the Englishman at his *best* one should watch him play tip-and-run.'

'You mean of course cricket?'

85

The Queen looked doubtful: she had retained of a cricket-match at Lord's a memory of hatless giants waving wooden sticks.

'I only wish it could have been a long engagement,' she abstrusely murmured, fastening her attention on the fountains whitely spurting in the gardens below.

Valets in cotton jackets and light blue aprons, bearing baskets of crockery and *argenterie*, were making ready beneath the tall Tuba trees a supper *buffet* for the evening's Ball.

> 'Flap your wings, little bird,
> Oh flap your wings——'

A lad's fresh voice, sweet as a robin's, came piping up.

'These wretched workpeople——! There's not a peaceful corner,' the Queen complained, as her husband's shape appeared at the door. He was followed by his first secretary—a simple commoner, yet with the air and manner peculiar to the husband of a Countess.

'Yes, Willie? I've a hundred headaches. What is it?'

'Both King Geo and Queen Glory are wondering where you are.'

'Oh, really, Willie?'

'And dear Elsie's asking after you too.'

'Very likely,' the Queen returned with quiet complaisance, 'but unfortunately, I have neither her energy nor,' she murmured with a slightly sardonic laugh, 'her appetite!'

The Countess of Tolga tittered.

'She called for fried-eggs and butcher's-meat, this morning, about the quarter before eight,' she averred.

'An excellent augury for our dynasty,' the King declared, reposing the eyes of an adoring grandparent upon an alabaster head of a Boy attributed to Donatello.

'She's terribly foreign, Willie ... ! Imagine ham and eggs ...' The Queen dropped her face to her hand.

'So long as the Royal-House——' The King broke off, turning gallantly to raise the Countess d'Omptyda, who had sunk with a gesture of exquisite allegiance to the floor.

'Sir ... Sir!' she faltered in confusion, seeking with fervent lips her Sovereign's hand.

'What is she doing, Willie!'

'Begging for Strawberry-leaves!' the Countess of Tolga brilliantly commented.

'Apropos of Honours ... it appears King Geo has signified

his intention of raising his present representative in Pisuerga to the peerage.'

'After her recent *Cause*, Lady Something should be not a little consoled.'

'She was at the début of the new diva, little Miss Helvellyn (the foreign invasion has indeed begun!), at the Opera-House last night, so radiant.'

'When she cranes forward out of her own box to smile at someone into the next, I can't explain . . . but one feels she ought to hatch,' the Queen murmured, repairing capriciously from one couch to another.

'We neglect our guests, my dear,' the King expostulatingly exclaimed, bending over his consort anxiously from behind.

'Tell me, Willie,' she cooed, caressing the medals upon his breast. and drawing him gently down: 'tell me. Didst thou enjoy thy cigar, dear, with King Geo?'

'I can recall in my time, Child, a suaver flavour. . . .'

'Thy little chat, though, dearest, was well enough?'

'I would not call him crafty, but I should say he was a man of considerable subtlety . . .' the King evasively replied.

'One does not need, my dearest nectarine, a prodigy of intelligence, however, to take him in!'

'Before the proposed Loan, Love, can be brought about, he may wish to question thee as to thy political opinions.'

The Queen gave a little light laugh.

'No one knows what my political opinions are; I don't myself!'

'And I'm quite confident of it: But, indeed, my dear, we neglect our functions.'

'I only wish it could have been a *long* engagement, Willie. . . .'

꧁ *XV* ꧂

IN the cloister eaves the birds were just awakening, and all the spider scales, in the gargoyled gables, glanced fresh with dew. Above the Pietà on the porter's gate, slow-speeding clouds, like knots of pink roses, came blowing across the sky, sailing away in titanic bouquets towards the clear horizon. All virginal in the early sunrise, what enchantment the world possessed! The rhythmic sway-sway of the trees, the exhalations of the flowers, the ethereal candour of this early hour,—these raised the heart up to their Creator.

Kneeling at the casement of a postulant's cell, Laura de Nazianzi recalled that serene, and just thus, had she often planned must dawn her bridal day!

Beyond the cruciform flower-beds and the cloister wall soared the Blue Jesus, the storied windows of its lofty galleries aglow with light.

'Most gracious Jesus. Help me to forget. For my heart aches. Uphold me now.'

But to forget to-day was well-nigh, she knew, impossible. . . .

Once it seemed she caught the sound of splendid music from the direction of the Park, but it was too early for music yet. Away in the palace the Princess Elsie must be already astir . . . in her peignoir, perhaps? The bridal-garment unfolded upon the bed: but no: it was said the bed indeed was where usually her Royal-Highness's dogs . . .

With a long and very involuntary sigh, she began to sweep, and put in some order, her room.

How forlorn her cornette looked upon her *prie-Dieu*! And, oh, how stern, and 'old'!

Would an impulse to bend it slightly, but only so, *so* slightly, to an angle to suit her face, be attended, later, by remorse?

'Confiteor Deo omnipotenti, beatae Mariae semper virgini, beato Michaeli Archangelo (et *tibi* Pater), quia peccavi nimis cogitatione, verbo et opere,' she entreated, reposing her chin in meditation upon the handle of her broom.

The bluish shadow of a cypress-tree on the empty wall fascinated her as few pictures had.

'Grant my soul eyes,' she prayed, cheerfully completing her task.

It being a general holiday, all was yet quite still in the corridor. A sound as of gentle snoring came indeed from behind more than one closed door, and the new *pensionnaire* was preparing to beat a retreat when she perceived, in the cloister, the dumpish form of Old Jane.

Seated in the sun by the convent wall, the Porteress was sharing a scrap of breakfast with the birds.

'You're soonish for Mass, love,' she broke out, her large archaic features surcharged with smiles.

'It's such a perfect morning, I felt I must come down.'

'I've seen many a more promising sunrise before now, my dear, turn to storm and blast! An orange sky overhead brings back to me the morning that I was received; ah, I shall never forget, as I was taking my Vows, a flash of forked lightning, and a clap of Thunder (Glory be to God!), followed by a waterspout (Mercy save us!) bursting all over my Frinch lace veil. . . .'

'What is your book, Old Jane?'

'Something light, love, as it's a holiday.'

'*Pascal* . . .'

'Though it's mostly a *Fête* day I've extra to do!' the Porteress averred, dropping her eyes to the great, glistening spits upon the Cloister flags. It was her boast she could distinguish Monsignor Potts's round splash from Father Geordie Picpus's more dapper fine one, and again the Abbess's from Mother Martinez de la Rosa's— although these indeed shared a certain opaque sameness.

'Of course it's a day for private visits.'

'Since the affair of Sister Dorothea and Brother Bernard Soult, private visits are no longer allowed,' the Porteress returned, reproving modestly, with the cord of her discipline, a pert little lizard, that seemed to be proposing to penetrate between the nude toes of her sandalled foot.

But on such a radiant morning it was preposterous to hint at 'Rules.'

Beneath the clement sun a thousand cicadas were insouciantly chirping, while birds, skimming about without thoughts of money, floated lightly from tree to tree.

'Jesus—Mary—Joseph!' the Porteress purred, as a nun, with her face all muffled up in wool, crossed the Cloister, glancing neither to right nor left, and sharply slammed a door: for, already, the Convent was beginning to give signs of animation. Deep in a book of Our Lady's Hours, a biretta'd priest was slowly rounding a garden path, while repairing from a *Grotto-sepulchre*, to which was attached a handsome indulgence, Mother Martinez de la Rosa appeared, all heavily leaning on her stick.

Simultaneously the matin-bell rang out, calling all to prayer.

The Convent Chapel, founded by the tender enthusiasm of a wealthy widow, the Countess d'Acunha, to perpetuate her earthly comradeship with the beautiful Andalusian, the Doña Dolores Baatz, was still but thinly peopled some few minutes later, although the warning bell had stopped.

Peering around, Laura was disappointed not to remark Sister Ursula in her habitual place, between the veiled fresco of the 'Circumcision' and the stoup of holy-water by the door.

Beyond an offer to 'exchange whippings' there had been a certain coolness in the greeting with her friend that had both surprised and pained her.

'When those we rely on wound and betray us, to whom should we turn but Thee?' she breathed, addressing a crucifix, in ivory, contrived by love, that was a miracle of wonder.

Finished Mass, there was a general rush for the Refectory!

Preceded by Sister Clothilde, and followed, helter-skelter, by an exuberant bevy of nuns, even Mother Martinez, who, being short-sighted, would go feeling the ground with her cane, was propelled to the measure of a hop-and-skip.

Passing beneath an archway labelled 'Silence' (the injunction to-day being undoubtedly ignored), the company was welcomed by the mingled odours of tea, *consommé,* and fruit. It was a custom of the Convent for one of the Sisters during meal-time to read aloud from some standard work of fideism, and these edifying recitations, interspersed by such whispered questions as: 'Tea, or *Consommé?*' 'A Banana, or a Pomegranate?' gave to those at all foolishly or hysterically inclined a painful desire to giggle. Mounting the pulpit-lectern, a nun with an aristocratic though gourmand little face was about to resume the arid life of the Byzantine monk, Basilius Saturninus, when Mother Martinez de la Rosa took it upon herself, in a few patriotic words, to relax all rules for that day.

'We understand in the world now,' a little faded woman murmured to Laura upon her right, 'that the latest craze among ladies is to gild their tongues; but I should be afraid,' she added diffidently, dipping her banana into her tea, 'of poison, myself!'

Unhappy at her friend's absence from the Refectory, Laura, however, was in no mood to entertain the nuns with stories of the present pagan tendencies of society.

Through the bare, blindless windows, framing a sky so bluely luminous, came the swelling clamour of the assembling crowds, tinging the languid air as with some sultry fever. From the *Chausée,* music of an extraordinary intention—heated music, crude music, played with passionate élan to perfect time, conjured up, with vivid, heartrending prosaicness, the seething Boulevards beyond the high old creeper-covered walls.

'I forget now, Mother, which of the Queens it is that will wear a velvet train of a beautiful orchid shade; but one of them will!' Sister Irene of the Incarnation was holding forth.

'I must confess,' Mother Martinez remarked, who was peeling herself a peach, with an air of far attention, 'I must confess, I should have liked to have cast my eye upon the *lingerie* . . .'

'I would rather have seen the ball-wraps, Mother, or the shoes, and evening slippers!'

'Yes, or the fabulous jewels . . .'

'Of course Sister Laura saw the *trousseau*?'

But Laura made feint not to hear.

Discipline relaxed, a number of nuns had collected provisions and were picnicking in the window, where Sister Innez (an ex-Repertoire actress) was giving some spirited renderings of her chief successful parts—*Jane de Simerose, Frou-Frou, Sappho, Cigarette*. . . .

'My darling child! I always sleep all day and only revive when there's *a Man*,' she was saying with an impudent look, sending the scandalised Sisters into delighted convulsions.

Unable to endure it any longer, Laura crept away.

A desire for air and solitude led her towards the Recreation ground. After the hot refectory, sauntering in the silken shade of the old astounding cedars was delightful quite. In the deserted alleys, the golden blossoms of the censia-trees, unable to resist the sun, littered in perfumed piles the ground, overcoming her before long with a sensation akin to *vertige*. Anxious to find her friend, Laura turned towards her cell.

She found Sister Ursula leaning on her window-ledge all crouched up—like a Duchess on 'a First Night.'

'My dear, my dear, the *crowds*!'

'Ursula?'

'Yes, what is it?'

'Perhaps I'll go, since I'm in the way.'

'Touchy Goose,' Sister Ursula murmured, wheeling round with a glance of complex sweetness.

'Ah, Ursula,' Laura sighed, smiling reproachfully at her friend.

She had long almond eyes, one longer and larger than the other, that gave to her narrow, etiolated face an exalted, mystic air. Her hair, wholly concealed by her full coif, would be inclined to rich copper or chestnut: indeed, below the pinched and sensitive nostrils, a moustache (so slight as to be scarcely discernible) proved this beyond all controversy to be so. But perhaps the quality and beauty of her hands were her chief distinction.

'Do you believe it would cause an earthquake if we climbed out, dear little one, upon the leads?' she asked.

'I had forgotten you overlooked the street by leaning out,' Laura answered, sinking fatigued to a little cane armchair.

'Listen, Laura . . . !'

'This cheering racks my heart. . . .'

'Ah, Astaroth! There went a very "swell" carriage.'

'Perhaps I'll come back later: it's less noisy in my cell.'

'Now you're here, I shall ask you, I think, to whip me.'

'Oh, no. . . .'

'Bad dear Little-One. Dear meek soul!' Sister Ursula softly laughed.

'This maddening cheering,' Laura breathed, rolling tormented eyes about her.

A crucifix, a text, *I would lay Pansies at Jesus' Feet*, two fresh eggs in a blue paper bag, some ends of string, a breviary, and a birch were the chamber's individual if meagre contents.

'You used *not* to have that text, Ursula,' Laura observed, her attention arrested by the preparation of a Cinematograph Company on the parapet of the Cathedral.

The Church had much need indeed of Reformation! The Times were incredibly low. A new crusade . . . she ruminated, revolted at the sight of an old man holding dizzily to a stone-winged angel, with a wine-flask at his lips.

'Come, dear, won't you assist me now to mortify my senses?' Sister Ursula cajoled.

'No, really, no—!—!—!'

'Quite lightly. For I was scourged, by Sister Agnes, but yesterday with a heavy bunch of keys, head downwards, hanging from a bar.'

'Oh . . .'

'This morning she sent me those pullets' eggs. I perfectly was touched by her delicate sweet sympathy.'

Laura gasped.

'It must have hurt you?'

'I assure you I felt nothing—my spirit had travelled so far,' Sister Ursula replied, turning to throw an interested glance at the street.

It was close now upon the crucial hour, and the plaudits of the crowd were becoming more and more uproarious, as 'favourites' in Public life and 'celebrities' of all sorts began to arrive in brisk succession at the allotted door of the Cathedral.

'I could almost envy the fleas in the Cardinal's vestments,' Sister Ursula declared, overcome by the venial desire to see.

Gazing at the friend upon whom she had counted in some disillusion, Laura quietly left her.

The impulse to witness something of the spectacle outside was, nevertheless, infectious, and recollecting that from the grotto-sepulchre in the garden it was not impossible to attain the convent wall, she determined, moved by some wayward instinct, to do so. Frequently, as a child, had she scaled it, to survey the doings of the city streets beyond—the streets named by the nuns often 'Sinward ho.' Crossing the cloisters, and through old gates crowned by vast fruit-baskets in stone, she followed, feverishly, the ivy-masked bricks of the sheltering wall, and was relieved to reach the grotto without encountering anyone. Surrounded by heavy boskage, it marked a spot where once long ago one of the Sisters, it was said, had received the mystic stigmata. . . . With a feline effort (her feet supported by the grotto boulders), it needed but a bound to attain an incomparable post of vantage.

Beneath a blaze of bunting, the street seemed paved with heads. 'Madonna,' she breathed, as an official on a white horse, its mane stained black, began authoritatively backing his steed into the patient faces of the mob below, startling an infant in arms to a frantic fit of squalls.

'Just so we shall stand on the Day of Judgment,' she reflected, blinking at the glare.

Street boys vending programmes, 'lucky' horseshoes, Saturnalian emblems (these for gentlemen only), offering postcards of 'Geo and Glory,' etc., wedged their way, however, where it might have been deemed indeed impossible for anyone to pass.

And *he*, she wondered, her eyes following the wheeling pigeons, alarmed by the recurrent salutes of the signal guns, he must be there already: under the dome! restive a little beneath the busy scrutiny, his tongue like the point of a blade. . . .

A burst of cheering seemed to announce the Queen. But no, it was only a lady with a parasol sewn with diamonds that was exciting the rah-rahs of the crowd. Followed by mingled cries of 'Shame!' 'Waste!' and sighs of envy, Madame Wetme was enjoying a belated triumph. And now a brief lull, as a brake containing various delegates and 'representatives of English Culture,' rolled by at a stately trot—Lady Alexander, E. V. Lucas, Robert Hichens, Clutton Brock, etc.—the ensemble the very apotheosis of worn-out *cliché*.

'There's someone there wot's got enough heron plumes on her head!' a young girl in the crowd remarked.

And nobody contradicted her.

Then troops and outriders, and at last the Queen.

She was looking charming in a Corinthian chlamyde, in a carriage lined in deep delphinium blue, behind six restive blue roan horses.

Finally, the bride and her father, bowing this way and that . . .

Cheers.

'Huzzas . . .'

A hushed suspense.

Below the wall the voice of a beggar arose, persistent, haunting: 'For the Love of God . . . In the Name of Pity . . . of Pity.'

'Of Pity,' she echoed, addressing a frail, wind-sown harebell, blue as the sky: and leaning upon the shattered glass ends, that crowned the wall, she fell to considering the future—obedience—solitude—death.

The troubling *valse* theme from *Dante in Paris* interrupted her meditations.

How often had they valsed it together, he and she . . . sometimes as a two-step . . . ! What souvenirs. . . . Yousef, Yousef. . . . Above the Cathedral, the crumbling clouds had eclipsed the sun. In the intense meridian glare the thronged street seemed even as though half-hypnotised; occasionally only the angle of a parasol would change, or some bored soldier's legs would give a little. When brusquely, from the belfry, burst a triumphant clash of bells.

Laura caught her breath.

Already?

A shaking of countless handkerchiefs in wild ovation: from roof-tops, and balconies, the air was thick with falling flowers—the bridal pair!

But only for the bridegroom had she eyes.

Oblivious of what she did, she began to beat her hands, until they streamed with blood, against the broken glass ends upon the wall: 'Yousef, Yousef, Yousef. . . .'

July 1921, May 1922.
Versailles, Montreux, Florence.

Prancing Nigger

Prancing Nigger

~ *I* ~

LOOKING gloriously bored, Miss Miami Mouth gaped up into the boughs of a giant silk-cotton-tree. In the lethargic noontide nothing stirred: all was so still, indeed, that the sound of someone snoring was clearly audible among the cane-fields far away.

'After dose yams an' pods an' de white falernum, I dats way sleepy too,' she murmured, fixing heavy, somnolent eyes upon the prospect that lay before her.

Through the sun-tinged greenery shone the sea, like a floor of silver glass strewn with white sails.

Somewhere out there, fishing, must be her boy, Bamboo!

And, inconsequently, her thoughts wandered from the numerous shark-casualties of late to the mundane proclivities of her mother; for to quit the little village of Mediavilla for the capital was that dame's fixed obsession.

Leave Mediavilla, leave Bamboo! The young negress fetched a sigh.

In what way, she reflected, would the family gain by *entering Society*, and how did one enter it at all? There would be a gathering, doubtless, of the elect (probably armed), since the best Society is exclusive and difficult to enter. And then? Did one burrow? Or charge? She had sometimes heard it said that people 'pushed'... and closing her eyes, Miss Miami Mouth sought to picture her parents, assisted by her small sister, Edna, and her brother, Charlie, forcing their way, perspiring but triumphant, into the highest social circles of the city of Cuna-Cuna.

Across the dark savannah country the city lay, one of the chief alluring cities of the world: the Celestial city of Cuna-Cuna, Cuna, city of Mimosa, Cuna, city of Arches, Queen of the Tropics, Paradise—almost invariably travellers referred to it like that.

Oh, everything must be fantastic there, where even the very pickneys put on clothes! And Miss Miami Mouth glanced fondly down at her own plump little person, nude but for a girdle of creepers that she would gather freshly twice a day.

'It would be a shame, sh'o, to cover it,' she murmured drowsily, caressing her body; and moved to a sudden spasm of laughter, she tittered: 'No! really. De ideah!'

～ II ～

'SILVER bean-stalks, silver bean-stalks, oh hé, oh hé,' down the long village street from door to door the cry repeatedly came, until the vendor's voice was lost on the evening air.

In a rocking-chair, before the threshold of a palm-thatched cabin, a matron with broad, bland features and a big, untidy figure surveyed the scene with a nonchalant eye.

Beneath some tall trees, bearing flowers like flaming bells, a few staid villagers sat enjoying the rosy dusk, while, strolling towards the sea, two young men passed by with fingers intermingled.

With a slight shrug, the lady plied her fan.

As the Mother of a pair of oncoming girls, the number of ineligible young men or confirmed bachelors around the neighbourhood was a constant source of irritation to her.

'Sh'o, dis remoteness bore an' weary me to death,' she exclaimed, addressing someone through the window behind; and receiving no audible answer, she presently rose and went within.

It was the hour when, fortified by a siesta, Mrs. Ahmadou Mouth was wont to approach her husband on general household affairs, and to discuss, in particular, the question of their removal to the town; for, with the celebration of their pearl wedding close at hand, the opportunity to make the announcement of a change of residence to their guests ought not, she believed, to be missed.

'We leave Mediavilla for de education ob my daughters,' she would say; or, perhaps: 'We go to Cuna-Cuna for de finishing ob *mes filles*!'

But, unfortunately, the reluctance of Mr. Mouth to forsake his Home seemed to increase from day to day.

She found him asleep, bolt upright, his head gently nodding, beneath a straw hat beautifully browned.

'Say, nigger, lub,' she murmured, brushing her hand featheringly along his knee, 'say, nigger, lub, I gotta go!'

It was the tender prelude to the storm.

Evasive (and but half awake), he warned her. 'Let me alone; Ah'm thinkin'.'

'Prancing Nigger, now come on!'

'Ah'm thinkin'.'

'Tell me what for dis procrastination?' Exasperated, she gripped his arm.

But for all reply Mr. Mouth drew a volume of revival hymns towards him, and turned on his wife his back.

'You ought to shame o' you-self, sh'o,' she caustically commented, crossing to the window.

The wafted odours of the cotton-trees without oppressed the air. In the deepening twilight the rising moonmist already obscured the street.

'Dis place not healthy. Dat damp! Should my daughters go off into a decline . . .' she apprehensively murmured, as her husband started softly to sing.

> ' "For ebber wid de Lord!"
>   Amen; so let it be;
>   Life from de dead is in dat word,
>   'Tis immortality.'

'If it's de meeting-house dats de obstruction, dair are odders, too, in Cuna-Cuna,' she observed.

'How often hab I bid you nebba to mention dat modern Sodom in de hearing ob my presence!'

'De debil frequent de village, fo' dat matter, besides de town.'

'Sh'o nuff.'

'But yestiddy, dat po' silly negress Ottalie was seduced again in a Mango track—; an' dats de third time!'

> 'Heah in de body pent,
>   Absent from Him I roam,
>   Yet nightly pitch my movin' tent
>   A day's march nearer home.'

'Prancing Nigger, from dis indifference to your fambly, be careful lest you do arouse de vials ob de Lord's wrath!'

'Yet nightly pitch—' he was beginning again, in a more subdued key, but the tones of his wife arrested him.

'Prancing Nigger, lemme say sumptin' more!' Mrs. Mouth took

a long sighing breath. 'In dis dark jungle my lil jewel Edna, I feah, will wilt away. . . .'

'Wha' gib you cause to speak like dat?'

'I was tellin' my fortune lately wid de cards,' she reticently made reply, insinuating, by her half-turned eyes, that more disclosures of an ominous nature concerning others besides her daughter had been revealed to her as well.

'Lordey Lord; what is it den you want?'

'I want a Villa with a watercloset—' Flinging wiles to the winds, it was a cry from the heart.

'De Lord hab pity on dese vanities an' innovations!'

'In town, you must rememba, often de houses are far away from de parks;—de city, in dat respect, not like heah.'

'Say nothin' more! De widow ob my po' brudder Willie, across de glen, she warn me I ought nebba to listen to you.'

'Who care for a common woman, dat only read de *Negro World*, an' nebba see anyt'ing else!' she swelled.

Mr. Mouth turned conciliatingly.

'To-morrow me arrange for de victuals for our ebenin' at Home!'

'Good, bery fine,' she murmured, acknowledging through the window the cordial 'good-night' of a few late labourers, returning from the fields, each with a bundle of sugar-cane poised upon the head.

'As soon as marnin' dawn me take dis biznis in hand.'

'Only pramas, nigger darlin',' she cajoled, 'dat durin' de course of de reception you make a lil speech to inform de neighbours ob our gwine away bery soon, for de sake of de education ob our girls.'

'Ah sha'n' pramas nothin'.'

'I could do wid a change too, honey, after my last miscarriage.'

'Change come wid our dissolution,' he assured her, 'quite soon enuff!'

'Bah,' she murmured, rubbing her cheek to his: 'we set out on our journey sh'o in de season ob Novemba.'

To which with asperity he replied: '*Not for two Revolutions!*' and rising brusquely, strode solemnly from the room.

'Hey-ho-day,' she yawned, starting a wheezy gramophone, and sinking down upon his empty chair; and she was lost in ball-room fancies (whirling in the arms of some blond young foreigner) when she caught sight of her daughter's reflection in the glass.

Having broken or discarded her girdle of leaves, Miss Miami Mouth, attracted by the gramophone, appeared to be teaching a hectic two-step to the cat.

'Fie, fie, my lass. Why you be so *Indian*?' her mother exclaimed, bestowing, with the full force of a carpet slipper, a well-aimed spank from behind.

'*Aïe, aïe!*'

'Sh'o: you nohow select!'

'*Aïe. . . .*'

'De low exhibition!'

'I had to take off my apron, 'cos it seemed to draw de bees,' Miami tearfully explained, catching up the cat in her arms.

'Ob course, if you choose to wear roses. . . . '

'It was but ivy!'

'De berries ob de ivy entice de same,' Mrs. Mouth replied, nodding graciously, from the window, to Papy Paul, the next-door neighbour, who appeared to be taking a lonely stroll with a lanthorn and a pineapple.

'I dats way wondering why Bamboo no pass dis evenin', too; as a rule, it is seldom he stop so late out upon de sea,' the young girl ventured.

'After I shall introduce you to de world (de advantage ob a good marriage; when I t'ink ob mine!), you will be ashamed, sh'o, to recall dis infatuation.'

'De young men ob Cuna-Cuna (tell me, Mammee), are dey den so nice?'

'Ah, Chile! If I was your age again . . .'

'Sh'o, dair's nothin' so much in dat.'

'As a young girl of eight (Tee-hee!), I was distracting to all the gentlemen,' Mrs. Mouth asserted, confiding a smile to a small, long-billed bird, in a cage, of the variety known as Bequia-Sweet.

'How I wish i'd been born, like you, in August-Town, across de Isthmus!'

'It gib me dis taste fo' S'ciety, Chile.'

'In S'ciety, don' dey dress wid clothes on ebery day?'

'Sh'o; surtainly.'

'An' don't dey nebba tickle?'

'In August-Town, de aristocracy conceal de best part ob deir bodies; not like heah!'

'An' tell me, Mammee . . . ? De first lover you eber had . . . was he half as handsome as Bamboo?'

'De first dude, Chile, I eber had, was a lil, lil buoy, . . . wid no hair (whatsoeber at all), bal' like a calabash!' Mrs. Mouth replied, as her daughter Edna entered with the lamp.

'Frtt!' the wild thing tittered, setting it down with a bang: with her cincture of leaves and flowers, she had the éclat of a butterfly.

'Better fetch de shade,' Mrs. Mouth exclaimed, staring squeamishly at Miami's shadow on the wall.

'Already it grow dark; no one about now at dis hour ob night at all.'

'Except thieves an' ghouls,' Mrs. Mouth replied, her glance straying towards the window.

But only the little blue-winged bats were passing beneath a fairyland of stars.

'When I do dis, or dis, my shadow appear as formed as Mimi's!'

'Sh'o, Edna, she dat provocative to-day.'

'Be off at once, Chile, an' lay de table for de ebenin' meal; an' be careful not to knock de shine off de new tin teacups,' Mrs. Mouth commanded, taking up an Estate-Agent's catalgoue and seating herself comfortably beneath the lamp.

' "City of Cuna-Cuna," ' she read, ' *"in the Heart of a Brainy District* (within easy reach of University, shops, etc.). A charming Freehold Villa. Main drainage. Extensive views. Electric light. Every convenience." '

'Dat sound just de sort ob lil shack for me.'

∞ III ∞

THE strange sadness of the evening, the *détresse* of the Evening Sky! Cry, cry, white Rain Birds out of the West, cry . . . !

'An' so, Miami, you no come back no more?'

'No, no come back.'

Flaunting her boredom by the edge of the sea one close of day, she had chanced to fall in with Bamboo, who, stretched at length upon the beach, was engaged in mending a broken net.

'An' I dats way glad,' she half resentfully pouted, jealous a little of his toil.

But, presuming deafness, the young man laboured on, since, to support an aged mother, and to attain one's desires, perforce necessitates work; and his fondest wish, by dint of saving, was to wear on his wedding-day a pink, starched, cotton shirt—a starched, pink cotton shirt, stiff as a boat's-sail when the North winds caught it! But a pink shirt would mean trousers . . . and trousers would lead to shoes . . . 'Extravagant nigger, don't you dare!' he would exclaim, in dizzy panic, from time to time, aloud.

'Forgib me, honey,' he begged, 'but me obliged to finish while de daylight last.'

'Sh'o,' she sulked, following the amazing strategy of the sunset-clouds.

'Miami angel, you look so sweet: I dat amorous ob you, Mimi!'

A light laugh tripped over her lips.

'Say, buoy, how you getting on?' she queried, sinking down on her knees beside him.

'I dat amorous ob you!'

'Oh, ki,' she tittered, with a swift mocking glance at his crimson loincloth. She had often longed to snatch it away.

'Say you lub me, just a lil, too, deah?'

'Sh'o,' she answered softly, sliding over on to her stomach, and laying her cheek to the flats of her hands.

Boats with crimson spouts, to wit, steamers, dotted the skyline far away, and barques, with sails like the wings of butterflies, borne by an idle breeze, were bringing more than one ineligible young mariner back to the prose of shore.

'Ob wha' you t'inking?'

'Nothin',' she sighed, contemplating laconically a little transparent shell of violet pearl, full of seawater and grains of sand, that the wind ruffled as it blew.

'Not ob *any* sort ob lil t'ing?' he caressingly insisted, breaking an open dark flower from her belt of wild Pansy.

'I should be gwine home,' she breathed, recollecting the undoing of the negress Ottalie.

'Oh, I dat amorous ob you, Mimi.'

'If you want to finish dat net while de daylight last.'

For oceanward, in a glowing ball, the sun had dropped already.

'Sho', nigger, I only wish to be kind,' she murmured, getting up and sauntering a few paces along the strand.

Lured, perhaps, by the nocturnal phosphorescence from its lair, a water-scorpion, disquieted at her approach, turned and vanished amid the sheltering cover of the rocks. 'Isht, isht,' she squealed, wading after it into the surf, but to find it, look as she would, was impossible. Dark, curious and anxious, in the fast failing light, the sea disquieted her too, and it was consoling to hear close behind her the solicitous voice of Bamboo.

'Us had best be movin', befo' de murk ob night.'

The few thatched cabins that comprised the village of Mediavilla lay not half a mile from the shore. Situated between the savannah and the sea, on the southern side of the island known as Tacarigua (the 'burning Tacarigua' of the Poets), its inhabitants were obliged, from lack of communication with the larger island centres, to rely to a considerable extent for a livelihood among themselves. Local Market days, held, alternatively, at Valley Village or Broken Hill (the nearest approach to industrial towns in the district around Mediavilla), were the chief source of rural trade, when such merchandise as fish, coral, beads, bananas and loincloths would exchange hands amid much animation, social gossip and pleasant fun.

'Wha' you say to dis?' she queried as they turned inland through the cane-fields, holding up a fetish known as a 'luck-ball,' attached to her throat by a chain.

'Who gib it you?' he shortly demanded, with a quick suspicious glance.

'Mammee, she bring it from Valley Village, an' she bring another for my lil sister, too.'

'Folks say she attend de Market only to meet de Obi man, who cast a spell so dat your Dada move to Cuna-Cuna.'

'Dat so!'

'Your Mammee no seek ebber de influence ob Obeah?'

'Not dat I know ob!' she replied; nevertheless, she could not but recall her mother's peculiar behaviour of late, especially upon Market days, when, instead of conversing with her friends, she would take herself off with a mysterious air, saying she was going to the Baptist Chapel.

'Mammee, she hab no faith in de Witch-Doctor at all,' she murmured, halting to lend an ear to the liquid note of a peadove among the canes.

'I no care; me follow after wherebber you go,' he said, stealing an arm about her.

'True?' she breathed, looking up languidly towards the white mounting moon.

'I dat amorous ob you, Mimi.'

❧ *IV* ❧

IT was the Feast night. In the grey spleen of evening, through the dusty lanes towards Mediavilla county society flocked.

Peering round a cow-shed door, Primrose and Phœbe, procured as waitresses for the occasion, felt their valour ooze as they surveyed the arriving guests, and dropping prostrate amid the straw, declared, in each other's arms, that never, never would they find the courage to appear.

In the road, before a tall tamarind-tree, a well-spread supper board exhaled a pungent odour of fried cascadura fish, exciting the plaintive ravings of the wan pariah dogs, and the cries of a few little stark naked children engaged as guardians to keep them away. Defying an ancient and inelegant custom by which the hosts welcomed their guests by the side of the road, Mrs. Mouth had elected to remain within the precincts of the house, where, according to tradition, the bridal trophies—cowrie-shells, feathers, and a bouquet of faded orange blossom—were being displayed.

'It seem no more dan yestidday,' she was holding forth gaily over a goblet of Sangaree wine, 'it seem no more dan yestidday dat I put on me maiden wreath ob arange blastams to walk wid me nigger to church.'

Clad in rich-hued creepers, she was both looking and feeling her best.

'Sh'o,' a woman with blonde-dyed hair and Buddery eyes exclaimed, 'it seem no more dan just like yestidday; dat not so, Papy Paul?' she queried, turning to an old man in a raspberry-pink kerchief, who displayed (as he sat) more of his person than he seemed to be aware of.

But Papy Paul was confiding a receipt for pickling yuccas to Mamma Luna, the mother of Bamboo, and made as if not to hear.

Offering a light, lilac wine, sweet and heady, Miami circled here and there. She had a cincture of white rose-oleanders, and a bandeau of blue convolvuli. She held a fan.

'Or do you care for anyt'ing else?' she was enquiring, automatically, of Mr. Musket (the Father of three very common girls), as a melodious tinkle of strings announced the advent of the minstrels from Broken Hill.

Following the exodus roadward, it was agreeable to reach the outer air.

Under the high trees by the yard-door gate, the array of vehicles and browsing quadrupeds was almost as numerous as upon a market day. The quiet village road was agog, with bustling folk as perhaps never before, coming and going between the little Café of the 'Forty Parrots,' with its Bar, spelled *Biar* in twinkling lights. All iris in the dusk, a few loosely-loinclothed young men had commenced dancing aloofly among themselves, bringing down some light (if bitter) banter from the belles.

Pirouetting with these, Miami recognised the twinkling feet of her brother Charlie, a lad who preferred roaming the wide savannah country after butterflies with his net to the ever-increasing etiquette of his home.

'Sh'o, S'ciety no longer what it wa',' the mother of two spare lean girls, like young giraffes, was lamenting, when a clamorous song summoned the assembly to the festal board.

In the glow of blazing palm logs, stoked by capering pickneys, the company, with some considerable jostling, became seated by degrees.

'Fo' what we gwine to recebe de Lord make us to be truly t'ankful.' Mr. Mouth's low voice was lost amid the din. Bending to the decree of Providence, and trusting in God for the welfare of his house, he was resigned to follow the call of duty, by allowing his offspring such educational advantages and worldly polish that only a city can give.

'An' so I heah you gwine to leab us!' the lady at his elbow exclaimed, helping herself to a claw of a crab.

'Fo' de sake ob de chillen's schoolin',' Mr. Mouth made reply, blinking at the brisk lightning play through the foliage of the trees.

'Dey tell me de amount of licence dat go on ober dah—' she murmured, indicating with her claw the chequered horizon; 'but de whole world needs revising, as de Missionary truly say!'

'Indeed, an' dat's de trute.'

'It made me cry,' a plump little woman declared, 'when de Minister speak so serious on de scandal ob close dancing. . . .'

'Fo' one t'ing lead sh'o to be nex'!' Mr. Mouth obstrusely assented, turning his attention upon an old negress answering to the name of Mamma May, who was retailing how she had obtained the sunshade beneath which, since noon, she had walked all the way to the party.

'Ah could not afford a parasol, so Ah just cut miself a lil green bush, an' held it up ober my head,' she was crooning in gleeful triumph.

'It's a wonder, indeed, no one gib you a lif'!' several voices observed, but the discussion was drowned by an esoteric song of remote tribal times from the lips of Papy Paul:

> *'I am King Elephant-bag,*
> *Ob de rose-pink Mountains!*
> *Tatou, tatouay, tatou . . .'*

provoking from Miss Stella Spooner, the marvellous daughter of an elderly father, a giggle in which she was joined by the youngest Miss Mouth.

Incontestably a budding Princess, the playful mite was enjoying, with airy nonchalance, her initial experience of Society.

'Ob course she is very *jeune*,' Mrs. Mouth murmured archly, behind her hand, into the ear of Mr. Musket.

'It's de Lord's will,' he cautiously replied, rolling a mystified eye towards his wife (a sable negress out of Africa), continually vaunting her foreign extraction. 'I'm Irish,' she would say: 'I'm Irish, deah. . . .'

'Sh'o she de born image ob her elder sister!'

'De world all say she to marry de son ob ole Mamma Luna, dat keep de lil shop.'

'Suz! Wha' nex'?' Mrs. Mouth returned, breaking off to focus Papy Paul, apparently, already, far from sober. 'I hav' saw God, an' I hav' spoke wid de President, too!' he was announcing impressively to Mamma Luna, a little old woman in whose veins ran the blood of many races.

'Dair's no trute at all in *dat* report,' Mrs. Mouth quietly added, signalling directions to a sturdy, round-bottomed little lad, who had undertaken to fill the gap caused by Primrose and Phœbe.

Bearing a pannier piled with fruit, he had not got far before the minstrels called forth several couples to their feet.

The latest jazz, bewildering, glittering, exuberant as the soil, a jazz, throbbing, pulsating, with a zim, zim, zim, a jazz all abandon and verve that had drifted over the glowing savannah and the waving cane-fields from Cuna-Cuna by the Violet Sea, invited, irresistibly, to motion every boy and girl.

'Prancing Nigger, hab a dance?' his wife, transported, shrilled: but Mr. Mouth was predicting a banana slump to Mrs. Walker, the local midwife, and paid no heed.

Torso-to-torso, the youngsters twirled, while even a pair of majestic matrons, Mrs. Friendship and Mrs. Mother, went whirling away (together) into the brave summer dusk. Accepting the invitation of Bamboo, Miami rose, but before dancing long complained of the heat.

'Sh'o, it cooler in de Plantation,' he suggested, pointing along the road.

'Oh, I too much afraid!'

'What for you afraid?'

But Miami only laughed, and tossed her hand as if she were scattering dewdrops.

Following the roving fireflies and adventurous flittermice, they strolled along in silence. By the roadside, two young men, friends, walking with fingers intermingled, saluted them softly. An admirable evening for a promenade! Indescribably sweet, the floating field-scents enticed them witchingly on.

'Shi!' she exclaimed as a bird skimmed swiftly past with a chattering cry.

'It noddin', deah, but a lil wee owl.'

'An' it to make my heart go so,' she murmured, with a sidelong smiling glance.

He had a new crimson loincloth, and a blood-pink carnation at his ear.

'What for you afraid?' he tenderly pressed.

'It much cooler heah, doh it still very hot,' she inconsequently answered, pausing to listen to the fretting of the hammer tree-frogs in the dusk.

'Dey hold a concert, honey lub, all for us.'

Rig a jig jig, rig a jig jig. . . .

'Just hark to de noise!' she murmured, starting a little at the silver lightning behind the palms.

'Just hark,' he repeated, troubled.

Rig a jig jig, rig a jig jig. . . .

106

❧ *V* ❧

LITTLE jingley trot-trot-trot, over the Savannah, hey—!
Joggling along towards Cuna-Cuna the creaking caravan
shaped its course. Seated in a hooded chariot, berced by mule-bells,
and nibbling a shoot of ripe cane, Mrs. Mouth appeared to have
attained the heights of bliss. Disregarding or insensitive to the incessant groans of her husband (wedged in between a case of pineapples
and a box marked 'lingerie'), she abandoned herself voluptuously
to her thoughts. It was droll to contemplate meeting an old acquaintance, Nini Snagg, who had gone to reside in Cuna-Cuna long ago.
'Fancy seein' you!' she would say, and how they both would laugh.

Replying tersely to the innumerable 'what would you do ifs' of
her sister, supposing attacks from masked bandits or ferocious wild
animals, Miami moped.

All her whole heart yearned back behind her, and never had she
loved Bamboo so much as now.

' —if a big, shaggy buffalo, wid two sharp horns, dat long, were
to rush right at you!' Edna was plaguing her, when a sudden jolt of
the van set up a loud cackling from a dozen scared cocks and hens.

'Drat dose fowl; as if dair were none in Cuna-Cuna!' Mrs. Mouth
addressed her husband.

'Not birds ob dat brood,' he retorted, plaintively starting to sing.

'I t'ink when I read dat sweet story ob old,
  When Jesus was here among men,
  How He called lil chillens as lambs to His fold,
  I should like to hab been wid dem den!
  I wish dat His hands had been placed ahn my head,
  Dat His arms had been thrown aroun' me,
  An' dat I might hab seen His kind look when He said,
"Let de lil ones come unto Me!"'

'Mind de dress-basket don't drop down, deah, an' spoil our clo','
Mrs. Mouth exclaimed, indicating a cowskin trunk that seemed to be
in peril of falling; for, from motives of economy and ease, it had
been decided that not before Cuna-Cuna should rear her queenly
towers above them would they change their floral garlands for the
more artificial fabrics of the town, and Edna, vastly to her importance, go into a pair of frilled 'invisibles' and a petticoat for the first

107

amazing time; nor, indeed, would Mr. Mouth himself 'take to de pants' until his wife and daughters should have assumed their skirts. But this, from the languid pace at which their vehicle proceeded, was unlikely to be just yet. In the torrid tropic noontime, haste, however, was quite out of the question. Bordered by hills, long, yellow and low, the wooded savannah rolled away beneath a blaze of trembling heat.

'I don't t'ink much ob dis part of de country,' Mrs. Mouth commented. 'All dese common palms . . . de cedar-wood tree, dat my tree. Dat is de timber I prefer.'

'An' some,' Edna pertly smiled, 'dey like best de bamboo. . . .'

A remark that was rewarded by a blow on the ear.

'Now she set up a hullabaloo like de time when de scorpion bit her botty,' Mrs. Mouth lamented, and indeed the uproar made alarmed from the boskage a cloud of winsome soldier-birds and inquisitive paroquets.

'Oh my God,' Mr. Mouth exclaimed. 'What for you make all dat dere noise?' But his daughter paid no attention, and soon sobbed herself to sleep.

Advancing through tracks of acacia-shrub or groves of nutmeg-trees, they jolted along in the gay, exalting sunlight. Flowers brighter than love, wafting the odour of spices, strewed in profusion the long guinea-grass on either side of the way.

'All dose sweet aprons, if it weren't fo' de flies!' Mrs. Mouth murmured, regarding some heavy, ambered, Trumpet flowers with a covetous eye.

'I trust Charlie get bit by no snake!'

'Prancing Nigger! It a lil too late now to t'ink ob dat.'

Since, to avoid overcrowding the family party, Charlie was to follow with his butterfly net and arrive as he could. And never were butterflies (seen in nigger-boys' dreams) as brilliant or frolicsome as were those of mid-savannah. Azure Soledads, and radiant Conquistadors with frail flamboyant wings, wove about the labouring mules perpetual fresh rosettes.

'De Lord protect de lad,' Mr. Mouth remarked, relapsing into silence.

Onward through the cloudless noontide, beneath the ardent sun, the caravan drowsily crawled. As the afternoon advanced, Mrs. Mouth produced a pack of well-thumbed cards, and cutting, casually, twice, began interrogating Destiny with these. Reposing as

best she might, Miami gave herself up to her reflections. The familiar aspect of the wayside palms, the tattered pennons of the bananas,
the big silk-cottons (known, to children, as 'Mammee-trees'),
all brought to her mind Bamboo.

'Dair's somet'in' dat look like a death dah, dat's troublin' me,'
Mrs. Mouth remarked, moodily fingering a greasy ace.

'De Almighty forgib dese foolish games!' Mr. Mouth protestingly
said.

'An' from de lie ob de cards . . . it seem as ef de corpse were ob
de masculine species.'

'Wha' gib you de notion ob dat?'

'Sh'o, a sheep puts his wool on his favourite places,' Mrs. Mouth
returned, reshuffling slowly her pack.

Awakened by her Father's psalms, Edna's 'What would you do's'
had commenced with volubility anew, growing more eerie with
the gathering night.

' . . . if a Wood-Spirit wid two heads an' six arms were to take
hold ob you, Mimi, from behind?'

'I no do nothin' at all,' Miami answered briefly.

'Talk not so much ob de jumbies, Chile, as de chickens go to
roost!' Mrs. Mouth admonished.

'Or, if de debil himself should?' Edna insisted, allowing Snowball, the cat, to climb on to her knee.

'Nothin', sh'o,' Miami murmured, regarding dreamily the sun's
sinking dusk, that was illuminating all the Western sky with
incarnadine and flamingo-rose. Ominous in the falling dusk, the
savannah rolled away, its radiant hues effaced beneath a rapid tide
of deepening shadow.

'Start de gramophone gwine, girls, an' gib us somet'in' bright!'
Mrs. Mouth exclaimed, depressed by the forlorn note of the Twa-
oo-Twa-oo bird, that mingled its lament with a thousand night
cries from the grass.

'When de saucy female sing "My Ice Cream Girl," fo' sh'o she
scare de elves.'

And as though by force of magic the nasal soprano of an invisible
songstress rattled forth with tinkling gusto a music-hall air with a
sparkling refrain.

> 'And the boys shout Girlie, hi!
> Bring me soda, soda, soda,

(Aside, spoken) (Stop your fooling there and let me alone!)

For I'm an Ice Cream Soda Girl.'

'It put me in mind ob de last sugar-factory explosion. It was de same day dat Snowball crack de Tezzrazine record. Drat de cat!'

'O Lordey Lord! Wha' for you make dat din?' Mr. Mouth complained, knotting a cotton handkerchief over his head.

'I hope you not gwine to be billeous, honey, afore we get to Lucia?'

'Lemme alone. Ah'm thinkin'.'

Pressing on by the light of a large clear moon, the hamlet of Lucia, the halting-place proposed for the night, lay still far ahead.

Stars, like many Indian pinks, flecked with pale brightness the sky above; towards the horizon shone the Southern Cross, while the Pole Star, through the palm-fronds, came and went.

> '*And the men cry Girlie, hi!*
> *Bring me*—'

'Silence, dah! Ah'm thinkin'. . . .'

❧ VI ❧

CUNA, full of charming roses, full of violet shadows, full of music, full of Love, Cuna . . . !

Leaning from á balcony of the Grand Savannah hotel, their instincts all aroused, Miami and Edna gazed out across the Alemeda, a place all foliage, lamplight, and flowers. It was the hour when Society, in slowly parading carriages, would congregate to take the air beneath the pale mimosas that adorned the favourite promenade. All but recumbent, as though agreeably fatigued by their recent emotions (what wild follies were not committed in shuttered-villas during the throbbing hours of noon?), the Cunans, in their elegant equipages, made, for anyone fresh from the provinces, an interesting and absorbing sight. The liquid-eyed loveliness of the women, and the handsomeness of the men, with their black moustaches and their treacherous smiles—these, indeed, were things to gaze on.

'Oh ki!' Miami laughed delightedly, indicating a foppish, pretty youth, holding in a restive little horse dancing away with him.

110

Rubbing herself repeatedly, as yet embarrassed by the novelty of her clothes, Edna could only gasp.

'...,' she jabbered, pointing at some flaunting belles in great evening hats and falling hair.

'All dat fine,' Miami murmured, staring in wonderment around.

Dominating the city soared the Opera House, uplifting a big, naked man, all gilt, who was being bitten, or mauled, so it seemed, by a pack of wild animals carved of stone; while near by were the University, and the Cathedral with its low white dome crowned by moss-green tiles.

Making towards it, encouraged by the Vesper bell, some young girls, in muslin masks, followed by a retinue of bustling nuns, were running the gauntlet of the profligates that clustered on the kerb.

'Oh, Jesus honey!' Edna cooed, scratching herself in an ecstasy of delight.

'Fo' shame, Chile, to act so unladylike; if any gen'leman look up he t'ink you make a wicked sign,' Mrs. Mouth cautioned, stepping out upon the balcony from the sitting-room behind.

Inhaling a bottle of sal volatile, to dispel *de megrims,* she was looking dignified in a *décolleté* of smoke-blue tulle.

'Nebba do *dat* in S'ciety,' she added, placing a protecting arm around each of her girls.

Seduced, not less than they, by the animation of the town, the fatigue of the journey seemed to her amply rewarded. It was amusing to watch the crowd before the Ciné Lara, across the way, where many were flocking attracted by the hectic posters of 'A Wife's Revenge.'

'I keep t'inking I see Nini Snagg,' Mrs. Mouth observed, regarding a negress in emerald-tinted silk, seated on a public bench beneath the glittering greenery.

'Cunan folk dat fine,' Edna twittered, turning about at her Father's voice:

> 'W'en de day ob toil is done,
> W'en de race ob life is run,
> Heaven send thy weary one
> Rest for evermore!'

'Prancing Nigger! Is it worth while to wear dose grimaces?'
'Sh'o, dis no good place to be.'
'Why, what dair wrong wid it?'

'Ah set out to look fo' de Meetin'-House, but no sooner am Ah
in de street dan a female wid her hair droopin' loose down ober her
back an' into her eyes, she tell me to Come along.'

'Some of dose bold women, dey ought to be shot through dair
bottoms!' Mrs. Mouth indignantly said.

'But I nebba answer nothin'.'

'May our daughters respect dair virtue same as you!' Mrs. Mouth
returned, focusing wistfully the vast flowery parterre of the Café
McDhu'l.

Little city of cocktails, Cuna! The surpassing excellence of thy
Barmen, who shall sing?

'See how dey spell "Biar," Mammee,' Miami tittered: 'dey forget
de *i*!'

'Sh'o, Chile, an' so dey do. . . .'

'Honey Jesus!' Edna broadly grinned: 'imagine de ignorance
ob dat.'

❧ *VII* ❧

NOW, beyond the Alemeda, in the modish faubourg of Farananka, there lived a lady of both influence and wealth—the widow
of the Inventor of Sunflower Piquant. The *veto* of Madame Ruis,
arbitress absolute of Cunan society, and owner, moreover, of a
considerable portion of the town, had caused the suicide indeed of
more than one social climber. Unhappy, nostalgic, disdainful, selfish,
ever about to abandon Cuna-Cuna to return to it no more, yet never
budging, adoring her fairy villa far too well, Madame Ruiz, while
craving for the International-world, consoled herself by watching
from afar European Society going speedily to the dogs. Art-loving,
and considerably musical (many a dizzy venture at the Opera-house
had owed its audition to her), she had, despite the self-centredness
of her nature, done not a little to render more brilliant the charming
city it amused her with such vehemence to abuse.

One softly gloomy morning, preceding Madame Ruiz's first
cotillon of the Season, the lodge-keeper of the Villa Alba, a negress,
like some great, violet bug, was surprised, while tending the
brightly hanging grape-fruit in the drive, by an imperative knocking
on the gate. At such a matutinal hour only trashy errand-boys

shouldering baskets might be expected to call, and giving the summons no heed the mulatress continued her work.

The Villa Alba, half buried in spreading awnings, and surrounded by many noble trees, stood but a short distance off the main road, its pleasaunces enclosed by flower-enshrouded walls, all a-zig-zag, like the folds of a screen. Beloved of lizards and velvet-backed humming-birds, the shaded gardens led on one side to the sea.

'To make such a noise at dis hour,' the negress murmured, going grumblingly at length to the gate, disclosing, upon opening, a gentleman in middle life, with a tooth-brush moustache and a sapphire ring.

'De mist'ess still in bed, sah.'

'In bed?'

'She out bery late, sah, but you find Miss Edwards up.'

With a nod of thanks the visitor directed his footsteps discreetly towards the house.

Although not, precisely, *in* her bed, when the caller, shortly afterwards, was announced, Madame Ruiz was nevertheless as yet in dishabille.

'Tiresome man, what does he want to see me about?' she exclaimed, gathering around her a brocaded wrap formed of a priestly cope.

'He referred to a lease, ma'am,' the maid replied.

'A lease!' Madame Ruiz raised eyes dark with spleen.

The visit of her agent, or man of affairs, was apt to ruffle her composure for the day. 'Tell him to leave it and go,' she commanded, selecting a nectarine from a basket of iced fruits beside her.

Removing reflectively the sensitive skin, her mind evoked, in ironic review, the chief salient events of society, scheduled to take place on the face of the map in the course of the day.

The marriage of the Count de Nozhel, in Touraine, to Mrs. Exelmans of Cincinnati, the divorce of poor Lady Luckcock in London (it seemed quite certain that one of the five co-respondents was the little carrot-haired Lord Dubelly again), the last 'pomps,' at Vienna, of Princess de Seeyohl *née* Mitchening-Meyong (Peace to her soul! She had led her life). . . . The christening in Madrid of the girl-twins of the Queen of Spain. . . .

'At her time, I really *don't* understand it,' Madame Ruiz murmured to herself aloud, glancing, as though for an explanation, about the room.

113

Through the flowing folds of the mosquito curtains of the bed, that swept a cool, flagged floor spread with skins, showed the oratory, with its waxen flowers, and pendent flickering lights, that burned, night and day, before a Leonardo saint with a treacherous smile. Beyond the little recess came a lacquer commode, bearing a masterly marble group, depicting a pair of amorous hermaphrodites amusing themselves; while above, suspended against the spacious wainscoting of the wall, a painting of a man, elegantly corseted, with a violet in his moustache, 'Study of a Parisian,' and its pendant, 'Portrait of a Lady,' signed Van Dongen, were the chief outstanding objects that the room contained.

'One would have thought that at forty she would have given up having babies,' Madame Ruiz mused, choosing a glossy cherry from the basket at her side.

Through the open window a sound of distant music caught her ear.

'Ah! If only he were less weak,' she sighed, her thoughts turning towards the player, who seemed to be enamoured of the opening movement (rapturously repeated) of *L'Après-midi d'un Faune*.

The venetorial habits of Vittorio Ruiz had been from his earliest years the source of his mother's constant chagrin and despair. At the age of five he had assaulted his Nurse, and, steadily onward, his passions had grown and grown. . . .

'It's the fault of the wicked climate,' Madame Ruiz reflected, as her companion, Miss Edwards, came in with the post.

'Thanks, Eurydice,' she murmured, smilingly exchanging a butterfly kiss.

'It's going to be oh so hot to-day!'

'Is it, dear?'

'Intense,' Miss Edwards predicted, fluttering a gay-daubed paper fan.

Sprite-like, with a little strained ghost-face beneath a silver shock of hair, it seemed as if her long blue eyes had absorbed the Cunan sea.

'Do you remember the giant with the beard?' she asked, 'at the Presidency fête?'

'Do I?'

'And we wondered who he could be!'

'Well?'

'He's the painter of Women's Backs, my dear!'

'The painter of women's *what*?'

'An artist.'

'Oh.'

'I wanted to know if you'd advise me to sit.'

'Your back is charming, dear, *c'est un dos d'élite.*'

'I doubt, though, it's classic,' Miss Edwards murmured, pirouetting slowly before the glass.

But Madame Ruiz was perusing her correspondence and seemed to be absorbed.

'They're to be married, in Munich, on the fith,' she chirruped.

'Who?'

'Elsie and Baron Sitmar.'

'Ah, Ta-ra, dear! In those far worlds . . .' Miss Edwards impatiently exclaimed, opening wide a window and leaning out.

Beneath the flame-trees, with their spreading tops a mass of crimson flower, cooly white-garbed gardeners, with naked feet and big bell-shaped hats of straw, were sweeping slowly, as in some rhythmic dance, the flamboyant blossoms that had fallen to the ground.

'Wasn't little Madame Haase, dear, born Kattie von Guggenheim?'

'I really don't know,' Miss Edwards returned, flapping away a fly with her fan

'This villainous climate! My memory's going. . . .'

'I wish I cared for Cuna less, that's all!' Miss Edwards said, her glance following a humming bird, poised in air, above the sparkling turquoise of a fountain.

'Captain Moonlight . . . duty . . . (tedious word) . . . can't come!'

'Oh?'

'Such a dull post,' Madame Ruiz murmured, pausing to listen to the persuasive tenor voice of her son.

> 'Little mauve nigger boy,
> I t'ink you break my heart!'

'My poor Vitti! Bless him.'

'He was out last night with some Chinese she.'

'I understood him to be going to *Pelléas and Mélisande.*'

'He came to the Opera-house, but only for a minute.'

'Dios!'

'And, oh, dearest.' Miss Edwards dropped her cheek to her hand.

'Was Hatso as ever delicious?' Madame Ruiz asked, changing the topic as her woman returned, followed by a pomeranian of parts, 'Snob'; a dog beautiful as a child.

'We had Gebhardt instead.'

'In Mélisande she's so huge,' Madame Ruiz commented, eyeing severely the legal-looking packet which her maid had brought her.

'Business, Camilla; *how* I pity you!'

Madame Ruiz sighed.

'It seems,' she said, 'that for the next nine-and-ninety-years I have let a Villa to a Mr. and Mrs. Ahmadou Mouth.'

∾ *VIII* ∾

FLOOR of copper, floor of gold. . . . Beyond the custom-house door, ajar, the street at sunrise seemed aflame.

'Have you nothing, young man, to declare?'

' . . . Butterflies!'

'Exempt of duty. Pass.'

Floor of silver, floor of pearl. . . .

Trailing a muslin net, and laughing for happiness, Charlie Mouth marched into the town.

Oh, Cuna-Cuna! Little city of Lies and Peril! How many careless young nigger boys have gone thus to seal their Doom!

Although the Sun-god was scarcely risen, already the radiant street teemed with life.

Veiled dames, flirting fans, bent on church or market, were issuing everywhere from their doors, and the air was vibrant with the sweet voice of bells.

To rejoin his parents promptly at their hotel was a promise he was tempted to forget.

Along streets all fresh and blue in the shade of falling awnings, it was fine, indeed, to loiter. Beneath the portico of a church a running fountain drew his steps aside. Too shy to strip and squat in the basin, he was glad to bathe freely his head, feet and chest: then, stirred by curiosity to throw a glance at the building, he lifted the long yellow nets that veiled the door.

It was the fashionable church of La Favavoa, and the extemporary address of the Archibishop of Cuna was in full and impassioned swing.

'Imagine the world, my friends, had Christ been born a girl!' he was saying in tones of tender dismay as Charlie entered.

Subsiding bashfully to a bench, Charlie gazed around.

So many sparkling fans. One, a delicate light mauve one: 'Shucks! If only you wa' butterflies!' he breathed, contemplating with avidity the nonchalant throng; then perceiving a richer specimen splashed with silver of the same amative tint: 'Oh you lil beauty!' And, clutching his itching net to his heart, he regretfully withdrew.

Sauntering leisurely through the cool, mimosa-shaded streets, he approached, as he guessed, the Presidency. A score of shoeblacks lolled at cards and gossip before its gilded pales. Amazed at their audacity (for the President had threatened more than once to 'wring the Public's neck'), Charlie hastened by. Public gardens, brilliant with sarracenias, lay just beyond the palace, where a music-pavilion, surrounded by palms and rocking-chairs, appeared a favourite, and much-frequented, resort; from here he observed the Cunan bay strewn with sloops and white-sailed yachts asleep upon the tide. Strolling on, he found himself in the busy vicinity of the Market. Although larger and more varied, it resembled in other respects the village one at home.

'Say, honey, say'—crouching in the dust before a little pyre of mangoes, a lean-armed woman besought him to buy.

Pursued by a confusion of voices, he threaded his way deftly down an alley dressed with booths. Pomegranates, some open with their crimson seeds displayed, banana-combs, and big, veined water-melons, lay heaped on every side.

'I could do wid a slice ob watteh-million,' he reflected: 'but to lick an ice-cream dat tempt me more!' Nor would the noble fruit of the baobab, the paw-paw, or the pine turn him from his fancy.

But no ice-cream stand met his eye, and presently he resigned himself to sit down upon his heels, in the shade of a potter's stall, and consider the passing crowd.

Missionaries with freckled hands and hairy, care-worn faces, followed by pale girls wielding tambourines of the Army of the Soul, foppish nigger bucks in panamas and palm-beach suits so cocky, Chinamen with osier baskets, their nostalgic eyes aswoon, heavily straw-hatted nuns trailing their dust-coloured rags, and

117

suddenly, oh, could it be?—but there was no mistaking that golden waddle: 'Mamma!'

Mamma, Mammee, Mrs. Ahmadou Mouth. All in white, with snow-white shoes and hose so fine, he hardly dare.

'Mammee, Mammee, oh, Mammee. . . .'

'Sonny mine! My lil boy!'

'Mammee.'

'Just to say!'

And, oh, honies! Close behind, behold Miami, and Edna too: the Miss Lips, the fair Lips, the smiling Lips. How spry each looked. The elder (grown a trifle thinner), sweet *à ravir* in tomato-red, while her sister, plump as a corn-fattened partridge, and very perceptibly powdered, seemed like the flower of the prairie sugar-cane when it breaks into bloom.

'We've been to a Music-hall, an' a pahty, an' Snowball has dropped black kittens.' Forestalling Miami, Edna rapped it out.

'Oh shucks!'

'An' since we go into S'ciety, we keep a boy in buttons!'

Mrs. Mouth turned about.

'Where is dat idjit coon?'

'He stay behind to bargain for de pee-wee birds, Mammee, fo' to make de taht.'

'De swindling tortoise.'

'An' dair are no vacancies at de University: not fo' any ob us!' Edna further retailed, going off into a spasm of giggles.

She was swinging a wicker basket, from which there dangled the silver forked tail of a fish.

'Fo' goodness' sake gib dat sea-porcupine to Ibum, Chile,' Mrs. Mouth commanded, as a perspiring niggerling in livery presented himself.

'Ibum, his arms are full already.'

'Just come along all to de Villa now! It dat mignon an' all so nice. An' after de collation,' Mrs. Mouth (shocked on the servant's account at her son's nude neck) raised her voice, 'we go to de habadasher in Palmbranch Avenue an' I buy you an Eton colleh!'

'PRANCING NIGGER, I t'ink it bery strange dat Madame Ruiz she nebba call.'

'Sh'o.'

'In August-Town, S'ciety less stuck-up dan heah!'

Ensconced in rocking-chairs, in the shade of the ample porch of the Villa Vista Hermosa, Mr. and Mrs. Mouth had been holding a desultory *tête-à-tête*.

It was a Sabbath evening, and a sound of reedy pipes and bafalons, from a neighbouring café, filled with a feverish sadness the brilliantly lamp-lit street.

'De airs ob de neighbehs, dat dair affair; what matter mo' am de chillen's schoolin'.'

'Prancing Nigger, I hope your Son an' Daughters will yet take dair Degrees, an' if not from de University, den from Home. From heah.'

'Hey-ho-day, an' dat would be a miracle!' Mr. Mouth mirthlessly laughed.

'Dose chillens hab learnt quite a lot already.'

' 'Bout de shops an' cinemas!'

Mrs. Mouth disdained a reply.

She had taken the girls to the gallery at the Opera one night to hear 'Louise,' but they had come out, by tacit agreement, in the middle of it: the plainness of Louise's blouse, and the lack of tunes . . . the suffocation of the gallery . . . Once bit twice shy, they had not gone back again.

'All your fambly need, Prancing Nigger, is social opportunity! But what is de good ob de Babtist parson?'

Mr. Mouth sketched a gesture.

'Sh'o, Edna, she some young yet. . . . But Miami dat *distinguée*; an', doh I her mother, b'lieb me dat is one ob de choicest girls I see; an' dat's de trute.'

'It queer,' Mr. Mouth abstrusely murmured, 'how many skeeter-bugs dair are 'bout dis ebenin'!'

'De begonias in de window-boxes most lik'ly draw dem. But as I was saying, Prancing Nigger, I t'ink it bery strange dat Madame Ruiz nebba call.'

'P'r'aps she out ob town.'

'Accordin' to de paper, she bin habing her back painted, but what dat fo' I dunno.'

'Ah shouldn't wonder ef she hab some trouble ob a dorsal kind; same as me gramma mumma long agone.'

'Dair'd be no harm in sendin' one ob de chillens to enquire. Wha' you t'ink, sah?' Mrs. Mouth demanded, plucking from off the porch a pale hanging flower with a languorous scent.

Mr. Mouth glanced apprehensively skyward.

The mutters of thunder and intermittent lightning of the finest nights.

'It's a misfortnit we eber left Mediavilla,' he exclaimed uneasily, as a falling star, known as a thief star, sped swiftly down the sky.

'Prancing Nigger,' Mrs. Mouth rose, remarking, 'befo' you start to grummle, I leab you alone to your Jereymiads!'

'A misfortnit sho' nuff,' he mused, and regret for the savannah country and the tall palm-trees of his village oppressed his heart. Moreover, his means (derived from the cultivation of the *Musa paradisica,* or Banana) seemed likely to prove ere long inadequate to support the whims of his wife, who after a lifetime of contented nudity appeared to be now almost insatiable for dress.

A discordant noise from above interrupted the trend of his thoughts.

'Sh'o, she plays wid it like a toy,' he sighed, as the sound occurred again.

'Prancing Nigger, de water-supply cut off!'

'It's de Lord's will.'

'Dair's not a drop, my lub, in de privy.'

' 'Cos it always in use!'

'I b'lieb dat lil half-caste, Ibum, 'cos I threaten to gib him notice, do somet'in' out ob malice to de chain.'

'Whom de Lord loveth He chasteneth!' Mr. Mouth observed, 'an dose bery words (ef you look) you will find in de twelfth chapter an' de sixth berse ob de Book ob Hebrews.'

'Prancing Nigger, you datways selfish! Always t'inkin' ob your soul, instead ob your obligations towards de fambly.'

'Why, wha' mo' can I do dan I've done?'

Mrs. Mouth faintly shrugged.

'I had hoped,' she said, 'dat Nini would hab bin ob use to de girls, but dat seem now impossible!' For Mrs. Snagg had been traced to a house of ill-fame, where, it appeared, she was an exponent of the Hodeidah—a lascive Cunan dance.

'Understand dat any sort ob intimacy 'tween de Villa an' de *Closerie des Lilas* Ah must flatly forbid.'

'Prancing Nigger, as ef I should take your innocent chillens to call on po' Nini; not dat eberyt'ing about her at de *Closerie* is not elegant an' nice. Sh'o, some ob de inmates ob dat establishment possess mo' diamonds dan dair betters do outside! You'd be surprised ef you could see what two ob de girls dair, Dinah an' Lew. . . .'

'Enuf!'

'It isn't always Virtue, Prancing Nigger, dat come off best!' And Mrs. Mouth might have offered further observations on the matter of ethics had not her husband left her.

∽ X ∽

PAST the Presidency and the public park, the Theatres Maxine Bush, Eden-Garden and Apollo, along the Avenida and the Jazz Halls by the wharf, past little suburban shops, and old, deserted churchyards where bloom geraniums, through streets of squalid houses, and onward skirting pleasure lawns and orchards, bibbitty-bobbitty, beneath the sovereign brightness of the sky, crawled the Farananka tram.

Surveying the landscape listlessly through the sticks of her fan, Miss Edna Mouth grew slightly bored—alas, poor child; couldst thou have guessed the blazing brightness of thy Star, thou wouldst doubtless have been more alert!

'Sh'o, it dat far an' tejus,' she observed to the conductor, lifting upon him the sharp-soft eyes of a paroquet.

She was looking bewitching in a frock of silverish *mousseline* and a violet tallyho cap, and dangled upon her knees an intoxicating sheaf of the blossoms known as Marvel of Peru.

'Hab patience, lil Missey, an' we soon be dah.'

'He tells me, dear child, he tells me,' Madame Ruiz was rounding a garden path, upon the arm of her son, 'he tells me, Vitti, that the systole and diastole of my heart's muscles are slightly inflamed; and that I ought, darling, to be *very* careful. . . .'

121

Followed by a handsome borzoi and the pomeranian 'Snob,' the pair were taking their usual post-prandial exercise beneath the trees.

'Let me come, Mother dear,' he murmured without interrupting, 'over the other side of you; I always like to be on the right side of my profile!'

'And, really, since the affair of Madame de Bazvalon, my health has hardly been what it was.'

'That foolish little woman,' he uncomfortably laughed.

'He tells me my nerves need rest,' she declared, looking pathetically up at him.

He had the nose of an actress, and ink-black hair streaked with gold, his eyes seemed to be covered with the freshest of fresh dark pollen, while nothing could exceed the vivid pallor of his cheeks or the bright sanguine of his mouth.

'You go out so much, Mother.'

'Not so much!'

'So very much.'

'And he forbids me my opera-box for the rest of the week! So last night I sat at home, dear child, reading the Life of Lazarillo de Tormes.'

'I don't give a damn,' he said, 'for any of your doctors.'

'So vexing, though; and apparently Lady Bird has been at death's door, and poor Peggy Povey too. It seems she got wet on the way to the Races; and really I was *sorry* for her when I saw her in the paddock; for the oats and the corn, and the wheat and the tares, and the barley and the rye, and all the rest of the reeds and grasses in her pretty Lancret hat, looked like nothing so much as manure.'

'I adore to folly her schoolboy's moustache!'

'My dear, Age is the one disaster,' Madame Ruiz remarked, raising the rosy dome of her sunshade a degree higher above her head.

They were pacing a walk radiant with trees and flowers as some magician's garden, that commanded a sweeping prospect of long, livid sands, against a white-green sea.

'There would seem to be several new yachts, darling,' Madame Ruiz observed.

'The Duke of Wellclose with his duchess (on their wedding-tour) arrived with the tide.'

'Poor man; I'm told that he only drove to the church after thirty brandies!'

'And the *Sea-Thistle*, with Lady Violet Valesbridge, and, *oh*, such a crowd.'

'She used to be known as "The Cat of Curzon Street," but I hear she is still quite incredibly pretty,' Madame Ruiz murmured, turning to admire a somnolent peacock, with moping fan, poised upon the curved still arm of a marble mænad.

'How sweet something smells.'

'It's the China lilies.'

'I believe it's my handkerchief . . .' he said.

'Vain wicked boy; ah, if you would but decide, and marry some nice, intelligent girl.'

'I'm too young yet.'

'You're *twenty-six*!'

'And past the age of folly-o,' he made airy answer, drawing from his breast-pocket a flat, jewel-encrusted case, and lighting a cigarette.

'Think of the many men, darling, of twenty-six . . .' Madame Ruiz broke off, focusing the fruit-bearing summit of a slender areca palm.

'Foll-foll-folly-o!' he laughed.

'I think I'm going in.'

'Oh, why?'

'Because,' Madame Ruiz repressed a yawn, 'because, dear, I feel armchairish.'

With a kiss of the finger-tips (decidedly distinguished hands had Vittorio Ruiz), he turned away.

Joying frankly in excess, the fiery noontide hour had a special charm for him.

It was the hour, to be sure, of 'the Faun!'

'Aho, Ahi, Aha!' he carolled, descending half trippingly a few white winding stairs that brought him upon a fountain. Palms, with their floating fronds radiating light, stood all around.

It was here 'the creative mood' would sometimes take him, for he possessed no small measure of talent of his own.

His *Three Hodeidahs*, and *Five Phallic Dances for Pianoforte and Orchestra,* otherwise known as 'Suite in Green,' had taken the whole concert world by storm, and, now, growing more audacious, he was engaged upon an opera to be known, by and by, as *Sumaïa.*

'Ah Atthis, it was Sappho who told me—' tentatively he sought an air.

A touch of banter there.

'*Ah Atthis—*' One must make the girl feel that her little secret is out . . . ; quiz her, but let her know, and pretty plainly, that the Poetess had been talking. . . .

'Ah Atthis—'

But somehow or other the lyric mood to-day was obdurate and not to be persuaded.

'I blame the oysters! After oysters—' he murmured, turning about to ascertain what was exciting the dogs.

She was coming up the drive with her face to the sun, her body shielded behind a spreading bouquet of circumstance.

'It's all right; they'll not hurt you.'

'Sh'o, I not afraid!'

'Tell me who it is you wish to see.'

'Mammee send me wid dese flowehs. . . .'

'Oh! But how scrumptious.'

'It strange how dey call de bees; honey-bees, sweat-bees, bumble-bees an' all!' she murmured, shaking the blossoms into the air.

'That's only natural,' he returned, his hand falling lightly to her arm.

'Madame Ruiz is in?'

'She is: but she is resting; and something tells me,' he suavely added, indicating a grassy bank, 'you might care to repose yourself too.'

And indeed after such a long and rambling course she was glad to accept.

'De groung's as soft as a cushom,' she purred, sinking with nonchalance to the grass.

'You'll find it,' he said, 'even softer, if you'll try it nearer me.'

'Dis a mighty pretty place!'

'And you—' but he checked his tongue.

'Fo' a villa so grand, dair must be mo' dan one privy?'

'Some six or seven!'

'Ours is broke.'

'You should get it mended.'

'De aggervatiness'!' she wriggled.

'Tell me about them.'

And so, not without digressions, she unfolded her life.

'Then you, Charlie, and Mimi are here, dear, to study?'

'As soon as de University is able to receibe us; but dair's a waiting list already dat long.'

124

'And what do you do with all your spare time?'

'Goin' round de shops takes up some ob it. An' den, ob course, dair's de Cinés. Oh, I love de Lara. We went last night to see *Souls in Hell.*'

'I've not been.'

'Oh it was choice.'

'Was it? Why?'

'De scene ob dat story,' she told him, 'happen foreign; 'way crost de big watteh, on de odder side ob de world . . . an' de principal gal, she married to a man who neglect her (ebery ebenin' he go to pahtys an' biars), while all de time his wife she sit at home wid her lil pickney at her breas'. But dair anodder gemplum (a friend ob de fambly) an' he afiah to woe her; but she only shake de head, slowly, from side to side, an' send dat man away. Den de hubsom lose his fortune, an', oh, she dat 'stracted, she dat crazed . . . at last she take to gamblin', but dat only make t'ings worse. Den de friend ob de fambly come back, an' offer to pay all de expenses ef only she unbend: so she cry, an' she cry, 'cos it grieb her to leab her pickney to de neglect ob de serbants (dair was three ob dem, an old buckler, a boy, an' a cook), but, in de end, she do, an' frtt! away she go in de fambly carriage. An' den, bimeby, you see dem in de bedroom doin' a bit ob funning.'

'What?'

'Oh ki; it put me in de gigglemints. . . .'

'Exquisite kid.'

'Sh'o, de coffee-concerts an' de pictchures, I don't nebba tiah ob dem.'

'Bad baby.'

'I turned thirteen.'

'You are?'

'By de Law ob de Island, I a spinster ob age!'

'I might have guessed it was the Bar! These Law-students,' he murmured, addressing the birds.

'Sh'o, it's de trute,' she pouted, with a languishing glance through the sticks of her fan.

'I don't doubt it,' he answered, taking lightly her hand.

'Mercy,' she marvelled: 'is dat a watch dah, on your arm?'

'Dark, bright baby!'

'Oh, an' de lil "V.R." all in precious stones so blue.' Her frail fingers caressed his wrist.

'Exquisite kid.' She was in his arms.

'Vitti, Vitti!—' It was the voice of Eurydice Edwards. Her face was strained and quivering. She seemed about to faint.

⚭ *XI* ⚭

EVER so lovely are the young men of Cuna-Cuna—Juarez, Jotifa, Enid—(these, from many, to distinguish but a few)—but none so delicate, charming, and squeamish as Charlie Mouth.

'Attractive little Rose . . .' 'What a devil of a dream . . .' the avid belles would exclaim when he walked abroad, while impassioned widows would whisper 'Peach!'

One evening, towards sundown, just as the city lifts its awnings, and the deserted streets start seething with delight, he left his home to enjoy the grateful air. It had been a day of singular oppressiveness and, not expecting overmuch of the vesperal breezes, he had borrowed his mother's small Pompadour fan.

Ah, little did that nigger boy know as he strolled along what novel emotions that promenade held in store!

Disrelishing the dust of the Avenida, he directed his steps towards the Park.

He had formed already an acquaintanceship with several young men, members, it seemed, of the University, and these he would sometimes join, about this hour, beneath the Calabash-trees in the Marcella Gardens.

There was Abe, a lad of fifteen, whose father ran a Jazz Hall on the harbour-beach, and Ramon, who was destined to enter the Church, and the intriguing Esmé, whose dream was the Stage, and who was supposed to be 'in touch' with Miss Maxine Bush, and there was Pedro, Pedro ardent and obese, who seemed to imagine that to be a dress-designer to foreign Princesses would yield his several talents a thrice-blessed harvest.

Brooding on these and other matters, Charlie found himself in Liberty Square.

Here, the Cunan Poet, Samba Marcella's effigy arose—that 'sable singer of Revolt.'

Aloft, on a pedestal, soared the Poet, laurel-crowned, thick-lipped, woolly, a large weeping Genius, with a bold taste for draperies, hovering just beneath; her one eye closed, the other open, giving her an air of winking confidentially at the passers-by.

' "Up, Cunans, up! To arms, to arms!" ' he quoted, lingering to watch the playful swallows wheeling among the tubs of rose-oleanders that stood around.

And a thirst, less for bloodshed than for a sherbet, seized him. It was a square noted for the frequency of its bars, and many of their names, in flickering lights, showed palely forth already.

Cuna! City of Moonstones; how faerie art thou in the blue blur of dusk!

Costa Rica. Chile Bar. To the Island of June. . . .

Red roses against tall mirrors, reflecting the falling night.

Seated before a cloudy cocktail, a girl with gold cheeks like the flesh of peaches addressed him softly from behind: 'Listen, lion!'

But he merely smiled on himself in the polished mirrors, displaying moist-gleaming teeth and coral gums.

A fragrance of aromatic cloves . . . a mystic murmur of ice. . . .

A little dazed after a Ron Bacardi, he moved away. 'Shine, sah?' The inveigling squeak of a shoeblack followed him.

Sauntering by the dusty benches along the pavement-side, where white-robed negresses sat communing in twos and threes, he attained the Avenue Messalina with its spreading palms, whose fronds hung nerveless in the windless air.

Tinkling mandolins from restaurant gardens, light laughter, and shifting lights.

Passing before the Café de Cuna, and a people's 'Dancing,' he roamed leisurely along. Incipient Cyprians, led by vigilant, blanched-faced queens, youths of a certain life, known as bwam-wam bwam-wams, gaunt pariah dogs, with questing eyes, all equally were on the prowl. Beneath the Pharaohic pilasters of the Theatre Maxine Bush a street crowd had formed before a notice described 'Important,' which informed the Public that, owing to a 'temporary hoarseness,' the rôle of Miss Maxine Bush would be taken, on that occasion, by Miss Pauline Collier.

The Marcella Gardens lay towards the end of the Avenue, in the animated vicinity of the Opera. Pursuing the glittering thoroughfare, it was interesting to observe the pleasure announcements of the various theatres, picked out in signs of fire: *Aïda: The Jewels of the Madonna: Clara Novotny and Lily Lima's Season.*

127

Vending bags of roasted peanuts, or sapodillas and avocado pears, insistent small boys were importuning the throng.

'Go away; I can't be bodder,' Charlie was saying, when he seemed to slip; it was as though the pavement were a carpet snatched from under him, and, looking round, he was surprised to see, in a confectioner's window, a couple of marble-topped tables start merrily waltzing together.

Driven onward by those behind, he began stumblingly to run towards the Park. It was the general goal. Footing it a little ahead, two loose women and a gay young man (pursued by a waiter with a napkin and a bill), together with the horrified, half-crazed crowd; all, helter-skelter, were intent upon the Park.

Above the Calabash-trees, bronze, demoniac, the moon gleamed sourly from a starless sky, and although not a breath of air was stirring, the crests of the loftiest palms were set arustling by the vibration at their roots.

'Oh, will nobody *stop* it?' a terror-struck lady implored.

Feeling quite white and clasping a fetish, Charlie sank all panting to the ground.

Safe from falling chimney-pots and sign-boards (that for 'Pure Vaseline,' for instance, had all but caught him), he had much to be thankful for.

'Sh'o nuff, dat was a close shave,' he gasped, gazing dazed about him.

Clustered back to back near by upon the grass, three stolid matrons, matrons of hoary England, evidently not without previous earthquake experience, were ignoring resolutely the repeated shocks.

'I always follow the Fashions, dear, at a distance!' one was saying: 'this little gingham gown I'm wearing I had made for me after a design I found in a newspaper at my hotel.'

'It must have been a pretty old one, dear—I mean the paper, of course.'

'New things are only those you know that have been forgotten.'

'Mary . . . there's a sharp pin, sweet, at the back of your . . . *Oh!*'

Venturing upon his legs, Charlie turned away.

By the Park palings a few 'Salvationists' were holding forth, while, in the sweep before the bandstand, the artists from the Opera, in their costumes of Aïda, were causing almost a greater panic among the ignorant than the earthquake itself. A crowd, promiscuous rather than representative, composed variously of chauffeurs (making a wretched pretence, poor chaps, of seeking out their masters), Cyprians, patricians (these in opera cloaks and sparkling diamonds), tourists, for whom the Hodeidah girls would *not* dance that night, and bwam-wam bwam-wams, whose equivocal behaviour, indeed, was perhaps more shocking even than the shocks, set the pent Park ahum. Yet, notwithstanding the upheavals of Nature, certain persons there were bravely making new plans.

'How I wish I could, dear! But I shall be having a houseful of women over Sunday—that's to say.'

'Then come the week after.'

'Thanks, then, I *will.*'

Hoping to meet with Abe, Charlie took a pathway flanked with rows of tangled roses, whose leaves shook down at every step.

And it occurred to him with alarming force that perhaps he was an orphan.

Papee, Mammee, Mimi and lil Edna—the villa drawing-room on the floor. . . .

His heart stopped still.

'An' dey in de spirrit world—in heaven hereafter!' He glanced with awe at the moon's dark disk.

'All in dair cotton shrouds. . . .'

What if he should die and go to the Bad Place below?

'I mizzable sinneh, Lord. You heah, Sah? You heah me say dat? Oh, Jesus, Jesus, Jesus,' and weeping, he threw himself down among a bed of flowers.

When he raised his face it was towards a sky all primrose and silver pink. Sunk deep in his dew-laved bower, it was sweet to behold the light. Above him great spikes of blossom were stirring in the idle wind, while birds were chaunting voluntaries among the palms. And in thanksgiving, too, arose the matin bells. From Our Lady of the Pillar, from the church of La Favavoa in the West, from Saint Sebastian, from Our Lady of the Sea, from Our Lady of Mount Carmel, from Santa Theresa, from Saint Francis of the Poor.

129

～ *XII* ～

BUT although by the grace of Providence the city of Cuna-Cuna had been spared, other parts of the island had sustained irremediable loss. In the Province of Casuby, beyond the May Day Mountains, many a fair banana or sugar estate had been pitifully wrecked, yet what caused perhaps the widest regret among the Cunan public was the destruction of the famous convent of Sasabonsam. One of the beauties of the island, one of the gems of tropic architecture, celebrated, made immortal (in *The Picnic*) by the Poet Marcella, had disappeared. A Relief Fund for those afflicted had at once been started, and, as if this were not enough, the doors of the Villa Alba were about to be thrown open for 'An Evening of Song and Gala' in the causes of charity.

'Prancing Nigger, dis an event to take exvantage ob; dis not a lil t'ing, love, to be sneezed at at all,' Mrs. Mouth eagerly said upon hearing the news, and she had gone about ever since, reciting the names in the list of Patronesses, including that of the Cunan Archbishop.

It was the auspicious evening.

In their commodious, jointly shared bedroom, the Miss Lips, the fair Lips, the smiling Lips were maiding one another in what they both considered to be the 'Parisian Way'; a way, it appeared, that involved much nudging, arch laughter, and, even, some prodding.

'In love? Up to my ankles! Oh, yes.' Edna blithely chuckled.

'Up to your topknot!' her sister returned, making as if to pull it.

But with the butt end of the curling-tongs Edna waved her away.

Since her visit to the Villa Alba 'me an' Misteh Ruiz' was all her talk, and to be his reigning mistress the summit of her dreams.

'Come on, man, wid dose tongs; 'cos I want 'em myself,' Miami murmured, pinning a knot of the sweet night jasmine deftly above her ear.

Its aroma evoked Bamboo.

Oh, why had he not joined her? Why did he delay? Had he forgotten their delight among the trees, the giant silk-cotton-trees, with the hammer-tree-frogs chanting in the dark: Rig-a-jig-jig, rig-a-jig-jig?

'Which you like de best, man, dis lil necklash or de odder?'

130

Edna asked, essaying a strand of orchid-tinted beads about her throat. 'I'd wear dem both,' her sister advised.

'I t'ink, on de whole, I wear de odder; de one he gib me de time he take exvantage ob my innocence.'

'Since dose imitation pearls, honey,—he gib you anyt'ing else?'

'No; but he dat generous! He say he mean to make me a lil pickney gal darter: an', oh, won't dat be a day,' Edna fluted, breaking off at the sound of her mother's voice in the corridor.

'. . . and tell de cabman to take de fly-bonnets off de horses,' she was instructing Ibum as she entered the room.

She had a gown of the new mignonette satin, with 'episcopal' sleeves lined with red.

'Come, girls, de cab is waiting; but perhaps you no savey dat.'

They didn't; and, for some time, dire was the confusion.

In the Peacock drawing-room of the Villa Alba the stirring ballet music from *Isfahan* filled the vast room with its thrilling madness. Upon a raised estrade, a corps of dancing boys, from Sankor, glided amid a murmur of applause.

The combination of charity and amusement had brought together a crowded and cosmopolitan assembly and, early though it was, it was evident already that with many more new advents there would be a shortage of chairs. From their yachts had come several distinguished birds of passage, exhaling an atmosphere of Paris and Park Lane.

Wielding a heavy bouquet of black feathers, Madame Ruiz, robed in a gown of malmaison cloth-of-silver, watched the dancers from an alcove by the door.

Their swaying torsos, and weaving gliding feet, fettered with chains of orchids and hung with bells, held a fascination for her.

'My dear, they beat the Hodeidahs! I'm sure I never saw anything like it,' the Duchess of Wellclose remarked admiringly: 'that little one, Fred,' she murmured, turning towards the Duke.

A piece of praise a staid small body in a demure lace cap chanced to hear.

This was 'the incomparable' Miss McAdam, the veteran ballet mistress of the Opera-house, and inventrix of the dance. Born in the frigid High Street of Aberdeen, 'Alice', as she was universally known among enthusiastic patrons of the ballet, had come originally to the tropics as companion to a widowed clergyman, when, as she would relate (in her picturesque, native brogue), at the sight of

Nature her soul had awoke. Self-expression had come with a rush;
and now that she was ballet mistress of the Cunan Opera, some of
the daring *ensembles* of the Scottish spinster would embarrass even
the good Cunans themselves.

'I've warned the lads,' she whispered to Madame Ruiz, 'to cut
their final figure on account of the Archbishop. But young boys are
so excitable, and I expect they'll forget!'

Gazing on their perfect backs, Madame Ruiz could not but
mourn the fate of the Painter, who, like Dalou, had specialised
almost exclusively on this aspect of the human form; for, alas, that
admirable Artist had been claimed by the Quake; and although his
portrait of Madame Ruiz remained unfinished . . . there was still a
mole . . . nevertheless, in gratitude, and as a mark of respect, she had
sent her Rolls car to the Mass in honour of his obsequies, with the
crêpe off an old black dinner-dress tied across the lamps.

'I see they're going to,' Miss McAdam murmured, craning a little
to focus the Archbishop, then descanting to two ladies with deep
purple fans.

'Ah, well! It's what they do in *Isfahan*,' Madame Ruiz commented,
turning to greet her neighbour Lady Bird.

'Am I late for Gebhardt?' she asked, as if Life itself hinged upon
the reply.

A quietly silly woman, Madame Ruiz was often obliged to
lament the absence of intellect at her door: accounting for it as
the consequence of a weakness for negroes, combined with a
hopeless passion for the Regius Professor of Greek at Oxford.

But the strident cries of the dancers and the increasing volume
of the music discouraged all talk, though ladies with collection-
boxes (biding their time) were beginning furtively to select their
next quarry.

Countess Katty Taosay, *née* Soderini, a little woman and sure of
the giants, could feel in her psychic veins which men were most
likely to empty their pockets: English Consul . . . pale and interesting, he would not refuse to stoop and fumble, nor Follinsbe
'Peter,' the slender husband of a fashionable wife, nor Charlie
Campfire, a young boy like an injured camel, heir to vast banana
estates, the darling, and six foot high if an inch.

'Why do big men like little women?' she wondered, waving a
fan powdered with blue *paillettes*: and she was still casting about for
a reason when the hectic music stopped.

132

And now the room echoed briefly with applause, while admiration was divided between the super-excellence of the dancers and the living beauty of the rugs which their feet had trod—rare rugs from Bokhara-i-Shareef, and Kairouan-city-of-Prayer, lent by the mistress of the house.

Entering on the last hand-clap, Mr. and Mrs. Mouth, followed by their daughters, felt, each in their several ways, they might expect to enjoy themselves.

'Prancing Nigger, what a *furore!*' Mrs. Mouth exclaimed. 'You b'lieb, I hope, now, dat our tickets was worth de money.'

Plucking at the swallow-tails of an evening 'West End,' Mr. Mouth was disinclined to re-open a threadbare topic.

'It queah how few neegah dair be,' he observed, scanning the brilliant audience, many of whom, taking advantage of an interval, were flocking towards a buffet in an adjoining conservatory.

'Prancing Nigger, I feel I could do wid a glass ob champagne.'

Passing across a corridor, it would have been interesting to have explored the spacious vistas that loomed beyond. 'Dat must be one ob de priveys,' Edna murmured, pointing to a distant door.

'Seben, Chile, did you say?'

'If not more!'

'She seem fond ob flowehs,' Mr. Mouth commented, pausing to notice the various plants that lined the way: from the roof swung showery azure flowers that commingled with the theatrically-hued cañas, set out in crude, bold, colour-schemes below, that looked best at night. But in their malignant splendour the orchids were the thing. Mrs. Abanathy, Ronald Firbank (a dingy lilac blossom of rarity untold), Prince Palairet, a heavy blue-spotted flower, and rosy Olive Moonlight, were those that claimed the greatest respect from a few discerning connoisseurs.

'Prancing Nigger, you got a chalk mark on your "West-End." Come heah, sah, an' let me brush it.'

Hopeful of glimpsing Vittorio, Miami and Edna sauntered on. With arms loosely entwined about each other's hips, they made, in their complete insouciance, a conspicuous couple.

'I'd give sumpin' to see de bedrooms, man, 'cos dair are chapels, an' barf-rooms, beside odder conveniences off dem,' Edna related, returning a virulent glance from Miss Eurydice Edwards with a contemptuous, pitying smile.

133

Traversing a throng, sampling sorbets and ices, the sisters strolled out upon the lawn.

The big silver stars, how clear they shone—infinitudes, infinitudes.

'Adieu, hydrangeas, adieu, blue, burning South!'

The concert, it seemed, had begun.

'Come chillens, come!'

In the vast drawing-room, the first novelty of the evening—an aria from *Sumaïa*—had stilled all chatter. Deep-sweet, poignant, the singer's voice was conjuring Sumaïa's farewell to the Greek isle of Mitylene, bidding farewell to its gracious women, and to the trees of white or turquoise in the gardens of Lesbos.

'Adieu, hydrangeas——'

Hardly a suitable moment, perhaps, to dispute a chair. But neither the Duchess of Wellclose nor Mrs. Mouth were creatures easily abashed.

'I pay, an' I mean to hab it.'

'You can't; it's taken!' the duchess returned, nodding meaningly towards the buffet, where the duke could be seen swizzling whisky at the back of the bar.

'Sh'o! Dese white women seem to t'ink dey can hab ebberyt'ing.'

'Taken,' the duchess repeated, who disliked what she called the *parfum d'Afrique* of the 'sooties,' and, as though to intimidate Mrs. Mouth, she gave her a look that would have made many a Peeress in London quail.

Nevertheless, in the stir that followed the song chairs were forthcoming.

'From de complexion dat female hab, she look as doh she bin boiling bananas!' Mrs. Mouth commented comfortably, loud enough for the duchess to hear.

'Such a large congregation should su'tinly assist de fund!' Mr. Mouth resourcefully said, envisaging with interest the audience; it was not every day that one could feast the gaze on the noble baldness of the Archbishop, or on the subtle *silhouette* of Miss Maxine Bush, swathed like an idol in an Egyptian tissue woven with magical eyes.

'De woman in de window dah,' Mrs. Mouth remarked, indicating a dowager who had the hard but resigned look of the mother of six daughters in immediate succession, 'hab a look, Prancing Nigger, ob your favourite statesman.'

'De immortal Wilberforce!'

'I' s'poge it's de whiskers,' Mrs. Mouth replied, ruffling gently

her 'Borgia' sleeves for the benefit of the Archbishop. Rumour
had it he was fond of negresses, and that the black private secretary
he employed was his own natural son, while some suspected indeed
a less natural connexion.

But Madame Hatso (of Blue Brazil, the Argentine; those nights
in Venezuela and Buenos Ayres, 'bis' and 'bravas'! How the public
had roared) was curtseying right and left, and Mrs. Mouth, glancing
round to address her daughters, perceived with vexation that
Edna had vanished.

In the garden he caught her to him.

'Flower of the Sugar Cane!'

'Misteh Ruiz. . . .'

'Exquisite kid.'

'I saw you thu de window-glass all de time, an' dair was I!
laughing so silent-ly . . . .'

'My little honey.'

'. . . no; 'cos ob de neighbehs,' she fluted, drawing him beneath
the great flamboyants that stood like temples of darkness all around.

'Sweetheart.'

'I 'clar to grashis!' she delightedly crooned as he gathered her up
in his arms.

'My little Edna . . .? . . .? . . .?'

'Where you goin' wid me to?'

'There,' and he nodded towards the white sea sand.

A yawning butler, an insolent footman, a snoring coachman, a
drooping horse. . . .

The last conveyance had driven away, and only a party of 'b—d—y
niggers,' supposed to be waiting for a daughter, was keeping the
domestics from their beds.

Ernest, the bepowdered footman, believed them to be thieves,
and could have sworn he saw a tablespoon in the old coon's pocket.

Hardly able to restrain his tears, Mr. Mouth sat gazing vacuously
at the floor.

'Wh' can keep de chile? . . . O Lord . . . I hope dair noddin'
wrong.'

'On such a lovely ebenin' what is time?' Mrs. Mouth exclaimed,
taking up an attitude of night-enchantment by the open door.

A remark that caused the butler and his subordinate to cough.

'It not often I see de cosmos look so special!'

'Ef she not heah soon, we better go widout her,' Miami murmured, who was examining the visitors' cards on the hall table undismayed by the eye of Ernest.

'It's odd she should so procrastinate; but la jeunesse, c'est le temps où l'on s'amuse,' Mrs. Mouth blandly declared, seating herself tranquilly by her husband's side.

'Dair noddin', I hope, de matteh. . . .'

'Eh, suz, my deah! Eh, suz.' Reassuringly, she tapped his arm.

'Sir Victor Virtue, Lady Bird, Princess Altamisal,' Miami tossed their cards.

'Sh'o it was a charming ebenin'! Doh I was sorry for de duchess, wid de duke, an' he all nasty drunk wid spirits.'

'I s'poge she use to it.'

'It was a perfect skangle! Howebber, on de whole, it was quite an enjoyable pahty—doh dat music ob Wagner, it gib me de retches.'

'It bore me, too,' Miami confessed, as a couple of underfootmen made their appearance and, joining their fidgeting colleagues by the door, waited for the last guests to depart, in a mocking, whispering group.

'Ef she not here bery soon,' Miami murmured, vexed by the servants' impertinent smiles.

'Sh'o, she be here directly,' Mrs. Mouth returned, appraising through her fan-sticks the footmen's calves.

'It daybreak already!' Miami yawned, moved to elfish mirth by the over-emphasis of rouge on her mother's round cheeks.

But under the domestics' mocking stare their talk at length was chilled to silence.

From the garden came the plaintive wheepling of a bird (intermingled with the coachman's spasmodic snores), while above the awning of the door the stars were wanly paling.

'Prancing Nigger, sah, heah de day. Dair no good waitin' any more.'

It was on their return from the Villa Alba that they found a letter signed 'Mamma Luna,' announcing the death of Bamboo.

❧ *XIII* ❧

HE had gone out, it seemed, upon the sea to avoid the earth-quake (leaving his mother at home to take care of the shop), but the boat had overturned, and the evil sharks . . .

In a room darkened against the sun, Miami, distracted, wept. Crunched by the maw of a great blue shark: 'Oh honey.'

Face downward, with one limp arm dangling to the floor, she bemoaned her loss: such love-blank, and aching void! Like some desolate, empty cave, filled with clouds, so her heart.

'An' to t'ink dat I eber teased you!' she moaned, reproaching herself for the heedless past; and as day passed over day still she wept.

One mid-afternoon, some two weeks later, she was reclining lifelessly across the bed, gazing at the sun-blots on the floor. There had been a mild disturbance of a seismic nature that morning, and indeed slight though unmistakable shocks had been sensed repeatedly of late.

'Intercession' services, fully choral—the latest craze of society—filled the churches at present, sadly at the expense of other places of amusement, many of which had been obliged to close down. A religious revival was in the air, and in the Parks and streets elegant dames would stop one another in their passing carriages and pour out the stories of their iniquitous lives.

Disturbed by the tolling of a neighbouring bell, Miami reluctantly rose.

'Lord! What a din; it gib a po' soul de grabe-yahd creeps,' she murmured, lifting the jalousie of a sun-shutter and peering idly out.

Standing in the street was a Chinese laundrymaid, chatting with two Chinamen with osier baskets, while a gaunt pariah dog was rummaging among some egg-shells and banana-skins in the dust before the gate.

'Dat lil-fool-fool Ibum, he throw ebberyt'ing out ob de window an' nebba t'ink ob de stink,' she commented, as an odour of decay was wafted in on a gust of the hot trade wind. The trade winds! How pleasantly they used to blow in the village of Mediavilla. The blue trade wind, the gold trade wind caressing the bending canes. . . . City life, what had it done for any of them, after all? Edna nothing else than a harlot (since she had left them there was no other word), and Charlie fast going to pieces, having joined the Promenade of a notorious Bar with its bright particular galaxy of boys.

'Sh'o, ebberyt'ing happier back dah,' she mused, following the slow gait across the street of some bare-footed nuns; soon they would be returning, with many converts and pilgrims, to Sasabonsam, beyond the May Day Mountains, where remained a miraculous image of Our Lady of the Sorrows still intact. How if she joined them, too? A desire to express her grief, and thereby ease it, possessed her. In the old times there had been many ways: tribal dances and wild austerities. . . .

She was still musing, self-absorbed, when her mother, much later, came in from the street.

There had been a great Intercessional, it seemed, at the Cathedral, with hired singers from the Opera-house and society women as thick as thieves, '*gnats*,' she had meant to say (Tee-hee!), about a corpse. Arturo Arrivabene . . . a voice like a bull . . . and she had caught a glimpse of Edna driving on the Avenue Amada, looking almost Spanish in a bandeau beneath a beautiful grey tilt hat.

But Miami's abstraction discouraged confidences.

'Why you so triste, Chile? Dair no good at all in frettin'.'

'Sh'o nuff.'

'Dat death was on de cards, my deah, an' dair is no mistakin' de fac'; an' as de shark is a rapid feeder it all ober sooner dan wid de crocodile, which is some consolation for dose dat remain to mourn.'

'Sh'o, it bring not an atom to me!'

' 'Cos de process ob de crocodile bein' sloweh dan dat ob de shark—'

'Ah, say no more,' Miami moaned, throwing herself in a storm of grief across the bed. And as all efforts to appease made matters only worse, Mrs. Mouth prudently left her.

'Prancing Nigger, she seem dat sollumcholly an' depressed,' Mrs. Mouth remarked at dinner, helping herself to some guava-jelly that had partly dissolved through lack of ice.

'Since de disgrace ob Edna dat scarcely s'prisin',' Mr. Mouth made answer, easing a little the napkin at his neck.

'She is her own woman, me deah sah, an' *I* cannot prevent it!'

In the convivial ground-floor dining-room of an imprecise style, it was hard, at times, to endure such second-rate company as that of a querulous husband.

Yes, marriage had its dull side, and its drawbacks; still, where would society be (and where morality!) without the married women?

Mrs. Mouth fetched a sigh.

Just at her husband's back, above the ebony sideboard, hung a Biblical engraving, after Rembrandt, of the *Woman Taken in Adultery*, the conception of which seemed to her exaggerated and overdone, knowing full well, from previous experience, that there need not, really, be so much fuss. . . . Indeed, there need not be any: but to be *Taken* like that! A couple of idiots.

'W'en I look at our chillen's chairs, an' all ob dem empty, in my opinion we both betteh deaded,' Mr. Mouth brokenly said.

'I dare say dair are dose dat may t'ink so,' Mrs. Mouth returned, refilling her glass; 'but, Prancing Nigger, I am not like dat: no, sah!'

'Where's Charlie?'

'I s'poge he choose to dine at de lil Cantonese restaurant on de quay,' she murmured, setting down her glass with a slight grimace: how *ordinaire* this cheap red wine! Doubtless Edna was lapping the wines of paradise! Respectability had its trials. . . .

'Dis jelly mo' like lemon squash,' Mr. Mouth commented.

' 'Cos dat lil liard Ibum, he again forget de ice! Howebber, I hope soon to get rid ob him: for de insolence ob his bombax is more dan I can stand,' Mrs. Mouth declared, lifting her voice on account of a piano-organ in the street just outside.

'I s'poge to-day Chuesdy'? It was a-Chuesd'y—God forgib dat po' frail chile.'

'Prancing Nigger, I allow Edna some young yet for dat position; I allow dat to be de matteh ob de case but, me good sah! bery likely she marry him later.'

'Pah.'

'An' why not?'

'Chooh, nebba!'

'Prancing Nigger, you seem to forget dat your elder daughter was a babe ob four w'en I put on me nuptial arrange blastams to go to de Church.'

'Sh'o, I wonder you care to talk ob it!'

'An', to-day, honey, as I sat in de Cathedral, lis'nin' to de Archbishop, I seemed to see Edna, an' she all in *dentelles* so *chic*, comin' up de aisle, followed by twelve maids, all ob good blood, holdin' flowehs an' wid hats kimpoged ob feddehs—worn raddeh to de side, an' I heah a stranger say: "Excuse me, sah, but who dis fine marriage?" an' a voice make reply: "Why, dat Mr. Ruiz de million'r-

'r-'r," an' as he speak, one ob dese Italians from de Opera-house
commence to sing "De voice dat brieved o'er Eden," an' Edna she
blow a kiss at me an' laugh dat arch.'

'Nebba!'

'Prancing Nigger, "wait an' see"!' Mrs. Mouth waved prophetic-
ally her fan.

'No, nebba,' he repeated, his head sunk low in chagrin.

'How you know, sah?' she queried, rising to throw a crust of
loaf to the organ man outside.

The wind with the night had risen, and a cloud of blown dust
was circling before the gate.

'See de raindrops, deah; here come at last de big rain.'

'. . .'

'Prancing Nigger!'

'Ah'm thinkin'.'

~ XIV ~

IMPROVISING at the piano, Piltzenhoffer, kiddy-grand, he was
contented, happy. The creative fertility, bursting from a radiant
heart, more than ordinarily surprised him. 'My most quickening
affair since—' he groped, smiling a little at several particular wraiths,
more or less bizarre, that, in their time, had especially disturbed
him. 'Yes; probably!' he murmured enigmatically, striking an
intricate, virile chord.

'Forgib me, dearest! I was wid de manicu' of de fingeh-nails.'

'Divine one.'

She stood before him.

Hovering there between self-importance and madcapery, she
was exquisite quite.

'All temperament . . . !' he murmured, capturing her deftly
between his knees.

She was wearing a toilette of white *crêpe de chine*, and a large
favour of bright purple Costa-Rica roses.

'Soon as de sun·drop, dey set out, deah: so de manicu' say.'

'What shall we do till then?'

'. . . or, de pistols!' she fluted, encircling an arm about his neck.

'Destructive kitten,' he murmured, kissing, one by one, her red,
polished nails.

'Honey! Come on.'

He frowned.

It seemed a treason almost to his last mistress, an exotic English girl, perpetually shivering, even in the sun, this revolver practice on the empty quinine-bottles she had left behind. Poor Meraude! It was touching what faith she had in a dose of quinine! Unquestionably she had been faithful to *that*. And dull enough, too, it had made her. With her albums of photographs, nearly all of midshipmen, how insufferably had she bored him:—'This one, darling, tell me, isn't he—I, really—he makes me—and this one, darling! An Athenian viking, with hair like mimosa, and what ravishing hands!—oh my God!—I declare—he makes me—' Poor Meraude; she had been extravagant as well!

'Come on, an' break some bokkles!'

'There's not a cartridge left,' he told her, setting her on his knee.

'Ha-ha! Oh, hi-hi!
Not a light:
Not a bite!
What a Saturday Night!'

she trilled, taking off a comedian from the Eden Garden.

Like all other negresses she possessed a natural bent for mimicry and a voice of that lisping quality that would find complete expression in songs such as: 'Have you seen my sweet garden ob Flowehs?', 'Sst! Come closer, Listen heah,' 'Lead me to the Altar, Dearest,' and 'His Little Pink, proud, Spitting-lips are Mine.'

'What is that you're wearing?'

'A souvenir ob to-day; I buy it fo' luck,' she rippled, displaying a black briar cross pinned to her breast.

'I hope it's blessed?'

'De nun dat sold it, didn't say. Sho'o, it's dreadful to t'ink ob po' Mimi, an' she soon a pilgrim all in blistehs an' rags,' she commented, as a page-boy with bejasmined ears appeared at the door.

'Me excuse. . . .'

'How dare you come in, lil saucebox, widdout knockin'?'

'Excuse, missey, but . . .'

'What?'

Ibum hung his head.

'I only thoughted, it bein' Crucifix day, I would like to follow in de procession thu de town.'

141

'Bery well: but be back in time fo' dinner.'

'T'ank you, missey.'

'An' mind fo' once you are!'

'Yes, missey,' the niggerling acquiesced, bestowing a slow smile on Snob and Snowball, who had accompanied him into the room. Easy of habit, as tropical animals are apt to be, it was apparent that the aristocratic pomeranian was paying sentimental court to the skittish mouser, who, since her περιπέτεια of black kittens, looked ready for anything.

'Sh'o, but she hab a way wid her!' Ibum remarked, impressed.

'Lil monster, take dem both, an' den get out ob my sight,' his mistress directed him.

Fingering a battered volume that bore the book-plate of Meraude, Vittorio appeared absorbed.

'Honey.'

'Well?'

'Noddin'.'

In the silence of the room a restless bluebottle, attracted by the wicked leer of a chandelier, tied up incredibly in a bright green net, blended its hum with the awakening murmur of the streets.

'Po' Mimi. I hope she look up as she go by.'

'Yes, by Jove.'

'Doh after de rude t'ings she say to me—' she broke off, blinking a little at the sunlight through the thrilling shutters.

'If I remember, beloved, you were both equally candid,' he remarked, wandering out upon the balcony.

It was on the palm-grown Messalina, an avenue that comprised a solid portion of the Ruiz estate, that he had installed her, in a many-storied building, let out in offices and flats.

Little gold, blue, lazy and romantic Cuna, what chastened mood broods over thy life to-day!

'Have you your Crucifix? Won't you buy a cross?' persuasive, feminine voices rose up from the pavement below. Active again with the waning sun, 'workers,' with replenished wares, were emerging forth from their respective depots nursing small lugubrious baskets.

'Have you bought your cross?' The demand, when softly cooed by some solicitous patrician, almost compelled an answer; and most of the social world of Cuna appeared to be vending crosses, or 'Pilgrims' medals' in imitation 'bronze,' this afternoon, upon the kerb. At the corner of Valdez Street, across the way, Countess Katty Taosay (*née* Soderini), austere in black with Parma violets, was presiding over a depot festooned with nothing but rosaries, that 'professed' themselves, as they hung, to the suave trade wind.

> 'Not a light:
> Not a bite!
> What a———'

Edna softly hummed, shading her eyes with a big feather fan.

It was an evening of cloudless radiance; sweet and mellow as is frequent at the close of summer.

'Oh, ki, honey! It so cleah I can see de lil iluns ob yalleh sands far away b'yond de Point!

'Dearest!' he inattentively murmured, recognising on the Avenue the elegant cobweb wheels of his mother's Bolivian buggy.

Accompanied by Eurydice Edwards, she was driving her favourite mules.

'An' de shipwreck off de coral reef, oh, ki!'

'Let me find you the long-glass, dear,' he said, glad for an instant to step inside.

Leaning with one foot thrust nimbly out through the balcony-rails towards the street, she gazed absorbed.

Delegates of agricultural guilds bearing banners, making for the Cathedral square (the pilgrims' starting-point), were advancing along the avenue amidst applause: fruit-growers, rubber-growers, sugar-growers, opium-growers, all doubtless wishful of placating Nature that redoubtable Goddess by showing a little honour to the Church. 'Oh Lord, *not* as Sodom,' she murmured, deciphering a text attached to the windscreen of a luxurious automobile.

'Divine one, here they are.'

'T'anks, honey, I see best widdout,' she replied, following the Bacchic progress of two girls in soldiers' forage-caps, who were exciting the gaiety of the throng.

'Be careful, kid; don't lean too far. . . .'

'Oh, ki, if dey don't exchange kisses!'

But the appearance of the Cunan Constabulary, handsome youngsters, looking the apotheosis themselves of earthly lawlessness, in their feathered sun-hats and bouncing kilts, created a diversion.

'De way dey stare up; I goin' to put on a tiara!'

'Wait, do, till supper,' he entreated, manipulating the long-glass to suit his eye.

Driving or on foot, were the usual faces.

Seated on a doorstep, Miss Maxine Bush, the famous actress, appeared to be rehearsing a smart society rôle, as she flapped the air with a sheet of street-foul paper, while, rattling a money-box, her tame monkey, 'Jutland-ho,' came as prompt for a coin as any demned Duchess.

'Ha-ha, Oh, hi-hi!' Edna's blasted catches. 'Bless her,' he exclaimed, re-levelling the glass. Perfect, Good lenses these; one could even read a physician's doorplate across the way: 'Hours 2-4, Agony guaranteed'—obviously, a dentist; and the window-card, too, above, 'Miss—? Miss—? Speciality: Men past thirty.'

Four years to wait. Patience.

Ooof! There went 'Alice' and one of her boys. Bad days for the ballet! People afraid of the Opera-house . . . that chandelier . . . and the pictures on the roof. . . . And wasn't that little Lady Bird? running at all the trousers: '*have* you your crucifix! . . .? ?'

'Honey. . . .'

She had set a crown of moonstones on her head, and had moonstone bracelets on her arms.

'My queen.'

'I hope Mimi look up at me!'

'Vain one.'

Over the glistering city the shadows were falling, staining the white-walled houses here and there as with some purple pigment.

'Accordin' to de lates' 'ticklers, de Procession follow de Paseo only as far as de fountain.'

'Oh. . . .'

'Where it turn up thu Carmen Street, into de Avenue Messalina.'

Upon the metallic sheen of the evening sky she sketched the itinerary lightly with her fan.

And smiling down on her uplifted face, he asked himself whimsically how long he would love her. She had not the brains, poor child, of course, to keep a man for ever. Heigho. Life indeed was often hard. . . .

'Honey, here dey come!'

A growing murmur of distant voices, jointly singing, filled liturgically the air, just as the warning salute, fired at sundown from the heights of the fort above the town, reverberated sadly.

'Oh, la, la,' she laughed, following the wheeling flight of some birds that rose startled from the palms.

'The Angelus. . . .'

'Hark, honey: what is dat dey singin'?'

> *A thousand ages in Thy sight*
> *Are like an evening gone;*
> *Short as the watch that ends the night*
> *Before the rising sun.*

Led by an old negress leaning on her hickory staff, the procession came.

Banners, banners, banners.

'I hope Mimi wave!'

Floating banners against the dusk. . . .

'Oh, honey! See dat lil pilgrim-boy?'

> *Time like an ever-rolling stream,*
> *Bears all its sons away;*
> *They fly forgotten, as a dream*
> *Dies at the opening day.*

'Mimi, Mimi!' She had flung the roses from her dress. 'Look up, my deah, look up.'

But her cry escaped unheard.

> *They fly forgotten, as a dream*
> *Dies——*

The echoing voices of those behind lingered a little.

'Edna.'

She was crying.

'It noddin'; noddin' at all! But it plain she refuse to forgib me!'

'Never.'

'Perspirin', an' her skirt draggin', sh'o, she looked a fright.'

He smiled: for indeed already the world was perceptibly moulding her. . . .

'Enuff to scare ebbery crow off de savannah!'

'And wouldn't the farmers bless her.'

'Oh, honey!' Her glance embraced the long, lamp-lit avenue with supressed delight.

'Well.'

'Dair's a new dancer at de Apollo to-night. Suppose we go?'

Havana—Bordighera.

145

Valmouth: A Romantic Novel

Valmouth : A Romantic Novel

𝕴 *I* 𝕽

D)AY was drooping on a fine evening in March as a brown barouche passed through the wrought-iron gates of Hare-Hatch House on to the open highway.

Beneath the crepuscular, tinted sky the countryside stretched away, interspersed with hamlets, meads and woods, towards low, loosely engirdling hills, that rose up against the far horizon with a fine monastic roll.

Although it was but the third month of the year, yet, from a singular softness of the air, already the trees were in full, fresh leaf. Along the hedgerows hawthorns were in bloom, while the many wild flowers by the roadside scented in fitful whiffs an invigorating, caressing breeze.

Seated immediately behind the coachman in the shell-like carriage was a lady no longer young. Her fragile features, long and pointed, were swathed, quasi-biblically, in a striped Damascus shawl that looked Byzantine, at either side of which escaped a wisp of red, crimped hair. Her big, wide eyes, full of innocent, child-like wonder, were set off by arched auburn brows that in the twilight seemed almost to be phosphorescent.

By her side reclined a plump, placidish person, whose face was half concealed beneath a white-lace coalscuttle hat.

'Some *suppose* . . . while *others*——; again, I'm told . . . And in *any case*, my dear!' The voice came droning in a monotonous, singsong way.

Facing the ladies a biretta'd priest appeared to be perusing a little, fat, black, greasy book of prayers which he held aslant so as to catch the light. Every now and then he would raise a cold, hypnotic eye above the margin of his page towards the ladies *vis-à-vis*.

'Of whom are you so unkindly speaking, Mrs. Thoroughfare?' he enquired at length.

The head beneath the coalscuttle-shaped hat drooped confused.

'I? Oh, my dear Father——!'

'Yes? my dear child? . . .'

'I was only telling Mrs. Hurstpierpoint how——'

149

Mrs. Hurstpierpoint—the dowager of the gleaming brows—leaned forward all at once in the carriage and pulled the checkstring attached to her footman's arm.

'Benighted idiot!' she exclaimed.

The fellow turned towards his mistress a melancholy, dreamy face that had something of a *quia multum amavit* expression in its wizen whiteness, and raised stiffly to a frayed silk cockade a long, bare hand.

'Didn't I say, blunt-headed booby, to Valmouth?'

'To Valmouth?'

'By way of Fleet. *Pardon,* Thoroughfare,' the dowager murmured, 'you were saying——'

'Evil, evil, evil,' her companion returned. 'Nothing but slander, wickedness and lies. *N'est ce pas,* Father Colley?'

'What is your book, Father Colley-Mahoney?' Mrs. Hurstpierpoint asked.

'St. Stanislaus-Kostka, my child.'

'Kostka——! It sounds like one of those islands, those savage islands, where my big, handsome, strong—*and* delicate!—darling Dick stopped at once, just to write to his old mother,' Mrs. Thoroughfare declared.

'Where is he now, Eliza?'

'Off the coast of Jamaica. His *ship*——' she broke off as a voice full and flexible rose suddenly from behind a burgeoning quincunx of thorns:

'I heard the voice of Jesus say-y-y! Yahoo, to heel. Bad dog.'

'It's that crazy Corydon,' Mrs. Thoroughfare blinked.

'Which, dear, crazy?'

'David Tooke—the brother, you know, of that extraordinarily extraordinary girl.'

'Thoroughfare.'

'Father?'

'That tongue.'

'The last time Dick was at Hare, I thought——'

'*Meet me in glow-ry by the gate o' pearl.* Hi, Douce!' the voice irrelevantly veered, as, over a near meadow, barking lustily, sprang a shaggy sheep-dog. 'Hi, Douce boy?... Doucey! Douce!'

The Priest pulled the light merino carriage rug higher about his knees.

'How,' he addressed Mrs. Hurstpierpoint, whose chevelure in

the diminishing daylight was taking on almost the appearance of an aureole, 'how if the glorious Virgin required you to take this young fellow under your wing?'

Mrs. Hurstpierpoint bent thoughtfully her eyes to the somewhat 'phallic' passementerie upon her shawl.

'For the sake, I presume,' she queried, 'of his soul?'

'Precisely.'

'But is he ripe?' Mrs. Thoroughfare wondered.

'Ripe?'

'I *mean*——'

There was a busy silence.

Descending a narrow tree-lined lane the carriage passed into a leisurely winding road, bounded by market-gardens and the River Val. Through a belt of osier and alder Valmouth, with its ancient bridge and great stone church, that from the open country had the scheming look of an ex-cathedral, showed a few lit lamps.

Mrs. Thoroughfare twittered.

'I did require a ribbon, a roughish ribbon,' she announced, 'and to call as well at the music-shop for those Chopin sonatas.'

'A "roughish" ribbon?' Father Colley-Mahoney echoed in searching tones. 'And pray, might I ask, what is that?'

'It's—— Oh, Father.'

'Is it silk? Or satin? Or is it velvet? Is it,' he conscientiously pressed, 'something rose-leafy? Something lilac?... Eh? Or sky-blue, perhaps?... Insidious child!'

'Insidious, Father?'

'Prevaricating.'

'Pax, Father,' Mrs. Thoroughfare beseeched.

Father Colley-Mahoney gazed moodily above the floppy fabric of her hat at an electric two-seater that was endeavouring to forge by the barouche from behind.

As it came abreast of it the occupants, a spruce, middle-aged man, and a twinkling negress, who clasped in her arms a something that looked to be an india-rubber coil, respectfully bowed.

'Dr. Dee, and la Yajñavalkya!'

'Those appliances of hers——; that she flaunts!'

'In massaging her "cases," ' Mrs. Thoroughfare *sotto-voce* said, 'I'm told she has a trick of—um.'

'Oh?'

'And of—um!'

'Indeed?'

'So poor Marie Wilks' nurse told my maid . . .'

'When,' Father Colley-Mahoney murmured, '*was* Miss Wilks a hundred?'

'Only last week.'

'Nowadays,' Mrs. Hurtpierpoint commented, 'around Valmouth centenarians will be soon as common as peas!'

'The air,' Mrs. Thoroughfare sniffed, 'there's no air to compare to it.'

'For the sake of veracity, I should be tempted to qualify that.'

'I fancy I'm not the only one, Father, to swear by Valmouth air!'

'Valmouth air, Valmouth air.'

'At the Strangers' Hotel,' Mrs. Thoroughfare giddily went on, 'it seems there's not a single vacant bed. No; nor settle either. . . . Victor Vatt, the delicate *paysagiste*—the English Corot—came yesterday, and Lady Parvula de Panzoust was to arrive to-day.'

'I was her bridesmaid some sixty years ago—and she was no girl then,' Mrs. Hurstpierpoint smiled.

'She stands, I fear, poor thing, now, for something younger than she looks.'

'Fie, Thoroughfare!'

'Fie, Father?'

'*La jeunesse—hélas*,' Mrs. Hurstpierpoint softly said, '*n'a qu'un temps*.'

Father Colley-Mahoney looked absently away towards the distant hills whose outlines gleamed elusively beneath the rising moon.

Here and there, an orchard in silhouette, showed all in black blossom against an extravagant sky.

🐾 *II* 🐾

TROTTING before his master, the fire-flies singing his tale, ran the watch-dog Douce. From the humid earth beneath his firm white paws the insects clamoured zing-zing-zing. Nuzzling intently the ground, sampling the pliant grasses, he would return from time to time to menace some lawless calf or cow.

Following a broken trackway through the deserted corn-land, the herd filed lazily towards the town in a long, close queue. Tookes's

Farm, or Abbot's Farm, as it indifferently was called, whither they now were bent, lay beneath the decayed walls of St. Veronica, the oldest church in the town. Prior to the Reformation the farm buildings (since rebuilt and considerably dwindled) had appertained, like much of the glebeland around Valmouth, to the Abbots of St. Veronica, when at the confiscation of the monasteries by the Crown one Thierry Monfaulcon Tooke, tennis-master to the Court of King Henry VIII, feinting to injure himself one day while playing with the royal princesses, had been offered by Henry, through their touching entreaties 'in consideration of his mishap,' the Abbey farm of St. Veronica's, then recently vacated by the monks; from which same Thierry (in the space of only six generations) the estate had passed to his descendants of the present time. Now in the bluey twilight as seen from the fields the barns and outhouses appeared really to be more capacious than the farm itself. With its white-washed walls and small-paned latticed windows it showed poorly enough between the two sumptuous wheat-ricks that stood reared on either side. Making their way across the long cobble bridge that spanned the Val, the cattle turned into an elm-lined lane that conducted to the farmyard gates, where, pottering expectantly, was a tiny boy.

At a bark from Douce he swung wide a creaking cross-barred gate overspread by a thorn-tree all in flower.

With lethargic feet the animals stumbled through, proceeding in an automatic way to a strip of water at the far end of the yard into which they turned. By the side of it ran an open hanger upheld by a score of rough tarred posts. Against these precocious calves were wont as a rule to rub their crescent horns. Within showed a wagon or two, and a number of roosting doves.

Depositing his scrip in the outhouse the cowherd glanced around.

'Where's Thetis got?' he asked, addressing the small boy, who, brandishing a broken rhubarb-leaf, was flitting functionarily about.

'Thetis?... She's,' he hopped, 'standing in the river.'

'What's she standing there for?'

'Nothing.'

'... Must I thrash you, Bobby Jolly?'

'Oh, don't, David.'

'Then answer me quick.'

'When the tide flows up from Spadder Bay she pretends it binds

her to the sea. Where her sweetheart is. Her b-betrothed. . . . Away
in the glorious tropics.'

' 'Od! You're a simple one; you are!'

'Me?'

'Aye, you.'

'Don't be horrid, David, to me. . . . You mustn't be. It's bad
enough quite without.'

' 'Od.'

'What with granny——'

'She'll not be here for long.'

'I don't think she'll die just yet.'

'It's a cruel climate,' the young man ruefully said, looking
impatiently up through his eyelashes towards the stars.

It was one of the finest nights imaginable. The moon reigned full
in the midst of a cloudless sky. From the thorn-tree by the gate the
sound of a bird singing floated down exuberantly through the leaves.

'Aye, cruel,' he muttered, shouldering a pitchfork and going out
into the yard. As he did so the church clock rang out loudly in the
air above.

'Shall I find 'ee Thetis?'

'Nay. Maybe I'll go myself.'

Beyond the low yard wall gleamed the river, divided from the
farm by a narrow garden parcelled out in vegetables and flowers.

A cindered pathway sloping between spring-lettuces and rows of
early tulips whose swollen calyxes, milk-white, purple and red,
probed superbly the moon-mist, led to the water's edge where,
clinging to the branches of a pollard-willow, a girl was gently
swaying with the tide. On her head, slightly thrown back, and
slashed all over with the shadow of the willow leaves, was perched
a small sailor's toque adorned with a spread gannet's wing that
rose up venturesomely from the ribboned cord. Her light print
frock, carelessly caught about her, revealed her bare legs below the
knees.

The cowherd paused hesitant.

'Thetis—!' he called.

Self-absorbed, wrapped in enchanting fancies, she turned:
'H'lo?'

'Come in now.'

'I shan't.'

'Come in, Thetis.'

'I won't. I will not.'

'You'll catch your death!'

'What of it?'

'The-tis. . . .'

With a laugh, she whisked further out into the stream.

Through her parted fingers, in microscopic wavelets, it swept, all moon-plashed from the sea.

Laughing, she bent her lips to the briny water.

⚘ III ⚘

IN a little back sitting-room overlooking the churchyard Granny Tooke, in a high rush-chair, was sharing a basin of milk with the cat.

It was her 'Vibro day,' a day when a sound like wild-bees swarming made ghostly music through the long-familiar room. Above the good green trees the venerable wood dial of St. Veronica's great clock informed her that, in the normal course of things, Madam Yajñavalkya and her instruments should already be on their way.

'Was there ever a cat like ye for milk, Tom?' the old lady wondered, setting down the half-emptied bowl on the whatnot beside her, and following with a poulterer's discerning eye the careless movements of the farm pigeons as they preened themselves on the long gross gargoyles of the church.

Once, long ago, in that same building she had stood a round-cheeked bride. Alas for life's little scars! . . . Now, all wrapped up like a moulting canary, her dun, lean face was fuller of wrinkles than a withered russet. Nevertheless, it was good still to be alive! Old Mrs. Tooke sighed with self-complacence as her glance took in the grave-ground, in whose dark, doughy soil so many former cronies lay asleep. It was a rare treat for her to be able, without any effort, to witness from time to time a neighbour's last impressive pomps; to watch 'the gentlemen' in their tall town tiles 'bearing up poor fellows'; to join (unseen in her high rush-chair, herself in carpet-slippers) in the long, lugubrious hymn; to respire through the window chinks of her room the faint exotic perfume of aromatic flowers from a ground all white with wreaths.

Valmouth

But, to-day, there were no obsequies to observe at all.

Through the window glass she could see Maudie and Maidie Comedy, daughters of Q. Comedy, Esq., the local estate agent and auctioneer, amusing themselves by making daisy chains by the mortuary door, while within the church someone—evidently not the vicar's sister—was casting the stale contents of an altar-vase through a clerestory-window (sere sweet by sweet), quite callous of passers-by.

Mrs. Tooke blew pensively the filmy skin forming upon her milk. A long sunbeam lighting up the whatnot caused the great copper clasp of her Bible to emit a thousand playful sparks, bringing to her notice somewhat glaringly a work of fiction that assuredly wasn't hers. . . . Extending a horny hand towards it, she had hardly made out a line when her granddaughter looked languorously in.

'Your towels are nicely steaming,' she said, resting her prepossessing, well-formed face against the polished woodwork of the door.

Mrs. Tooke coughed drily.

'So far,' she murmured, 'Mrs. Yaj ha'n't come.'

'It's such a splendid morning.'

'Where's David?'

'He went out early with the barley-mow.'

'Any orders?'

'The hotel only—extra butter.'

'Be sure to say it's risen. Butter and eggs,' Mrs. Tooke dramatically declared, 'have gone up. And while you're at the Strangers' you might propose a pair of pigeons, or two, to the cook.'

Miss Tooke turned yearningly her head.

'You'd think,' she faltered, 'they were seagulls, poor darlings, up there so white.'

'If only I could get about the place,' Mrs. Tooke restively pursued, 'as once I did.'

'Maybe with the warmer weather here you will. This very night the old sweetbrier tree came out. The old sweetbrier! And none of us thought it could.'

'In heaven's name,' her grandmother peevishly snapped, 'don't let me hear you talk of thinking. A more feather-brained girl there never lived.'

'I often think, at any rate,' Miss Tooke replied, 'I was born for something *more brilliant* than waiting on you.'

156

'Impudent baggage! Here, take it—before I tear it.'

'My library book?'

'Pah to the library. I wish there was none.'

Miss Tooke shrugged slightly her shoulders.

'There's Douce barking,' she said, 'I expect it's Mrs. Yaj.'

And in effect a crisp rat-a-tat on the yard-door gate was followed by a majestical footfall on the stair.

'Devil dog, pariah! Let go of me,' a voice came loudly drifting from below; a voice, large, deep, buoyant, of a sonorous persuasiveness, issuing straight from the entrails of the owner.

Mrs. Tooke had a passing palpitation.

'Put the chain on Douce, and make ready the thingamies!' she commanded, as Mrs. Yajñavalkya, wreathed in smiles, sailed briskly into the room.

She had a sheeny handkerchief rolled round and round her head, a loud-dyed petticoat and a tartan shawl.

'Forgive me I dat late,' she began. 'But I just dropped off to sleep again—like a little chile—after de collation.'

'Howsomever!' Mrs. Tooke exclaimed.

'Ah! de clients, Mrs. Tooke!' The negress beamed. 'Will you believe it now, but I was on my legs this morning before four! . . . Hardly was there a light in the sky when an old gentleman he send for me to de Strangers' Hotel.'

Mrs. Tooke professed astonishment.

'I understood you never "took" a gentleman,' she said.

'No more do I, Mrs. Tooke. Only,' Mrs. Yajñavalkya comfortably sighed, 'I like to relieve my own sex.'

'Up at four!' Mrs. Tooke archly quavered.

'And how do you find yourself to-day, Mrs. Tooke? How is dat sciatica ob yours?'

'To be open with you, Mrs. Yaj, I feel to-day as if all my joints want oiling!'

'What you complain ob, Mrs. Tooke, is nothing but stiffness—due very largely from want ob par. Or (as we Eastern women sometimes say) from want ob vim. Often de libber you know it get sluggish. But it will pass. . . . I shall not let—you hear me?—I shall not let you slip through my fingers: Oh no, your life wif me is so precious.'

'I can't hope to last very much longer, Mrs. Yaj, anyway, I suppose.'

157

'That is for me to say, Mrs. Tooke,' the imperious woman murmured, beginning to remove, by way of preliminary, the numerous glittering rings with which her hands were laden.

'Heysey-ho!' the old lady self-solicitously sighed, 'she's getting on.'

'And so's de time, Mrs. Tooke! But have no fear. Waited for as I am by a peeress ob distinction, I would never rush my art, especially wif you. No; oh no.You, my dear, are my most beautiful triumph! Have I not seen your precious life fluttering away, spent? Den at a call . . . I . . . wif my science—wif dese two hand have I not restored you to all de world's delights?'

'Delights,' Mrs. Tooke murmured, going off into a mournful key. 'Since the day my daughter-in-law—Charlotte Carpster that was—died in child-bed, and my great, bonny wild-oat of a son destroyed himself in a fit of remorse, there's been nothing but trouble for me.'

'And how is your young grandchild's erot-o-maniah, Mrs. Tooke? Does it increase?'

'God knows, Mrs. Yaj, what it does.'

'We Eastern women,' Mrs. Yajñavalkya declared, drawing off what perhaps was once her union-ring, 'never take lub serious, And w'y is dis, Mrs. Tooke?—Because it is so serious!'

'Love in the East, Mrs. Yaj, I presume, is *only* feasible indoors?'

'Nobody bothers, Mrs. Tooke. Common couples wif no place else often go into de jungle.'

'Those cutting winds of yours must be a bar to courting.'

'Our cutting winds! It is you who have de cutting winds. . . . It is not us. . . . No; oh no. In de East it is joy, heat!'

'Then where do those wicked blasts come from?'

'Never you mind now, Mrs. Tooke, but just cross dose two dear knees ob yours, and do wot I bid you. . . . Dis incipient pass,' the beneficent woman explained, seating herself in the window-bench facing Mrs. Tooke's arm-chair, 'is a daisy. And dat is sure, O Allah la Ilaha,' she gurgled, 'but I shall have you soon out in de open air again, I hope, and den you shall visit *me*. . . . De white acacia-tree in my back garden is something so beautiful dis year; at dis season it even eclipse my holly. . . . Ah, Mrs. Tooke! Whenebber I look at a holly it put me in mind ob my poor Mustapha again. It has just de same playful prickle of a mastodon's moustache. Husband and wife ought to cling together, Mrs. Tooke; if only for de sake ob de maintenance; it's hard often, my dear, for one in de professional-way to make both ends meet; clients don't always pay; you may rub your arms off for some folk (and include all de best specifics), but never a dollar will you see!'

'Howsomever,' Mrs. Tooke exclaimed, eyeing mistrustfully her granddaughter, who had re-entered the room unobtrusively with the towels.

She had a sun-hat on, equipped to go out.

'Where are you off, so consequential?' the old lady interrogatively said.

'Nowhere in particular.'

'In that big picture-hat——? Don't tell me!'

'I shall be back again, I dare say, before you're ready,' Miss Tooke replied, withdrawing on tiptoe from the room.

'Dat enlarged heart should be seen to, Mrs. Tooke. Do persuade her now to try my sitz-baths. I sell ze twelve tickets ver cheap—von dozen only for five shillings,' the young girl could hear the mulattress murmur as she closed the door.

Taking advantage of her grandame's hour of treatment, it was her habit, whenever this should occur, to sally forth for a stroll. Often she would slip off to Spadder Bay and lie upon the beach there, her pale cheek pressed to the wet sea-shingle; oftener perhaps she would wander towards Hare-Hatch House in the hope of a miraculous return.

This morning her feet were attracted irresistibly towards Hare.

Crossing the churchyard into the Market Square, where, above booths and shops and the flowered façade of the Strangers' Hotel, towered the statue of John Baptist Daleman, *b.* 1698, *ob.* 1803, Valmouth's illustrious son, Miss Tooke sauntered slowly across the old brick bridge that spanned the Val. Here, beneath a cream canvas sunshade traced at the borders with narrow lines of blue, sat Victor Vatt, the landscape artist, a colour-box upon his knee. At either side of him crouched a pupil—young men who, as they watched the veteran painter's hand, grew quite hot and red and religious-looking.

Bearing on, Miss Tooke branched off into an unfrequented path that led along the river-reach, between briers and little old stunted pollard-willows, towards Hare. Kingfishers emeralder than the grass passed like dream-birds along the bank. Wrapped in fancy, walking in no great hurry, she would pause, from time to time, to stand and droop, and dream and die. Between the sodden, creaking bark of pollard-willows, weeping for sins not theirs, the sea, far off, showed pulsating in the sun.

> 'I loved a man
> And he sailed away,
> Ah hé, ah hé,'

she sang.

From Valmouth to Hare-Hatch House was reckoned a longish mile. Half buried in cedar woods, it stood on high ground above the valley of the Val, backed by the bluish hills of Spadder Tor. Ascending a zigzag track she entered a small fir plantation that was known by most people thereabouts as Jackdaw Wood; but, more momentously, for her it was '*the*' wood. How sweetly he had kissed her in its kindly gloom. . . . On those dead fir-needles hand in hand, his bright eyes bent to hers (those dear entrancing eyes that held the glamour of foreign seaports in them), he had told her of her goddess namesake of Greece, of the nereid Thetis, the sister of Calypso, and the mother of Achilles, the most paradoxical of all the Greeks. On these dead fir-needles he had told her of his ship—the *Sesostris*—and of his middy-chum, Jack Whorwood, who was not much over fifteen, and the youngest hand on board. 'That little lad,' he had said, with a peculiar smile that revealed his regular pointed teeth, 'that little lad, upon a cruise, is, to me, what Patroclus was to Achilles, and even more.'

Ruminating, she roamed along, brushing the rose-spiked self-heal and the red-thimbled fox-gloves with her dress. Upon a fitful breeze a wailing repeated cry of a peacock smote like music on her ear and drew her on. Striking the highway beyond the little copse she skirted the dark iron palings enclosing Hare. Through the armorial great gates—open as if expectant—the house lay before her across a stretch of drive.

Halting she stood, lost in amorous conjectures, surveying with hungry eyes the sun-bleached, mute façade.

Oh, which amongst those tiers of empty windows lit his room?

Above each tall window was a carved stone mask. Strange chiselled faces, singularly saturnine . . . that laughed and leered and frowned. His room perhaps faced the other way? Her eyes swept the long pseudo-classic pile. Above the gaunt grey slates showed the tops of the giant cryptomerias upon the lawn.

She had never penetrated there.

160

To one side of it on a wooded hillock rose a garden temple open to the winds, its four white columns uplifting each a bust.

Beneath the aerial cupola three people at present were seated, engaged in tranquil chat.

Transfixed, Miss Tooke considered them. She was there, in spirit, too, 'holding her own,' as her grandmother would have said, with those two patrician women and the priest.

🐦 *IV* 🐦

THEY were ringing the angelus. Across the darkling meadows, from the heights of Hare, the tintinnabulation sounded mournfully, penetrating the curl-wreathed tympanums of Lady Parvula de Panzoust.

'There's the dinner-bell, coachman!' her ladyship impatiently exclaimed, speaking through the ventilator of her cab. 'Please to get on.'

Whipping up his horse with an inventive expletive, the driver started forward at a trot.

Lady Parvula relaxed.

The invitation to dinner at Hare-Hatch House had included her daughter, the Hon. Gilda Vintage, as well; a fair girl whose vast fortune as sole heiress of the late Lord de Panzoust caused her to be considered one of the most tempting present *partis* in the land. Bring Gilda, Mrs. Hurstpierpoint had written to Lady Parvula, 'so that, not unlikely,' her ladyship blissfully mused, 'Captain Thoroughfare will be there!'

Captain Thoroughfare.

There were rumours, to be sure, he was above Love.

Lady Parvula studied dreamily her hands. (She had long, psychic, pallid, amorous fingers, much puffed at the tips and wrinkled.)

'Oh, how I wish *I* were!' she reflected. 'But that is something I never was. . . . Who was that I saw by the ditch just now? *Quel ioli garçon!* Quite—as Byron said of D'Orsay—a *"cupidon déchaîné."* . . . Such a build. And such a voice! Especially, when he called his horrid dog to heel. *I heard the voice of Jesus say, yahoo—yahoo, bad dog!'*

Lady Parvula threw a little palpitating smile towards the evening star.

161

'He must be mine,' she murmured, 'in my manner . . . in my way . . . I always told my dear late Lord I could love a shepherd—peace be to his soul!'

A grey-haired manservant, and a couple of underfootmen wearing the violet vestments of the House-basilica (and which for moral reasons they were requested of an evening to retain), were meanwhile awaiting the arrival of the Valmouth cab, while conversing in undertones among themselves as servants sometimes do.

'Dash their wigs!' the elderly man exclaimed.

'What's the thorn, Mr. ffines?' his colleague, a lad with a face gemmed lightly over with spots, pertly queried.

'The thorn, George?'

'Tell us.'

'I'd sooner go round my beads.'

'Mrs. Hurst cut compline, for a change, to-night.'

' . . . She's making a studied toilet, so I hear.'

'Gloria! Gloria! Gloria!'

'Dissenter.'

'What's wrong with Nit?'

The younger footman flushed.

'Father Mahoney sent for me to his room again,' he answered.

'What, *again*?'

'Catch me twice——'

'*Veni cum me in terra coelabus!*'

'S-s-s-s-s-s-sh.'

'*Et lingua . . . semper.*'

'On the whole,' the butler said, 'I preferred Père Ernest.'

'And so did half the maids.'

'Although his brilliance here was as you may say wasted.'

' 'Pon my word! It's a deadly awful place.'

'With the heir-presumptive so much away it's bound to be slow and quiet.'

'Why,' George gurgled, 'the Captain should be heir of Hare I never could make out!'

'Mr. Dick's dead father,' Mr. ffines replied, 'was a close relative of Mrs. Hurst.'

'The Admiral?'

'And it was as good as a combination . . .' he further explained, 'only he was too poor. And things fell out otherwise.'

'There'd be a different heir, I s'pose, if missis married ag'in?'

' 'Tisn't likely. Why she'll soon be a centenarian herself.'

'You've only to change her plate,' Nit, with acumen, said, 'to feel she's there.'

'So I should hope!'

'And as to Father Colley. My! How he do press!'

The servitors waxed silent, each lost in introspection, until the rattle of the Valmouth cab announced the expected guest.

Alighting like some graceful exotic bird from the captivity of a dingy cage, Lady Parvula de Panzoust hovered a moment before the portal as much to manipulate her draperies, it seemed, as to im-breathe the soft sweet air.

The sky was abloom with stars. . . .

In the faint elusive light flitter-mice were whirling about the mask-capped windows, hurtling the wind-sown wallflowers embedded in the fissure of each saturnine-hewn face.

'Come back for me again by ten o'clock, remember,' her ladyship commanded her coachman, prior to following the amaranthine skirts of the two footmen into the house.

Passing through the bleak penumbra of the hall and along a corri-dor bristling with horns of every description, she was shown into a deep, T-shaped, panelled room profusely hung with pictures.

There seemed at present to be no one in it.

'The mistress, I presume, is with the scourge,' the butler an-nounced, peering impassably around.

Lady Parvula placed her fan to her train.

'Let her lash it!' she said. 'In this glorious room one is quite content to wait.'

And indeed there could not be the least doubt that the drawing-room at Hare-Hatch House was sufficently uplifting to be alone in without becoming dull.

Here were the precious Holbeins—the finest extant—and the Ozias Humphry in its original oval frame, while prominent above the great Jacobean fireplace, with a row of lamps shining footlight-wise beneath it, was the youthful portrait of the present mistress from the hand of Ingres.

Garbed in Greek draperies, she was seen leaning her head against a harpsichord, whose carved support rose perpendicularly from end to end of the canvas like some flower-wreathed capital.

Less redoubtable perhaps were an infinity of Morlands, fresh and fragrant, in their oblong, cross-ribboned frames, a Longhi or two—

a Piazza, a Punchinello in a little square, and a brilliant croquis signed *Carmontelle* of a Duchess trifling with a strawberry.

By a jaguar-skin couch far down the room an array of long-back chairs in the splendid upholstery of the seventeenth century suggested to Lady Parvula's mind an occasional 'public' correction. And everywhere ranged fortuitously about were *faïence* flower-tubs bearing large-leaved plants that formed tall canopies to the white, pensive statues grouped patiently beneath.

She was just passing a furtive hand over the promising feet and legs of a Discobolus, broken off, unfortunately, at the height of the loins, as Mrs. Thoroughfare entered.

All billowing silks and defenceless embroideries, she was looking to-night like a good-natured sphinx—her rather bulging, etiolated cheeks and vivid scarlet mouth expanded in a smile.

'I know of no joy,' she airily began, 'greater than a cool white dress after the sweetness of confession.'

Lady Parvula cast an evasive eye towards the supine form of a bronze hermaphrodite, whose long, tip-tilted, inquisitive nose protruded snugly above a smart Renaissance quilt.

'No! Really! Elizabeth!' she exclaimed.

Mrs. Thoroughfare breathed in a way that might have been called a sigh.

'And where is Gilda?' she asked.

'Gilda . . . Gilda's still at school!'

'Oh!'

'And Dick?'

'Dick . . . Dick's still at sea!'

'Wicked fellow.'

'A crate of some wonderful etherised flowers,' Mrs. Thoroughfare informed, pivoting with hands outspread, about a tripod surmounted by a small braziero, 'came from him only this afternoon, from Ceylon.'

Lady Parvula plied her fan.

'Even at Oomanton,' she murmured, 'certain of the new hybrids this year are quite too perfect.'

'Eulalia and I often speak of the wondrous orchids at Oomanton Towers.'

Lady Parvula expanded.

'We're very proud of a rose-lipped one,' she said, 'with a lilac beard.'

'A lilac . . . *what*?' It was Mrs. Hurstpierpoint's voice at the door. 'Eulalia!'

'Is it Sodom?' she enquired in her gruff, commanding way, coming forward into the room.

She had a loose, shapeless gown of hectically-contrasted colours—one of Zenobia Zooker's hardiest inspirations—draped from the head à l'Evangile.

Lady Parvula tittered.

'Goodness, no,' she said.

'Because Father Mahoney won't hear of it ever *before* dessert.'

'How right.'

'He seems to think it quite soon enough,' the mistress of Hare murmured, passing an intimate arm about her old friend's waist.

Lady Parvula cooed half-fluttered. In a time-corroded mirror she could see herself very frail, and small, and piquant in its silver-sheeted depth.

'To be continually beautiful, like *you,* dear,' her hostess said. 'How I wish I could. . . .'

'Yet I date my old age,' Lady Parvula replied, 'from the day I took the lift first at the Uffizi!'

'You dear angel.'

'One's envious, almost, of these country clowns, who live, and live, and live, and look so well!'

'Many find the climate here trying to begin with,' Mrs. Hurstpierpoint said, 'owing to the amount of cosmic activity there is; but the longevity of the Valmouthers attracts all kinds of visitors to the town.'

'At the Strangers' a Contessa di Torre Nuevas has the room next to me—and *oh*! how she snores!'

'Do they make you comfortable?'

'Most.'

'You must miss the society of your girl.'

'Dear child. She is training under Luboff Baltzer—in Milan.'

'To what end?'

'Music. And she is in such cruel despair. She says Luboff insists on endless counterpoint, and *she* only wants to play valses!'

'She hardly sounds to be ambitious.'

'It depends; measured by Scriabin's *Quasi-Valse,* or the *Valse in A flat major,* she may have quite intricate idylls. . . .'

Mrs. Thoroughfare simmered. 'I do so love his *Étrangeté*,' she said.

'Was it you, Betty,' Mrs. Hurstpierpoint demanded, 'before Office I heard amusing yourself in Our Lady?'

'I am sure, Eulalia, I forget.'

Lady Parvula's hand wandered vaguely towards the laurel-leaf fillet that encompassed irresponsibly her pale, liver-tinted hair.

'After the Sixtine Chapel,' she remarked, 'I somehow think your Nuestra Señora de la Pena is the one I prefer.'

'You *dear* you! You should have been with us Easter Day! Our little basilica was a veritable bower of love.'

'Have you any more new relics?'

'Only the tooth of St. Automona Meris, for which,' Mrs. Hurstpierpoint, in confidence, was moved to add, 'I've had my tiara-stones turned into a reliquary.'

'You funny animal!'

'If we go on as we go on,' Mrs. Thoroughfare commented as dinner was ceremoniously announced, 'we'll be almost *too* ornate!'

It was what they, each in their way, were ready for.

'I adore dining *en petit comité*,' Lady Parvula exclaimed, accepting gaily her hostess's propellent arm.

It was past blue, uncurtained windows to the dining-room, that remained, too, uncurtained to the night.

In the taper-lit, perhaps pre-sixteenth-century room—a piece of *Laughing and Triumphing* needlework in the style of Rubens completely hid the walls—the capacious oval of the dinner-table, crowned by a monteith bowl filled with slipper-orchids, showed agreeably enough.

'Where can Father be?' Mrs. Hurstpierpoint wondered, sinking to her chair with a slight grimace. Rumour had it that she wore a bag of holly-leaves pinned to the lining of her every gown; it even asserted that she sometimes assumed spiked garters.

'He went to the carpenter's shop, Eulalia,' Mrs. Thoroughfare replied, 'to give "a tap or two," as he said, to your new *prie-dieu*.'

'And so you've lost Père Ernest,' Lady Parvula murmured, humbling a mitred napkin with a dreamy hand.

'Alas! our stationariness soon bored him. He preferred flitting about the world like you.'

'I go about,' Lady Parvula admitted, 'as other fools, in quest of pleasure, and I usually find tedium.'

'If I recollect,' Mrs. Hurstpierpoint said, 'the Valmouth cattle-show was *our* last gaiety.'

'Your pathetic-eyed, curious oxen . . . it's a breed you don't see everywhere! My husband—my Haree-ee-ee' (either from coquetry or from some slight difficulty she experienced in pronouncing her y's, Lady Parvula pronounced 'Harry' long) 'tried them, in the park down at Oomanton Towers; but they didn't do.'

'No?'

'They got leaner and leaner and leaner and leaner in spite of cakes and cakes and cakes and cakes. . . . Poor Haree-ee-ee, my dearly beloved lord, even allowed them on to the lawn, where they used to look in at the ground-floor windows. One dreadful evening —we were taking tea—a great crimson head and two huge horns tossed the cup I was holding out of my hands, which sent me off— I'm just all over nerves!—into a state of *défaillance*; the last thing you may imagine I wanted, as it was Gilda's last night at home.'

'You should consult local advice.'

'It's what I intend doing.'

'We hear of several of our hidalgos having been immortalised lately, thanks to Victor Vatt.'

Mrs. Thoroughfare smiled indulgently.

'Those disciples of his,' she demurely said, 'oh; are they all they seem?'

'Lady Lucy Saunter swears not!'

'Is Lady Lucy at Valmouth?'

'Indeed she is. . . . And *so* poorly and *so* run-down. She says her blood is nothing but rose-water.'

'I suppose the town is full of imaginary invalids *comme toujours*?'

'My dear, one sees nothing else. So many horrid parliament-men come here apparently purely to bask.'

Mrs. Thoroughfare's face lit.

'Like our two whips!' she made chucklingly rejoinder. 'Last Epiphany in a fit of contrition we sent a tiny *enfant du chœur* (a dangerous, half-witted child . . . but pious: pious . . . ! And with the sweetest face; oh hadn't Charlie a witching face last Epiphany, Eulalia? His hair's good yet, and so are his taper hands, but his voice has gone, and so too have his beautiful roses) into town for a couple of whips. They duly appeared. But two such old vote-hunters. . . . "My God," Eulalia said, "we asked for whips and Thou sendest *scourges*." '

'Well! Quite a harum-scarum, one of the Vile-islands, sits for Oomanton, who pretends, I believe,' Lady Parvula breathed, 'to be an advocate for Gilda; but if *I* ever venture to propose an alliance to my ewe-lamb usually she answers: "I don't want to marry *any*-one, thank you, mama! I prefer to be free." She has no real cognisance, dear lambkin, of anything at all.'

'Sooner or later she'll make her choice!'

'Men, men! . . . "They are always there," dear, aren't they, as the Russians say?'

Mrs. Hurstpierpoint repressed a grimace.

'Nowadays,' she murmured, 'a man . . . to me . . . somehow . . . oh! he is something so wildly *strange*.'

'Strange?'

'Unglimpsable.'

'Still, some men are ultra-womanly, and they're the kind I love!' Mrs. Thoroughfare chirruped.

'I suppose that none but those whose courage is unquestionable can venture to be effeminate?' Lady Parvula said, plunging a two-pronged fork into a 'made' dish of sugared-violets served in aspic.

'It may be so.'

'It was only in war-time, was it, that the Spartans were accustomed to put on perfumes, or to crimp their beards?'

'My dear, how your mind seems to dwell upon beards.'

'Upon *beards*?'

'It's perfectly disgusting.'

'In the old days do you remember "Twirly" Rogers?'

'Out with the Valmouth Drag,' Mrs. Thoroughfare sighed, 'how well he looked in his pink coat!'

Lady Parvula assented.

'Those meets,' she said, 'on the wintry cliffs above the world had a charm about them. One could count more alluring faces out with the Valmouth, my husband used to say, than with any other pack. The Baroness Elsassar—I can see her now on her great mauve mount with her profile of royalty in misfortune—never missed. Neither, bustless, hipless, chinless, did "Miss Bligh"! It was she who so sweetly hoisted me to my saddle, when I'd slid a-heap after the run of a "fairy" fox. We'd whiffed it—the baying of the dogs is something I shall never forget; dogs always know!—in a swede-field below your house from where it took us by break-neck, rapid stages—(oh! oh!)—to the sands. There, it hurried off along the sea's edge, with the harriers in full cry; all at once, near Pizon Point, it vanished. Mr. Rogers, who was a little ahead, drew his horse in with the queerest gape—like a lost huntsman (precisely) in the *Bibliothèque bleue.*'

'It's a wonder he didn't vomit.'

'I and Miss Bligh lay on the beach for hours——!'

'With a *dominus vobiscum*,' Mrs. Hurstpierpoint remarked, turning her head at the silken swish of her chaplain's gown.

Flecked with wood shavings, Saint Joseph-wise, it brought with it suggestions of Eastern men in intriguing, long burnooses; of sandalled feet; of shadûf singing boys; of creaking water-wheels and lucerne-laden camels.

Bowing her face before the stiff, proud thumb and crooked fore-finger raised to bless, Mrs. Hurstpierpoint remained a moment as if in transport, looking, with her figured veils and fuzzed hair-wreath-ings, like some Byzantine peacock searching for fleas.

'Lulu Veuve? Veaujolais? Clos Voukay? Or Château-Thierry!' the butler broke the silence.

Lady Parvula hesitated.

'If only not to be too like everyone else, *mon ami*,' she murmured, her perfervid, soul-tossed eyes wandering towards the priest, 'you shall give me some of each.'

Father Colley-Mahoney launched a dry, defensive cough, involuntarily starting Nit.

'How incomparable their livery is!' Lady Parvula commented.

'It has a seminary touch about it,' Mrs. Hurstpierpoint conceded, 'though at Headquarters it's regarded (I fear!) as inclining to modernism, somewhat.'

'Pray what's that?'

'Modernism? Ask any bishop.'

Lady Parvula rippled.

'I once,' she said (resolutely refusing a stirring salmis of cocks'-combs *saignant* with *Béchamel* sauce), 'I once peeped under a bishop's apron!'

'Oh . . . ?'

'And what ever did you see?' Mrs. Thoroughfare breathlessly asked.

'Well . . . I saw,' Lady Parvula replied (helping herself to a few *pointes d'asperges à la Laura Leslie*), 'I saw . . . the dear Bishop!'

Father Mahoney kindled.

'Apropos,' he said, 'his Eminence writes he is offering an ex-voto to Nuestra Señora of a silver heart.'

'In any particular intention?'

'No. Its consecration he leaves to our discretion.'

'He owes, they say,' Mrs. Thoroughfare murmured, consulting the menu with Spanish gravity, 'to women at least the half of his red hat. . . .'

Lady Parvula's glance explored the garden.

A hyacinthine darkness flooded the titanic cedars before the house above whose immemorial crests like a sad opal the moon was rising.

'Parvula,' her hostess evinced concern, 'you're tasting nothing.'

'I shall wait,' Lady Parvula made answer, 'Eulalia, for the *Madeleines en surprise*!'

'An abbess, and one of my earliest penitents,' Father Mahoney said, 'professed to find "delicious" small slips of paper traced thickly across with holy texts.'

'Really? . . . It sounds like parlour games!'

Mrs. Hurstpierpoint was moved to sigh.

'No one remembers cribbage now,' she lamented, 'or gleek, or bi-ri-bi.'

'No; or ombre. . . .'

'Or lansquenet. . . .'

'Or spadille. . . .'

'Or brelan. . . .'

'But for cards, country evenings would be too slow!'

'Indeed, when Father reads us Johnny Bunyan after dinner I fall asleep,' Mrs. Thoroughfare declared.

'Have you nothing brighter than that?'

'We read here,' Father Mahoney interpolated, 'books only of a theological trend. Not that,' he disconsolately added, 'the library upstairs doesn't contain a certain amount of Rabelaisian literature, I regret to say.'

'Rabelaisian, Father?' Mrs. Hurstpierpoint faintly shrieked.

'I don't choose, my child, to think of some of the "works" we harbour.'

'Those Jacobean dramatists, and the French erotic works of the eighteenth century, of course, would be free . . . but Père Ernest didn't reject them; many a stern metaphor have I heard him draw from *Dr. James's Powders* and *Mr. Foote's Tea*—and all the rest of it.'

Lady Parvula considered with a supercilious air the immaterial green of a lettuce-leaf.

'Oh, well,' she said, 'even at Oomanton, I dare say, there are some bad books too; in fact, I know there are! Once my ewe-lamb came to me with what appeared to be a medieval lutrin. "Oh, mama," she said, "I've found such a funny word." "What is it, my precious?" I said. "——, mama!" she answered with the most innocent lips in life . . . which sent me off—I'm just all over nerves! —into a fainting state; fairly scaring my lambkin out of her wits.'

Mrs. Hurstpierpoint extended towards her guest a hand that was not (as Lady Parvula confided afterwards to the Lady Lucy Saunter) too scrupulously clean.

'Those fainting-fits,' she said, motioning an order to Nit as he flitted by with an ingenuity of tartelettes, 'should be taken in time. For my sake, allow Dr. Dee of Valmouth to systematically overhaul you.'

'Overhaul me! What for?'

But Mrs. Thoroughfare uttered a cry.

'Oh poor wee mothlet!' she exclaimed, leaning forward to extricate a pale-winged moth, struggling tragically in one of the sconces of a candelabra. . . .

'If ffines to-night was not enough to infuriate an archangel!' Mrs. Hurstpierpoint commented, resplendently trailing (the last tooth-some dish having been served) towards the holy-water stoup of old silver-work behind the door.

Lady Parvula joined her.

'After your superexcellent champagne,' she exclaimed, 'I feel one ought to go with bared feet in pilgrimage to Nuestra Señora and kindle a wax light or two.'

'My dear, I believe you've latent proclivities!'

'Eulalia!'

'Parvula!'

'Never.'

'Ah, don't say that.'

'Dearest,' Lady Parvula perversely marvelled, 'what a matchless lace berthe!'

'It was part of my corbeille——'

'Like *doubting Thomas*, I must touch with my hands.'

'Touch! Touch!'

Father Mahoney fidgeted.

171

'Beyond the vigil-lamp,' he objected, 'Nuestra Señora will be quite obscure.'

'Then all the more reason, Father, to illumine it!' Lady Parvula reasoned.

'Are you resolved, Parvula?'

'Of course. And I'm agog to see the tooth, too, of St. Automona Meris (Do you imagine she ever really ate with it horrid Castilian garlic *olla cocida*? Or purple *pistos insalada*? She and Teresa together, in some white *posada*, perhaps, journeying South), and your Ghirlandajo and the miracle-working effigy, and afterwards, until the fly comes round, you shall teach me gleek!'

'You dear angel . . . it's very simple!'

'Then let us play for modest points.'

Mrs. Hurstpierpoint crossed herself with her fan.

'As if,' she horror-struck said, 'I should consent to play for immodest ones! Are you coming, Elizabeth, too?' she asked.

'In one moment, Eulalia; I must speak to Father first,' Mrs. Thoroughfare replied, folding her arms lightly across the back of her chair.

'Don't, dear, desert us!' Mrs. Hurstpierpoint, withdrawing, enjoined.

There was a short pent silence.

'Do you think, Father,' Mrs. Thoroughfare broke in at last, 'she suspects?'

'Rest assured, my poor child,' Father Mahoney answered, 'your confession to me to-night exceeds belief.'

'Was there ever such a quandary!' Mrs. Thoroughfare jabbered.

'They obeyed the surge of their blood—what else?' Father Mahoney dispassionately said.

Mrs. Thoroughfare's full cheeks quivered.

'Oh, my darling boy,' she burst out, 'how *could* you!'

'My poor child, try not to fret.'

'It makes one belch, Father—belch.'

'They're joined irremediably, I understand?'

'From what he writes I conclude the worst.'

'Won't you show me what he says?'

'The card,' she murmured, drawing it from her dress, 'is covered, I fear, by the chemicals that were in the crate, gummed to the stem as it was of a nauseating lily.'

'Decipher the thing, then, to me—if you will.'

Mrs. Thoroughfare adjusted a lorgnon tearfully to her nose.

' "These are the native wild-flowers," he writes (what, I wonder, Father, must the others be!), "the native wild-flowers of my betrothed bride's country. Forgive us, and bless us, mother. Ten thousand loves to you all." '

'O, wretched boy.'

'O, Father.'

'That ever any Black woman should perform the honours at Hare!'

Mrs. Thoroughfare smiled mirthlessly.

'Well—if it comes to that—Eulalia, *herself*, to-night, is more than grubby,' she said.

ᛈ V ᛈ

THE installation of a negress at the 'Nook,' Mrs. Yajñavalkya's old-style dwelling in the Market Square, came to Valmouth, generally, as a surprise.

Almost from the outset of her arrival in the town, soft-muted music, the strange, heart-rending, mournful music of the East—suggestive of apes, and pearls, and bhang, and the colour blue—was to be heard, surging from the Nook in monotonous improvisation.

Madame Mimosa, the demi-mondaine, the only 'one' there was thereabouts, hearing it from the Villa Concha, next door, fancied she detected rivalry, competition—*the younger generation*—and took to her *bravura* (cerise chiffon, and a long, thick, black aigrette) before the clock told noon. Nurse Yates, hard by, heard 'zithers' too, and flattered herself the time was ripe to oust Mrs. Yajñavalkya from the town, 'automatically' capturing her clients as they dropped away. Mrs. Q. Comedy, *née* Le Giddy, ever alert to flare an auction, told her Quentin she supposed Mrs. Yajñavalkya would shortly be giving up her house and going off into Valopolis, or New-Valmouth, where she might conduct a *bagnio* with more facility, perhaps, than beneath the steeple of the church. While all the time, shining smiles, Mrs. Yajñavalkya herself went about affairs much in her usual way.

Of a morning early she would leave the Nook followed by a

little whey-faced English maid, to whom she allowed twelve pounds
a year 'because she is so white,' to take her way towards the provision
stalls encamped beneath John Baptist Daleman's virile, but rudi-
mentary, statue in the square, where, flitting from light to shade,
she would exchange perhaps a silver coin against a silver fish, or
warm-leafed cauliflower, half dead on the market stones. Sometimes,
quickly dismissing her little Gretchen, she would toddle off up
Peace Street into Main Street, and enter, without knocking, the
house of Dr. Dee, but more frequently mistress and maid would
return to the Nook together, when almost immediately from her
chimneys would be seen to rise a copious torrent of smoke.

From the Strangers' Hotel across the way Lady Parvula de
Panzoust, like the local residents themselves, had been a puzzled
spectator of the small particular coterie at the Nook, since, to her
ever-deepening vexation, her shepherd-with-the-dog was a constant caller there.

Had he anything, then, the matter? His constitution, was it not
the mighty thing it seemed? His agile figure (glowing through co-
duroys and hob-nailed boots; his *style d'amour*), was it nothing but a
sham? Or had he an intrigue, perhaps, with one or other of the
women of the house?

Now and then a dark face framed in unbound hair would look
out through a turret window of the Nook, as if moved to home-
sickness at the cries of a beautiful cockatoo that hung all day in the
window of Sir Victor Vatt's sitting-room at the hotel.

'Dear Vatt,' the bird would say with sonorous inflections, taking
off some artist, or sitter perhaps, 'dear Vatt! He is splendid; so
o-ri-gi-nal and exuberant; like an Italian Decorator.' Or, *vivo*:
'Now, Vatt! Do me a Poussin.' Or, the inflection changing *languido
dolce*: 'Come, Vatt! Paint me in a greenhouse ... in a st-oove; a
little exotic; paint me (my little Victor!) like Madame Cézanne!
They say,' *meno languido*, 'they say he gave her one hundred and
fifteen sittings! Pretty Poll!'

Loiterers in the Market Square, observing the attentive negress
trim the window, smiled and called her a caution, more cautious-
like, said they in the local vernacular, than 'Old Mrs. Rub-me-down,'
inferring Mrs. Yajñavalkya. Lady Parvula de Panzoust, alone, a
sure connoisseur of all amative values, was disposed to allow the
negress her dues, divining those ethnologic differences, those uneasy
nothings, that again and again in the history of the world have tempted

mankind to err. She descried, therefore, whenever the parrot's loquaciousness induced the negress to look out, a moon-faced girl with high-set, scornful eyes almost in her forehead and bow-curved pagan lips of the colour of rose-mauve stock. Her anatomy, singularly independent in every way, was, Lady Parvula surmised, that of a little *woman* of twelve. Was it, she asked herself, on this black Venus' account Adonis visited the Nook? Or was it for other reasons, graver, sadder ones . . . such as, for instance, dressing the gruesome injury of the boar?

One sunny May-day morning, full of unrest, Lady Parvula de Panzoust left the hotel for a turn on the Promenade. It was a morning of pure delight. Great clouds, breaking into dream, swept slowly across the sky, rolling down from the uplands behind Hare-Hatch House, above whose crumbling pleasances one single sable streak, in the guise of a coal-black negress, prognosticated rain.

'Life would be perfect,' she mused, 'if only I hadn't a corn!' But the Oriental masseuse was the sole proficient of the chiropodist's art at Valmouth, and Lady Parvula de Panzoust felt disinclined to bare her tender foot to the negress's perspicacious gaze. Yet after going a few painful yards this is what she realised she must do. 'After all,' she reflected, 'I may perhaps ascertain her pastoral client's condition, and so free my mind from doubt!'

She was looking charmingly matinal in a simple tweed costume, with a shapely if perhaps *invocative* hat, very curiously indented, and well cocked forward above one ear. She held a long ivory-handled sunshade in the form of a triple-headed serpent, and a book that bore the irreproachable Christian title *Embrassons Nous*.

'And who knows,' she sighed, lifting Mrs. Yajñavalkya's sun-fired knocker with a troubled hand, 'he may even be there himself!'

The little chalk-faced maid that answered the door said her mistress was in, and preceding the evident 'London lady' up a short flight of stairs, ushered her with a smile of triumph into a small but crowded cabinet whose windows faced the Square.

'Is it for a douche, m'm,' she asked, 'or ought I to start the steam?'

'Not on *my* account!' Lady Parvula murmured with dilated retinas, scanning the signed diplomas and framed credentials displayed upon the walls. A coloured 'Insurance' almanac, privately marked with initials and crosses—engagements no doubt of Mrs. Yajñavalkya's—gladdened gaily their midst.

'Chance me finding her,' she reflected, moving involuntarily towards a brilliant draped mirror above the chimney-place, where a tall piece of branched coral was stretched up half-forbiddingly against the glass.

Through its pink sticks she could see reflected in the room behind part of a calico-covered couch with the negress's bureau beyond, on which at present stood a half-eaten orange and a jar of white pinks.

A twitter of negro voices was shrilly audible through the wood partition of the wall.

'*Yahya!*'

'*Wazi jahm?*'

'*Ah didadidacti, didadidacti.*'

'*Kataka mukha?*'

'*Ah mawardi, mawardi.*'

'*Jelly.*'

'A breeze about their jelly!' Lady Parvula conjectured, complacently drawing nearer the window.

Before the Villa Concha, a little curtained carriage attached to an undocked colt with a bell at its ear signified that Madame Mimosa was contemplating shortly a drive.

Through what blue glebe or colza-planted plains would her rainbow axles turn?

Mrs. Yajñavalkya's ambling step disturbed her speculations.

'Have I not de satisfaction?' she ubiquitously began, 'ob addressing Milady Panzoust?'

Lady Parvula nodded.

'I believe you do chiropody?' she said.

'Dat is a speciality ob de house—de cultivation ob de toes. Vot is dair so important? O wen I consider de foot . . . de precious precious foot! For de foot support de body; it ber de burden ob ten thousand treasures! . . . *Kra*. And dat's vot I alvays say.'

'Undoubtedly,' Lady Parvula assented, 'whatever there *is*, it bears.'

'It gib gentle rise to ebberything,' Mrs. Yajñavalkya pursued.

'Perhaps—sometimes—it carries charms.'

'*Ukka-kukka!*' the negress broke off, dropping darkly to the floor. 'My niece, Niri-Esther, she fill de flower vases so full dat de water do all drip down and *ro-vine* de carpet.'

'Then of course she's in love?'

'Niri-Esther!'

'Now and then an interesting patient must wish to approach you.'

'I alvays,' Mrs. Yajñavalkya blandly yapped, 'decline a gentleman. Often ze old greybeards zey say, "Oh, Mrs. Yaj," zey say, "include our sex." And I laugh and I say, "I've enough to do wif my own!"'

Lady Parvula surrendered smilingly her shoes.

'Still, I sometimes see,' she said, 'call here a young tall man with his dog.'

'He call only to fetch de fowls dat flit across to my acacia-tree from de farm.'

'Is that all?'

'Being so near de church, de house is open to ebbery passing ghoul. De incubes and de succubes dat come in, and are so apt to molest . . . ob an evening especially, ven de sun fall and de sky turn all caprice, I will constantly dispatch my little maid to beg, to implore, and to beseech dat Dairyman Tooke will remove his roosters.'

'Dairyman Tooke?'

'Or his prize sow, maybe—a sow! Ah, dat is my abomination!'

'Probably the antipathy springs through the belief in reincarnation.'

'No doubt at all dat is one ob de causes.'

'The doctrine of Transubstantiation must often tell on your nerves.'

'When I die,' Mrs. Yajñavalkya said, her eyes disappearing expiringly in their sockets, 'I would not wish to be transubstantiated into a horse or a cow or a sheep or a cat. No; oh no! I will wish to be changed into a little bird, wid white, white feathers; treasuring,' she wistfully added, 'meantime de poet's words:

' "My mother bore me in the southern wild,
And I am black, but O! my soul is white." '

'Your songsters, too,' Lady Parvula said, 'have also their poignance.'

'Ah! when Niri-Esther read Tagore,' Mrs. Yajñavalkya glowed, 'dat is something beautiful! Dat is something to make de tears descend.'

'To hear her render the love lyrics of her country, just the most typical things, would interest me immensely if it might some day be arranged.'

'But why not?'

'A *séance* in your garden amidst the acacia leaves——Mademoiselle Esther and I! And when the young man came to retrieve his birds, I vow he'd find no turkey!'

'Believe me,' Mrs. Yajñavalkya murmured, indrawing succulently her cheeks and circumspectly toying with her file, 'believe me, he's awfully choice.'

'He has youth.'

'He's awfully, awfully choice!' the negress murmured, admiring the intricate nerve-play of her patient's foot.

'It's just a Valmouth type,' Lady Parvula observed.

'Ah! It is more dan dat.'

'How?'

'Much more in ebbery way.' Mrs. Yajñavalkya looked insoluble.

'I don't I fear follow . . .' Lady Parvula gasped.

'I have known what love is, I!' The negress heaved. 'Dair are often days ven I can neither eat, nor drink, nor sleep, ven my fingers hab no strength at all (massage den is quite impossible)—I am able only to groan and groan and groan—ah, my darling!'

'A nigger?'

'A nigger! No. He was a little blond Londoner—all buttoned-and-braided, one ob de *chasseurs* at your hotel.'

'Thank you.' Lady Parvula looked detached.

'De dear toe,' the operatress raised a glinting, sooty face, 'is quite inflamed! De skin,' with unwitting cynicism she theorised, 'may vary, but de Creator ob de universe has cast us all in de same mould; and dat's vot I alvays say.'

'In what part, tell me, is your home?'

'Here!' the negress lisped.

'Geographically, I mean.'

'Geographically, we're all so scattered. Von ob my brother, Djali, he in Ujiji Land. *Kra.* He a Banana-Inspector. Official. He select de virgin combs from off de tree; dat his Pash-on, dat his Cult. Other brother, Boujaja, he in Taihaiti. He a lady-killer, well-to-do-ish; he three wives, *kra*; and dose three women are my sisters-in-law. . . . De Inspector, he no marry; I don't know why!'

'Then your niece,' Lady Parvula pressed, 'is from Taihaiti?'

But Mrs. Yajñavalkya was abstruse.

'Do you care to undergo a course ob me?' she asked. 'For de full course—I make you easy terms; and I alvays try,' she airily cozened, 'to end off wid a charming sensation.'

'Massage merely as sensation does not appeal to me:—and otherwise, thank you, I'm perfectly well.'

'I gib a massage lately to de widowed Duchess ob Valmouth for less! Yajñavalkya, she laugh and say after I had applied my court cream (half a crown; five shillings): "Yajñavalkya, your verve, it's infectious." "My what, your grace?" I say. "Your verve," she reply; "it's so *catching*." '

'I always admired her,' Lady Parvula remarked, 'you'd almost say she was a man.'

'Her testimonial is on my bureau dair.'

'You must be proud of your tributes.'

'Zey come from all sides. . . . Queen Quattah, she write again and again for my balsam ob mint, or my elixir ob prunes; but my greatest discovery, milady, my dear, was de use ob tiger-lily pollen for "superfluous hair." '

Lady Parvula moved uncomfortably in her chair. She was sufficiently alert to feel the animal magnetism from a persistent pair of eyes.

'*Wushi!*' Mrs. Yajñavalkya turned too.

'*Kataka?*' a voice came from the door.

'My relative Niri-Esther,' Mrs. Yajñavalkya explained, 'she ask me what I do.'

'She seems,' Lady Parvula commented, 'to have been crying.'

'She cry for a sting ob a wasp dat settle on her exposed bosom. I tell her—at de window—she shouldn't expose it!'

'Oh?'

'De wasps dis year dey are a plague.'

'*Kataka . . . ; kataka mukha?*'

Advancing with undulating hesitation, the young black girl brought with her a something of uttermost strangeness into the room.

Incontestably, she was of a superior caste to Mrs. Yajñavalkya, albeit her unorthodox values tended, perhaps, to obscure a little her fundamental merit.

She wore a dishabille of mignonette-green silk and a bead-diapered head-dress that added several inches to her height; her finger-slim ankles were stained with lac and there were rings of collyrium about her eyes.

With one hand clasped in the other behind her back, she stood considering Lady Parvula de Panzoust.

'*Chook*,' Mrs. Yajñavalkya grumbled.

'*Owesta wan?*'

'*Obaida.*'

'She has the exuberance of an orchid,' Lady Parvula cried. 'Could Sfax—he is my gardener down at Oomanton Towers—behold her now, he'd exclaim, "A Urania Alexis, your ladyship!" and pop her into a pot.'

'Niri-Esther's clothes, I sometimes venture to tink, are a little too vainglorious! ! ! At her age,' Mrs. Yajñavalkya retailed, 'and until I was past eighteen, I nebber had more in de course ob a year dan a bit ob cotton loincloth. You may wear it how you please, my poor mother would say, but dat is all you'll get! And so, dear me, I generally used to put it on my head.'

'She eyes one like a cannibal.'

'Are you quite well?' the young black woman waveringly asked.

Lady Parvula answered with a nod.

'Come here and show me,' she said.

'I drop de *mushrabiyas*—; so nobody den can see in!'

'Why O, why O,' Mrs. Yajñavalkya complained, 'will dat *hetæra's* horrid coachman draw up always just opposite to my gate?'

'She is later dan usual to-day,' her relative rejoined.

'Wears her horse,' the elder negress demanded, 'a rose?'

'De poor unhappy thing; he wear both a favour and a strap.'

'The looser the mistress . . . the tighter the bearing-rein!' Lady Parvula remarked.

Mrs. Yajñavalkya languished.

'She dribe her chestnut for day work, and reserbe a white for evening use. Not dat,' she amplified, 'one move more rapidly dan de other; no, oh no; Madame Mimosa refuse to dribe her horses fleet! She seldom elect to aribe betimes; she say it "good" to keep de clients waiting. It's a question ob policy wif her dat "two hours late."'

'I suppose simply to engender suspense.'

'*C'est une femme qui sait enrager. Allez!*'

'You know French?'

'Like ebberything else!'

Lady Parvula expanded.

'I said to my maid this morning: "Oh, Louison!" I said, "what does

180

the prommy place here remind you of?" "Of nothing, your lady-ship," replied she. "Oh, *doesn't* it?" I said; "well, it does me! It reminds me of the Promenade des Sept Heures at Spa." '

'Ah, de dear spot!'

'For brio, and for beauty and from the look of the trees, I said to her, it reminds me of the Promenade des Sept Heures at Spa.'

'You may go far before you will find a prettier place dan dis is.'

'True, I never go out but I see someone sketching.'

Mrs. Yajñavalkya was convulsed.

'A certain Valmouth widow, living yon side de church, found a Francis Fisher lately lying in her ditch (some small *plein-air* ob his, I suppose, he had thrown away), so she forwarded it to London just to ask what it would fetch, and sold it to a dealer for more dan fifty pounds.'

'Bravo. I must try to pick up a Vatt!'

'Curious how he faber de clodhopper type. Who would want to hang a beggar on his walls? Dair are enough in de world without. Believe me.'

'Indeed there are.'

'An artist I alvays admire, now,' the negress murmured, retying with coquetry her patient's shoe-string, 'is Mr. FitzGeorge! All his models are ladies ... daughters ob clergymen, daughters of colonels ... and even his male sitters are,' she twittered, 'sons ob good houses.'

'Someone should paint your niece!' Lady Parvula rose remarking.

'*Fanoui ah maha?*'

'*Tauroua ta.*'

'*Yahya.*'

'What's that she says?'

'That she will be glad to make music for you at any time.'

'That will be delightful.'

'And I, also,' the dark-skinned woman assumed her silkiest voice, 'will endeavour to have a few fugitive fowls over from de farm. De dogs shall bark, and de birds shall fly (de sky is full ob de whirring ob wings), but de lover and his beloved shall attain Nirvana.'

'Nirvana?'

'Leave it to me and you and he shall come together.'

'Oh, impossible.'

'Leave it to me.'

'I never run *any* risks,' Lady Parvula babbled.

'Risks! Vot risks? Risks?... O Allah la Ilaha! Shall I tell you vot de Yajñavalkya device is? Vot it has been dis thousand and thousand ob year? It is *bjopti. Bjopti!* And vot does *bjopti* mean? It means *discretion. S-s-s-s-s-s-s-s-s-s-s-s-s-s-s-s-s-s-s-s-s-s-sh!*'

Lady Parvula toyed reflectively with her rings.

'At balls in a quilted skirt and with diamonds in my hair I've often been hugely admired as a shepherdess,' she said. 'I well remember,' she tittered, 'the success I had one evening—it was at the British Embassy in Paris—as a shepherdess of Lely. I had a lamb (poor, innocent darling, but so heavy and so hot; worse than any child) with me, that sprang from my arms quite suddenly while I was using my powder-puff and darted bleating away beneath the legs of Lord Clanlubber (at that time ambassador) out into the Champs-Élysées, where it made off, I afterwards heard, towards the Etoile. And *I* never saw it again! So that you see,' she murmured, depositing her benefactress's fee vaguely upon the couch, 'I've a strong bond with shepherds, having myself, once, lost a lamb. . . .'

'In a like rig-up you would stir de soul ob Krishna, as de milk-maid Rádhá did!'

'I'm quite content to "stir" my neighbour instead.'

'Believe me,' the dark-skinned woman murmured, following her visitor to the stairhead, with a sigh that shook the house, 'he's awfully, awfully choice!'

'——...'

'He has a wee mole—on de forehead.'

'Ah, and he has another: yes! in the deep pool above his upper-lip—; the channel affair. . . .'

'He's *awfully* choice!'

'*C'est un assez beau garçon,*' Lady Parvula answered with a back-ward æsthetic glance.

Leaning from the hand-rail, like some adoring chimpanzee, Mrs. Yajñavalkya watched her recede, the wondrous crown of the vanishing hat suggesting forcibly the peculiar attributes of her own tribal gods.

The shadow upon the forewall of her little English maid descending the staircase with a chamber-pot from above recalled her to herself.

'Ah, *zoubé kareen pbf!* Why weren't you in readiness, Carry, to open de door?' she enquired, returning thoughtfully towards her sanctum with the intent to sterilise her tools.

On a spread kerchief, pitcher-posture, upon the floor her relative was bleaching idly her teeth with a worn bit of bone, while turning round and round like a water-wheel in her henna-smeared fingers the glass hoop-clasp at her abdomen.

Mrs. Yajñavalkya gave way to a joyous chuckle.

'Mrs. Richard Thoroughfare, Mrs. Richard Thoroughfare!' she addressed the prostrate belle.

'*Chakrawaki—wa?*'

'Mrs. Dick, Mrs. Thorough-dick, Mrs. Niri fairy!'

'*Suwhee?*'

With an eloquent listening eye, Mrs. Yajñavalkya laid a hand to her ear.

'De bridal litter,' she playfully announced, 'from Hare-Hatch House, is already at de far corner ob de adjacent street!'

The water-wheel ceased as the mauve lips parted.

'Ah, Vishnu!' the young black girl yawned. 'Vot den can make it come so slow?'

๙ *VI* ๙

A CAMPAIGN of summer storms of a quasi-tropical nature was delaying the hay harvest that in Valmouth, as in the neighbouring Garden Isles, was usually celebrated before the last week in May.

Not since the year 17—, when milord Castlebrilliant's curricle was whirled to sea with her ladyship within, had there been such vehement weather.

At Hare-Hatch House, the finest hornbeam upon the lawn had succumbed, none too silently, while in the park several of the centennial cedars were fallen, giving to the grounds somehow a tragic, classic look.

And indeed, with her favourite hornbeam, Mrs. Hurstpierpoint's nerves had also given way.

One afternoon, just as the bell of Nuestra Señora was sounding Terce, the lament of the peacocks announced a return of the storm. Since mid-day their plangent, disquieting cries had foretold its approach. Moving rapidly to and fro in their agitation, their flowing fans sweeping rhythmically the ground, they traced fevered curves beneath the overarching trees, orchestrating, with barbarity, as they did so, their strident screech with the clangour of the chapel bell that seemed, as it rang, to attract towards it a bank of tawny gold, cognac-coloured cloud, ominously fusing to sable.

Sauntering up and down in the shadow of the chapel wing the mistress of the manor, this afternoon, was also mingling her voice, intermittently, as though a plaintive, recurring motif in a slightly trying musical score, with her birds and her bell. 'Eliza! Eliza!' she called.

Seated upon the fallen hornbeam, Mrs. Thoroughfare was regarding distraitly the sky.

Ever since the windy weather a large pink kite like a six-humped camel had made above the near wood its extraneous appearance. To whom, Mrs. Thoroughfare asked herself, bewildered, could such a monstrous toy belong? There was something about it that alarmed her, alarmed her more than all the storm-clouds put together.

'Elizabeth!'

As if cleft by passing lightning the name on the tense hot air writhed lugubriously away amid the trees.

'In, in,' Mrs. Thoroughfare beseeched.

But Mrs. Hurstpierpoint had already turned towards the house, where an under-footman was busily closing the ground-floor windows against the dark, shining spots of falling rain. And falling too, Mrs. Thoroughfare noted, came the bewildering kite, head-foremost, as though jerked smartly earthward in the flyer's hand. A burst of near thunder sent her perforce to join her friend, whose finer, more delicate nature was ever apt to be affected by a storm.

She found her in a corner of the vast drawing-room clasping a 'blessed' rosary while listening in a state of compressed hysterics to the storm.

'I'm an old woman now': she was telling her beads: 'and my only wish it to put my life in order—was that another flash?'

'Darling.'

'Is that you, my little Lizzie?'

'Tchut! Eulalia.'

'Oh-h-h-h! . . . Betty dear! The *awful* vividness of the lightning!' Mrs. Hurstpierpoint wailed.

Through the nine tall windows with their sun-warped, useless shutters, like violet-darting swallows, the lightning forked.

'Let us go,' Mrs. Thoroughfare said in a slightly unsteady voice, 'shall we both, and confess?'

'Confess!'

'Father's in Nuestra now.'

'My dear, in my opinion, the lightning's so much more ghastly through the stained-glass windows!'

Mrs. Thoroughfare pressed her hands lightly to her admired associate's humid brow.

'Dear mother was the same,' she cooed. 'Whenever it thundered she'd creep away under her bed, and make the servants come and lie down on top . . . (it was in the eighteenth century of course . . .) so that should the brimstone burst it must vent its pristine powers on them. Poor innocent! It was during a terrific thunderstorm at Brighton, or *Brighthelmstone* as they called it then, that several of the domestics fell above her head. . . . And the fruits of that storm, as I believe I've told you before, Eulalia, are in the world to-day.'

'My dear . . . every time the weather breaks you must needs hark back to it.'

Mrs. Thoroughfare showed pique.

'Well *I*,' she said, ambling undeterred towards the door, 'intend to pray.'

'Who knows but our prayers may meet?' Mrs. Hurstpierpoint murmured, returning to her beads, that in the sombre brilliance of the darkened room shed different pale and supernatural lights as they swung from side to side in her nerveless hands.

'Adorable Jesus,' her mouth moved faintly beneath the charcoal shadow of her moustache, 'love me even as I do Thee, and I,' she deeply breathed, 'will land Thee a fish! I will hook Thee a heretic; even though,' her tongue passed wistfully over her lips, 'to gain an open sinner I should be impelled to go to London, O Lord; for I will bend to Thy Sovereign Purpose (irrespective of my little kitchen-maid whom I most certainly mean to force) a thorough-going infidel; something very putrid . . . very lost. And so, O my Saviour Dear,' beatifically she raised her face, 'I will make Thee retribution for the follies of my youth.'

Her lips grew still.

From the adjacent chapel soft, insinuating voices assailed agreeably the ear.

'Victories . . .' 'Vanquish . . .' 'Virtue . . .' 'Virgin . . .'

Mrs. Hurstpierpoint's veiled glance dropped from her rafters,

hovering with a certain troubled diffidence over the ruff and spade-
beard of a dashing male portrait, until it dwelt on the face of the
time-piece on the commode below, so placed as to exclude as far as
possible the noble arch of her kinsman's shapely legs. The slow beat
of the flower-wreathed pendulum usually filled the room.

Long ago, it was related, it had been consulted in an hour of most
singular stress. And it was as if still some tragic pollen of anguish-
staring eyes clung to the large portentous numerals of the Louis-
Sixteenth dial. Two steel key-holes in the white full face loomed
now like beauty patches in the flickering light.

'I feel I'm ready for my tea,' Mrs. Hurstpierpoint reflected, taking
up an invalidish posture on the jaguar-skin couch.

The inebriating, slightly acrid perfume of a cobra lily, wilting
in its vase, awoke solicitous thought within her of her distant heir.

Soon the dear lad would give up his junketings, she mused, and
take to himself a wife.

Her eyes absorbed fondly the room.

'Ah! Ingres!' she sighed, 'your portrait of me is still indeed most
like . . . more like and much more pleasing, I think, than the marble
Dalou did. . . .' And fearful lest she should fall a victim to her own
seductiveness, against the peevish precepts of the church, she averted
her eyes towards the young naval officer in the carved Renaissance
frame, into whose gold-wrapped, slim-wristed hands, with the long
and lissom fingers swelling towards their tips like big drop pearls,
Hare-Hatch House and all its many treasures would one day pass.

A flare of dazzling brightness on the wainscoting caused her to
knit her brows, and like a tall reed, wrapped in silk, her maid,
wheeling a light chaufferette, advanced towards her.

'Is the worst of the storm yet over, Fowler, do you consider?'
Mrs. Hurstpierpoint gently groaned.

The maid's sallow-face, flame-lit, looked malign as she drooped
her trim-coiffed head.

'Now that the wind has deprived the statues of their fig leaves,
'm,' she replied, 'I hardly can bear to look out.'

'Oh? *Has* it? What? Again?'

'All around the courtyard and in the drive you'd think it was
October from the way they lie!'

'Sister Ecclesia will be distressed going home, I fear. Even *an
altar-cupid*—— She's so sensitive,' Mrs. Hurstpierpoint remarked.

'It's mostly dark 'm, before she's done.'

186

'Unless the summer quickly mends the Hundred Club's fête must be postponed!'

'It's odd, 'm,' the waiting woman answered, adding a pinch of incense to the fire, 'how many a centenarian seems more proof against exposure than others not yet in their prime. Only a short while since my Lady Parvula's maid—she's been spending the day here among us—got caught in the wet while taking a turn with Miss Fencer and Nit; and now there she is, sitting before the kitchen range, in borrowed hose, with a glass of hot toddy.'

'I dare say her licentious stories have brought on this storm!'

'She was very full to be sure at meal-time of a fraudulent marriage, saying how no one or nothing was inviolate or safe.'

'The sole dependable marriage is the Spiritual marriage! On that alone can we implicitly rely.'

'And she was very full, too, of her ladyship's jewelled pyjamas.'

'Holy Virgin!'

'The storm sounds almost above us.'

'Lift the lid of the long casket—and pick me a relic,' Mrs. Hurstpierpoint enjoined, surveying apprehensively the dark clumps of wind-flogged trees upon the lawn.

'Any one in particular, 'm?' the maid enquired, slipping, with obedient alacrity, across the floor.

'No; but not a leg-bone, mind! A leg-bone relic somehow——' she broke off, searching with her great dead eye dreaming the sad camphor-hued hills for the crucifix and wayside oratory that surmounted the topmost peak.

'You used to say the toe, 'm, of the married sister of the Madonna, the one that was a restaurant proprietress (Look alive there with those devilled kidneys, and what is keeping Fritz with that sweet-omelette?), in any fracas was particularly potent.'

'Yes . . . bring the toe of the Madonna's married sister, and then come and read to me out of Père Pujol,' her mistress answered, it being one of her chosen modes of penance (as well as a convenient means of paving the way to papalism) to call from time to time on her servants to come and read to her aloud. How often afterwards, in the soundless watches of the night, must the tonic words of a Pujol, or a brother Humphrey Caton, recur to dull procrastinating minds linked, made earthly in souvenir, with her own kind encouraging looks! Indeed, as a certain exalted churchman had excellently expressed it once, Oral-punishment, the mortification of the sparkling ear, was more delightful to heaven inasmuch as frequently it was more far-reaching than a knot in a birch or a nail in a boot.

But with Fowler, one of the earliest converts of the house, there was no need any more to push to extremes.

'*Figlia mia*,' she jarringly began with a great thick 'G' fully equal, her mistress reckoned, to a plenary indulgence alone, '*figlia mia*, examine your conscience, ask your heart, invoke that inner voice which always tells the truth, and never, no, never, betrays us! For the spark will live through the rains, lighting up dead fires: fire which is still fire, but with purer flame. . . .'

'Lest your cap-pin kindles, *presto* there. Never,' Mrs. Hurstpierpoint intervened, 'read of bad weather during storm!'

'One day St. Automona di Meris, seeing a young novice yawning, suddenly spat into her mouth, and *that* without malice or thought of mischief. Some ninety hours afterwards the said young novice brought into the world the Blessed St. Elizabeth Bathilde, who, by dint of skipping, changed her sex at the age of forty and became a man.'

'A *man*—! Don't speak to me of *men*. Especially one of that description!' Mrs. Hurstpierpoint rapped. 'Inflict something else.'

'Something more poetical perhaps?'

'What is that thick, twine-coloured linen book I see the back of, beneath the young mistress's shawl?'

'Anthropology again, I expect, 'm,' Fowler answered.

'This craze for anthropology with her is something altogether new.'

'It frets her to form no idea of the tribes the Captain's been among.'

'It only makes her dream. She was talking so (being forced to fly to my little rosewood night-stool, I overheard her) in her sleep again.'

'Miss Fencer was saying so, too. Only this morning (in calling her) she heard her say: "I will *not* go in beads to the opera." (Or was it "berries" she said?) "Tell King Mbmonbminbon so!" Anyway, Miss Fencer was so completely seized she just emptied the early tea vessel on to the floor.'

Mrs. Hurstpierpoint exchanged with her maid a lingering, expressive glance.

'I *know* she's worried! I *know* she's keeping something from me! and I *know* she'll tell me in the end!' so the dependent, who was apt to read her mistress's face with greater accuracy than she did her books, interpreted the glance.

'The volume I find, 'm, beneath the shawl,' she said, 'is the *Tales from Casanova.*'

'Child that my soul's treasure is!' There was a second significant glance.

'Well, well; for St. Francis's sake,' Mrs. Hurstpierpoint said, steeling herself to listen, 'an Italian story is always permitted at Hare.'

'There was once upon a time two sisters,' Fowler falteringly began, 'named Manette and Marton, who lived with a widowed aunt, a certain Madame Orio, in the city of Venice. The disposition of these fair Venetians was such that——, such——,' she floundered.

'Their disposition? . . . Yes? It was such?'

'Such——'

'That?'

' . . . Well, I declare!'

'How often, Fowler,' Mrs. Hurstpierpoint said with some asperity, 'must I beg you not to employ that ridiculous phrase in my hearing?'

'Very good, 'm, but it's all Portuguese to *me*! . . . And wagged his Persian tail.'

'Go on.'

'One evening,' she went on, 'while Madame Orio was fast asleep in her little belvedere (it being the good old lady's habit to repair there to rest after a bottle or two of red Padua wine), Manette and Marton left the widow's house noiselessly in the Campo San Zobenigo, and made their way running towards the Piazza of St. Mark's. It was a radiant night in early April. All Venice was in the open air. The moon, which——'

Listening with detached attention lest her ears should be seduced and tickled rather than soundly chastened, Mrs. Hurstpierpoint's mind turned somewhat sombrely to her future connection with her heir's fiancée. Some opinionated, wrong-headed creature, *une femme mal pensante*, in the house, she mused, would be indeed tormenting. While on the other hand, of course, Dick's bride *might* add a new interest to the place; in which case Elizabeth's attitude too would be sure to change.

Mrs. Hurstpierpoint plied speculatively her beads, catching between her *Aves* just enough of the tale to be able to follow its drift.

Music, she heard. Those sisters ✠ a ripe and rich marquesa ✠ strong proclivities ✠ a white starry plant ✠ water ✠ lanterns ✠ little streets ✠ Il Redentore ✠ Pasqualino ✠ behind the Church of ✠ Giudecca ✠ gondola ✠ Lido ✠ Love ✠ lagoon ✠ Santa Orsola ✠ the Adriatic——

With a sigh at the mutability of things, she realised that with a young daughter-in-law of her own Elizabeth would no longer be towards her her same gracious self. With the advent of Dick's wife a potential disturbing force would enter Hare. New joy would bring new sorrow. Whoever he might choose to marry, intrigue, jealousy would seldom be far away. Should Gilda Vintage be the *partie,* the Lady Parvula de Panzoust with her irrelevant souvenirs would be a constant figure at Hare: she would 'come over' probably quite easily—sooner, even, than her daughter! 'And her *First* Confession,' Mrs. Hurstpierpoint ruminated with a crucial, fleeting smile, 'if (by some little harmless strategy) I could arrange it, I should dearly love to hear!'

Her cogitations were interrupted by the return of Mrs. Thoroughfare, leading by the hand a reluctant Poor Clare for a cup of tea.

Proscribed by her Order to Silence, and having nothing in her physiognomy to help her out, Sister Ecclesia's position at present was one of peculiar difficulty and constraint.

In the Convent of Arimathæa, at Sodbury hard by Hare whence she came, her indiscreet talkativeness had impelled a wise, if severe, Mother-Superior to impose upon her the *Torture* of Silence—which supplice had led her inevitably into tricks; Sister Ecclesia had contracted mannerisms therefrom. Though uttering no audible word her lips seldom were till. Strangers sometimes took her to be a saint, in touch with heaven. Bursting to speak she would frequently, when in society, shake clenched hands in the air impotently like a child. Sometimes, in order to find an outlet to her pent emotions, she would go as far as to kick and to pinch, and even to dance (her spirited hornpipes with Captain Thoroughfare were much admired at Hare), while with a broomstick she was invaluable—a very tigress—drawing blood directly. Indeed, as Mrs. Hurstpierpoint was wont to say, her arm seemed born for a birch. Thrice a year Sister Ecclesia was allowed the use of her tongue when instead of seeking intercourse among the nuns she would flit off quite alone towards the sea-shore and blend her voice with the errant gulls until her unrestrained cries and screams frequently caused her to faint.

With vacuous, half-closed lids, Mrs. Hurstpierpoint accepted her generous shower-bath of Eau Bénite.

'Out? Already,' she murmured, simultaneously offering her hand on one side while abandoning her lips on the other.

'And oh! Eulalia,' Mrs. Thoroughfare's voice shook with inflections, 'who should one find in Nuestra Señora . . . (in the Capella Love of the Salutation) but Lady Violet Logg? Lady Violet! Elegant to tears, and with two such wisps of boys! Boys of about seventeen —or eighteen, Eulalia! Like the mignons of Henry the Third.'

'I suppose . . . no umbrella.'

'And I am sure that Edie's pricked.'

'I know of more than one in the house to be wobbling!' Fowler averred as with rush-like gait at the view of the butler's crane-like legs, harbinger of the tea-board (in the dark of his mind might he not aspire to build with her? Swoop! Fly to church with her: make a nest of her? Snatch at her? Bend her, break her—God knew how!— to his passions' uses?), she flexibly withdrew.

'If anyone calls, ffines,' Mrs. Hurstpierpoint said, rousing herself and running a hand to her half-falling hair, 'better simply say I'm out.'

'Les-bia—ah-h . . . !' Mrs. Thoroughfare struck a few chords airily on the open piano.

'And, ffines . . . an extra cup.'

'An extra, 'm?'

'Insensate!'

'Hitherto, 'm (and I've seen some choice service I am sure) I always gave entire satisfaction.'

'You never saw choicer service (I am quite sure) than with *me*, ffines,' Mrs. Hurstpierpoint said, complacently adjusting a pin. 'And I'd have you to remember it!'

'Julia, Duchess of Jutland thought the world of me.'

'And so do I, ffines. I think the world of you too—*this* world! . . ."

'White Mit-y-lene . . .' Mrs. Thoroughfare broke melodiously in, 'where the gir——'

'What was that song about lilacs, Lizzie?' Mrs. Hurstpierpoint, turning to her, asked.

'*Lilacs*, Eulalia?'

'Something to do with lilacs: *lilas en fleur*; an old air of France.'

'Le temps des lilas et le temps des roses,
Ne reviendra plus à ce printemps ci.
Le temps de lilas et les temps des roses
Est passé, le temps des œillets aussi.

Le vent a changé les cieux sont moroses,
Et nous n'irons plus courir et cueillir
Les lilas en fleur et les belles roses;
Le printemps est triste et ne peut fleurir.

Oh, joyeux et doux printemps de l'année
Qui vint, l'an passé, nous ensoleiller,
Notre fleur d'amour est si bien fanée.
Las! que ton baiser ne peut l'eveiller.

Et toi, que fais-tu? pas de fleurs écloses,
Point de gai soleil ni d'ombrages frais;
Le temps des lilas et le temps des roses
Avec notre amour est mort à jamais.'

Mrs. Thoroughfare's voice ebbed.

'May a woman know, dear,' Mrs. Hurstpierpoint softly said, 'when she may receive her drubbing?'

'Oh I've no strength left in me to-day, Eulalia, I fear, for anything,' Mrs. Thoroughfare answered.

'Positively?'

'Ask Ecclesia!'

But with the French song over Sister Ecclesia had edged, with much wild grace, from the room.

'She's returned to her prayers, I suppose.'

'Or to Father.'

'Happily, quite in vain!'

'*Chè volete?*'

'I miss Père Ernest,' Mrs. Hurstpierpoint sighed, leisurely sipping her tea.

'Yes, dear, but he had too many ultramontane habits. . . . There was really no joy in pouring out one's sins while he sat assiduously picking his nose.'

'Which reminds me,' Mrs. Hurstpierpoint serenely said, 'to gather my nectarines. . . .'

192

'Your nectarines . . . ?'

'Sir Victor begs me for a few nectarine models. Nectarines meet to sit to him. Not *too* ripe.'

'I should think he only wanted them for himself,' Mrs. Thoroughfare cooed, opening wide a window that commanded an outlook of the lawns.

The atmosphere was clearer now. Before the house the mutilated statues and widowed urns showed palely white against a sky palely blue through which a rainbow was fast forming. By the little garden pergola open to the winds some fluttered peacocks were blotted nervelessly amid the dripping trees, their heads sunk back beneath their wings: while in the pergola itself, like a fallen storm-cloud, lolled a negress, her levelled, polecat eyes semi-veiled by the nebulous alchemy of the rainbow.

'What are you doing fiddle-faddling over there, Elizabeth?' Mrs. Hurstpierpoint asked.

'Look, Eulalia,' Mrs. Thoroughfare said, catching her breath, 'someone with a kite is on our lawn!'

Mrs. Hurstpierpoint was impelled to smile.

'In the old days,' she murmured, brushing a few crumbs from her gown, 'sailing a kite heavenward was my utmost felicity. No ball of string, I remember, was ever long enough!'

'This is no christian and her kite, Eulalia, or I'm much mistaken. . . .'

'No christian, Elizabeth?'

'It's a savage.'

Mrs. Hurstpierpoint sank humbly to her knees.

'*Gloria in Excelsis tibi Deo!*' she solemnly exclaimed.

৯ৼ *VII* ৯ৼ

THE plaintive pizzicato of Madame Mimosa's Pom pup 'Plum Bun' aroused Mrs. Yajñavalkya one triumphal summer morning while lying in the voluminous feather-bed that since lately she shared with her niece.

'*Zbaffa pbf!*' she complained, addressing an ape-like image, cut in jade, that stood at the bed-end, its incensed arms and elongated eyes defensively alert. Beside her Niri-Esther, indiscreetly *enceinte*, was still asleep.

'O de worries!' the negress murmured, leaving indolently her bed and hitching higher the blind.

It was Market morning. . . . Beneath a mottled sky some score or so of little carts covered in frail tarpaulins of unnamable sun-scorched colours were mustered before the Daleman Memorial where already a certain amount of petty chicanery had begun.

'Dat is a scene now which somehow make me smile,' Mrs. Yajñavalkya commented. 'Ya Allah, but whenever I see a Market I no longer feel Abroad. . . . And w'y, I wonder, is de reason ob dis? . . . Because human nature is de same ebberywhere.'

'Any old flint glass or broken bottles for a poor woman to-day?' a barrow-hawker smote into her reflections from below.

Mrs. Yajñavalkya indrew her head.

It was one of her fullest mornings, being the eve of Mrs. Hurst-pierpoint's reunion in honour of the centenarians of the place, who together with their progeny assembled yearly in the closed drawing-rooms, or beneath the titanic cedars, of Hare.

And for these annual resuscitations Mrs. Yajñavalkya's invigor-ating touch was deemed almost indispensable.

Consulting her tablets, she found Tooke's Farm to be first on her list, when it might be that the dairyman himself would be about. Disheartening contretemps had followed hitherto her every intri-guing effort. He had responded to her summons to 'take a look at the Vine' in the small grape-house at the extremity of the garden, politely, if unorthodoxly enough, bringing with him, with Mrs. Tooke's 'compliments,' a sumptuous barrowful of well-seasoned offal, whereat Lady Parvula de Panzoust, poised like a Bacchante amid the drooping grapes, had taken to fastidious heels in alarm.

'If I cannot throw dem both together,' she brooded, 'be it only out ob doors . . . I will be obliged to quench lub's fever wif a sedative.'

The venerable dial of St. Veronica's wood clock, and a glimpse of Nurse Yates' under-sized form crossing the Square, advised her not to dawdle, and soon she, too, was threading her way amid the arguing yokels and the little carts.

Beneath a strip of awning that shook slightly in the soft sea air a sailor with eyes like sad sapphires was showing a whale caught in the bay, to view which he asked a penny. Partially hid within a fishing creel it brought back to Mrs. Yajñavalkya the unfaithful wives of her own native land who were cast as a rule to the sharks.

Refusing payment only to revive poignant memories of aunts and cousins, sisters and sisters-in-law, as well as a close escape of her own, Mrs. Yajñavalkya disdainfully moved away.

In a cottage garden at the corner of the market-place she could distinguish the sexton of St. Veronica's meandering round his beehives in a white paper mask. From his shuffling step and obvious air of preoccupation, it was as though in some instinctive way he was aware that the consequences of the Hare-Hatch rout would shortly drive him to 'resume' his spade.

Flitting fleetly by, Mrs. Yajñavalkya attained the weather-beaten farmyard gate where, grinning as he watched her approach, stood Bobby Jolly.

'Is your master in, you little giggling Valmouth goose?' she enquired.

'David? He won't be back till evenfall.'

'Oho?'

'He's felling trees in Wingley Woo,' the child replied, looking up quizzically into the negress's face.

Between his long curly lashes were blue eyes—not very deep: a slight down, nearly white, sprouted below a dainty little nose, just above the lip at the two corners.

'No matter. So long as the dear dowager has not gone with him,' Mrs. Yajñavalkya replied, jauntily entering the yard. On the dung-hill that rose against the church to the sill of the clerestory-windows lay Douce—treacherously asleep, his muzzle couched on a loose forepaw.

'He leave behind de dog?'

''Cos of pheasants.'

Mrs. Yajñavalkya shaded her brow from the sun with her hand. Through an open barn she could trace the River Val winding leisurely coastward through cornfields white with glory. A hum of bees from the flower plat by the garden wall filled the air with a ceaseless sound and raised the mind up to Allah.

She chanced on Mrs. Tooke essaying the effect of a youthful little cap before the glass.

'Charming,' the negress cried. 'Delicious!'

Decked with silk bandstrings and laces, the old lady's long bluish profile, calcined on the grave-ground without, recalled to Mrs.

Yajñavalkya one of the incomparable Dutch paintings assigned to Franz Hals, in Evadne, Duchess of Valmouth's boudoir.

'Faith, my dear,' Mrs. Tooke exclaimed, 'but you frightened me.'

'And how do you find yourself, Mrs. Tooke, to-day?' the negress archly asked.

Troubled at being surprised in an act of vanity, a thing she professed to abhor, Mrs. Tooke was inclined to be captious.

'To-day I feel only passably well, Mrs. Yaj,' she replied.

'I've seen you worse, Mrs. Tooke.'

'I fear I shall soon become now a portion for foxes.'

'Dat is for me to say, Mrs. Tooke.'

'I ha'n't the constitution at all that I had.'

'De prospect ob a function may have occasioned a touch ob fever; nothing but a little cerebral excitement, de outcome ob neurasthenia, which my methods, I hope, will remove.'

'I wish I hadn't a wen, Mrs. Yaj! A sad hash your methods made of it.'

'De more you cauterise a wen, Mrs. Tooke . . . Besides, wot's de good ob worry? Not poppy, nor mandragora, nor all the drowsy syrups of the world, shall ever soothe it or medicine it away. Remember.'

Mrs. Tooke sighed submissively.

'Where did I put my Bible?' she plaintively asked, peering around the long-familiar room.

'I wonder you're not tired ob your Bible, Mrs. Tooke.'

'Fie! Mrs. Yaj. You shouldn't speak so.'

'You should read de Talmud for a change.'

'It sounds a poor exchange.'

'Do you really believe now, Mrs. Tooke my dear, in de Apostolic Succession? Can you look me in de eyes and say you do?'

'I ha'n't paid any heed lately to those chaps, Mrs. Yaj; I'm going on to Habakkuk.'

'Was not he de companion ob de Prodigal son?'

'Maybe he was, my dear. He seems to have known a good many people.'

'Dat is not de name now ob a man, Mrs. Tooke, to observe a single wife, nor even a single sex. . . . No! Oh no; a man wif a name like dat would have his needs!'

'Heysey-ho! We most of us have our wants.'

'From all one hears, Mrs. Tooke, your grandson hasn't many.'

'Yoiks, Mrs. Yaj! He was at me just now for a Bull.'

'And do you tell me so, Mrs. Tooke?'

'A farm's no farm without a Bull, says he; and t'other day 'twas a shorthorn milcher he'd have had me buy.'

'He seems insensitive to women, Mrs. Tooke! I think, my dear, he never was truly enmeshed.'

'He's unimpressionable, I'm thankful to say.'

'I know ob one now, Mrs. Tooke, who would be glad to be on his two legs again to-morrow night—and who *will* be, my dear, I dare say, although I did refuse him.'

Mrs. Tooke evinced detachment.

'They tell me Doris Country's dress is being edged with ermine,' she observed, fastening her eye on a piece of old Valmouth ware representing a dog with a hen in its mouth, that occupied the dresser.

'You'll need your *boa* as de nights are chilly.'

' 'Od: I've no ermine skin myself!'

'Dair are furs besides ermine, Mrs. Tooke. Wot is dair smarter dan a monkey's tail trimmed in black lace?—wid no stint mind to de strings; dat is a combination dat always succeed.'

'Belike.'

'In my land ermine, you know, is exclusive to de khan or, as you would say, de king.'

'His Majesty, the Can!' the old lady shyly marvelled.

'He my beloved sovereign.'

'And your Queens (I presume) are Pitchers?'

'Never you mind now, Mrs. Tooke, never you mind! but just let me rub a little ob dis on de seat ob your ovaries; de same as I did once to a Muscovite princess. . . . "Your magic hand, my dear," she say, "it bring such joy and release. . . ." '

'I wish I had your brawn, Mrs. Yaj!'

'Noble, or ignoble, Mrs. Tooke, I treat my clients just de same!'

'You old black bogey, what should I do without you?'

'*Inshallah!*' The negress shrugged, glancing over her shoulder at a sudden sneeze from Miss Tooke behind her.

Bearing in her arms the sacrificial linen, she waded forward in a ray of dusty sunlight, as if fording in fancy the turbid Val that should transport her to Love's transcendent delights, in illimitable, jewelly seas.

'It's a hard thing, Mrs. Yaj,' Mrs. Tooke observed, 'to be depen-

dent on a wench who spends half her life in the river! If *I* was a
fish I'd snap at her legs.'

'I've no doubt you would, Mrs. Tooke, but joking, my dear,
apart, unless as a finish to a douche cold water I always discom-
mend. Dair (in moderation no doubt) it is good; otherwise in my
opinion it is injurious to de circulation, impeding and clogging de
natural channels and so hampering de course ob de blood, and
often even gibbing excuse to de body's worst enemy ob all—I mean
de gastric juices.'

Mrs. Tooke's brows knit together. She scowled.

'Let her keep her distance,' she exclaimed, 'with her contagious
heavy cold!'

'I am sure I've no will to come near you,' Miss Tooke replied with
a desolating sigh as she fell to earth.

She was looking restless and pale and strangely avid for love.

'You'll not die in an old skin if you fret it so, Thetis girl, ah,
that ye won't.'

'What's the use of living then? Life is only acceptable on the
condition that it is enjoyed.'

Mrs. Tooke blinked, eluded.

'Belike,' she said, 'by God's grace to-morrow night we'll both
have a bit of a fling. Oh-ay, I do mind the nestful of field-mice we
had in the spring-cart last year. I had been out all day among the
clover, but, Lord! I never knew 'twas full of they mice, till a satyr,
in livery, shoved his hand (like a sauce-box) into the cart, under
pretext of helping me down, when pouf! out they all hopped from
under my train, furnishing the tag-rag and bobtail there was standing about with all manner of *immund* remarks. . . .'

'And where was this, Mrs. Tooke?' the negress aloofly asked.

'Why at Hare, Mrs. Yaj, last year.'

Miss Tooke sighed again, and drawing a cut citron from her
apron pocket she applied it gently (as directed by 'Susuva' in
The Woman's Friend) to the roots of her nails.

> 'When I am dead
> Ah bring me flow-ers,
> Spread roses and forget-me-nots,'

she somewhat hectically hummed.

'You bits of raw shoots seldom hark to any sense, though 'twere
better often to be a primrose in the wilderness than a polyanthus in

a frame. And you'll remember, maybe, I said so, when I'm grassed down in the earth and gone,' Mrs. Tooke declared, riveting her attention on the tombstones below.

Several of the nearer epitaphs were distinctly legible through the farmstead windows, such as '*Josephine—first wife of Q. Comedy Esqre died of Jealousy, March 31st 1898: Remember her*,' while the rest, monotonously identical, for the most part betokened 'inconsolable widows' and were nothing, according to Mrs. Tooke (who had eyes for a wedding as well as for a funeral), but 'a "——" tangle of lies!' One gaunt, tall cross, however, half hidden by conifers, a little apart, almost isolated, solitary, alone, was, to the excellent English-woman, in its provocativeness, as a chalk egg is to a sensitive hen. Here lay Balty Vincent Wise, having lived and died—*unmarried*. Oh what a funny fellow! Oh what a curious man! . . . What did he mean by going off like that? Was no woman good enough for him then? Oh what a queer reflection to be sure; what a slur on all her sex! Oh but he should have settled; ranged himself as every bache-lor should! Improper naughty thing! He should be exorcised and whipped: or had he loved? Loved perchance *elsewhere* . . . ? The subject of many a fluttered reverie he gave, by his eccentric manes, just that touch of mystery, that piquant interest to the churchyard that inwardly she loved—Balty!

'There are times, Mrs. Yaj, when I find the look-out cheerless.'

'Still! Radder dan see "Marsh-lights" . . .'

'Ah . . . I shall never forget how Mr. Comedy (when he lost his first wife) passed the night in the graveyard, crying and singing and howling, with a magnum of Mumm. . . .'

With a wry little laugh Miss Tooke turned and moved away.

'Since you've all, then, you need,' she said, 'I'll take a pail of clams and yams, I think, to feed the pigs.'

'Let 'em farrow if they choose, and keep clear of the river, mind; don't let me hear of you in the Val again to-day.'

'The Val! You ought to see the Ganges, Mrs. Tooke! Ah, dat is some river indeed.'

'In what way, Mrs. Yaj?'

'A girl may loiter there with her amphora and show her ankles to de fleets of sailing sampans often to her advantage. . . . Many a match-making mother have I known, my dear, to send her daughter to stand below some eligible Villa with instructions to toy for an hour with her crock.'

'As I'm a decent widow, Mrs. Yaj, you negresses are a bad lot, I'm afraid.'

'O w'y?'

'I expect it's something to do with your climate.'

'We Eastern women love the sun . . . ! When de thermometer rise to some two hundred or so, ah dat is de time to lie among de bees and canes.'

'I could never stand the stew——, it would take all *my* stamina.'

'My little maid, Carry, is de same as you. De least spell ob warmth prostrate her wid de vertigoes.'

'You've had her some time now, Mrs. Yaj.'

'So I have, Mrs. Tooke, so I have; dô I say often I've a mind to take a page; but a growing boy in de house, my dear—you *know* what dey are! However, Carry I soon shall have to dismiss. . . . She dat otiose! She dat idle! She will read by de hour from my medical dictionary, dô I defend her eber to open it, because dair are tings she is perhaps better without de knowledge ob! *Kra*. And how she wreck my china! Before I came to dis place I had no stylish services; but I would go out and pick myself a plate ob a fresh green leaf, and den wen it had served its purpose, after each course, I would just throw it away; and like dat dair was no expense, and none ob dese breakages at all.'

'Well, there are plenty of pleasant trees round Valmouth, Mrs. Yaj, I'm sure; and you're welcome to flower-leaf or vegetable from these acres, my dear, at any time; you shall sup off Dock a-Monday, and Cabbage Tuesday, Violet-hearts on Wednesday, Ivy Thursday, Nettle Friday, King Solomon's seal Saturday, and Sunday, you old black caterpillar, you can range as you please through the grass.'

'I have my own little garden, Mrs. Tooke, my dear, you forget: but dat white calf now out yonder . . . my niece beg me to say she'd buy it, as she desire to sacrifice it to a certain goddess for private family reasons.'

'For shame, Mrs. Yaj. It makes me sad to hear you talk like a heathen.'

'Such narrow prejudice; for I suppose it will only go to de butcher in de end?'

'Disgusting.'

'Butchers are so brutal, Mrs. Tooke . . . ! Dair hearts must be so unkind . . . men without mercy! And dat's wot I alvays say.'

'Ts!'

'And remember dis, my dear. It is for her deity and not for herself she seek the calf.'

'Be quiet.'

'Niri-Esther only relish roots, a dish ob white roots and fruits—unless dis last few day, when she express a fancy for water-melon jam! But where I say in Valmouth can you find water-melon jam? O de worries, Mrs. Tooke!'

'I ha'n't seen her kite so much lately, Mrs. Yaj.'

'Babies are so tender. . . . Little children are so frail . . .' the negress said to herself aloud.

'What's that, my dear?'

'I miss a mosque, Mrs. Tooke, and de consolation ob de church; but when I turn to Allah, I suppose de Holy Mihrab near to me and den,' the negress murmured, bestowing a parting pinch upon the aged dame, 'all is well.'

Her day indeed was but begun. In many a cloud-swept village bespattering the hills her presence was due anon.

Issuing from the farm-house she hovered to consider the itinerary ahead—culminating picturesquely (towards sunset) in a ruined stomach—some six miles from the town. Deliberatingly traversing the yard, where, here and there, fowl were pecking negligently at their shadows, she recognised in the penumbra of a cart-shed the arrowy form of Lady Parvula de Panzoust.

She wore a dress of becoming corduroy and a hat all rose-pink feathers, the little basket upon her arm signifying, evidently—*eggs*.

Following her (with more perhaps than his habitual suspicion) was churlish Douce.

'Poor, dear, beautiful, patient beast!' the negress could hear her say in tones of vivacious interest as she fondled the dog's supple back and long, soft, nervelessly drooping ears. Then suddenly stooping, she exclaimed vehemently, as if transported: 'Kiss me, Bushy!'

𝕯ॡ *VIII* ॡ𝕯

IT was the auspicious night when as to a Sabbat the centenarians of Valmouth, escorted by twittering troops of expectant heirs and toad-eating relatives, foregathered together, like so many warlocks and witches, in the generously loaned drawing-rooms and corridors of Hare.

Originating in the past with the corporation, as a subtle advertisement to the salubrity of the climate, these reunions were now in such high favour that the Valmouth Town Hall, a poor poky place, was no longer capable of holding so numerous an attendance, obliging the municipality to seek a more convenient rendezvous elsewhere; hence the cordial offer of the Hare ladies to 'throw open' their doors annually had been accepted officially with a thousand pleasant thanks; and by degrees, by dint of some acted *Mystery*, played to perfection by the Nuns of Sodbury and the Oblates of Up-More, these reunions had afforded full scope for the diplomatic furtherance of Rome.

Something of Limbo, perhaps, was felt by those at present gathered in the long salon, bafflingly lit by an old-fashioned chain-chandelier that threw all the light upwards, towards the ceiling, leaving the room below (to the untold relief of some) in semi-obscurity; but, the night being fine, many preferred to wander out attracted by the silken streamers of a vast marquee.

Leaning on the arm of a swathed tangerine figure, Mrs. Hurst-pierpoint, decked in wonderful pearls like Titian's Queen of Cyprus, trailed about beneath the mounting moon, greeting here and there a contemporary with vague cognition. She seemed in charming spirits.

'Your ladyship dribbles!' she complacently commented, shaking from the curling folds of her dress a pious leaflet, *The —— of Mary,* audaciously scouting the Augustinian theory 'that the Blessed Virgin conceived our Lord through the Ears.'

Looking demurely up she saw wide azure spaces stabbed with stars like many Indian pinks.

The chimeric beauty of the night was exhilarating.

In the heavy blooming air the rolling, moon-lit lawns and great old toppling trees stretched away, interfusing far off into soft deeps of velvet, dark blue violet, void.

'The last time I went to the play,' the tangerine figure fluted, 'was with Charles the Second and Louise de Querouaille, to see Betterton play Shylock in *The Merchant of Venice*.'

'Was he so fine?' Mrs. Hurstpierpoint asked, her query drowned in a dramatic dissonance from the pergola—climax to a blood-stirring waltz.

On the lawn-sward couples were revolving beneath the festooned trees that twinkled convivially with fairy lamps, but the centre of attraction, perhaps, at present was the Mayor.

'Congratulations,' his voice pealed out, 'to Peggy Laughter, Ann and Zillah Bottom, Almeria Goatpath, Thisbe Brownjohn, Teresa Twistleton, Rebecca Bramblebrook, Junie Jones, Susannah Sneep, Peter Palafox, Flo Flook, Simon Toole, Molly Ark, Nellie Knight, Fanny Beard, May Thatcher, May Heaven, George Kissington, Tircis Tree, Gerry Bosboom, Gilbert Soham, Lily Quickstep, Doris Country, Anna Clootz, Mary Teeworthy, Dorothy Tooke, Patrick Flynn, Rosa Sweet, Laurette Venum, Violet Ebbing, Horace Hardly, Mary Wilks——'

'*In saeculum saeculi,* apparently!' Mrs. Hurstpierpoint shrugged.

On the fringe of the throng, by a marble shape of Priapus green with moss, Lady Parvula de Panzoust was listening, as if petrified at her thoughts, to the Mayor.

'I shall never forget her,' the tangerine bundle breathed, 'one evening at Salsomaggiore——!'

'For a fogy, she's not half bad, is she, still?'

'I consider her a charming, persuasive, still beautiful, and *always* licentious woman. . . .'

'And with the art . . . not of returning thistles for figs?'

'There are rumours—I dare say you know—of an affair here in the town.'

'Poor Parvula . . . ! a scandal, more or less, it will make no difference to her whatever,' Mrs. Hurstpierpoint answered lucidly, turning apprehensively at the sound of a jocose laugh from Mrs. Yajñavalkya.

Très affairée, equiped in silk of Broussa, she was figurable perhaps to nothing so much as something from below.

'That little black niece of hers, my dear, is extremely exciting. . . .'

'Divinely voluptuous.'

Mrs. Hurstpierpoint tossed a troubled leaflet.

'She is ravishing,' she declared, wafting a butterfly kiss to the Abbess of Sodbury—Mère Marie de Cœurbrisé. Née a Begby of 'Bloxworth,' Mère Marie's taste for society was innate, and her petits goûters in the convent parlour were amazing institutions, if Sister Ecclesia, before her lips were bound, was to be believed.

'It puts me in mind of Vauxhall when I was a girl,' she chuckled.

'Oh—oh!'

'*Wunderschön! Bella, bella.*'

Her old orchidised face, less spiritualised than orchidised by the convent walls, in the moonlight seemed quite blue.

'And my birch, the blessed broom. . . . Is it iɪ Ttaly? Has His Holiness complied with the almond-twigs?' Mrs. ɪurstpierpoint enquired, drawing her away just as Mrs. Yajñavalkya, believing the leaflet to be as fraught with meaning as a Sultan's handkerchief, dispatched her niece to pick it up.

Such an unorthodox mode of introduction could not but cause the heart a tremor.

'In de case ob future advance,' Mrs. Yajñavalkya enjoined her niece (smiling impenetrably at her thoughts), 'be sure to say de dear billet shall receive your prompt attention.'

'*Paia!*' Niri-Esther assented.

She was looking vanquishing in a transparent, sleeveless tunic over a pair of rose-mauve knickers of an extraordinary intensity of hue. In her arms she held a sheaf of long-stemmed, pearl-white roses—*Soif de Tendresse*.

'We shall enter de palace by de garden gate . . . by de gate ob de garden . . .' Mrs. Yajñavalkya reflected, her eyes embracing the long, semi-Grecian outline of the house.

Before the mask-capped windows, Lady Parvula de Panzoust pointed sharply the dusk with a shimmering fan.

'Your Diana,' the negress, approaching, coughed, 'we speak ob as Hina. But she is de same; she is de moon.'

'Ah?'

'She is de moon. . . .'

'Soon, again, she'll be dwindling.'

'May you enjoy ambrosia: a lover's tigerish kisses, ere she disappears.'

Lady Parvula braced nervously her shoulders.

'Who is the woman in the cerements?' she inconsequently wondered.

'Dat dair she some stranger.'

'It amuses one to watch their dying flutters. . . .'

'You should take notice ob de wife ob de Mayor. Dô she be a hundred and forty, and more, yet she hardly look de age ob "consent"!'

'Have you nothing else—more interesting—to tell me?' Lady Parvula asked, motioning to the shade of the nearest tree.

Valmouth

'Assuredly,' the negress answered, following towards the dark-spreading Spina-Christi over against the house.

I, I, I, I! A night-bird fled on startled wings.

'Like the cry of an injured man!' Lady Parvula murmured, sinking composedly to a garden chair.

'Like de cry ob a djinn!'

'Well; is one any nearer? does he seem in a coming-on stage?' her ladyship blithely asked.

The oriental woman swelled.

'De way he questioned me concerning you, milady,' she unctuously made reply, 'was enough to make a swan bury its head beneath de water.'

'Silly fellow and is he crazy about me, you say? Dear boy. Well.'

'He say he ready to eat you.'

'To—what?'

'Ah de rogue!'

'Eat me . . . and when does he wish to devour me?' Lady Parvula touched nervously the white plumes and emeralds in the edifice of her hair.

'Ah de wretch!'

'Doesn't he say?'

'Al-ways he is hungry, de ogre!'

'The great, big, endless fellow!'

'Al-ways he is clamouring for a meal.'

'Let him guard as he can those ambered freckles!'

'Dey would draw de mazy bees.'

'I so feared he was going to be shy.' With pensive psychic fingers the enamoured Englishwoman toyed with a talismanic bagatelle in New Zealand jade.

'Believe me, he only play de part ob de timid youth de better to surprise you.'

'Simple angel!'

'He resist.'

'I once made a grand resistance—and oh! don't I regret it now . . . the poor dear was of low birth: humble origin: no condition: my husband's amanuensis! But oh! oh! !'

'Dose villain valets. Dey are de very men wif dair fair hard hair and dair chiselled faces. . . .'

'This was a paid secretary. . . . But oh, oh! Even my Lord. He could hardly spell. . . .'

'His face was his fortune?'

'Possibly. But I never was careless of appearances, as I told you I think once before. To my good name I cling. Mine, I congratulate myself, is entirely proof. No one has ever really been able to make a heroine out of me! The bordomette of circumlocution one submits to meekly perforce. In the Happy East you live untrammelled by the ghouls of our insular convention.'

Mrs. Yajñavalkya shook a stiff forefinger.

'Sho,' she muttered, allowing soft, discarnate voices to articulate and move on.

'Her great regret you know . . .' the murmur came, 'she is . . . God forgive her . . . the former Favourite of a king; although, as she herself declares, *only* for a few minutes. Poor darling! . . . Yes! My poor Love! She gave herself to an *earthly* crown. . . .'

'An ex-mistress of a king: she has the air.'

'It is Eulalia's *constant torment*!' The voices ebbed.

Lady Parvula looked down at the blue winter-violets in the front of her dress.

'Her sway was short!' she wondered.

She was all herself in a gown of pale brocade with a banana pattern in gold fibre breaking all over it.

'In an affair ob kismet—for it is kismet; what (I ask you to tell me) is reputation? What is it, reputation, in a case ob dis discription? Dis Smara. Dis Mektoub. Dis Destiny!'

'Sound him again. Put out final feelers,' Lady Parvula murmured, waving dismissal with a tap of her fan.

With a wise expressive nod the negress turned away.

Picking her way over the contorted roots of the trees she shaped her course towards the house, pausing to admire a universe of stars in a marble basin drip drop dripping, drip drip dropping, over with the clearest water.

'Væa, væa,' she mused, 'satufa lu-lu fiss.'

Looking up she perceived David Tooke, as if in ambush behind a statue of Meleager that resembled himself.

'Vot do you dair so unsocial?' she demanded in her softest gavroche speaking voice.

The young yeoman smiled slowly.

'Is it true,' he abstrusely answered, 'that in your country bulls consort with mares, and rams seek after cows, and the males of partridges do curious things among themselves?'

'Whoebber told you so told lies.'

'Told lies?'

'Dey told you only ob de few exceptions.'

'Ah.'

He seemed a trifle moonstruck.

'But ob vot importance is it? . . . Suppose *dey do*? Come on now, and hitch your wagon to a star.'

'I'll hitch my wagon where I choose.'

'Up wid dose dear shafts.'

'Tiddy-diddy-doll!' ungraciously he hummed.

'You marry her—and be a Lord!'

'Be off! Don't pester me.'

'Come on now.'

'Heart and belly: not I!'

'Must I *pull* you?'

'Pull me?'

'Drag you to milady.'

'Don't make me a scene, because my nerves can't stand it!'

'Vas dair ebber a eunuch like you?'

'Why does she want to come bothering me?'

'I have nebber heard of such contempt ob de peerage,' Mrs. Yajñavalkya fairly snorted.

'Here's Granny,' he breathed.

And indeed rounding a garden path on her grand-daughter's arm Mrs. Tooke was making a spirited progress of the grounds.

'Glad am I, my dear,' the negress cried, 'to see you're still so able . . .'

'Isht! My legs gae all tapsalteerie!'

'Dat is nothing but Nature's causes. What is wobblyness ever but de outcome simply ob disuse?'

'Just hark to my joints! I'm positively tumbling to bits!'

'And where are you off to, Mrs. Tooke?'

'To make a beau-pot, Mrs. Yaj.'

'What do you call a *beau-pot*, Mrs. Tooke?'

'A posy, Mrs. Yaj.'

'And vot's a posy, Mrs. Tooke?'

'A bunch of flowers, my dear.'

'In de East dair is a rose, deep and red, dat wen she open go off, pop, pop, pop—like de crack ob a gun!' and relinquishing her quarry, with a meaning glance, the negress strolled away.

'He is frigid. Dat I will admit: and bearish a little, too. But de boy is not such a fool,' she philosophised, gazing around her for a sign of her niece.

Through a yew-hedge, thinner at the bottom than at the top, she could see the feet of the dancers as they came and went.

A drowsy Tzigane air, intricate, caressing, vibrated sensuously to the night.

'May I have the pleasure . . . ?' a mild-faced youth, one of the Oblates of Up-More, addressed her.

'Delighted,' she answered, with equanimity, accepting his arm.

'Your countrywoman doesn't dance,' he observed, signalising Niri-Esther astride the seat-board of a garden swing, attached to the aerial branches of a silver fir.

She was clinging mysteriously to the ropes as though her instinct told her they had known the pressure of the palms of someone not altogether indifferent to her heart.

'Just at present . . .' the negress shrugged, submitting to be borne off by the will of a man.

'Ga—ga,' Niri-Esther gurgled, rubbing her cheek languorously against the cord.

'A push is it?' Mrs. Hurstpierpoint aborded her with a smile. 'Is it a push you wish for, dear child? Is that,' she dismantlingly ogled, 'what you're after?' and taking silence for assent, she resolutely clasped the black girl from behind below the middle.

Niri-Esther fetched a shout.

'Oh! Eulalia! ! !' Mrs. Thoroughfare approached *à pas de loup*. 'What are you up to, Eulalia? What are you doing?'

'Go away, Thoroughfare. Now, go away.'

'Oh, Eulalia.' Mrs. Thoroughfare shrank.

'Is not that *heavenly*, dear child?' the formidable woman queried, depositing a rich muff of Carrick-macross lace, bulging with propaganda, upon the ground.

'Stop!'

'Was not that divine, my dear? Didn't you like it?' The hieratic woman pressed, passing her tongue with quiet but evident relish along her upper lip.

Niri-Esther turned aside her head.

The constipated whiteness of a peacock in the penumbra of the tree was disquieting to her somewhat.

'Bird! !' Mrs. Hurstpierpoint chuckled.

'Ours at home are much bigger.'

'Are they, dear child?'

'Much.'

'I want us to be friends. Will you?'

'Why?'

'Ah, my dear ... "why"? Because,' Mrs. Hurstpierpoint quavered, leaning forward to inhale the singularly pungent perfume proceeding from the negress's person, 'because you're very lovable.'

'Eulalia!' Mrs. Thoroughfare reimportunated.

'Yes, Elizabeth!'

'I'm anxious to speak to you for a moment privately, Eulalia.'

'Well——'

'Oh, Eulalia!' Mrs. Thoroughfare faltered. 'Madame Mimosa is here ... exercising her calling ...'

'What?'

'Oh, Eulalia. ...'

'ffines! And turn her out.'

'At least, darling, she was arm-in-arm ... entwined, Eulalia.'

'Prude Elizabeth. Was that all you had to say?'

Mrs. Thoroughfare cast a grim glance towards Niri-Esther.

'Oh, she's a monstrous kid, Eulalia! ... Isn't she just?'

'I don't agree with you there, Elizabeth, at all.'

'Oh, she's a nutty girl; she's a bit of all right.'

'Why are you so down on her, Eliza?'

'I, Eulalia? I'm not down. I think her charming.'

'I'm glad you do.'

'She has her immaturity. I divine this and that.'

'Pho.'

'I guess a great deal.'

'How dear Richard would have admired her.'

'Dick would? How?'

Mrs. Hurstpierpoint lifted her shoulders slightly.

'Your son has a many-sided nature to him, Elizabeth,' she observed; 'which I suppose is not surprising when one thinks of you!'

'What do you mean, Eulalia?'

'What I say, darling. Dick's a man of several facets—no specialist! Thank the Lord!'

'Her habit of covering up her mouth with her hand when not speaking isn't exactly pretty.'

'She needs debarbarising, of course.'

'She'd still be black, Eulalia!'

'Black or no, she's certainly perfectly beautiful.'

'She may appeal to your epicurism, dear, although she mayn't to mine.'

'She was telling me—only fancy, Lizzie—that the peacocks in her land are much bigger——!'

'I should think they were, Eulalia. I should imagine they would be.'

'I found her so interesting.'

'I've no doubt of that, Eulalia.'

'But where is she?'

Apparently, like the majority of persons present, she had sauntered over to where a wordless passional play performed by mixed religious seemed to be scoring a hit.

On an overt stage ranged beneath the walls of *Nuestra Señora de la Pena* brilliantly lit within, two pretty probationers, Mystylia and Milka Morris, protégées of the ladies of the house, were revealing themselves to be decidedly promising artists, while gathered in a semi-circle about the stage the audience was finding occasion to exchange a thousand casuistries relative to itself or to the crops.

There uprose a jargon of voices:

'Heroin.'

'Adorable simplicity.'

'What could anyone find to admire in such a shelving profile?'

'We reckon a duck here of two or three and twenty not so old. And a spring chicken *anything to fourteen*.'

'My husband had no amorous energy whatsoever; which just suited me, of course.'

'I suppose when there's no more room for another crow's-foot, one attains a sort of peace?'

'I once said to Doctor Fothergill, a clergyman of Oxford and a great friend of mine, "Doctor," I said, "oh, if only you could see my——" '

'*Elle était jolie! Mais jolie! . . . C'était une si belle brune . . . !*'

'Cruelly lonely.'

'Leery. . . .'

'Vulpine.'

'Calumny.'

'People look like pearls, dear, beneath your wonderful trees.'

'. . . Milka, to-night—she is like a beautiful Cosway.'

'Above social littleness. . . .'

'Woman as I am!'

'Philanthropy.'

'. . . A Jewess in Lewisham who buys old clothes, old teeth, old plate, old paste, old lace. And gives very good prices indeed.'

' 'Er 'ealth I'm pleased to say is totally established.'

'If she pays her creditors *sixpence* in the *pound* it's the utmost they can expect.'

'Wonderful the Duchess of Valmouth's golden red hair, is it not?'

' "You lie to me," he said. "I'm not lying, and I *never* lie," I said. "It's *you* who tell the lies." Oh! I reproached him.'

'I'm tired, dear, but I'm *not* bored! . . .'

'What is a boy of twenty to me?'

'It's a little pain-racked face—not that she really suffers.'

Sister Ecclesia chafing at her Vows, martyred to find some outlet to expression, was like to have died, had not Nature inspired her to seek relief in her sweetest, most inconsequent way.

'I give her leave,' Mère Marie de Cœurbrisé said, 'to demand "the Assembly's pardon." '

Drawn by this little incident together, Lady Parvula de Panzoust and Mrs. Q. Comedy, a lady with white locks and face—the only creature present in a hat—had fallen into an animated colloquy

'These big show seats,' Lady Parvula sighed, 'are all alike: insanitary death-traps!'

The local land-agent's wife sent up her brows a little.

'Were you ever over Nosely?' she interjected.

'The Lauraguays'? Never!' Lady Parvula fluttered a painted fan of a bouquet of flowers by Diaz.

'My husband has the letting of it, you know.'

'Ah, hah—? Well, I always admire Richard the Third, who leased his house in Chelsea to the Duchess of Norfolk for the yearly rental of one red rose.'

Mrs. Comedy's mouth dropped.

'But that was hardly business!' she remarked.

'Who knows though? Perhaps it was,' Lady Parvula answered, appraising her Corydon through the eyelits of her fan.

'I've a sure flair for a figure,' she mused, 'and this one is prodigious.'

'Some say they find the country "warping." '

'Oh, but I feel I want to kiss you!' Lady Parvula ecstatically breathed.

'Madam?' Mrs. Comedy recoiled.

Just at this juncture, over the lawn-party, appeared the truant poll-parrot of Sir Victor Vatt. Wheeling round and round the chapel cross in crazy convolutions, the bird was like something demented.

'Dear Vatt,' it cried, 'he is splendid: so o-ri-gi-nal: and exuberant; like an Italian Decorator. Come, Vatt! Paint me in a greenhouse . . . in a st-oove; a little exotic! . . . Where's my bloody Brush?'

'I forget,' the Abbot of Up-More (a man like a sorrowful colossus) said, fingering fancifully the ring of red beard that draped his large ingenious face, 'if Vatt is for us or no.'

'He is to be had,' Mrs. Hurstpierpoint answered. 'In my private-list I have entered him as "Shakeable": Very: he will come for a touch . . .' she added, wincing at some shooting stars that slipped suddenly down behind the house.

'As Othniel prevailed over Chushanrishathaim so ought likewise we, by self-mortification and by abstinence, to proselytise all those who, themselves perhaps uncertain, vacillate ingloriously upon the brink,' the Abbot cogently commented.

With angelic humour Mrs. Hurstpierpoint swept skyward her heavy-lidded eyes.

'I thought last night, in my sleep,' she murmured, 'that Christ was my new gardener. I thought I saw Him in the Long Walk there, by the bed of Nelly Roche, tending a fallen flower with a wisp of bast. . . . "Oh, Seth," I said to Him . . . "remember the fresh lilies for the alter-vases. . . . Cut all the myosotis there is," I said, "and grub plenty of fine, feathery moss. . . ." And then, as He turned, I saw of course it was not Seth at all.'

'Is Seth leaving you?'

'He leaves us, yes, to be married,' Mrs. Hurstpierpoint replied, acknowledging a friendly little grimace from Niri-Esther, who appeared to be comporting herself altogether unceremoniously towards Thetis Tooke over the matter of a chair.

'Nowadays, the young people sit while their elders stand!' the Abbot succinctly said, riveting a curly-pated enfant de chœur lolling coxcombically beneath the nose of a doating Statilia.

Mrs. Hurstpierpoint kicked out the fatigued silver folds of her Court train with some annoyance.

'Charlie,' she beckoned.

'Here, 'm,' the child chirped, coming up.

'Where's your chivalry, Charlie? Your respect to the ladies?'

The lad looked down abashed.

'Come nearer, Charlie. (Quite close, Little-Voice!) Is that ink, on your head, I see?'

'Probably. . . . Father often wipes his pen in my hair,' the boy replied, darting off down a gravel path, where, having strayed away from the rest, Mrs. Tooke was dropping curtsies to the statues.

'She's loose.'

'Oh! At her time?'

'Very, very loose.'

The Abbot caressed his beard.

'Indeed, she looks a squilleon,' he raptly conjectured.

'She's *shakeable*, Abbot, I mean: in other words one could have her . . .' Mrs. Hurstpierpoint explained.

'Ah: I see.'

'My tongue is over-prone perhaps to metaphor. My cherished friend sometimes scolds me for it; only a fellow-mystic—some saint, would ever know, she says, what I'm driving at often. . . . Dear Lizzie. . . . If I could but influence her to make a Retreat; a change from Hare seems highly expedient for her; and at Arimathæa she would have still her Confessor! For something, I fear, is weighing on her mind; some sorrow she tells me nothing of; and it makes her so difficult. Just now we almost quarrelled. Yes. She grew jealous. And of a negress. Not the old one, "Dina-dina-do." I mean the girl in drawers. So I feel somehow Sodbury is the place for my poor angel. Just for a time. They have there, I believe, at present, Julie Bellojoso, and her sister, Lady Jane Trajane—also little Mrs. Lositer; Grouse Dubelly that was; she, of course, a fixture! . . . Thus my excellent, exquisite friend would have comradeship: and she would return here, I trust, softened, chastened, and with a less dingy outlook on life. For her talk, lately, Abbot, has been anything but bright. Indeed, she frightens me at times with her morose fits of gloom. Entre nous I lay the blame on the excellence of the garden as much as anything else! Our wall-fruit this year has been so very delicious; were not those dark Alphonsos perfection? Dear Father Notshort, though, forgets my wicker basket! But he was always a favourite of mine; and one hears he has great authority with the Duchess. I hope she will decide to make the plunge from

Hare. Her little starveling flower-face almost makes me want to cry. I feel as if I wanted to give her straight to Jesus. She is here some-where to-night. With her triste far look. I often say she has the instinct for dress. Even a skirt of wool with her feels to shimmer. . . . Lady Violet Logg also is somewhere about: my Poor Heart found her the other day—the day, it was, of the appalling storm—in *Nuestra Señora*, practically on her knees—and with *both* her boys.' Mrs. Hurstpierpoint diffusely broke off, directing her glance towards the municipal marquee.

Emerging from it amid a volley of laughter, came a puny, little old, osseous man of uncertain age, brandishing wildly to the night an empty bottle of Napoléon brandy.

'Ho! broder Teague,' his voice flew forth, 'dost hear de decree?

> 'Lilli burlero, bullen a-la.
> Dat we shall have a new deputie,
> Lilli burlero, bullen a-la.
> Lero lero, lilli burlero, lero lero, bullen a-la,
> Lero lero, lilli burlero, lero lero, bullen a-la.
>
> Ara! but why does he stay behind?
> Lilli burlero, bullen a-la.
> Ho! by my shoul 'tis a protestant wind.
> Lilli burlero, bullen a-la.
> Lero lero, lilli burlero, lero lero, bullen a-la,
> Lero lero, lilli burlero, lero lero, bullen a-la.
>
> Now, now de heretics all go down,
> Lilli burlero, bullen a-la.
> By Chrish' and Shaint Patrick, de nation's our own—"

But with quick insight the maître d'orchestre had struck up a capricious concert waltz, an enigmatic *au delà* laden air: Lord Berners? Scriabin? Tschaikovski? On the wings of whose troubled beat were borne some recent arrivals.

Entering the garden from the park, they would have reached the house, perhaps, unheeded, but for a watchman upon his rounds.

'A fine night, Captain!' The armed protector Mrs. Hurstpierpoint saw fit to employ against itinerant ravishers or thieves addressed his master.

'A delicious night indeed!'

'A little rain before morning maybe . . .'

For Captain Thoroughfare had found his way home again, anxious yet diffident enough to introduce his bride to her new relations: while to lend a conciliatory hand Lieutenant Whorwood himself had submitted to pass a few days at Hare, his cajoling ways and prepossessing face having quite melted Mrs. Hurstpierpoint upon a previous visit.

And, indeed, as he lagged along in the faint boreal light behind his friend he resembled singularly some girl masquerading as a boy for reasons of romance.

He had a suit of summer mufti, and a broad-brimmed blue beaver hat looped with leaves broken from the hedgerows in the lanes, and a Leander scarf tucked full of flowers: loosestrife, meadowrue, orchis, ragged-robin.

But it was due to Thetis Tooke that their advent was first made known.

'Oh! Is it y-you, Dick?' she crooned, catching sight of her lover: 'dear, is it you? Oh, Dick, Dick, Dick, my life!' She fell forward with a shattering cry.

ᛨ IX ᛨ

IT was in the deserted precincts of a sort of Moorish palace in the purlieus of the town that Lady Parvula de Panzoust and David Tooke were to come together one afternoon some few days subsequent to the Hare-Hatch fête.

In the crazy sunlight the white embattled Kasbahs of the vast rambling villa (erected by a defunct director of the Valbay Oyster-beds, as a summer resort, towards the close of the eighteenth century) showed forcefully, albeit, perhaps, a little sullenly, above the frail giraffe-like trunks of the birch-trees, and the argent trembling leaves of the aspens, that periodically shaded the route.

'I know I should despise myself, but I don't!' Lady Parvula told herself, unrolling a bruised-blue, sick-turquoise, silk sunshade very small like a doll's. 'Such perfect cant, though, with four "honeymoons" in the hotel, to be forced oneself to take to the fields . . . ! Oh, Haree-ee-ee,' she flashed an œillade up into the electric-blue dome of her parasol, 'why did you leave me? Why did you leave your tender "Cowslip" by the wayside all alone? Do you hear me,

Valmouth

Haree-ee-ee? Why did you ever leave me? And Gilda too, my girl. Oh, my darling child . . . do you know the temptation your mother is passing through? Pray for her . . . excuse her if you can. . . . . We shall be like the little birds to-night. Just hark to that one: *tiara, tiara, tiara*. It wants a tiara!'

Her aphrodisiac emotions nicely titillated, Lady Parvula de Panzoust was in her element.

'The Roman bridge in Rimini, the *Long* bridge in Mantua . . .' she murmured to herself erotically, dreamily, as she crossed the Val.

She wore a dress of filmy white stuff, embroidered with bunches of pale mauve thistles, a full fichu, and a large mauve hat with wide mauve ribbons, tied in front in a large knot where the fichu was crossed on her bosom.

'Such red poppies, such blue hills and sea, I never saw!' she reflected, entering a luxurious lime alley leading to the house.

A sign-board bearing the words 'commodious residence,' with the name of Mr. Comedy subjoined, struck a passing chill.

Evidently he was not yet come.

'I shall scream if he turns up in a dreadful billycock, or plays stupid pranks,' she murmured, pursing forward her lips that showed like a ripe strawberry in a face as whitened as a mask of snow.

Beneath the high trees there was a charming freshness.

'Kennst du das Land, wo die Citronen blühen?' she vociferated lightly, glancing up at the sun-fired windows of the house.

'It might suit me, perhaps,' she sighed, sinking down on an old green garden-seat with the paint peeling off in scales.

But to one of her impatient character expectance usually makes substantial demands upon the vitality.

' "Oui, prince, je languis, je *brûle* pour Thésée—Je l'aime," ' she lyrically declaimed.

Mightn't he be, perhaps, lurking close somewhere out of sight?

' "Laissez-moi ma main . . ." ' she languidly hummed (affecting Carré in Manon).

After all there was no need, it seemed, to have put herself in quite such a hurry.

'I begin now to wish I'd worn my little bombasine,' she mused, 'notwithstanding the infernal quantities of hooks. It's too late to turn back for it, I suppose? I feel all of a-twitter. . . . These accidental affairs . . . I said I know I never would. I can't forget the caïquejee on the Golden Horn; since that escapade my nerve has

216

gone completely. How quiet the rooks are to-day. I don't hear any.
Why aren't they chanting their unkydoodleums? Swing high, swing
low, swing to, swing fro, swing lal-lal-lal-la. What keeps him ever?
Some horrid cow? I can't bear to think of the man I love under
some cow's chidderkins. Oh, Haree-ee-ee, Haree-ee-ee! Why did you
leave me, Henry, to this sort of thing?'

She peered about her.

In the shade of a tree, a book, forgotten, doubtless, by some
potential tenant, was lying face downwards, open upon the grass.

With a belief in lovers' lightest omens, Lady Parvula de Panzoust
was tempted to rise.

'*Un Document sur l'Impuissance d'Aimer*,' she pouted, pricking
the brochure of Jean de Tinan with the point of her parasol.

'I seem to receive a special warning to take steps. . . . He may
require inciting,' she deliberated, dropping very daintily to a grassy
slope.

The turquoise tenderness of the sky drew from her heart a happy
coo.

Overhead a wind-blown branch, upheld in its fall by another
branch below, flecked precociously, with hectic tints, the heavy
midsummer greenery.

Half sitting, half reclining, she settled herself reposefully against
the tree-bole—limp, undefensive, expectant.

'I shall be down to-morrow with lumbago I dare say,' the latent
thought flashed through her.

Nevertheless, the easy eloquence of the pose was worth while,
perhaps, preserving.

A weasel, 'with a face like a little lion,' she told herself, skipped
from behind a garden dial—paused, puzzled at the diaphanous
whiteness of her gown,—turned tail, and disappeared briskly
beneath a fissure in the plinth.

The words, '*Donec eris felix, multos numerabis amicos, Tempora si
fuerint nubila, solus eris!*' traced thereon, irritated her somehow.

Pulling out a letter from her dorothy bag she beguiled the tedious-
ness of waiting by perusing distraitly its contents.

'The *première* of Paphos,' she read. 'Castruccio . . . Delmé. The
choruses made me weep. The Carmen Nuptiale was wholly divinely
given. I fear these few months in Milan have been all in vain. My
glory my voice. An old diva, a pupil of Tiejens . . . *Ah, fors' è lui!*
Purity of my . . . No Patti, or Pasta . . . Signor Farsetti . . . thrilling

shake . . . *Caro Nome*. Lessons. Liras. One of the pensionnaires. . . .
From Warsaw . . . worship . . . Mademoiselle Lucie de Cleremont
Chatte. Lucie . . . Lucie . . . Lucie.'

Her head flopped forward beneath her heavy hat, her apathetic
eyelids closed. . . .

When at length she looked up, the fretted shadow of the house
had sloped far toward the south.

Something broke the stillness.

An object that to her perplexity resolved itself into a large pink
kite was being dragged slowly past her over the grass. Preceding it,
the forms of Captain Thoroughfare and Niri-Esther were to be
descried retreating together into the dusk. Catching itself in the
garden weeds like a great maimed bird, the kite tore its way along
in the wake of an insouciant pair, followed discreetly a few yards
to the rear by the sorrowing figure of Thetis Tooke.

Lady Parvula was still meditating on what she had seen, when
Mrs. Yajñavalkya presented herself from beneath the shade of the
boskage.

Her downcast eyes and rapid respiration prepared Lady Parvula
to expect the worse.

'What brings you?' she faintly asked.

'Milady P.!' the negress clasped perfervidly beneath her chin her
white-gloved hands. 'It is a case ob *unrequited love* . . . but dat does
not mean to say you shall not be satisfied. No; oh no. On my honour.'

'The affair then'—Lady Parvula de Panzoust broke a pale-veined
leaf, and bit it—'proves abortive?'

'He will offer no opposition. . . . But on de other hand, he pretend
he cannot guarantee to make any advance!'

Her ladyship's lip curled.

'I fear he must be cold, or else he's decadent? . . .' she said, 'for
I have known men, Mrs. Yajñavalkya—yes, and *many men* too!—
who have found us little women the most engrossing thing in
life——'

'He has abjured, he says, de female sex.'

'Abjured us? Oh impossible!'

'However! he will content your caprice on one condition.'

'Let me hear it.'

'Marriage.'

'Marriage ! ! ! ! !'

Lady Parvula wrapped herself in her dignity.

'He seems to *me* to be an unpublished type,' she said severely.

'De great, sweet slighter.'

'I try to follow his train of feeling—but I can't.'

'He is inhuman, milady, and dat is sure.'

Lady Parvula followed absently with her glance a huge clock-beetle, exploring restively the handle to her parasol.

'At once. Where is he?' she demanded.

'I left him yonder at de gate.'

'You got him to the gate!'

'And dair we just parted. "Come along, now," I said, "for wif-out you I refuse to budge." '

'Well, what made you leave him then?'

'*Kra.*'

'As he is a shy, mistrustful misanthrope . . . an inverted flower . . .'

' "Why won't you come?" I say to him. "Do I ask de impossible?" *Kra!*'

'Oh . . . I want to spank the white-walls of his cottage!'

'Vot is von misadventure.'

'Do you really believe candidly there's *any* chance?'

'Dis but a hitch!'

'A disappointment, Mrs. Yajñavalkya——'

'Take what you can get, milady . . . Half a loaf is better dan no bread! Remember; and dat's vot I alvays say.'

'Nonsense—; he must trot out—; I want more than crumbs.'

'I get you both de crust *and* de crumb. I obtain you all you desire: only give me de time,' the negress wheezed.

Lady Parvula looked malicious.

'Of course he's *stable*,' she remarked.

'*Inshallah!*'

'Since seeing him in his shirt-sleeves with the peak of his cap turned over his neck, and redolent, upon the whole, of anything but *flowers* . . . he no longer thrills me,' she alleged, 'to the former extent.'

'I could get you de cousin.'

'What cousin?'

'De Bobby Jolly boy.'

' . . . Too young!'

'He twelve.'

'Go on! He's not eight.'

'Dat child is a king's morsel.'

Lady Parvula had a headshake.

'In the depths of the wilds you'd think young folk were bound to be more or less pent up,' she reflected, in tearful tones.

Mrs. Yajñavalkya smiled beneficently.

'It is not right, my dear,' she declared, 'you should be bilked. . . . Vot do you say to de captain ob a ketch? Beyond de Point out dair I have in mind de very goods.'

'As a rule that class is much too Esau. You understand what I mean.'

'Or; have you ever looked attentively at de local school-master?'

'No; I can't say I have.'

'Den you certainly should!'

'A schoolmaster—there's something so very *dredged*——'

'I sometimes say to Doctor Dee he put me in mind ob Dai-Cok.'

'Dai-Cok?'

'De Japanese God ob Wealth.'

'Well—; I dare say he would do as a poor *pis aller*,' Lady Parvula tittered, retouching her cheeks lightly with a powder-ball.

Not a breath of wind was stirring the trees. High up in the incandescent blue the whitest of moons was riding.

'Hina has lit her lamp. Hina here.'

'Damnation! ! ! !'

'Come with me now, my beautiful darling. Come. Come. Be brave. Be patient,' the negress begged.

Lady Parvula rose stiffly to her feet.

'I'll come perhaps a short way with you,' she said, regarding speculatively the interchanging fires of the lighthouse, that revealed, far off, their illusive radiance round the Point.

'How I wish, my dear, I could bow to your wishes!'

'You?'

'Supply de need.'

'I have reconsidered——' Lady Parvula breathed. 'Tell me . . . This captain of a ketch . . . Has he . . . (There are one or two petty questions I would like to put to you quietly as we go along . . . !)'

Valmouth

✿ X ✿

THE sky was empurpled towards the west, and the long, desolate, road, winding seaward, was wrapped in shadow; and desolate equally, was her heart.

'I loved you, Dick—: I asked for nothing better, Dear, than to be the wool of your vest . . .' Thetis softly wailed.

Her pale lips quivered.

'I would have done it yesterday,' she moaned, 'only the sea was as smooth as a plate!'

Yet now that it was slashed with little phantom horses it affrighted her. To be enveloped utterly by that cold stampede! Recalling the foolishness they had talked of her naiad namesake, she spat.

A fleet white pony and a little basket-wagon, with Maudie and Maidie, the charming children of Mrs. Q. Comedy, rattled by, returning from a picnic on the beach.

'I'd have blacked myself, Dick, for you. All over every day. There would have been such delight, Dear, in my aversion. . . . But you never told me your tastes. You concealed what you cared for from me. And I never guessed. . . . No; you never trusted me, Dick. . . . Besides! Everything's useless now,' she soliloquised, inclining to decipher the torn particles of a letter, littering the high road beneath her feet.

Willows near Pavia——

Weeping-willows near Pavia——

Pavia University——

Pavia——

Her bruised mind sought comfort . . . (vainly) . . . amid the bits——

'Yes. Everything's useless now. For very soon, Dick, I'll be dead!'

From a bank of yellowing bracken, a beautiful cock-pheasant flew over her with a plaintive shriek.

'Dead. . . . I suppose they'll put out the Stella Maris and dredge the Bay. But the tide will bear me beyond the Point; fortunately; I'm so lightsome! Seven stone. If that . . . oh dear, oh dear. When Nellie Nackman did the same she never left the rocks. It's a matter of build purely.'

Two bare-footed men—Up-Moreites—passed her with a 'famished' stare.

'I have a lovely figure. Totally superior to hers. He doesn't know what I am . . . . Poor Dear. How should he? My honey-angel . . . . Oh, Dick, Dick, Dick, Dick. . . . I ought to curse you, my darling.'

A labourer striding fugitively along in front of her, a young spruce-fir on his back (its bobbing boughs brushing the ground), perplexed her briefly.

'But I can't, I can't curse you, Dick. . . . Dear one, I can't. Neither, I find, can I forgive you. . . . I hope your brats may resemble their mother—that's all.'

As in a stupor, forging headlong forward she was overtaken in the vicinity of Valopolis by the evening voiture of Madame Mimosa, the lady's monogram, 'Kiki,' wreathed in true-love-knots, emblazoning triply the doors and rear. Presumably the enchantress was returning from the parsonage there—her penchant for Canon Wertnose being well known.

Canon Wertnose, Thetis's thoughts ran on, would bury her were she to be cast ashore. The beach was considered as his 'domain.' . . . Canon Wertnose would call at the Farm. Her grandmother would put on her cap to receive his visit with the whiskerage appended. Canon Wertnose would caress the cat. There would be talk of Habakkuk. . . .

She started.

Seated on a mileage-stone near the road's end was Carry, the little slavey of Mrs. Yajñavalkya, her head sunk low over a book.

She had in her hands a huge bright bouquet of Chinese asters, sunflowers, chrysanthemums and dahlias, which she inhaled, or twisted with fabulous nonchalance in the air as she read. . . . She appeared to be very much amused.

'What are you laughing for, Carry Smith?' Thetis made question.

'Me?' the negress's little apprentice tittered. . . . 'Oh, Miss! . . . I know at last. . . .'

'What futility have you discovered now?'

'I know *at last*—about the gentlemen.'

'About what gentlemen?'

'I know all about them.'

'So do I—traitors.'

'Oh, miss!'

'Don't be a fool, Carry Smith.'

'I know, miss, about them.'

'You may think you do.'

'Ah, but I *know*.' The child kissed her two frail hands to the first white star.

'Pick up your flowers, Carry Smith, and don't be a dilly,' Thetis advised, turning from her.

Day was waning.

The retreating tide exposed to view the low long rocks, encrusting sombrely the shore. Towards the horizon a flotilla of fishing-boats showed immutable, pink-lacquered by the evening sun.

'I shall remove my hat I think,' she cogitated. 'It would be a sin indeed to spoil such expensive plumes. . . . It's not perhaps a head-piece that would become everyone;—and I can't say I'm sorry!'

Her gaze swept glassily the deserted strand.

'It exasperates me though to think of the trouble I gave myself over maquillage. Blanching my face and fingers (and often my neck and arms . . .) surreptitiously in the cream-cans, before their con-signment to Market, when all the while,' she mumbled, fumbling convulsively amid the intricacies of her veil, 'he'd sooner have had me black!'

A little sob escaped her.

'Yes, he'd sooner I'd have been black,' she pursued, approaching determinedly the water's brink, when, from the shade of a cruciform stone, stepped Ecclesia, the Nun.

It was her 'Day.'

Mingling her voice with the planing gulls, winding her way dolorously amid the harsh bare rocks, she approached Thetis Tooke as if divinely impelled.

From the grey headland, where the stone Pharos cast through the gloom its range of shimmering light, a coastguard was surprised to see two women wrestling on the beach below, their outlines dim against the western sky.

ﯼ XI ﯼ

CLAD in a Persian-Renaissance gown and a widow's tiara of white batiste, Mrs. Thoroughfare, in all the ferment of a *Marriage Christening*, left her chamber one vapoury autumn day and descending a few stairs, and climbing a few others, knocked a trifle brusquely at her son's wife's door.

Through the open passage windows scent-exhaling Peruvian roses filled the long corridors with unutterable unrest, their live oppressive odour quickening oddly the polished assagais and spears upon the walls.

'Yahya?'

'It's me, dear.'

'Safi?'

'May Mother come in?'

'N . . . o.'

'Hurry up, then, Esther—won't you?' Mrs. Thoroughfare made reply, continuing resourcefully her course towards the lower regions of the house.

A tapestry curtain depicting *The Birth of Tact*, in which *Taste* was seen lying on a flower-decked couch amid ultra-classic surroundings, divided the stairway from the hall.

'Her eye was again at the keyhole,' Mrs. Thoroughfare reflected, pausing to glare at ffines, who was imparting technicalities relative to the Bridal-breakfast to his subordinates.

All was hurry and verve, making the habitual meditation in *Nuestra Señora* a particular effort to-day.

Yet, *oremus*—there being, indeed, the need.

Beyond a perpetual vigil-lamp or two the Basilica was unlit.

Glancing nervously at the unostentatious (essentially unostentatious) font, Mrs. Thoroughfare swept softly over a milky-blue porcelain floor (slightly slithery to the feet) to where her pet prie-dieu, laden with pious provender like some good mountain mule, stood waiting, ready for her to mount, which with a short sigh she did.

'Teach me to know myself, O Lord. Show me my heart. Help me to endure,' she prayed, addressing a figurine in purple and white faience by Maurice Denis below the *quête*.

Through the interstices of the be-pillared nave (brilliant with a series of Gothic banners) the sunlight teemed, illuminating the numerous *ex-votos,* and an esoteric little altar-piece of the 'School' of Sodoma.

'O grant me force!' she murmured, unbending a shade at sight of the gala altar-cloth where, crumpled up amid paschal lilies and *fleurs-de-luce,* basked an elaborate frizzed lamb of her own devoted working, the smart sophisticated crown displayed by the creature ablaze with Mrs. Hurstpierpoint's unset precious stones.

'Our nuptial bouquets (hers and mine) I like to think are con-
served below,' she mused, laying her cheek to her hands and smiling
a little wistfully towards a statue of the Virgin—*Nuestra Señora de la
Pena*—standing solitary under the canopy of the apse, her heart a
very pin-cushion of silver darts.

'Hail, Mary . . . !' she breathed, ignoring a decanter of sherry
and a plate of herring-sandwiches—a contrivance akin to genius
in drawing attention to an offertory-box near by.

From the sacristy the refined roulades of a footman (these
'satanic' matches!) reached her faintly:

> 'Oh I'm his gala-gairle . . .
> I'm his gala child,
> Yes,' etc.

Useless, under the circumstances, to attempt a *station*! 'Besides,'
Mrs. Thoroughfare speculated, trailing her Ispahanish flounces over
to the dapper, flower-filled chapel of the Salute, 'I bear my own
cross, God knows. . . .'

The mystic windows, revealing the astonishing Life of Saint
Automona Meris, smouldered brightly.

Automona by way of prelude lolling at a mirror plein de chic, her
toes on a hassock, reading a billet-doux. Automona with a purple
heartsease, pursuing a nail-pink youth. Automona with four male
rakes (like the little brown men of Egypt)—her hair down, holding
an ostrich-fan. Automona, in marvellous mourning and with
Nile-green hair, seated like a mummy bolt upright. Automona
meeting Queen Maud of Cassiopia:—'You look like some rare plant,
dear!' Her growing mysticism. She meets Mother Maïa: 'I'm not
the woman I was!' Her moods. Her austerities. Her increasing dow-
diness. Her indifference to dress. She repulses her couturier: 'Send
her away!' Her founding of Sodbury. Her end.

'Dear ardent soul!' Mrs. Thoroughfare commented, her spirit
rejoicing in the soft neurotic light.

Seldom had the Basilica shown itself as seductive.

From a pulpit festooned fancifully in prelatial purple the benediction of Cardinal Doppio-Mignoni would shortly fall.

The last time the Cardinal had preached at Hare had been for
the harvest festival, when a pyre of wondrous 'wurzels' had been
heaped so high on the pulpit-ledge that he had been almost hidden
from sight. Whereupon, dislodging a layer, His Eminence had

deplaced the lot—the entire structure, Mrs. Thoroughfare remembered well, rattling down like cannon-balls on to the heads of those below.

Glancing round, her eyes encountered a taper-lighting acolyte—Charlie, revolving with an air of half-cynical inquiry before a *Madeleine Lisante,* attributed to the 'Master of the Passion,' usually kept veiled, but to-day exposed to view.

Dipping a grimly sardonic finger in the vase of holy water by the door, Mrs. Thoroughfare withdrew, halting mechnically just outside to lend a listening ear to a confused discursive sound—the eternal *she she she* of servants' voices.

' . . . She . . . she . . .'

Through a service hatch ajar the chatter came.

'She . . .'

'There's the Blue-Room bell!'

'Confound it.'

' . . . Well, dear . . . as I was saying . . . Never before was I so insulted or outraged! Just catch me taking any more topsy freedoms from her.'

'I should keep my breath to cool my porridge. In your shoes, Sweetie.'

'Sweetie? Who's your sweetie? . . . I'm not your sweetie.'

'No? I shouldn't think you was.'

'In your shoes . . . I'd put-myself-out to school, I would, and be taught some grammar!'

'Hurry up, please. . . . Come on now with the samovar—and make haste sorting the letter-bag.'

'His Eminence. His Eminence: didn't someone say Cardinal Mignoni's correspondence passed first through Monsignor Girling? . . . Lord Laggard . . . Lady Laggard. Her Ladyship. Her ladyship. . . . Mademoiselle Carmen Colonnade—; *do, re, mi, fa.* . . . Signora Pinpipi. The Mrs. The Mrs. . . .'

'I always know instinctive when the Mrs. has on her spiked garters.'

'Do you, dear? . . . And *so* do I.'

'You could hear her a-tanning herself before cock-crow this morning in her room. Frtt! but she can swipe.'

'Those holly-bags, too, must tickle one's hams.'

'Now her sister's visiting Valmouth, you'd have thought it was Penance enough!'

'Who are the sponsors beside Lady Laggard?'

'What's that, my dear, to you?'

'There's the Blue-Room bell again!...'

> 'I'll be your little blue-bell
> If you'll be my little bee.'

'And *don't* forget Mrs. Thoroughfare.'

'... What Mrs. Thoroughfare? Which Mrs. Thoroughfare?... the white Mrs. Thoroughfare? The black Mrs. Thoroughfare?'

'I've seen a mort o' queer things in my day' (the voice was ffines's), 'but a *negress*; oh deary me!'

'Give me strength, my God, to bear this cross. Uphold me, Holy Mary, or I fail,' Mrs. Thoroughfare inwardly breathed, retreating softly towards the drawing-room door.

The renowned room was completely bathed in sun, revealing equally the qualities and defects of the numerous baptismal or bridal gifts set out to be admired.

Bending over a charming little mirror of composite precious woods, Mrs. Thoroughfare detected Lieutenant Whorwood grooming assiduously his romantical curls.

Embarrassed at being taken thus unawares, the young man blushed up to the *rose-mauve* of his lips.

'I realise,' said he, 'I'm one of those who, at the last Trump, would run their hand across their hair!'

'Ah? Really—; would you? Why?'

'Probably,' he replied, 'because I'm naturally vain.'

'I adore your hair:—and so does Dick.'

'Did he say so?'

'My boy is very fond of you.'

'And I'm very attached to him.'

'I know you are—and that *is why* I can talk to you about my son,' Mrs. Thoroughfare said, keeping the lieutenant's hand captive in her own a moment longer, perhaps, than was actually required.

'After the ceremony, I trust you'll all at length be easy.'

'Their re-union in my opinion,' Mrs. Thoroughfare declared, 'is nothing but nonsense, but Eulalia seemed so fidgety and nervous —oh! she's so particular now about the least flaw or hitch——! And we thought it best, perhaps, to humour her.'

'Those black weddings are rarely *en règle*.'

'I would give the whole world willingly for the poor fellow to repudiate the affair altogether—; *get out of it*! Such a marvellous opportunity ... But no; he's utterly infatuated by his wife, it seems;—too much, alas, I fear ...'

'Dear Mrs. Thoroughfare,' the lieutenant sympathetically said, 'don't think I can't understand. I do ... absolutely.'

Mrs. Thoroughfare looked appreciative.

'I wish I was more stoic, Lieutenant Whorwood,' she replied, 'I wish I had less heart. ... But I'm super-sensitive. So I suffer like a fool!'

'It isn't my business of course,' he said, 'to meddle in souls. But Father Colley-Mahoney should be skilled to advise.'

'I've an inkling that Father very soon may be resigning his post,' Mrs. Thoroughfare returned. 'Such a pity! None of the chaplains ever stay long. ... They seem to dislike Eulalia hauling them out of bed o' nights to say Midnight Masses for her.'

'But *does* she?' the lieutenant murmured, ensconcing himself in an easy-chair.

'Oh, my dear, she's merciless. ... Eulalia's inexorable. ... Dom Jonquil, Père Ernest des Martelles, she wore them *out*. You're aware of course about THE KING ...'

'The old story?'

'For Eulalia with her glowing artist mind—she is a born artist—she reminds me often of Delysia—it is anything but "old." Her poor spirit, I fear, is everlastingly in the back of the Royal Box that ghastly evening of Pastor Fido: or was it in a corner of it she was? She is so liable to get mixed.'

'I understand at any rate she projects presenting Mrs. Richard herself at one of the coming courts.'

'Oh, she's very full of plans—although she tells *me* none of them now.'

'She has been consulting me instead!'

'You remind her of a pet *cicisbeo* she had on her wedding tour—so she pretends.'

'She designs a trip to Paris, and to Vienna too, and Rome; and she has a wild delicious scheme even of visiting *Taormina*.'

'She'll be all over the place now I suppose. I shouldn't wonder if she didn't marry again.'

'It's for little Mrs. Richard presumably that she goes.'

'It's ridiculous how she spoils her. But it's useless to remonstrate. One would have thought she'd have shaved her head and put on mourning. One would have thought she would have received her death-blow. I've known her to take to her bed for a mere black-beetle. Yes, oh, I have . . . blubbering and lamenting like a great frightened silly. But for a hulking *black* savage! not a bit of it! She enjoys all the kudos of a heathen's conversion (a "double conversion," as she says, on account of the child) and forgets altogether the discreditable connection.'

'It's really not such a discreditable one after all.'

'I'll refuse to believe this little madcap negress was ever born a Tahaitian princess. No, Lieutenant Whorwood, or that Mrs. Yajñavalkya of Valmouth is only her nurse.'

'At Tarooa we knew quite well the brother—the banana man . . . employed on King Jotifa's estate.'

'Beuh!'

'The bride's credentials anyway will probably be examined; as Mrs. Hurstpierpoint declares she shall know "no rest" until she has secured for her *the precedence of the daughter of an earl*.'

'Through the Laggard's wire pulling, I wonder.'

'He's vastly struck by her.'

'She provokes him. . . . He finds her piquant.'

'If only she wouldn't run at one quite so much and rumple one's hair!'

'Last night after dinner when *we* all withdrew she amused herself by smacking the hermaphrodite. . . . So Eulalia's full of hopes, she says, that she will sometimes take a hand with the broom. . . .'

'She made a sudden dash for my b-t-m. Greatly to my amazement.'

'Oh, she's a regular puss; my word she is! A regular *civet* if ever there was,' Mrs. Thoroughfare wickedly commented.

'She's perhaps a little too playful.'

'Having torn to piecemeal Eulalia's copy of *Les Chansons de Bilitis* and "mis-used" my set of dear Dumas the Elder, one might say in truth—she was destructive.'

'A book is anathema to her.'

'Even a *papier poudré* one; for when I gave her my little precious volume, my little inseparable of *blanc de perle* in order to rub her nose, she started grating her teeth at me—to my utter terror! Rolling her eyes; lolling out her tongue——'

'One has to feel one's way with her.'

'I'm sure I meant it kindly!'

'A negress never powders.'

'Why not?'

'Because she *knows* it's useless,' the lieutenant lucidly explained.

'Her chief pleasure she seems to find in digging about among the coco-nut fibre in the conservatory with her hands.'

'She's very fond of gardening.'

'And she is also very fond, I fear, of betel. Yes, I fear my boy is married to a betel-chewer. But of course *that* is nothing. . . . "De worst ob dis place," she said to us last night, "is dat dair is no betel! No betel at all;—not ob any discription!" "Are you a betel-chewer, then, my dear?" I asked, *aghast*. "Oh yes," she answered without winking. "How I do crave for some." '

'It's likely to be injurious to her babe at present.'

'*Which?* She's expecting a second enfantement, you know, immediately . . . Oh she's such a quick puss.'

'A prettier, more câline mite than Marigold I never saw.'

Mrs. Thoroughfare exchanged a quick glance with heaven.

'It's a pity the servants don't think so,' she said, 'for none of them will go near her! Baby has had three nurses in one fortnight; not that she perhaps is altogether to blame. The new woman, Mrs. Kent, that came only yesterday (I got her too through the columns of "Femina") Eulalia seems all against. She can't "abide" her, in fact, as they say in Papiete.'

'So soon?'

'Oh Eulalia's so difficult. And she goes far too much to the Nursery. . . ! And unfortunately she isn't *mealy-mouthed*. . . . Eulalia says what she thinks,' Mrs. Thoroughfare murmured, her voice discreetly sinking as an old maid-servant of the house peered into the room—ostensibly only to sneeze twice—and out again.

'It disturbs her,' the young man ventured, 'that you don't get on better with Mrs. Dick!'

Mrs. Thoroughfare's eyes wandered ruefully to a superlatively sensitive miniature—one of the numerous wedding-gifts—portraying Niri-Esther, radiant with wax-white cheeks, as seen through the temperament of a great artist.

'There'd be more affection, perhaps, between us,' she returned sadly, 'if she resembled that.'

'It's rather a gem— Who did it?'

'Sir Victor . . .'

'It's quite inspired!'

With pensive precision Mrs. Thoroughfare drew on a pair of long, primrose-tinted gloves.

'To surprise Eulalia,' she murmured, 'I've commissioned him—only don't let it go further—to compose a Temptation of Saint Anthony for *Nuestra Señora*, a subject she has ever been fond of, it being so full of scope. He proposes inducing the local Laïs, Madame Mimosa, to pose as the Temptation; but I say, she isn't seductive enough. . . . No "Temptation": at least, *I* shouldn't find her one.'

'But why be dull and conventional; why be banal; why should you have a female model?'

'Why, what else, Lieutenant,' Mrs. Thoroughfare shifted a cameo bangle dubiously from one of her arms to the other, 'would you suggest?'

'Oh! A thousand things . . .' the lieutenant was unprecise.

'No; if he can't find a real temptation, a proper temptation, an irresistible temptation—I shall put him "off" with a little flower-piece, some arrangement, perhaps, of *flame-coloured roses* and tell Eulalia it's the "Burning Bush." '

'The Nation should prevent his old Mother from leaving the country.'

'Oh . . . why? What has she done?'

'Nothing—His masterpiece, I meant.'

'I understood him, once, I think, to say that *that* was the *Madame Georges Goujon with Arlette and Ary.* . . .'

'Oh he has so many. His drawing of a Valmouther getting over a stile is something I could covet.'

'They say his study of the drawer of the Bawd's Head Hostelry here is worthy of Franz Hals,' Mrs. Thoroughfare related.

But the entry of Mrs. Hurstpierpoint bearing a long-clothes baby put an end to the colloquy.

Out of courtesy to the bride, and perhaps from some motive of private thanksgiving, her face was completely covered by a jet-black visard. Big beaded wings rose from her back with a certain moth-like effect.

'Tell me, Elizabeth,' she asked, 'will I do?'

'Do! ! Eulalia—I never saw anything like you.'

'I hope the dear Cardinal won't tell me I'm unorthodox; or do you think he will?'

'Take it off, Eulalia,' Mrs. Thoroughfare begged.

'I shall not, Elizabeth!'

'Take it off!'

'No.'

'But why should you conceal yourself behind that odious mask?'

'I wear it, dear, only because a white face seems to frighten baby,' Mrs. Hurstpierpoint explained.

'Eulalia, Eulalia.'

'Mind, Elizabeth. . . . Be careful of my wings.'

'You're beyond anything, Eulalia.'

Mrs. Hurstpierpoint sat down.

'Sister Ecclesia has just been giving me an account, in dumb show, of the young woman whom she saved from drowning. . . . But for her the sea would have absorbed her. . . . However, she is now comfortably installed in the Convent of Arimathæa, and already shows, it seems, signs of a budding vocation! So peradventure she will become a Bride of the Church.'

'Let us hope so, anyway. But talking of "brides," Eulalia, *where's Esther?*'

'She was outside, dear, a moment ago. . . .'

'In *toilette de noce*?'

'And so excited! She's just floating in happiness—floating, swimming, sailing, soaring, flying. The darling! She is happy. So hap-py! Oh——'

'Really, dear, it's you that seem elated.'

'Your boy has my condemnation, Bessy; but he has also my forgiveness,' Mrs. Hurstpierpoint blandly declared.

'Oh! Eulalia, you're too subtle for me.'

'Call her in, darling, do, or she may perhaps take cold, and a bride ought not to do that. I had such a cold on *my* honeymoon I remember, I never really ceased sneezing.'

'Oh, she'll come in I dare say when she wants to, Eulalia.'

'You amuse me, Eliza. . . . What makes you so unaccommodating?'

'It's odd you should ask, Eulalia!'

'Our friendship is unalterable, my little Lizzie, nothing has changed, or come between.'

'Mind Marigold, Eulalia.'

'What is it she wants? I expect it's her bobo!'

'No she doesn't, Eulalia. She doesn't want it at all.'

'Esther has no notion yet of managing a child. . . . Although she appears to have any number of quixoticisms.'

'I fear we shall find she has her own little black ideas about everything, Eulalia.'

'Well, well; if she has, she must drop them.'

'Naturally,' the lieutenant interposed, 'her intellectual baggage is nil—simply nil,' he added, lighting complacently a cigarette.

'Father wouldn't agree with you there at all; and he has had her, remember, daily, for pious Instruction.'

'I fear, Eulalia, she was won as much as anything by our wardrobe of stoles.'

'Father seems half in awe of her. . . . "Is an *egregious* sin a *mortal* sin?" she asked him quite suddenly the other day.'

'Oh! Eulalia!'

'She's devoted, though disrespectful, he tells me,' Mrs. Hurstpierpoint murmured, blowing a kiss to the bride who was passing the windows just then.

'Rain fell steadily in the night; the grass must be drenched.'

'Oh, Esther—your feet.'

'When the Spina-Christi sheds its leaves my God what sorrow and stagnance,' Mrs. Thoroughfare sighed oppressed.

'Shall you want the horses, do you think, this evening, Elizabeth?'

'I don't want them, Eulalia.'

'Are you sure, Elizabeth?'

'Perfectly, Eulalia.'

'The evening drive is almost an institution of the past. . . .'

Mrs. Thoroughfare assented.

'Here we are too with winter upon us,' she observed.

'Yes; and this is not the Tropics, my mignonne Niri!' Mrs. Hurstpierpoint reminded her convert as she came forward into the room.

'In de winter,' the negress lisped, 'our trees are green wif parrots.'

'Are they, my dear?'

'Green!'

'Think of that now, dear child.'

'Green wif dem.'

'Did you hear, Elizabeth, what she said?'

'No, Eulalia.'

'It appears their trees are never bare. Always something.'

'Her salvation, in my estimate, Eulalia, should be equivalent quite to a Plenary-perpetual-Indulgence.'

'And so *I* think too.'

'Had she been more accomplished: wives should second their husbands; if not, perhaps, actually lead them. . . .'

'She does not want abilities, I can assure you, Eliza. She knows how to weave grasses. She can make little mats. She's going to teach me some day: aren't you, Esther? She and I are going to make a mat together. And when we've made it, we'll spread it out, and kneel down on it, *side by side*; won't we, Esther!'

'Yaas!' the negress answered, fondling playfully the Hare hermaphrodite.

'You may look, dear, but don't touch. Esther! Pho pet. My *dear*, what next?'

'There's a mean in all things . . . really.'

'Giddy.'

'Incorrigible.'

'You must learn to recollect yourself, dear child, or else I shall return the Lord Chamberlain our Cards.' Mrs. Hurstpierpoint made show of rising.

'Oh, she'd better be presented in Ireland, Eulalia. Dublin Castle to *begin* with—afterwards we'll see——! !'

'Ireland?'

'What do you say, Lieutenant Whorwood?'

The lieutenant laid whimsically his face to a long cylindrical pillow of cloth of silver garnished with beaded-flowers.

'What do *I* say?' he echoed, half closing his eyes and flicking the cigarette-end from his knees, when a discharge of bells from *Nuestra Señora*, and the arrival of the vanguard of the bridal guests, prevented further discussion.

'Her Grace, the Duchess of Valmouth; the Honourable Mrs. Manborough of Castle Malling"—ffines' voice filled the room.

'You shall hold Baby, Lieutenant, while I——' Mrs. Hurstpierpoint flapped expressively her loose-winged sleeves.

'Sir William West-Wind, Mr. Peter Caroon, Mrs. Trotter-Stormer, Sir Wroth and Lady Cleobulina Summer-Leyton, Sir Victor Vatt, Master Xavier Tanoski, Lady Lucy Saunter, Miss à Duarté, Miss Roxall, Lady Jane Congress, Lady Constance Cadence-Stewart, Mrs. Q. Comedy, Lady Lauraguay, Lady Lukin de Lukin, Mrs. Lumlun, Mr. Argrove, Mrs. Lositer, General George Obliveon, Lady Parvula de Panzoust.'

Exhaling indescribably the esoteric gentillezze of Love, she was looking almost girlish beneath a white beret de Picador, enwreathed with multifarious clusters of silken balls, falling behind her far below the waist. Wearing a light décolleté day-dress, her figure since her previous visit to Hare had perceptibly grown stouter.

She was eyeing her hostess with wonder unrestrained when a dowager with a fine film of rouge wrapped in many shawls sailing up to her said:

'Persuade my sister do to take off her mask. Can't you persuade her to doff it?'

Lady Parvula dimpled.

'If you, Arabella, can't—why how,' she returned, 'should I?'

Lady Laggard shook censoriously her shawls.

'I fear,' she observed, 'my poor sister will be soon a *déclassée*. She has been a sore grief to us—a sad trial! But when she begged me to be a godmother to the little Aida, I could hardly say no.'

'Cela va sans dire.'

'Her escapade with King Edred was perfectly disgraceful! She got nothing out of him, you know, for anyone—like the fool that she was. And to see her to-day going about be-winged, be-masked . . .'

'Sad, isn't it, how the old Hare days seem completely gone: vanished.'

'She conceals her upper-lip, one must allow,' Lady Laggard commented. 'But there was no—or *next* to no—was there—to *speak* of—about the eyes? . . . And nothing, nothing to excuse all that long fall of dreary lace.'

'Really she looks so quaint I can hardly help laughing,' Lady Parvula declared.

'She must be bitterly mortified, I imagine, by this marriage.'

'It shows though, I think, her savoir faire, to put the best construction on it.'

'The old Noblesse—where is it now?'

'Ah! I wonder.'

'With a woman like that his career is closed.'

'You may be sure they'll soon be separated!'

Lady Laggard removed an eyelash.

'They're not really married yet, you know,' she alleged.

'N . . . o?'

'The ceremony before I gather was quite null and void.'

'In . . . deed?'

'Their own rites, so it seems, are far simpler. All they do is *simply* to place each a hand to the torso of the Beloved. And that's as far—will you *believe it*, dear?—as we are at present!'

'Your sister spoke of "special licence." '

'She would; she has the tongue of a Jesuit.'

'I didn't of course realise . . .'

'We were pumping the bride, Lord Laggard and I, and she told us, poor innocent, she was not married yet,' Lady Laggard averred, shaking long tremulous earrings of the time of Seti II of Egypt.

'I notice she likes lights and commotion, which goes to show she has social instincts!'

'Well, it's some time I suppose since there's been a negress——'

'All the fair men—the blondes, she will take from us. . . .'

'I wish I'd a tithe of your charms, dear.'

'But I don't really mind! . . . So long as *I* get the gypsies. . . .'

'They should forbid her from repeating a horrid equivocal epigram of old Dr. Dee's—on the Masseuse, La Yajñavalkya.'

'What was it, Arabella?'

'Her brains are in her arms.'

'And are they?'

'I don't know, dear, where they are. Such a pity *hers* aren't anywhere. Her incessant "Wot for dis?" gets so on my nerves.'

'I don't wonder. It would on mine. I'm such a nervous woman! Now I've no Haree-ee-ee to look after me I get so fluttered. . . .'

'All these priests in the house I find myself a strain. The old Cardinal, with his monstrous triple-mitre, one goes in terrors of. He was in the passage just now as I came through waiting for someone. And last night—there's only a panel door between our rooms—I heard him try the handle.'

'Their last chaplain—Père Ernest—I remember was a danger. A perfect danger! He could have done anything with me, Arabella, had he willed. I was plastic wax with him.'

'With their faggots of candles (and their incense) they seek to render imbecile our poor sex. Coming by Nuestra, I assure you, I was almost *poisoned*. Or, to use a juster metaphor, perhaps,' Lady Laggard corrected herself, 'suffocated,' she added, 'by the fumes.'

'Monsignor Vanhove, Father O'Donoghue, Frater Galfrith, Brother Drithelm, Père Porfirio'—ffines insistently continued in his office until, in sweeping purple and scarlet biretta, Cardinal Doppio-Mignoni himself passed valedictionally through the rooms.

In the extravagant hush, following on his transit, a prolonged peacock's wail sounded electrifying from the park: *Nijny-Novgorod, Nijny-Novgorod*—creating among the younger bridesmaids an impression of 'foreboding.'

Only Mrs. Hurstpierpoint, to judge by her rich enveloping laugh, seemed really happy or serene.

'I always intended to visit *Walt Whitman*, didn't I, Lizzie? Poor old Walt! . . . I wrote: "Expect me and my maid. . . . I'm coming!" I said. . . . It was the very spring he died.'

Involving some interesting, intellectual trips, she was descanting lightly to right and left.

'I remember you intended once to visit me,' the Bolshevik member for Valmouth, Sir William West-Wind, softly remarked.

'You, Sir William? And when did I ever intend to visit you, I wonder?'

'There was a time,' Sir William murmured, 'when I confess I expected you.'

'Have you any intention, Eulalia,' a *douairière* enquired, 'of visiting the present châtelaine of Nosely?'

'You dear angel—I wasn't aware even it was let.'

'To a field-marshal's widow.'

'My brother,' one of the bridesmaids giggled, 'was his favourite *aide-de-camp*.'

'And what is *she* like?'

'He describes her as lissom as a glove, lively as a kid, and as fond of tippling as a Grenadier-Guard.'

'She sounds a treasure,' Mrs. Hurstpierpoint declared, with a glance backward over her wings.

'Go to Vivi Vanderstart—and say I sent you!' the Duchess of Valmouth was saying.

'Very well, dear, I will.'

'Her boast is, she makes only "Hats for Happy Women." '

'I always pin my faith in Pauline Virot. . . .'

'One should pin one's faith only in God,' Mrs. Hurstpierpoint commented blithely.

'Only where, Eulalia?'

'Only with Him.'

'I remember,' Mrs. Thoroughfare dryly laughed, ' when Eulalia's God was *Gambetta*.'

'Gambetta, Betty—what next will you say, naughty, naughty angel?'

But what Mrs. Thoroughfare subsequently would have said was lost amid Church canticles.

It was the call to the altar.

Oscillating freely a long chain incense swinger, a youthful server, magnificent in white silk stockings and Neapolitan-violet maroquin shoes, presented himself on the threshold in a fragrant veil of smoke.

Venite.

Followed by Charlie with the Holy Pyx and by Father Colley-Mahoney and various officiating priests, he traversed from end to end, amid much show of reverence (crossing and crouching), the vast salon.

'Grant she shall find,'

(Pinpipi with her great male voice from 'Nuestra' was waking the echoes beyond)

'On Yniswitrins altars pale,
The gleaming vision of the Holy Grail.'

'Yes; grant Lord her *soul* shall find,' Mademoiselle Carmen Colonnade, the beloved of the Orpheum, Scala, San Carlo, Costanzi, simultaneously (more or less) struck in, her soft vocal flourishes and pimpant variations soaring, baby-like, high above the strong soprano voice of the severe Pinpipi.

''*Es, gwant 'Ord 'er 'oul*—
Grant it shall find—
On Ynis-wi-trins walters—
Altars—
WALTERS PALER!
The gleaming vision—
—*dazzling*—
Of—
The Holy Grail-a!'

'Come, Esther,' Mrs. Hurstpierpoint murmured, dashing a tear from her mask.

'Yield the *pas* to a negress! *Never!*' Lady Laggard looked determined.

'Oh, Eulalia!' Mrs. Thoroughfare touched her arm.

'You dear queen.'

'Have you seen my boy, Eulalia?'

'No, Elizabeth—; not to-day.'

'No one can find him.'

'Ah les oiseaux amoureux,' Mrs. Hurstpierpoint began a series of seraphic giggles, 'chers oiseaux . . . paradise uccellinis . . . delicious vogels. . . .'

'I feel half-worn-out.'

'Come, Esther child, to church!'

But Niri-Esther had run out of the house (old, grey, grim, satanic Hare) into the garden, where, with her bride's bouquet of malmaisons and vanessa-violets, she was waywardly in pursuit of—a butterfly.

FAREWELL

The Artificial Princess

The Artificial Princess

IN WHICH A LADY BEGS ANOTHER TO PERFORM A SERVICE

'YOU take the white omnibus in the Platz,' murmured the Princess, 'but do not forget to change into an ultramarine on reaching the Flower Market, or you will find yourself in the "Abattoirs." Had it been any other day, I would have sent you in the incognito glass-coach—the one my poor sister used when she ran away with the little chorister—but I have ordered that, since it is my birthday, the royal horses shall pass the day lying down. To-night, they shall be led out to see the fireworks, and possibly the stars. . . . But, Baroness, you are not eating any of these delicious sweets—that purple one looks irresistible. I think it is a crystallised Orchid; or this wee pink one; I think it is a Wild Rose. In spite of the Revolution the dear President never forgets my birthday.'

The Baroness Rudlieb declined, and then accepted; it was a way of hers. . . . Seated at the piano she had accompanied the Princess's directions to a brilliant Rhapsody by Liszt, her eyes fixed theatrically upon a Coronation of the Virgin that adorned the ceiling. In silence she swallowed both sweets, and then expressed herself by a bewildered sigh.

The Princess's economies were ridiculous. The white omnibus! And then a vulgar blue one! It was an indignity, but it was characteristic of the Princess to be so mean.

'A hired landau,' the Baroness ventured to suggest, 'would look less conspicuous. . . .'

The Princess lifted her shoulders slightly. 'No, dear, I think you had better take the bus.'

There was a firmness, honey-sweet, about the voice that was not intended to disguise the pill.

At Court the Princess was considered exquisite—a Largillière . . . but her mother, the Queen, had never doubted her to be a Minx.

'We have never heard of the painter,' the Maids of Honour would say, curtseying, and opening very wide their eyes: but the Mistress of the Robes, who was considered intellectual (she had

241

written several volumes white-washing famous Sinners, and an extravaganza to be performed that evening in the Princess's honour), had more than once declared that the Princess possessed all the delicacy of expression, and radiancy of colouring, only to be found in the later manner of a Minx.

'I know; I like his pictures; they are so exquisitely unreal,' the Queen usually agreed. 'I admire the fantastic grandeur of his backgrounds, his looped-back portières, and towering storm-clouds . . . so sweet!' She was the first cynical Queen to reign just there for many hundreds of years; indeed, she may have been the very first, for her predecessor could only be judged from her postures in a masquerade, embroidered in certain medieval tapestries, representing the extreme exclusiveness of Semiramis, Queen of Babylon and her own particular set. The Queen in consequence was often misunderstood; many people considered her to be extremely foolish. 'But intellect,' they said, 'was seldom found under a yellow fringe.'

The Princess was seventeen—except on those days when she went to play at Mah-Jong in the Casino. On these occasions she would powder her hair in front, put on diamond earrings, and say she was twenty-two. 'Such fascinating insolence!' The amiable beauties who frequented the place adored her.

People either admired the Princess very much, or they didn't admire her at all. Like a Virgin in a missal her figure lacked consequence—sex.

'My tall-tall schoolboy,' her mother would usually call her in her correspondence with neighbouring Queens.

Realising to the full the drawbacks of an extreme finesse, the Princess's choice of gowns was nearly always indiscreet; but happily reckless toilettes suited her.

To-day, the wicked thing wore masses of lace with twists of riband termed 'Inspirations' and no particular sleeves; her slender arms like the stem of flowers fainting away to the pointed finger-tips that seemed to evaporate and lose themselves in æther.

Evidently she was not at all plain; she looked like some radiant marionette.

The Baroness was a thin weary person, with the air of a passée Madonna. She had that faint consumptive colouring that connoisseurs so admire, and nervous mystical hands that might have belonged to an El Greco Saint. Her nose, ever so little to one side, suggested ruse, a capacity of deception. In her day it was said that

she had provoked great passions, and it was known that she possessed love-letters in three different languages which she kept
on her dressing-table in a silver box. In a woman whose appeal had
been so gloriously universal, graciously unhampered by politics,
her charm was naturally elusive. But probably her secret lay simply
in her untidiness; she had made it a study. Untidiness, with her, had
become a fine art. A loose strand of hair . . . the helpless angle of a
hat; and, to add emphasis, there were always quantities of tiny
paste buttons in absurd places on her frocks that cried aloud to be
fastened, giving her an air of irresponsibility which the very young
Courtiers seemed to find quite fascinating.

Super-sensitive, exquisitely impressionable, it was part of her
temperament to fall under a new influence every quarter of an hour.
She could draw all the beauty from a face, and for the space of a
Rainbow make it her very own. Often the fugitive marvels of the
Sunset would linger with her in an afterglow entirely personal,
and some of her lunar effects were extremely fine. Unfortunately,
she was equally sensitive to ugliness, and she had made many enemies
among plain people through an almost telegraphic abruptness,
excessively wounding, and it had been often remarked that, after
chatting with the King, or dining with the Prime Minister, her
beauty invariably waned.

'She is so splendidly feminine,' the Courtiers would say. 'What
fastidious joie de vivre!' 'She is a Cobra,' thought her maid, who
understood her to perfection.

She had put on that morning, in honour of the Princess's birthday, a cloth costume, in a new and mysterious art-shade, embroidered capriciously with sprays of Oleander-flower in brightest pink.
A sly short train, much ruched, coiled serpent-like about her
Louis XV heels.

Seated on the edge of a threadbare music-stool, she appeared
now to delicate advantage; her indeterminate profile, fugitive
against the insinuating masterpieces upon the walls. Mechanically,
with a heavy black fan, she stirred up the air. From the piano,
surrounded by Iris, an idol in a professional pose, considered her
with a look of golden indulgence; in life, only a diplomatist could
look so much, and mean so little.

The Princess raised her eyes sleepily to an oval portrait of an
ancestress, known to history as 'Queen Beryl the Bad.' The Queen,
with a star in her hair, clad in a French dinner-gown, was leading,

by a chain of frail Convolvulus, a prancing war-horse. The portrait was by Nattier.

'It is two o'clock,' remarked the Princess. 'All the town is at siesta; it is an hour more secret than midnight,' and she slightly shivered.

'You forget the Queen, dear,' sighed the Baroness. (The Baroness was privileged to call the Princess 'dear' whenever she chose.) 'She went out motoring only an hour ago. It would be *so* awkward if I should meet her!'

'Mamma is too wrapped up in herself,' returned the Princess, 'to be really dangerous, besides, you could open your sunshade when you see her coming.'

The Queen had a passion for motoring. She would motor for hours and hours with her crown on; it was quite impossible to mistake her . . . she was the delight of all those foreigners, and especially Americans, who came to her Capital to study Art.

'To tell the truth, darling,' began the Baroness, 'I have a severe headache; I noticed it this morning when I got up; I fancy, before evening, we may expect a storm.' And throwing down her fan, and removing some rings, she commenced a melancholy fugue.

'A storm!' mocked the Princess, lighting a cigarette and heightening a trifle the blind (to sit in a strong light was against all her principles), 'alas! there will be nothing so interesting; but if you *must* play, dear, couldn't you manage to be a little less sinister.' And she added mysteriously: 'You may play that to me, if you like, after *he* is dead.'

Outside, under the Palace windows, the sun shone down on the meek boughs of the lime trees that waved about a green pool where a Dolphin bubbled heedlessly and warmed the strangely shaped beds and borders, strictly floral, which, woven through the grass, suggested patterns on an Oriental shawl. Here and there where the foliage dipped, you could see the blue-washed Wellen Range, hill over hill, along whose veins flashed the splendid automobiles. Overhead the sky was so pale that it appeared to have been powdered all over with poudre-de-riz. The scent of Lime flower wafted through the open windows, filled the long corridor-room where the Princess sat, surrounded by faded royal furniture, and mingled pleasantly with Tea Cigarettes from China, which it was her pleasure to inhale.

What an elegant view! What deceptive expanse! Who could have guessed that behind the swaying curtain of the trees, stood the curly wrought-iron gates, with prowling Sentinels in gay plumed hats, and sun-fired swords; while beyond, the white town, with its countless Spires and gold domed Opera House, its Theatres and spacious streets, its Cafés, from whence, sometimes, on still nights, you might hear the sound of violins, trailing capriciously, like a riband, upon the wind. Who could have guessed at such gaieties, looking down from the Palace windows at the quiet Dolphin, as it bubbled heedlessly, amid its reeds and lilies; staring foolishly up at the Royal window-panes, indifferent to the swirling dance of Butterflies, or to the occasional leaping of a Carp. What an elegant view! What deceptive expanse! So much, contained in so little, suggested a landscape painted delicately upon a porcelain cup or saucer, or upon the silken panel of a fan.

'This cigarette . . . my nerves . . . the hour,' faltered the Baroness with uncourageous fingers pressing her heart.

'Nonsense, Teresa!' the Princess said, quite sharply, 'I had not thought you such a coward. See! here is the letter; take it, there is no danger. It is as obscure as the second part of "Faust"; indeed it is a good deal more so.'

The envelope, lilac, narcissi-scented, was addressed to:

St. John Pellegrin,
Villa Montoni.

'Villa Montoni!' The Baroness rolled up her eyes in resignation to the barocco ceiling, tucking as she did so the envelope into a fold of her gown. 'Of course,' she said, 'darling, you must do just as you please, I never advise anybody, but if I were you, I certainly should not dream. . .'

'The Villa is two miles beyond the town,' continued the Princess, nestling her head deep into an incredibly shaped cushion, 'but the tram passes the gate. It is surrounded by a low wall which is plastered all over with inartistic announcements in the worst possible taste. There are pomegranate-trees on either side of the door; such stately ones; he also keeps pets. Lovely plump pigeons that take his letters; and run little errands of mercy for him through the sky. Only last night I noticed two of his birds fly over the Palace with a pair of stockings. His garden they say is full of tropical flowers even in the winter, and it is rumoured that strawberries ripen there all the year. Do not forget to take a basket with you nor, in your emotion, to admire the fruit.'

The Baroness fixed enormous eyes on a Crucifixion by a pupil of Félicien Rops—a pale woman seen stretched upon a Cross in a silver tea gown, with a pink Rose in her powdered hair; the pearls about her throat bound her faster to the cross, and splendid lace draped her bleeding hands and feet. At the foot of the Cross lay a fan, a letter, and a handkerchief, tortured into a knot till it looked like a white flower; behind her spread the sky grey and ashen, gashed with flame, whilst rain-drops fell slowly, slowly, as though scattered through fingers . . . For a moment the Baroness seemed lost in thought, imagining the martyred woman's lover.

'He must have been very young to be so cruel,' she told herself. 'I should not be surprised if he were quite a boy. *She* might be any age; a powdered wig is so deceptive. What secretive eyes! I do not like her look!—I am wondering,' she said at length, after a pause just long enough for an Angel to pass, flying slowly, 'what I shall wear. I hope the man is shy and not at all forward; think! dear, if he should molest me! I cannot forget poor Gilda's fate in that very faded Opera we saw last night.'

'Hush!' the Princess exclaimed, drawing in voluptuously a long slow breath—a breathing exercise known familiarly to herself and the Baroness as 'a soul flutter.' 'He is a Saint, you forget that! And if that were not sufficient, his mother, I believe, was an *Italian Countess*.'

The Baroness looked less suspicious, it was a comfort to think that the creature had not begun life as an acrobat or with a concertina, she began to feel almost excited.

'Should I,' she enquired, 'wear the little gown I wore at poor Eulalia's funeral, or dare I wear a heavenly thing—Scenes from the Decameron painted upon chiffon, and an enormous sombrero with silver strings?'

'I do not mind what you wear,' replied the Princess, 'but oh, Teresa, whatever you put on, do not return without his promise that he will come to my party to-night. How I should care to be a new Salomé! And why pray should I not be? Indeed the position in which Fate has placed me, to hers, exactly corresponds. Let us review the situation, and you will see that all I need is to develop my style.'

The Princess loved colouring her retrospect. She would do it indeed aloud by the hour, ignoring altogether that the patient Baroness had nearly always been present at the original occurrence.

'When dear Papa died at Montreux seven years ago,' she began, —'he died holding a bottle of absinthe,—Mamma erected a mundane-looking angel to his memory and accepted his brother's, the King's invitation to weep away the remainder of her life at Court. How pretty Mamma looked as a widow, with her thin rouged cheeks, and her black feather boa! and how dreadfully she worried over her pink pearl earrings with permanent clasps that would not take off. In doing so she mercifully quite forgot poor, poor Papa. What an unenjoyable journey that was; Mamma prostrate with presentiments. Each time the basket of Arums and Orchids (eked out with Gypsophila) that the Station Master at Montreux had presented her with, rolled to the ground, Mamma screamed, and said she was certain that she would be assassinated within the year, which naturally reminded her of the fatal gala performance given to poor Aunt Caroline—*requiescat in pace*.

"Did you never hear of the Duchess of Malfi," my Governess asked mysteriously, in tones that robbed us of our circulation, and without any more warning began to recite: "What would it pleasure me to have my throat cut with diamonds? or to be smothered with Cassia? or to be shot to death with pearls?" Personally, I was almost paralysed by the idea of a long drive on our arrival through crowded thoroughfares in an open landau, and being stared at, in an ugly crêpe hat trimmed with crêpe buttercups, my hair in a knot like a Chinaman's tail. It was a beautiful June evening, the blues and reds of the sunset combining in an exquisite mauve. The sky was then decidedly mauve, which, as night came on, turned to subdued violet. We passed through fields of white clover, bounded by canals of purple water, and hurried by windmills that turned and turned in the dusk like revolving Crucifixes. The white oxen returning from the fields were washed in violet light, and the pink powder on the end of my governess's nose turned violet too. As we drew near the Capital, Mamma became terribly unstrung, and began to laugh immoderately.

'The King met us at the Railway station with his Crown on, and at the sight of him, poor Mamma lost all control of herself and laughed till she wept: "He looks like a piece off a chess-board!" she gasped. "How totally sweet!"

247

'The train was late, and the King already annoyed.

"Quiet your mother for the love of God, and a box of chocolates, little cat-thing," he whispered to me, and turning to Mamma he said: "The public has been standing since daybreak to catch a glimpse of you, while many people have gone to the expense of taking balconies to watch the Procession pass. They will certainly feel disappointed if you do not look stricken, shed public tears, and behave in a general way as though you are very much upset.'

"Can you not see that I am?" cried Mamma ... "But, really ... an ovation? How delightful! No; of course I shan't disappoint them. Is my hat on straight? How does my veil droop?" And all the way back to the Palace she flung herself about amid a storm of sympathetic applause. She went down to dinner that night in a lovely black cashmere, sewn with sparkling Lilies, an *uraeus* diadem of diamonds outstretched wingwise in her hair. I was standing at the window as she entered watching the sentinels pace slowly to and fro; the night was so still that I could hear them swear. I think the moon looked like a piece of Majolica-Ware as it hung above the trees, and I remember the fire-flies darting in the garden below were a new experience for me; you see, dear Papa would never stay anywhere unless there was a Casino; he loved the dazzling life of Casino Towns, and would find poetry in the cool shuttered rooms, whilst outside the sun poured louis on the sea. In the afternoons Mamma and I would go and drink tea in lace frocks in the public salons, and listen to the Viennese band, and even in those days, she held a gay little court. She would often scold me for looking too old and said that no nice girl ever looked more than eight; and she would never take me about with her unless I carried a silly woolly lamb until I was past fourteen.

'It was foolish of me, but I confess I felt just a wee bit lonely that first evening as I stood at the window recalling it all. How gloomy the Palace seemed! I missed the glamour, the feeling of possible adventure that you get at twilight in a large hotel, for not unfrequently (as Mamma knows!) I would manage to find at least *one* small boy to pay me his respectful love. It was the hour when we were accustomed to music, when it was my habit to hide behind a curtain or a tub of flowers and watch the people as they wandered down to dine. One could hear often the waves of the sea, like some great chagrin, unclasping themselves without, and when a door opened catch a glimpse of it, stretched like a strip of tight silk, across a window as a blind.

'How gloomy the Palace seemed! How still! You know, dear, when we first came, they put me all alone up a horrid tower; the same apartments poor Queen Beryl had before they dragged her out to die.

"How foolish of us to come and live in such a Barrack," I exclaimed bitterly, for in spite of Mamma always grumbling about dinner in Restaurants—"Snatching Meals" she used to say,—I knew she really loved it, when suddenly, behind me, I heard the movement of her gown.

'Directly I saw her smart frock I knew why we had come. She read my thoughts, and pressing a finger to her lips, and pointing to heaven with her fan, she hurried from the room without a word.

'Six months later the Crown jewels had been all re-set and Mamma was Queen. She was married quite quietly in a corner of the Ballroom ... before an Empire table, without a bridesmaid, without a flower. Just the Lord's Prayer in B and a chapter that sounded as though it were taken from Jean Cocteau or Maurice Rostand mumbled over their heads! Of course I have never believed it to be properly binding. And I am sure that he will think so too. And when I asked Mamma why she wasn't married in State at the Cathedral, she told me not to ask questions, but that it was on account of the roof.

"That is what I call perfect candour!" I said, "but you cannot deceive me; you wished to escape the Procession."

'Whereupon she displayed vexation and screamed: "Impudent!" in French, and predicted that one day I should make a *mésalliance*, and that is why I have gone and engaged myself to that horrid-horrid Crown Prince, but of course nothing, nothing, nothing shall ever make me marry him.'

The Baroness smiled, twisting her mouth sideways like La Taxeira in an invalid rôle ... the monotony of these daily outbursts! 'The resemblance *is* remarkable,' she agreed, tactfully, 'your mother, like Herodias, *did* marry her brother-in-law, but somehow I had never thought of them together before. I don't know why!'

'Ah! but you will,' the Princess declared, 'after *he* has denounced her. Moreover there is something in Mamma's appearance that recalls Herodias, especially in the afternoon when she wears her furs. You will never know how bored I am, Teresa, nor how I long for a little excitement, and now that there seems to be a faint chance of having some, it would be cruel of you to spoil any trifling amusement the dear Devil sends my way. Charming Man! He neglects our Court ever since Fräulein Anna Schweidler giggled so disrespectfully at a Black Mass. She attributes her laugh to nervousness, but you know what Anna is! She should never have gone.'

'After all,' said the Baroness soothingly, 'it is delicious to lie still. Excitement, particularly when it is diabolic, always tells. Not that life is really so very dull . . ."

'Naturally,' replied the Princess rather spitefully, 'as one grows old, one likes to be quiet,' and seating herself, with the unreasonable look of an Iphigenia, upon a brittle, tattered and ornate throne, she began to hum a certain air by Strauss.

These cast-off Thrones were one of the features of the Palace. Whenever a throne began to look worn-out or the silk got 'shrill,' it was hurried off to a spare bedroom in the visitors' wing and used as a chair. Whenever a Grand Duchess came to stay, she was sure to be late for dinner, leaning back on her seat in a regal pose before her dressing-table, her combs arranged 'en couronne,' forgetful of time, the Queen's temper and the cold soup—dreaming, dreaming. . . . The Princess also shared the same weakness. Leaning back now, her index finger pressed against her cheek, she felt like a married woman, as she studied herself attentively in a mirror. 'Alas!' she presently exclaimed. 'Why are present-day sins so conventional—so anaemic? A mild, spectacled priest could trample them out with a large pair of boots. I prefer a Prophet who will insult me! It is then a pleasure to retaliate. I have always suspected mine to be a Salomesque temperament. Naturally, it would be treason to speak with candour of the King, but he would make a superb Herod. He has the same suspicious walk and the incurable habit of prodding curtains and expecting an ambush round every corner. So silly of him! and a constant disappointment as well. He is an old darling, and spoils me, but really his character is frightfully weak. What ever will History say? But he never troubles about that, and he will certainly be made into an Opera after he is dead, and I daresay I shall be dragged into it, too. And now, since Fate has placed us—how events repeat themselves—King, Queen, Princess—improbable people like ourselves, with a Prophet at our very gate, and the whole

Court languishing for something new, it would be ungrateful not to take advantage of the opportunity and make hay whilst. . .'

'Hay!' The Baroness looked sceptical. 'I am afraid you deceive yourself, dearest,' she said, 'about this man, he may not be all you suppose; I have made enquiries, and even quite foolish people think him foolish . . . And then remember, darling, that you *really are* affianced to the young man from Bucharest—The Crown Prince. If it should get into the papers . . . this adventurousness may end in some dreadful scandal. I cannot forget an old maxim of my mother's! "You cannot," she used to say, "be too careful until after you are dead." Remember how jealous your fiancé looked in his yellow uniform at the Review only the other day; I am sure he could be terrible when roused.'

'Do not speak of him, I hate him, and will never marry him, I would rather die,' declared the Princess, dramatically.

She had been brought up on this speech, so to say, from her earliest years. It came in most of the Classical plays at children's matinées, and sometimes the heroine would speak it from her closet whither she had been confined in disgrace, or sometimes through the keyhole of her dungeon, to an invisible person without, usually her mother, trembling lest her outraged lord should surprise her in forbidden intercourse. If the play happened to be an opera this scene gave splendid scope for a long duet.

'I would rather die,' repeated the Princess.

'Think of yourself alone with him, on a desert island,' the Baroness said, drearily, after a sententious pause.

'Ah! Don't, Teresa, how can you be so cruel.'

'Cruel! My dear' it is the only way to think about a man. Consider, what would a young girl of parts, fresh from her convent, do under similar circumstances. The first day on the Island she would (if she were at all distinguished) refuse to speak to him, and withdraw to some Oasis with a book. The second day, she would find herself watching him out of the corner of her eyes; still, she would not admit it. And when he tried to tell her that the desert winds had given her an infinitely better complexion than her married sister— who went out far more than was good for her—she would force a tired, distrustful smile and go away to write letters for the after-noon-tide. But the third evening, after she had finished dessert, and there were a few stars shining, she would probably feel a nervous flutter, a positive emotion at his approach. And why? Simply because he would be the *only man* . . . and the uglier he was, the more terrible the fascination! And fascination is really far more binding than love. I contend the Desert Island is the proper way of looking at every wealthy man; especially if he be a Prince. All you need, dear, is just the will to shut your eyes to everybody else and tell yourself there is only *one* man, and that you have been lucky enough to secure him all-to-yourself, and then, with a little coaxing, Love is bound to come . . .' And the Baroness, looking wise, took out her powder-ball and used it with an elegance that could not have been exceeded even in the flowery days of the Petit Trianon.

'Dear Teresa,' exclaimed the Princess. 'You are so wonderful! But you have had so many experiences. I feel I could never really love anyone unless he was pale, but pale . . . with violet rippling hair, and had eyes, blue, but blue, as skies in May, and could boast a big-big, Oh,' she abstrusely broke-off,' 'have you ever loved anyone just like that, Teresa?'

'Several,' answered the Baroness, recklessly. And as the Princess expressed a wish to know more, she was obliged to rise to her feet. These sentimental talks she usually learned to repent.

From the mantelpiece came a sudden 'whirr' from an unconcerned Sèvres shepherdess; a coquettish silence, followed by the florid chiming of a clock.

'Very well, dear,' she said, 'if you really wish me, and I absolutely must, I will be ready in an hour. Nothing discreditable, I hope, may come of it. I shall put on all my amulets; it would be difficult to harm me when I'm wearing my Winged Victories—and long earrings are being worn just now.'

'Bless you,' the Princess purred transported; and she added, sweetly: 'Remember the jewelled girdle that shall be yours if you set your nets with tact.'

The Baroness blinked as she withdrew. 'Nets! Alas! I have none, but the jewelled girdle . . . you spoil me, dear.'

'Poor Teresa,' reflected the Princess, sounding idly a harp with jade stops and rose-red strings, 'she is a dreadful hypocrite, but I am very fond of her all the same.'

When the Baroness returned an hour later she was all feathers and nerves. She was looking angelic in a gown three shades of grey, with silver embroideries and improvised knots and falling tassels, partly concealing the 'heavenly aquarelles,' which was perhaps just as well. Quantities of tiny painted buttons ran hither and thither, quite aimlessly, going nowhere, all undone. Like yellow butterflies the Winged Victories hovered from her ears, and a string of filmy stones, obviously spells, peeped furtively, like watchful eyes, waiting to operate at a moment's warning, in ways best known to themselves. She was looking pale, and unusually weary, under an enormous structure of feathers and orchids, weighed down on one side in artistic collapse. In her delicate Greco hands, cased in stiff white kid, she carried the frailest of wicker baskets and tucked under her arm an elaborate sunshade of geranium pink.

'How nice you look!' the Princess said, as she kissed her on either cheek. 'And, oh! What a smart hat. And how sensible of you to wear grey—it is always *safe*. Black, if it is well-made looks so fast. And now, don't forget, dearest, to bring me back in your basket an enormous water-melon, the kind they have in Palestine; and, if it were possible, I should so love a light green Rose. Up to now I have seen them only in hats, when they look like cabbages, or in paper sometimes at bazaars.'

The Baroness seemed too overcome, with the perils of her mission, to articulate; a soul-flutter was her only comment. She received her mistress's embrace with a nervous calm, never lifting her eyes higher than the royal shoe. When at length she had actually disappeared the Princess gave vent to her relief and performed a riotous valse. Up and down the room she whirled, past the famous Master-pieces (hung by a gardener, one might have said, skilled in Herbaceous lore) past Madonnas and frowning Queens, and Favourites shivering on sofas in airiest batistes and 'Awkward Surprises,' and 'Storms at Sea,' and enormous paintings of bouquets of flowers, all satiny, on varnished boards, over which the gold dust poured. Presently, exhausted by her transports, she collected her hairpins and seated herself on a conventional Empire stool, with a conventional book, from a conventional Aunt, with conventional love, for a conventional birthday. The conventional book was 'The Home Life of the Queen of Sheba.'

'So far,' she told herself, 'it isn't a bit amusing to be a débutante. I believe I almost wish I were back in the Schoolroom again with old Miss Littleclaud, although I called her such an odious woman at the time.'

But what was that heavy persistent perfume that lingered amorously on the air, enfeebling the moral senses, undoing good resolutions—supposing any to have been made? The Princess sniffed.

Lime Flower? No. Acacia Blossom? Hardly. Tuber Rose? Perhaps. She rose suddenly to her knees, her mind full of a horrible suspicion. Could it be what the Queen most abhorred, what the King most objected to; what she herself most particularly disliked because she was forbidden to employ? Could it possibly be . . . *scent*?

Yes, it was, indeed, and of a particularly execrable kind—'Vieille Cocotte' she pronounced it. A woman with such a pocket handkerchief could have no prestige.

Pacing to and fro, she pondered the matter. Here was some mystery brewing; some intrigue to unveil.

Teresa? It was unthinkable. 'Knowing, as she knows,' she murmured, 'Mamma's horror of all essence she would never dare. . . .'

But there was no mistaking it; the room was drenched with the pungent smell. It *was* Vieille Cocotte! You could get it at the Casino in small green bottles tied up with gay-gay ribands, at an unusually beautiful Kiosque with 'Madam Carmen' painted across the door. Madam Carmen, a remarkable looking person, sat there all day long, in a paste necklace and earrings, smiling always at her own amusing thoughts, her face so powdered that it seemed to be smothered in flour. But how had the Baroness managed to procure the guilty stuff? And now, through a spiral of inconsequences, the Princess recollected. Last night at the Theatre the Baroness had begged leave during an entr'acte. . . .

'I love,' she had said, 'wandering on the terrace at night. The City looks really queenly with its white houses, glittering water, and arching trees!' and with the smiled permission she had gone.

'Artistic creature!' the King had said, quite loudly, as she left the box.

On her return, her manner had seemed strange—she must have procured it then.

The Princess crossed to the windows and flung them open. How irritating the Dolphin looked below as it stared up at her, bubbling needlessly, its mouth wide open like a person who had committed a fault. Beneath the shadow of the trees men were erecting a vast Marquee, and bringing forth refreshments for the ball. Trays laden with sparkling sweetmeats and champagne bottles, reclined imprudently in the sun (how irresponsible those impassive bottles would make folk when the stars came out!) and a forest of empty glasses packed tight together like flowers grown for sale, suggested Dutch gardens glowing with all the colours of rarest Tulips. Scattered over the lawn were majestic dishes, and piles of plates, more gorgeous even than the flower beds they were set among.

'Let the crockery be representative!' the Queen had said, 'as the Ambassadors will be here.' And she had also added: 'Do not turn on the fountains before you perceive the first guest.'

Oh! What a variety of porcelain there was! Looking down upon it it was like assisting at a fancy dress ball. There was gala Dresden (which showed the imperfections of their own national faïence) and Crown Derby and Biscuit, and Urbino, and Delft. There were things Japanese, and things Chinese, and whole regiments of mysterious pots and pans which, unless turned over and their marks examined, refused to be known. There were festoons of flags, too, to correspond, and hampers of roses (white Miss Missingham and dark red Mrs. Steeple) all the way from the King's country seat in the Wellan Range, whose Ogreish towers and sinister Minarets, just visible, served to scare the disobedient children in the capital beneath.

Fluttering out upon the balcony, the Princess became absorbed. There was something exquisitely Eastern about all these bustling servants that suggested slaves. 'I am afraid the sunset will be a failure,' she remarked presently regarding anxiously the sky. And as she spoke a bird skimmed past her with a satin quilt.

O Charity! She watched it, spellbound, soar above the trees. In some cosy cottage garden *his* gift would fall like a bolt from the blue. Only the Flemish Primitives could do justice to the surprise.

How the elder Brueghel would have delighted in the scene.... The fence, the rows of stiff hollyhocks, the invalid at her casement, the children rolling in the dust, the father busy digging, the immodest courtship in the back-yard, and the sudden appearance of the struggling bird over the low thatched roof.

What an admirable Primitive it would have made! What scope for amazement! for flinging up of hands! And to think of it all wasted. She sighed, and turned her eyes to heaven at the loss.

Although the Princess had been expensively brought up, she could not prevent herself from uttering a scream. Gazing down upon her from the floor above, her Grandmother (an old lady almost past everything but making mischief) stared straight into her eyes. In her great mob cap she looked like some dreadful gargoyle. Could it be an evil omen? How often the King had said at the noonday-meal, that his mother had been the Ruin of the Country....

'My dear,' the old lady called down in her crotchety voice, 'did you notice that irregular looking bird? I'm afraid it means *we are about to have a War.*'

With an unamiable reply, the Princess returned to the Corridor-room, but the scent of Vieille Cocotte did not soothe her; it dawdled ridiculously, lingering on as its name implied, and it was some time before it could make up its mind to depart and escape by the window.

Ablaze with suspicions, there was to follow for her a period of considerable suspense.

Of course! She might have guessed it. The Baroness would try and dazzle the Saint. In imagination already she saw her seated on the Saint's knee, a perfervid arm about the prophet's neck. It was not to be endured. Deliberately, she cast her glance about for something to destroy. Marie Leszczinska, in her robes of Fleur-de-lys, stared at her from over the fireplace in cold dismay.

Stiffening her fingers, and dilating the pupils of her eyes, the Princess examined herself carefully in a mirror. What fatal beauty! What a wonderful expression! But, of course! Only dull relations or stupid courtiers could fail to notice the very close resemblance....

*   *   *

Ten minutes later the whole palace was in an uproar. The Princess had commanded a warm bath à la reine de Saba, and before she had it, she wished to *speak with the King.*

𝄢 *II* 𝄢

IN WHICH THE DEVIL HIMSELF INTERVENES

IN the Platz under the Linden trees stood the white omnibus, less white than the Princess had supposed. Catching her skirts closely about her the Baroness seated herself in the furthest corner, shielding herself from the public gaze behind the pages of the Court Gazette.

How the bees hummed among the Linden flowers, and how dull it was hiding behind the Court Gazette! After a few moments the

Baroness made a window in her newspaper—a long Gothic one—and peered out.

The Platz seemed almost deserted. There was an afternoon atmosphere about everything difficult to define. Even the equestrian statue of the King, with his fierce expression and brandished sword, seemed to unbend a little to the influence of the hour, while his bronze charger, so imposing by moonlight, looked almost gentle as it pranced into the blue-pale air.

In the shadow of the Linden trees a few children played, in subdued manner, the National game—Whipping Tops—and near by a Vendor of Images appeared asleep before his tray.

Birds flew past and butterflies loitered, and in their formal borders, the town flowers languished in stately rows. How close it was! Small risk to get down and sit on the bench outside . . . but to manœuvre one's hat twice through that narrow door . . . No! better sit still and essay to be amused as best one might. How stout the conductor was! . . . really there was lots to see.

Beneath the great *West* door of the Cathedral (where she had ripped her gown at the Coronation of the first Queen), a lady, all in raptures and a guide book, stood admiring the façade, whilst a gardener, too young to be allowed a can, busy watching her, seemed to be watering his feet, and almost along the very rails of the tram from behind his remarkable structures, an artist, in a shady hat, sat painting the Image-seller.

The Baroness would have given a crystal rosary to know whether the Image-seller was only posing or actually asleep. 'I shall never know,' she reflected mournfully, and just as she thought she detected an eyelid tremor faintly, the tram cruelly carried her away.

In the Flower Market she descended.

It was a delightful spot, with its lazy fountain designed from an early drawing of Verrocchio, round which, under monster parasols, the market-women clustered before their fragrant wares, idly dreaming, perhaps, of deceiving their husbands, or posing to Foreign artists at a shilling an hour. But in Medieval times, so history said, this delightful spot had been used for other ends than flowers.

'My little dressmaker lives quite close,' the Baroness murmured, ' and I do so want a tinsel rose . . . and a few yards of spangled net. I hear she has some transcendently foppish gauzes just now, and the smartest plumes. But, alas! I suppose I haven't time.' She could not resist, however, purchasing a beautiful bouquet of 'Cottage' lilies—a suitable offering she considered for the Saint.

The charming caress of her frock, the cottage-lilies, and the strange afternoon atmosphere, gave her a vague and soothing sensation wholly delightful. Contrary to what might have been supposed, the Baroness did not 'glide'; far from it, she walked as if the heel of one shoe were a trifle higher than the other; not that this was so; it was merely style. Catching sight of herself in a shop-window, she reminded herself of an Angel of the Annunciation—a Carlo Dolci.

But there was no time to indulge in roadside-sensations, and putting up her lorgnon she peered about her for the blue tram.

There it was; and *what* a conspicuous blue. 'Really, my dear,' she said to herself, 'it is too crude.' The Mistress of the Robes had a dinner-gown in exactly the same shade.

'There are already two people inside; it is crowded,' she murmured, as she got in.

In a corner of the tram sat a Priest, reading a Book of Hours—not her own dear, charming, delightful Monsignor Parr, but such a *hard*-looking man, who looked as if he might be a little relentless towards his Penitents; and although she rustled her gown a great deal, and changed her position twice, he *never* looked up from his book. The other occupant was an impressionable-looking youth in a blue smock, picturesquely patched in conventional places. (. . .) He had profusions of golden hair, and eyes as hard as flints.

'He is charming,' thought the Baroness. 'I think him all too sweet.' And lowering her eyes at his insistent stare, she commenced a long voyage on the silver laces that adorned her gown.

She was at Thebes, and preparing to start for Tunis, when he suddenly interrupted her innocent pastime and asked her the name of the flowers she was wearing in her hat.

To talk *chiffons* to such a person was out of the question, so she answered a trifle stiffly: 'I beg your pardon, did you ask for the time? It is not yet half-past four.' Can he be mad, she wondered, looking at him with interest. Psychologically, an imbecile was not to be despised.

'He has pretty eyes,' she told herself, 'and looks wonderfully robust (. . .) but I cannot afford to risk anything just now in returning glances with a lunatic,' and with an annihilating look at the golden-haired youth, she left the interior of the tram and climbed on top.

How delightful it was on top!

The branches of the chestnut trees drooped above her listlessly, wrapt in summer haze. Here and there the town doves, looking like plump white pearls, threaded through the heavy foliage, cooed capriciously as they plumed themselves, dropping down feathers and platitudes on the passers-by.

They were inadequately supported by the State, and would certainly have died long before, but for the charitable assistance of foreign tourists. They lived to be photographed; posing for picture-postcards, and 'souvenirs,' hovering, and doing their best, over the heads, or at the feet, of anybody who would throw them sufficient corn—As indifferent to the Nationality, as to the quality of the hand that threw; more callous even than the pert *meretrix* who flaunted beneath them when evening fell. They were not particular, but they were acutely bored with their professions, and took it in turns, when, for a livelihood, a bourgeois destiny obliged them to disport themselves and show the lining to their wings. Sweet things! They had never heard of Venice.

To be up among the cream and pink chestnut flower, like a bird, had seemed to the Baroness a foolish dream. Yet suddenly, unexpectedly, it had happened.

The warm wind, passing across the Flower Market, brought with it, in rhythmic waves, the scent of narcissi and violets, and above, great fleecy clouds hung low in the sky as though they were going to fall. Opening her parasol, the Baroness looked about her vaguely expecting to see the Queen.

The Queen always insisted while motoring on mending her punctures herself, and it was no uncommon sight to see her sitting with her crown on in the dust. Her reasons for doing so were complex; probably she found genuine amusement in making herself hot and piggy; but it is not unlikely that the more Philistine motive of wishing to edify her subjects was the real cause. She had been called a great many things, but nobody had ever said she was proud; this was her pride. . . .

But the Queen was nowhere in sight. Indeed, nobody of any note seemed to be about. A few pious persons threaded their way towards the Cathedral on emotions bent. A girls'-school passed with its escort of Nuns, and fantastic Demons flying above them

The Artificial Princess

(invisible) criss-cross through the air; (these summer days! how irksome they were ... even quite fervent prayers would fall swooning to earth, too tired to rise) whilst at the corner of 'Looking Glass Street,' over the new Beauty Shop, where, unembarrassed, you might buy other things as well, they were hammering the Royal Arms up over the door.

'Surely these things ought to be done at night,' the Baroness mentally reflected, as she watched the swaying emblem, when suddenly the refined sound of horses' hoofs, and a superb rumble of heavy wheels, broke the apathy of the hour (such a magnificent noise, dear reader, could only be produced at great expense, and indicated an elegant establishment, a number of servants, flattering friends, and family skeleton, none of which, of course, just then, one was privileged to see) and the Mistress of the Robes clattered by in her painted coach. She was off to attend a last rehearsal of her play and was evidently so late that the most she could hope for would be to arrive in time to witness all her characters lying dead in each other's arms.

Fortunately for the Baroness, it was impossible for the great woman to see sideways without turning her head, for her profile was entirely hidden behind a huge Leghorn hat, perched completely on one side, smothered with Jericho roses and Autumn leaves. Severely perpendicular, she carried in her dimpled hands an imprudently small parasol in the loveliest shade of sunset silk. Two black pages in powdered periwigs, and liveries couleur de rose, displayed their vocation by clinging with amazing agility to the swaying splashboard, ducking and bobbing in the most ingenious fashion so as to avoid being wound up in the meshes of her voluminous veil that streamed behind.

As she swept past the Baroness she suddenly let fall her sunshade and stretched out an impulsive arm with considerable coquetry, the palm of her hand turned inwards, as if—any student of the theatre would recognise the movement—to ward off some disgraceful proposition made by an indelicate person, invisible to the eyes, yet mentally no doubt an abomination of sin. She was evidently fussing over a stage gesture for her forthcoming play.

'I call her impossible,' reflected the Baroness. 'I daren't think what are her thoughts; but I always knew she had a criminal mind.'

The tram, after several false starts on account of absurd people who *would* come late, gesticulating wildly as they waddled up with enormous baskets of flowers, or vegetables, at last got under way, and the Baroness endured as best she might the jolting motion, and the uninventive naïvetés of a playful breeze. 'This is life,' she told herself at each fresh jolt. 'This is life.'

But the opportunity that came with solitude was not to be missed, and producing her faithful vanity-bag she administered to her complexion. 'He may be very handsome,' she told herself, 'or he may be only a frump; but in any case there is no harm in looking my best.'

The young man who came and sold her a sordid-looking ticket, seemed a dear, and almost made amends for the trouble it was to find her purse. He had brown, delicate hands (the backs amply strewn with fine blonde hair) and a reckless look about his eyes.

'Quite too graceful,' she described him.

'Cripples' Gate?' he asked her, with a charming smile.

'No! No! The Barrier.' And whilst he clipped her ticket *with a bell*, she could not help asking him a thousand questions. Who lived in that great-big-ugly house? (It was her own.) Was the Queen really liked? And didn't it get just a wee bit monotonous always being on a tram? And why was the tram painted blue? ? ? Surely heliotrope or palest amber would attract more passengers? What! colour made no difference! No? How strange! She felt quite sorry when the time came for her to alight and say farewell to the conductor.

To her dismay, the Princess had looked at an old time-table, and it was necessary to change her tram and take a pink. It was too tiresome; she would have some time to wait.

But, oh! How lovely it was to be in the Country again! !

'I would love to sit down on some shady bank,' she thought, 'and put daisies in my hair, and throw away this heavy-heavy hat, and drown it in a lilied-pool; and people passing by would think some poor unhappy woman was wearing it underneath."

Now, at that moment, the Devil, who had felt wounded, slighted, pained, at the Princess's complaints that afternoon, was hurrying incognito towards the Palace disguised as a sleek black Crow. Recognising the Baroness, with some faint surprise, he circled above her, deeply meditating. Here was a woman who interested him. He had long kept his eye upon her. He admired her languid style, her way; more than once, moreover, he had been vastly entertained by some of her conversations with Monsignor Parr.... He would have been pleased to have nominated her an extra Perpetual-lady of the Bedchamber (with the Eternal precedence of the Marchioness), at his own Infernal Court.

'Where she is,' he murmured, 'she is wasted.' But, as he was well aware, she belonged to that slithery type, which, alas! too often slipped through his fingers by the merest riband. How many delightful creatures had eluded him at the last moment by a sudden whisk! Here was an opportunity not to be missed. Wheeling several times above her, he plucked a feather from his breast and willed . . .

Ambling up and down beneath, the Baroness was growing impatient for the pink tram. Such unpunctuality was a scandal! It was monstrous! It was a perfect bore!

Already the sun had dipped below the hills, and the sky was streaked with crimson like a china rose. Just where the sun had dipped there lingered a mild yellow glow, producing that curious *Sunday effect* only to be found in Turner's water-colours; it made her think immediately of *Chepstowe*.

The sudden sound of an automobile behind her made her turn— if it should be the Queen!

To be found wandering at shut of day on the high-roads would require considerable explanation, and as she herself (to use her own expression) had more than once declared: 'I always feel that nobody ever believes me as soon as I start to explain.' She looked about her. How much lively gossip might yet be avoided if only by chance she could hide. Such an adventure, too, would delight the Princess; with a little embellishment it would make the most piquant story. 'The growing dusk, the rising moon, and there, my dear, was I . . .'

Already the Baroness indeed had begun to exaggerate, She had seen half a dozen cars go by, and had some interesting information to give about the occupants of each . . . 'and little did they guess, the wicked things! that at that very moment there, my dear, was I . . .'

But there was not a second to lose. Happily, there was not far to go; over there behind those Silver Fir she would find safety; an ambush there was even nearer, but—'No! No! "she shuddered", *not* that dreadful ditch.'

To pick up her things and rush blindly towards the advancing automobile was due partly to that femininity for which she was

The Artificial Princess

admired. 'One is so handicapped,' she panted, as she flew, 'with the wind snatching at one's hat. How exhilarating it is to feel oneself pursued! but oh! oughtn't I to be going the *other* way?'

It was impossible to doubt. To rush past the automobile would give the impression of a person steeped in guilt. Her chief chance was to stand still and look dazed and feign to be the sole-survivor of an accident. Promptly she struck a pose. Putting up her lorgnon, with a wretched look of broken bones, she began to stare very hard into a hedge.

'Theresa!' Through a thin veil of dust the bright countenance of a young man whom her husband had often sworn to kill, smiled at her in delighted surprise.

Although the Baron had often sworn vengeance, he was constantly offering his victim cigars and lending him his box at the Opera. It was difficult to know what quite were his intentions.

'Thérèse!'

'Max!' she gasped. 'Oh: You sweet thing! No, I'm not hurt—only very much shaken . . .'

He led her with solicitude to the car. 'Poor dearest!' he said, 'she is dazed.'

His manner was so charming, she felt it would be almost rude to resist. Besides it was delicious to give way to him, and nothing could be more to her taste than an escapade when frankly egotistical. But the letter . . . duty . . . it was demoralising.

'My dear,' she said, realising that she was being carried off all willingly-unwillingly like a creature in a Rape. 'I have a tiresome errand; a note to leave; I cannot go with you another yard,' and as she spoke there was a flash of diamonds, and the Queen whirled by in a cloud of dust. Like a shot Cameo she passed—all glimmering stones and pale mimosa hair, and wide dilated eyes.

'Never mind,' he exclaimed: 'Give me your note; the chauffeur can take it, and we will steal an hour . . . one little hour.'

She demurred, consulted a pet Saint (a neglected long-shelved creature, one of her own discoveries: St. Aurora Vauvilliers). 'Oh! dear St. Aurora, watch over me in this imprudence, and keep me from all calumny, Amen.' And, since she was about it, she added a few urgent words for a certain tardy frock: 'delivered by to-night, dear Saint,' *etc.* Then, acquiescing feebly, she rearranged her hat. 'I suppose your man could leave it just as well as I?' she murmured. 'And certainly the country, this evening, looks irresistible.'

263

There arose a fleeting dialogue as to time and place.

'I don't mind,' she said. 'But we must be careful to avoid the Romantic Valley; half the Court have gone there to a picnic. And we must be careful to avoid the road to Fort Little; it is just the hour when the Officers are likely to be hastening towards the Capital—gracious knows for what! And we must be careful to avoid ... but, really, I don't mind; everywhere in my present mood is equally delicious.'

He proposed Sand Dunes, Lanes; those towards Vermillionville? The Sea Shore ...

She became suddenly wildly romantic.

'There is an old haunted Inn on the Wellan road,' she began, 'with a parlour hung in flapping tapestries, and a painting by Vermeer in the front hall, and an entrancing garden beyond, full of Hollyhocks and Fruit blossom, and a running stream ... We might go there for an hour; the Fête, at the Palace, does not begin till quite late to suit the moon. Nobody well can miss me. From the number of invitations sent out the Banquet is certain to be a terrible crush; last year it was dreadful!'

They pulled up before a signpost, looking like a very thin Pierrot, as it pointed a white arm backwards, towards the Capital. The wind had fallen and the Roses on the hedges hung motionless on the thick blue air, as though posing for a study in Still-life for a Flower painter who had failed to come. Along the fertile Wellans, the fields lay like spread silks. In pale stripes ran the Cuckoo flower; in wavy lines coiled the Daisies; here and there, weary with sweetness, stretched patches of ruffled Clover, and once or twice, something more richly brittle—a speckled Orchid. Above, wrapped in evening haze, rose the loftier slopes, like rubbed-out charcoal where they touched the sky.

While he gave directions to the man, she meditated how she should fill her empty basket with fruit for the Princess. Doubtless, one would find Cherries, and Melons, at the Inn. 'Little fool, she will never know,' she thought. 'But the Green Rose—alas!' and she tittered.

Observing the chauffeur for the first time, she was pleased with his unintelligent expression; he had the obtuse look of a village Barber in a Comic Opera; she could see him dancing in a pair of sabots between two windmills, whilst the Prima Donna chatted archly at a lighted window, staring vivaciously into the boxes.

'Here,' she murmured, proffering him a whole sheaf of dainty, pansy-coloured notes, 'this is for your pains. Be careful not lose the letter, nor to soil the envelope. There is no answer, but remember to say that the Baroness Rudlieb would be glad if the Saint would kindly telephone *to her* whether he is able to accept . . . I think that is all. Do not bandy words with other servants, but when you have done your duty go and watch the moonrise from a hill.'

They set off at a reckless speed. 'Indecent haste, disgraceful empressement,' thought the chauffeur—whose face was his fortune —and looked about him for the nearest Tavern where he could get a drink. A sleek black Crow followed the Car for a while cawing 'lost—lost.'

How helpless the Baroness looked in the hurrying twilight! An unfinished masterpiece, suggesting delicious possibilities. Her plumed hat seemed sliding from her head, and her heavy coil of chestnut hair looked so loosely wound that anybody uninitiated in the Craft-mysteries of an experienced maid, would have said that it *must* fall as inevitably as a shower of Autumn leaves. O Magical Untidiness! O never-failing Charm! 'She looks like a Nun come into a sudden fortune,' he thought, 'did one ever see such a frock!' and the little empty basket in her tired white hands went straight to his heart. She leaned against his sleeve with the lightness of a moth. How wonderful the trees were, as they swept past them in the failing light, and the blue chain of hills reaching endlessly beyond, how peaceful!

'I can so well understand,' she mused, 'why the Saints flew to the hills. Some day I shall do the same, as St. Aurora did.'

And her thoughts returned to the adventurous history of Aurora de Vauvilliers. Aurora, who till the age of thirty-nine had been a celebrated courtesan when (by celestial design) an overturned carriage, and some injured limbs, had put a finish to her irregular mode of life. Aurora who had vowed (should she ever recover) to mend her ways, and make an expiatory pilgrimage as far as Palestine (with commissions to gather Roses at places of interest for the good Nuns of Forbonnais, and to fill bottles with water from well-known founts for the dear Monks at Istres). Aurora who had contemplated setting up a shop . . . Aurora who had set sail one languid summer evening with just a faithful maid and a Book of Hours . . . Aurora who, before she had been at sea a week, was captured by Pirates, and after enduring untold horrors made her escape on a loose board disguised as a man. Aurora who was tossed about for many days on a pitiless sea. Aurora who was cast at length upon a desolate shore, where she led for five years the Simple Life. Aurora who returned at length to her own dear France, with wonderful silver hair, more captivating than she had ever been before. Aurora who became the rage, attended fashionable assemblies, and who, whilst on a round of visits to the Châteaux in Touraine, had expired quite beautifully, one All Hallows Eve, at the Castle of Loches.

How often had the Baroness pondered the life of this adorable being (as set forth in the sympathetic biography of Monsignor Parr) and found extreme profit thereby in her own self-scrutinies.

'After all,' she murmured to herself, excusingly, '*we* may have an accident, too. He is driving very badly. . . .'

She leaned back, her face almost grey, the sins and sorrows of all the world gathered for an instant in her tired green eyes.

The warm air swept past them; the scent of flowers rose up from the fields. A startled cow grazing knee-deep in the long blue grass— like a creature in a Noah's Ark—looked up with a martyred glance expecting milk-pails, effrontery. Above hung a solitary star. What a lonely existence! The Crow followed yet, murmuring 'lost—lost.' Its effect was Japanese against the clear pistachio of the sky. On the outskirts of a wood a white goat fled into a thicket. 'Stop, stop,' she cried, 'I think I see Pan,' and round a bend suddenly appeared the Haunted Inn, with Pink Hollyhocks sleeping before the door. How dark it was inside. The Vermeer (a chaste Suzanne) was in eclipse. He ordered Champagne in the tapestry parlour, and they wandered out into the garden while the landlord groped for the wine.

She had exaggerated the beauties of the garden. It was full of Yews, strange lichened Statues, brown Owls . . . there was an air of witchcraft about the place; from the little stream floated up a thin mist.

She began to feel anxious; after risking so much, she was almost afraid that he was going to be dull. The twilight she felt sure laid too great stress on the *Madonna* side of her, he needed encouragement; she gave an artificial shudder, and took his arm. 'Everything seems so creepy,' she remarked, 'so immaterial in this light—black upon rose!'

They sauntered away down a meditative-looking path that twisted and twirled like a by-way in a legend.

The Artificial Princess

How dim it was under the trees, and how still. It was exceptionally sweet of Nature to allow her to trouble the silence sola, with the silken murmuring of her gown.

The Statues in the dusk looked terribly emotional as they clung to each other in immortal love. How fervent they seemed. Quite candidly, it was absurd to be alive and yet more cold than they. How dark it was! The ground sank away in profoundest purple under their feet; profoundest purple with a phosphorescent flicker, here and there; fortunately atmosphere left no stain . . . or what would Zellie say—without actually *leaning* she felt she might exact from him a further slight measure of support. It was a most disappointing path. Instead of hurrying to a comfortable summer-house (as she had certainly supposed) it went only a short way before it began to repent. In a moment they were back again before the Inn. A light twinkled from the parlour window. All around the Statues showed unflagging in the dusk. . . .

'Have we made the most of our opportunities?' she asked herself doubtfully as they wandered in.

Inside, all was candle-light and gloom. The parlour at any other time, and with anybody else, would have been disenchantment, for where was any tapestry? But the simmering wine, and the mellow light were things to be grateful for.

After all one did not expect to enjoy these adventures much at the *time*; it was only afterwards, from a sofa, in recollection, to the sound of a piano that they began to seem delightful; and just now, the landlord, she was afraid, was likely to be a thorn. He lingered insufferably.

Seating herself at the table, she drummed her fingers with impatience.

'What a pity,' she murmured desperately, 'that Goya never painted Fans.'

*　　　*　　　*

Far off, in the Palace, the Princess, who had obtained the King's word, that she might ask, during dessert, for anything she pleased, had risen from her bath, and was dancing a Tarantella before the Mirror, in just a bracelet and a rope of pearls.

The *Artificial Princess*

ℰ III ℱ

WALPURGIS—(POLITE)

THE Mistress of the Robes had lost her temper. The première danseuse from the Opera House, who was to have taken part in her al fresco extravaganza, refused to dance in the dew. 'I cannot do so,' was all the reason she gave.

'Obstinate creature,' the great lady stormed. 'Amateur!' she taunted her, but all in vain.

Nothing could have been more inconvenient. Failure, fantastic and Dureresque, stared at her and chilled her to the marrow. There could be no Ballet . . . the Ballet could not take place.

Oh! everyone knew how fond the King was of a little dancing, especially after a Banquet . . . to think that an abandoned wretch had it in her power to refuse to wobble her clumsy legs. To postpone the play at the eleventh hour and fifty-ninth minute, whilst a double throne, upholstered in gamboge, stood gaping before the sweetest of stages, was impossible.

Heaven alone could solve the embarrassment, and rolling up her eyes, she prayed with all the fervour of an horticulturer, for rain, or sudden hurricane. 'A steady downpour, dear Christ,' she implored, 'a Second Deluge!'

But unfortunately the weather was adorable; above, the night was a marvel of serenity, the air clearer than beaten silver; around her stood the trees motionless, like massive candelabra tipped with stars.

The Overture had already commenced. The Mistress of the Robes was in despair. Whenever she closed her eyes, she could see a skeleton dancing in the moonlight, clapping grave-bones, and cutting capers too harrowing to describe; it was no wonder, for she was thoroughly unstrung. It was remarked that in her agitation she had misquoted Lucretius during supper, and dropped her fan into the soup.

'All this strain will take her an extra month at Carlsbad,' a voice was heard to lament. 'I shall not get my holiday this year.'

Standing now midway on the flight of grassy stairs (the King was so tired of marble!) that led to the gardens, chatting with dangerous politeness to the French Ambassador, as she drew on her long white gloves, the Mistress of the Robes was the cynosure of all eyes.

'You mix them with olives and a little cognac,' she was telling him. 'Naturally it is a speciality, but it is quite my favourite dish.'

Flushed to the colour of a Malmaison, she was looking conspicuous in silver tissue and diamonds, her long train spread, shimmering, over the steps behind, with the exquisite restraint of a waterfall in a poem. Above, from the fortifications of a lofty tiara, an Ostrich feather fluttered in her hair, as from a Citadel. What radiancy! The moths caught themselves in her crown, and beat their soft wings against the crystals on her gown; with a scream she felt their cold caress upon her throat and breast.

'Flatterer,' she breathed, trying not to hiss. 'Personal magnetism indeed! Charms exposed? Help me, or I shall faint'; and the Ambassador bending gallantly over her, removed them one by one.

'He is taking liberties with her, before all the world,' murmured those who did not understand.

Clearly she was a Rubens, with her ample figure, florid colouring, and faintly pencilled moustache, a Rubens on the verge of becoming a Jordæns from a too ardent admiration of French cooking, and a preference for sleep. To all suggestions, kindly meant or otherwise, she would reply, indiscriminately: 'It is too sweet of you, still! I wrote the play, and you must admit that I know best.' And to the well-meaning entreaties of the extremely épanouie wife of a Court official 'to do a little Moorish dance,' she answered evasively, 'Thanks, dear, I dare say I could flop about myself.'

'How waspish!' murmured those who were standing near enough to hear.

She was not popular like the late Mistress—a polite woman—who, when one had said that she was too fond of gay colours, and was always insinuating the untruest things about everyone, was an angelic creature who would exclaim: 'thank you *so* much,' even for a pin.

On the terrace above the Rose Garden where the stage was set, stood a tumult of Servants, Operatic in liveries that included all the colours that may be found in a child's paint-box between white and black. How self-conscious they looked! fidgeting, whispering. Like a Chorus waiting outside some Cathedral for the Prima Donna; their poor hands aching for somebody at whom to point. Above them towered the Palace, looking like yards and yards of purple satin, stitched upon blue; a puff of air, one felt, would fill the whole thing out like a sail: the lack of perspective and needless quantities of Stars suggested an ambitious drop scene. Behind the servants, gleamed the startled eyes of the Princess's horses; their behaviour during the fireworks had caused censure and surprise. 'They will go into disgrace for a fortnight,' said the lugubrious Lord Chamberlain, which meant they might run about exactly as they pleased. 'There,' he added, addressing the horses in rebukeful tones, 'should be your model,' and he waved a soft white hand, and some wonderful cameo rings. Through the trees, a bronze horse leapt lightly into the night, bearing a dainty Queen arrayed in wind-blown draperies and stone-rosettes. She carried a fan, and an enormous key. The key was so fantastic, that people had come from all parts of the world to look at it, obliging the King to throw open his gardens on Thursdays from two to four. After a pedantic controversy, it was agreed that the key opened nothing more particular than the doors of her heart.

There were Roses in the Rose Garden, which was remarkable where all was paradox, and from every Rose bush hung a Chinese lantern; between these, the Maids of Honour tripped about, looking like Easter Lilies, they were enjoying themselves immensely, and giggled a great deal; but nobody smiled at the absurd antics of the King's Dwarf. A young boy, with a tired white face, wandered about among the Terminal figures and the Rose trees, playing in the remotest fashion upon a violin. No voice could reach the silver region where he *began*, and he would trail deliciously away until he evaporated imperceptibly into silence.

In the chiaroscuro of a shrubbery, a Society Crystal gazer, swathed in many shades of violet, was predicting misfortunes by the light of the Stars.

The summit of her dreams was to look 'uncanny'; this (for she succeeded perfectly) was her solitary secret.

'People won't come to one in a peach-charmeuse trimmed with Point,' she had often lamented. 'One requires Moonstones, Veils, and a ghoulish cut to one's skirt . . . it is so tiresome not to be able to wear out one's professional clothes in the street.'

She wore, this evening, an Amethyst chain, a high Aigret in her hair, and concealed her face behind a Mauve Satin Mask. The Maids of Honour shivered, and quarrelled about their turns: 'She

The Artificial Princess

is not very definite, and muddles her dates,' was the verdict of those who had already been.

Under the quivering detail of the Limes, the Stone Dolphin bubbled heedlessly, it looked in the moon-mist like a large white Rose. The night was so warm that conversation languished, many people chose to nibble ethereally-tinted sweets, and sip Elixir Vitæ, and say nothing at all, waiting until the extravaganza should begin, but a select group of Matrons, Mothers to Maids of Honour, or Pages in Waiting, drew themselves aside to gossip with Monsignori, or whispered scandals about the Statues, dispassionately, behind their fans.

In spite of the Princess's wish that there should be 'no old people much,' the Queen had replied: 'My dear they *have* to come!'

Here and there, from a tree, hung a caged Nightingale—professional birds, with trained voices, and a grand manner of rounding off their notes with a marvellous shake. The wild Nightingales, unable to express their sentiments with such perfect finish, were silent from respect.

A loud crash of porcelain, and a smothered scream from behind the brocaded curtain, was a signal that the extravaganza was soon to begin.

The Mistress of the Robes closing her eyes saw flowers of alabaster and flame, and felt the earth as it revolved beneath her. Quite perceptibly she slipped a yard.

The King and Queen sat on a dais apart, the King with glazed eyes, the Queen amiably austere (so far everything naturally had to be a little stiff) watching a continuous stream of Mothers and débutantes trip forth by twos from a lighted Marquee, as from an Ark. The débutantes dipped a careless knee, while their mothers bowed down and enjoyed a delicious grovel. The Queen felt herself growing more beautiful every minute, it consoled her to be worshipped. Life with the King and his tiresome old mother was not all Violets, and when the ceremony was over she was feeling quite her best.

The Princess reclined gracefully at the Royal feet, looking incomparable in a Louis Quinze skirt, with the most interesting paniers, a corsage of a later period, and a cluster of wired gardenias (worn like a married woman), festooned with pearls. It was one of her Infanta Nights. One longed to make her stand up to see what she really had on. Her hair, like the tower of Pisa, leaned all one way,

271

caught together by a gemmed stiletto, smouldering fire. Now and then she would hold up a rose-red fan, painted by Conder, slantwise across the night: it pleased her to watch whole planets gleam between the fragile sticks; she had a capacity for dreams.

The Queen's expression was distinctly worried.

'I keep wondering, Theodore,' she kept saying to the King, 'whether there will be enough for them all to eat! I had not meant the refreshments to be served until *after* the play, and it looks as though everything would be consumed *before*. It is mortifying to be obliged to think constantly of expense, and to have to bargain, but now that the Army is being increased, and the uniforms have been changed from lemon and silver to periwinkle and violet, one must do what one can. But never forget this, dear, I will walk with you to the last under the same parasol.'

The King appeared unaffected by this fond outburst; if anything he seemed a trifle vexed.

'To-morrow,' the Queen went on, 'we will begin our economies. The Court shall have *Rabbits* for dinner. So good for them.'

'Nonsense!' growled the King, who looked like a tired Viking under an elaborate arrangement of jewels. 'It is bourgeois to think seriously about one's food; but if you meditate economy, let it not be in the *Cuisine*, Madam, for we forbid it,' and with a look of fixed horror he stared up into the hollow of the moon, murmuring 'Rabbit' in a deranged voice, as if it were a plot, or the name of a poison.

Although the Queen was a Colonel in several dashing regiments, she looked quite fearful. She wept and laughed with an equal facility and found an equal enjoyment in doing either; if she had any choice she preferred to weep; it was more refined.

'I am sure I do my best,' she murmured, leaning back carefully on her throne, on account of her puffed hair, 'and I am tired of doing it; tired, *tired*. It is impossible to scramble along on our small income. There are *not* enough taxes, although of course one cannot say so. My poor friend, you will never really be popular and you may just as well get what you can. If not, I dare say, one day, I shall be forced to pawn my pearls!' And dilating the pupils of her eyes she gazed wanly up at the tall-tall windows of the Palace, so large in winter, so tiresome in times of war.

The Queen loved to provoke a scene in public; it was a means to an end.

The Artificial Princess

She desired to create a permanent pose, to be symbolical.

She wished History to speak of her sadly as 'ill-used,' 'ill-starred,' 'the wretched Queen of a Tyrant.' She sought the warm tears of posterity, at the risk of being considered unsympathetic during her own life; to kindle enthusiasm, to leave a glamour, these were her ambitions; if it were not for the pain of it, she would have liked to have been executed.

'Mon Dieu! Que de cancans!' murmured the Princess, lowering her fan and fidgeting with the bouquet at her heart: 'Tell me, Papa, are the wires turning my Gardenias brown?'

'No, little-cat-thing,' replied the King, bending amicably over her.

'I am afraid *there is something* . . .' thought the Queen and she said quite icily: 'How often have I told you that I object to the child being called by any other name than Mary. *Another word,* and I will make the girl a Nun.'

'A Carmelite, dear, perhaps?' enquired the Princess unruffled, 'or a Poor Clare. Tell me, for I should like to know.'

The King threw a look of complete indifference at the Queen, and the conversation came to a close. The King had a glass eye, and it was difficult to say which was which.

'He has only one eye, and I never know which is looking at me,' the Queen would sometimes complain. 'His stare is quite a Medusa's one; it is most uncomfortable. Ah! If that were the least of my grievances I might bear with it. But, unfortunately,' . . . and she would float away into a delicate psychology of her wrongs.

In Court circles men were mostly 'sorry for her' and thought her 'far too good' for the King.

'He is getting senile,' they would say. 'What a pity she is so constant. She lives for History—it will have nothing to say.'

The Queen was considered very lovely, but the relations of the King's first wife, and especially the Dowagers of the ancient régime, never ceased whispering about the individual style of her dress.

Rumour had it that she slept in a hat garnished with Roses, Plumes and Pearls. 'Her style seems a little too "emancipated," ' certain ladies would purr, 'and smacks too much of "*those women*" or at best "a Prima Donna." Ah! Poor King Theo!' And they would sigh.

To-night, the Queen was looking like a column in a white velvet dinner gown, with a delicate spiral of silver leaves that wound up her dress, towards her hair. Except for her hands, Providence had been unusually kind. Her hands, large like a gladiator's, were her most sensitive point; it was useless to bury them in rings, or squeeze them in gloves; she was obliged to carry a perpetual muff. Her feet . . . but one could only suppose. There was a donjon, rumour had it, prepared for the Bootmaker who should reveal her size.

But the play had already begun, and by degrees all chatter ceased.

Everybody modelled their expression from the Queen. The expression was not too difficult to imitate, for it was elementary . . . a languid interest.

Under the Rose Trees the critics sat upon the ground. They had been presented with diamond scarf pins by the Mistress of the Robes as soon as they arrived, so they knew just what they had to say. 'In her play,' wrote one, 'four persons faint at the same moment. With what economy of means does she bring this about?—A simple telegram.'

Notwithstanding the lateness of the hour, the Baroness had not yet appeared. When the Princess turned her head towards the Palace, she could see her Teresa's window ablaze with light, and now and then caught a glimpse of her passing shadow across the blind.

'She is probably putting on an over-emphasis of rouge,' she thought, 'and painting circles under her eyes. Poor dear! She is always so extravagant on gala nights.'

From the attic leaned her grandmother, looking, as earlier in the day, exactly like a gargoyle. A lighted candle beneath her chin threw the light uppermost à la Gerard Dow. Overcome with delight at the Fireworks she had waved her handkerchief at the Roman Candles, Flower Pots and Catherine Wheels. Beside her stood a Parrot, and a faithful maid. The Parrot's reflections, limited to 'Rubbish!' and 'Oh, how sweet!' could be heard plainly in the garden below, and the actors, perplexed, thought the critics must be composing their notices aloud.

On the stage, a pretty actress, in a pearl satin nightgown, and a bandeau of orange blossom, was dictating to herself an impassioned telegram. She was a huge success. Unquestionably she had learned her art from frescoes and tapestries; her poses were those of the figures on the best embroideries.

'Superb,' everyone agreed. 'Prodigious.' And the King was pleased to say: 'She is a lovely Nymph.'

The Artificial Princess

An immoderate laugh made the whole Court turn. The Mistress of the Robes was enjoying her own play.

'It is so witty,' she cried. 'What satire! And, oh, do look at the Paramour behind the curtain.' And, leaning against a young attaché, she collapsed into his arms a heap of quivering diamonds.

Under the trees, wrapped in nature's indigo, an orchestra, composed entirely of Zithers, commenced a serenade, and just then the Baroness appeared gliding between the Chinese lanterns that adorned the grass. It was a conspicuous entry, for, at a sudden silence from the parrot, everybody had turned on their chairs. The women, with their long necks curved, looked like spiteful swans. The Baroness seeing the whole Court turn towards her, imagined herself irremediably lost.

She had foreseen an ordeal; and was prepared to meet it. To be a taper in a wind showed inexperience, a shallow nature. Praise to St. Aurora, she had greater strength than that. She knew the power of being aloof, the effect of night-shade on sugar for the soul. A puff of air could not quench the electric force, the wrap of dreams, that flowed within. On returning to the Palace she had sprayed her face with spirits of Roses and read a chapter from *The Way of Perfection* of Theresa of Jesus. Under such circumstances, St. Aurora she found was too exciting, but the sublime Theresa never failed to restore her to complete peace.

After reading her words of blue-pale fire, she felt as though the waves of the sea had swept over her, obliterating any traces of emotion, reinforcing her, leaving her cheeks waxen as delicate shells.

Only for an instant, startled at the flash of stones as long necks curved enquiringly towards her, did her soul misbehave itself, and the stronger feelings flit to the surface, above the elaborate look-of-peace she had laid on as with a trowel. For a moment she lost her mask, and her guilt tripped forth, a ripple, and was gone, She felt suddenly a little masculine, that she was wearing his lips, his eyes, his way. . . .

It was irritating. To compose herself she thought of Carpaccio's St. Ursula in Venice, a woman without a trace of expression, with the veiled, crêpe-de-chine-look of a Sphinx. 'Whoever said the Sphinx *had* a secret?' she wondered; and at this wonderful thought she was lifted into realms of abstract speculation, and was saved.

She wore a gown neither blue nor green, like the egg-shell of a thrush, and a wreath of flat silver Vine leaves fastened across her hair. In her gracile fingers, long like a bunch of ribands, she carried a bouquet of full white tulips, and slung from her waist an enormous fan of sea-gulls' wings. She walked very slowly, with the artful unconsciousness of a Prima Donna wandering in a forest before a crowded house, examined, spied upon, through countless malicious glasses.

'Can she be in love *again*?' whispered the Lord Chamberlain. 'Impossible!' cried the Court Physician, 'only yesterday she declared that she was tired of love.' 'Tired of love?' The Court Matrons positively sniffed. 'She cares only about Statues now,' said a Maid of Honour. 'She has married herself to a Marble Pan in the middle of a wood; she told me so last night.'

'She is frightfully made up,' murmured the King's favourite.

'Her eyes are full of belladonna,' remarked the Queen's favourite.

'She is growing old,' whispered others.

'In the blue twilight of a garden all is permissible," smiled the Queen.

The Princess moved aside. She had not seen her Teresa to speak to, since her return, though she had sent her a thousand messages.

The Baroness had crept into the Palace by a side door, used as a rule by the Royal Family as an emergency exit in times of Revolution. She had gone straight to her room, rung for her maid, and locked herself in.

At that moment, it chanced that the Princess with her hair half-finished was seated at her bedroom window amusing herself by frightening the passing Bats with a rope of pearls. It was a pastime she never wearied of.

She was arrayed in a Chinese wrapper, embroidered with Junks riding on a sea of flowers, whose foam turning to Plum-blossom, blew right in at the open doors of the Pagodas, that peeped provokingly through wisps of cloud. The wrapper was a birthday gift, from a Sailor cousin; a boy with the glamour of foreign sea-ports in his eyes.

The night was full of Bats and purple Butterflies, they trembled by in a shadowy stream.

She had startled not a few, when the stealthy frou-frou of silken petticoats beneath her window aroused her girlish curiosity.

'Some Marguerite perhaps hurrying to her doom? The wear and tear to one's heart must be simply tremendous.' She leaned suspiciously out; curiosity with her was strongly hereditary . . .

The Artificial Princess

The trees in the garden had turned to blackened-emerald; the air seemed smeared with bloom.

The footsteps wavered, ceased. Someone with a marvellous shadow (what bravura in the angle of the hat!) was concealing herself behind a statue.

'Poor darling,' murmured the Princess with a seraphic smile. 'Trust me! I shall not move.' And folding her hands, she warbled plaintively some words by a Court Poet.

> 'I am disgusted with Love,
> I find it exceedingly disappointing.
> Mine is a nature that craves for more
> elusive things,
> Banal passions fail to stir me.
> I am disgusted with Love.'

It was not really a popular air with vulgar persons, but it was a privilege to hear her sing; judging from the timbre of her voice one might have supposed her to be a child of six. She paused, and picking up the rare first edition of Unlikely Conversations, flung it out into the night.

There was a movement.

'Teresa?' the Princess called, surprised.

The Baroness, for it was she, wavered, looked up, gave a stage-start and vanished, apparently into a sentry-box.

A quarter of an hour later came a gentle knock at the Princess's door.

'Sesame!' called the Princess, who was mixing something in a jar, but it was only a maid with a note in the Baroness's flower-like hand—all loops and tumbling blossoms and faint stems bearing unformed buds. Tearing the envelope, she read: 'Patience, dear, he is capricious, but *I believe* that he will come.'

A basket of unripe fruit accompanied the note.

'How is the Baroness,' enquired the Princess; 'I hope not tired?'

'She has asked for ice, and hot water,' the maid had answered, 'and seems very much upset.' And this was the beginning of the thousand messages.

'Am I dreadfully late?' murmured the Baroness, as she hurried up. 'I did all I could to be in time when I heard there was a creature practising Black Art in the shrubberies. Are her methods really those of the witch of Endor, as they say they are. And, oh, ma chère,

The Artificial Princess

where is she?' and opening wide green eyes, and pretending to be a little out of breath, she fearfully scanned the shadows.

The Princess was accustomed to intricate temperaments, everyone at Court had one; ignoring the Baroness's remarks she said in calm but firm tones: 'Do not be tiresome' Teresa, but come and tell me all about him.'

At such direct mode of speech, the Baroness visibly winced.

'Come and tell me all about him.' Exactly what one house-maid would say to another after an evening out. After all, it was scarcely astonishing; the Princess's lineage was perplexingly mixed.

'My dear,' the Baroness murmured in her most mundane voice. 'What more is there to tell? My maid wore holes in her shoes, running to and fro on our enigmatical correspondence. As I said, I cannot possibly describe him, but I daresay he would like look a Donatello in his bath.'

The Princess evinced interest.

'We must stir him up to say dreadful things about Mamma,' she cooed. 'How like Herodias she looks to-night! And how step-Papa's glass eye shines! I am sure something terrible is going to happen.'

'Not necessarily,' murmured the Baroness, uneasily, catching at the heart-shaped, sensitive leaves of a Headache Bush. She felt that she was standing in a Quagmire, and to recover her equilibrium she *imagined* Pico de la Mirandola saying his prayers. She put him in a window with a distant view of Florence seen through the casement; the Tower of the Signoria, the dome of the Cathedral, and just the tip of Santa Maria Novella all visible through the stems of the tall white lilies that grew upon the sill. From the way she lit the picture the hour would be Tierce.

'Modern landscapes are all sky,' she murmured, taking an invisible step backwards to admire her work, 'but here you really see the town.'

'Would you say that his eyes were stern?' queried the Princess in a Baa-lamb voice that would have rejoiced the Queen. Like an invalid, she could harp cleverly upon a single string.

'Il est bon, il est doux,' the Baroness gurgled, seeking refuge in Massenet. 'But see,' she murmured, 'His Majesty is observing us'; and she added in louder tones, to be heard by all: 'Tell me, dear, do you think the Nightingale's song is really sad?'

On the stage, standing at her dressing-table, draped like an altar

278

with rows of flickering candles, rocking gently in a drowsy breeze that seemed to spring straight from the heart of a bouquet of Sweet-briar, the pretty actress, suddenly become the most vivacious of widows, was recklessly throwing objects into a satin-lined box, preparing to leave for Venice there and then with the Paramour.

This was the climax in the play, and the Baroness's interlude on the subject of Nightingales was greeted with a loud 'Sh!' and an 'à la porte' from an insignificant page.

Under the Rose-trees, wearing their diamond scarf pins, the critics wrote indefatigably.

'Nature, by some mechanical process,' wrote one, 'can produce dew, but it takes Art to produce tears.'

The Princess, drawing her Teresa's arm through hers, ambled lightly away, hoping, by a few naive questions, to arrive at the truth. But the Baroness was not to be duped.

They seated themselves on a low seat overlooking the Japanese garden.

It was quite a charming garden.

None of the flowers grew in the earth, but lived in celibacy in China pots, packed closely together, and divided symmetrically by formal paths made out of porcelain tiles, in patterns of rose and gold. In the centre a miniature lake, dotted with sacred lilies, lapped the smooth shores of an Island, presided over by the Goddess Kwannon, in a tight frock, and still tighter shoes.

She stood ever before the doors of a shuttered temple, whose gates were far too small to let her in, looking down into the unemotional waters of the lake with narrow sidelong eyes; the temple was pleasantly situated at the foot of an artificial mountain capped with snow.

Through the garden, lanterns glimmered, strangely huge, and fountains spurted, strangely high, and all the flowers in their lonely bowls, stiffly in bloom, smelled strangely sweet.

A City of Flowers, and Lights!

Whole troops of phantom eerie things, fluttered noiseless down the porcelain streets.

'What voluptuous flowers!' murmured the Baroness with a wave of her fan, 'and what a languid night; not since I was a girl have I seen a more audacious moon.'

But the Princess was anxiously watching the airy movements of a

Page, as he tripped towards her, bearing a note on a cushion, at an angle considerably higher than his head.

He wore the dainty trappings of a page in a Benozzo Gozzoli, and was paid a large wage to look wilful, and to stand about corridors and pout. The expression, as was natural, ended in a sulky frown.

'Thanks, little dear,' said the Princess taking the note. And whilst the child lingered for the answer, the Baroness, with great sweetness of manner, retied his sash.

'Not bad news, I hope?' she enquired carelessly as she finished her bow.

'It is from the Bravados, dear. They have thrown me over; it seems that they have trouble of their own. I engaged them just to stroll about and to be at what they term, professionally, "a beck and call."'

The Baroness took the Princess's hand in her own, and sympathetically pressed it.

'You *poor* thing! *How* awkward! But I daresay they were only dreadful Meissonier-people after all.'

At that moment, a barbaric blast of trumpets from the King's Heralds, sustained as long as their breath would permit, announced the arrival of a belated guest.

For a timid person such an entry must have been extremely trying.

The Baroness pressed a hand to her heart. 'Mercy!' she exclaimed, 'it must be he! Hold me, dearest, I believe I'm going to faint.'

'Don't, dear, until something has actually happened,' the Princess implored, darting forward to meet her guest.

'Very well,' the Baroness called after her, 'I will put it off until after supper, and choose a more frequented spot'; and wreathing her arms about a sundial, resting in the moonlight, she unburdened herself in an intimate soliloquy, raising the dial to the dignity of a Mute Confidante in a 'periwig' play.

'It would look so strange,' she meditated, opening a fan that was a sensuous delight, 'to faint and then to eat a substantial supper; and after my long day I can no longer disguise it from myself—I feel slowly sinking. How I reproach myself for this afternoon! ... little puss! She will dredge the truth from her poppy-haired Saint, before it were possible to exclaim "Spinoza!" Great Booby! ... probably not even a picturesque man, or he would live in a cave

280

on a sun-parched plateau and swathe savage skins as Iokanaan about his loins. He would have no chance against the machinations of the Princess. She would flatter; she would bleat; she would make him feel that it was he that held the crook—until he began to make use of it, when—becoming suddenly contralto—she would spring.'

Some words from an 'Everywoman's Criminal' fluttered to her mind.

'Spread the threads of your Cobweb with enough sequins, scintillating enticingly like a lamp-lit street. Carefully veil the Monument at the end. Amuse your victim. When you have gone far enough, turn suddenly and thrust!'

Hush! What was that? Voices surely upon the dilettante breeze. . .

'The Baroness was enchanted with your garden; and thank you so much for your heavenly flowers.'

His silly look of amazement, reproduced upon the air, caused the first Autumn leaf to fall.

She shivered. It was merely, of course, that she was overwrought.

'My mind is a bonfire; my feet are brass,' she told herself. 'Only a salamander could feel as I. A little supper. A little champagne,' she mused, 'and I shall feel less enervated. And then, a long, delicious faint in some nice man's arms.'

She smiled, a faint unholy smile, and with a charming sigh wandered slowly away examining the moon's disk through her lorgnon; it looked like a disembodied spirit above the big top-heavy trees.

'Surely,' she murmured as she walked towards it, 'I think I see the violet cassock of Monsignor Parr.'

The Princess, in the meanwhile, had powdered her neck and arms with poudre Rachel and captured her Saint midway on the flight of natural stairs.

She was surprised, and not displeased, to notice that he wore a Gardenia in his buttonhole, and that his hair—a dusky gold—seemed decidedly waved.

'He looks clever,' she thought, as she rushed up to him.

It was an unfortunate meeting-place, for the chaperons, grouped about the steps in tiers, were idling the hours, patiently awaiting the first streaks of dawn.

'Griffins!' murmured the Princess, shuddering her paniers, but never wavered. 'Did you get my message!' she asked sweetly, as he

kissed her hand. 'It was delightful of you to come. This is my birthday: isn't it provoking to have to be a débutante?' And, looking into his eyes, she threw him a bewitching glance intended to be
demure.

It had been her intention to lead off with a little speech, previously
prepared. But somehow (oh, why?) things seldom turn out just as
you suppose . . . and the rows of staring chaperons were decidedly
disconcerting.

'Where can she have picked him up?' asked a tired dowager.
'Who is he?'

To recollect the speech by message was out of the question, so
she continued hurriedly: 'But won't you take me to the buffet; I
am sure you must need refreshment, and *I* am longing for an ice.
When I knew you were coming I wired for Lampreys; I thought
they might tempt you. What is a Lamprey? Well, really, I scarcely
know; surely a sort of *Locust*,' she enquired with a searching look.
'But we will go and see.'

The play was over. Everyone was circling about the Mistress of
the Robes to congratulate her on her success. She stood simpering
depreciatively between two Rose trees, trying to convey—by a
sorrowful surface smile—that there were greater depths in her than
she allowed the world to see.

'I wrote the play between dinner and prayers,' she was telling
everyone; and allowing the smile to fade, looked sadly away to the
Palace, as though it were a hospital.

'Your theories on death?' asked Madame Storykoff, the wife of a
rising Privy Councillor, catching her mood. (She was on the staff
of four newspapers and considered 'dangerous.')

The great woman looked at her.

'I think when wicked people die they become sheep,' she replied
airily, and, pivoting slightly, indicated her disapproval by the angle
of her bust.

The English Ambassadress, Melissa, Lady Lostwaters, trailed
slowly across the scene.

'Can you tell me,' she was enquiring, vaguely, 'has anybody
seen him? I am looking everywhere for *Sir Oliver* Scott.'

Nearby the King was bestowing the Order of King Sigismond II
on the principal actors, in 'recognition' of their Art.

In her riding habit and a feather boa, contentedly sipping champagne, the very pretty actress stood chatting with extreme animation

The Artificial Princess

to the Prime Minister. 'I do hope the horses won't bolt,' she remarked a little anxiously, 'or behave badly in any way. I am so suspicious of quadrupeds ever since the shock I sustained once on tour! It was when I was playing "La Dame aux Camélias" in the desert. In the middle of the great scene—you remember where I have the trying interview with *his father*—I noticed creeping up behind the Audience an enormous lion. Just fancy! Of course I said nothing; I remained true to my author.'

'Did it spring?' enquired the Prime Minister.

'Of course it sprang,' answered the actress; 'well, naturally!'

And the great man listened spellbound to her narrative, supporting himself against a tree, his mouth ajar, till his wife observing him, and fearing a pernicious influence—for she knew his frailness—came and dragged him away.

Just then, a loud peal of laughter, and clapping of hands from a Pavilion, came floating across the garden. The King's Favourite, an intensely plain, rather impudent-looking woman, already, perhaps, *sur le retour,* was singing comic songs accompanying herself on a guitar. She was the type of person who, in a former age, would have probably ended her career on the scaffold, or by being poisoned; for nobody liked her.

Among the majestic or dove-like Beauties of the Court, beauty in time became a weariness, and the Favourite's plainness positively a distinction—hence a danger. 'Odd,' 'weird,' 'bedraggled,' were the courtesy-titles usually used to describe her, whilst many spared their brains in finding descriptive symbols and pronounced her merely 'vulgar.' One could suppose her dangling a ball-slipper over a cliff and murmuring, 'Shall I?' in a voice irresistibly cajoling. Her sallow cheeks, alert eyes, and malicious mouth, made a vivid contrast to the frail vestal type that the Queen admired.

'She is the only distinguished woman at Court,' the King was in the habit of saying. 'She is so *Spanish.*'

In her gold trailing skirts, the Favourite pirouetted amidst a ring of bottle-nosed Dowagers who were urging her on to wilder follies, garnering up the while a stock of conversation to last them over many a drowsy evening. 'She is calling the Attachés "pets,"' they murmured, delightedly, fanning themselves at a tremendous pace, and they thrilled.

The Queen watched the lady from a distance, and presently, smiling suavely, wandered away into the chiaro-oscuro of the

Shrubbery to enquire of the crystal gazer the date and hour of the Favourite's fall.

Meanwhile, in the Refreshment Tent, the Princess was exploring her Saint. 'How delicious these Lampreys are,' she was saying, making a charming grimace. 'Put some honey with them; aren't they far nicer than Locusts?' And holding out a hand, powder-white: 'Oh, do give me some more Champagne.'

They were drinking Champagne out of Limoges enamel Ewers, decorated by Jean Limousine, and Suzanne Court, with scenes from the lives of Castor and Pollux.

The Champagne was completely spoiled, but there was intoxication in the delicate naked figures, in their rumbling cars, seen through the sparkle of the wine.

From the garden came a lazy ripple of strings, like waves breaking uncertainly on some veiled coast, a pause, a troubled stillness, and in a key infinitely remote, the violins broke imperceptibly, inevitably, into a slumberous Valse.

The Baroness peered in at the tent door, sweeping aside like a handful of Honeysuckle the voluminous fringes that adorned the entry. She was looking for a partner . . . For an instant she hovered on the threshold, admiring her pose in an unexpected mirror.

Behind her, showed reflected in the glass, a patch of lamp-black sky crowded behind the unschooled draperies of a tree, while beyond, fluttering in the rhythm of the dance, like figures on a bas-relief, the Maids of Honour in their long white frocks appeared and disappeared between huge tubs of flowers.

The Baroness hastily dropped the fringe, such a full background made her feel quite dizzy. She was looking extremely pale. News had just reached her that the Princess's note had not been delivered.

The better for wine, it seemed the chauffeur had left the letter at some Inn, to be delivered by some stable-boy, at some time during his convenience, who, in turn, had entrusted the letter to a van passing the Saint's doorstep on the course of its rounds, laden with the creations of the 'Maison Greuze.'

At the Schloss of the Countess Elsassar, the wife of the Chancellor of the Exchequer, the van had been driven back to the capital almost by swords to fetch a piece of passementerie, and the driver had been so harassed thereat that he had forgotten altogether the Princess's note. With the unopened letter scorching her bosom the Baroness was at a loss.

The Artificial Princess

To screen herself, she felt, could best be done by warning the Princess of her mistake. Yet how?

Already the Princess seemed to have commenced a pious flirtation. 'When I asked her to describe you,' the Baroness could hear her say, 'she said: "he has a long straight nose, a determined chin, and would look like a Donatello when in certain lights." '

'What on earth am I to do?' wondered the Baroness. 'Nothing perhaps, until after I've had some supper; it will choke me, I know, and I'm certain to be dull. I shall go in with another woman'; and catching up her train over her arm, and calling herself 'Coward,' she left the tent looking more helplessly untidy than she had ever looked before.

She stepped straight into the arms of the King and the English Ambassadress, who were patrolling slowly up and down in deep confabulation. The Ambassadress was complaining, in French, of the mice at the Embassy whilst the King was telling her of some quite wonderful mouse-traps, intermixed with the history of the house. Detaining the Baroness, they forced her to join them, too. Their ill-assorted shadows, falling on the grass, suggested Early Abyssinian Art,—'persons returning from a lion-hunt.' Music came towards them on little puffs of air, strange languid, passing suavely through the myriad small openings of boughs and brambles, twining round the sleeping heads of flowers, blown through the philharmonic fingers of the statues; the violins, heavy, stifling as black velvet, made everybody long to sit down.

The Conductor's wand, mesmeric, swayed sensuously to and fro, falling, climbing, till his hands seemed full of stars. With a delicious dissonance the Valse unexpectedly ceased.

The dancers crushed streaming by into the tent, where a frugal 'Theatre Supper' was being served. The battle for precedence before the mirror was, in several cases, the commencement of a life-long feud.

There came a babel of voices: 'Such a cat! I would, dear, if I could only move my poor hips.'

'Insolence!'

' . . . As if I were no more than the wife of an Aide-de-camp!'

'Above social littleness.'

'Those "Isolde" cocktails make one very amorous!'

'Would you mind not hurting me with your fan?'

'Oh! Be careful there, Countess, of some horses' offal.'

285

'I hear that your wife and my wife . . . but I fancy there's nothing in it . . .'

The Princess turned to her companion. 'I am afraid our Court life must strike you as dreadfully hollow,' she said.

'Not at all,' he answered, 'I'm enjoying myself immensely.'

The Princess staggered. Was it possible that this man had a common nature? She would not believe it.

'You are a dear, excellent creature,' she murmured, touching his arm, 'and you think of us far too well. If you could see us in the searching light of morning you would condemn us in fiery words. But you must come to lunch . . . Although, even now, I daresay if you look about you will find bribery and corruption in our very midst.'

In a hurricane of silver, and swinging chains, leaning solidly on the arms of two of her most formidable critics, the Mistress of the Robes approached the buffet; flushed and triumphant. Apparently, she was revealing the plot of her next play. 'In the last act,' they could hear her say, 'she confesses her guilt; she departs, and crossing a rickety wooden bridge, falls into the river and is drowned.'

'A merciful end,' the Baroness breathed, glancing up into the blue of the night.

Certainly the affair was now beyond ker keeping: the Princess must be allowed to discover the error as she might.

'The man must be a hardened opportunist,' she reflected, sinking with wan philosophy to a seat.

A wild Hawaiian melody, evoking exuberance and glamour, fell engagingly upon her ear.

'You are not dancing, Baroness?' An elderly gentleman with a toothbrush-moustache and a sapphire ring made blandly question.

'I? Oh, Sir Oliver,' the Baroness started.

'You prefer, perhaps, looking on?'

The Baroness nodded, her glance following some shooting stars that slipped suddenly down behind the palace.

'There,' she observed with half-closed eyes, 'went Ursa Major!'

'Never! Ursa's over there . . .'

'What; Ursa is?' she murmured, wondering if her own fall from royal favour and grace would be equally rapid.

It seemed indeed quite certain that a season of disesteem was upon her; 'I shall let my house and go abroad,' she brooded,

bestowing a smile of sleepy sadness at her rings—London! Paris!
Madrid! perhaps further still! 'Tell me, Sir Oliver,' she demanded,
'have you ever been to Greece?'

'More than once,' Sir Oliver dryly replied, 'I even married, *en
secondes noces,* a Lesbian . . .'

'A native of Lesbos? Just fancy that!' the Baroness marvelled,
appraising a passing débutante, a young girl in a mousseline robe
of palest Langue de chat.

'*Née* a Demitraki.'

'A demi what?' the Baroness abstrusely twittered, blinking at
the intermittent lightning in the sky.

'A Demitraki.'

'Hark.'

'What is it?'

'Only,' the Lady answered, raising her face into the soft dream
morning, already pointing, '*a cock.*'

'A cock?'

'Chanticleer,' she added suavely, for the sake of euphony:
'Chanti . . .'

* * *

'Cock-a-doodle, doooooooooooooooooooooooooooooooooooooo
oooooooooooooooooooooooooooooooooooooooooooooooooooo'

'(Cluck-cluck?)'

'Cock-a-doodle. . . .'

Concerning the Eccentricities
of Cardinal Pirelli

Concerning the Eccentricities
of Cardinal Pirelli

HUDDLED up in a cope of gold wrought silk he peered around. Society had rallied in force. A christening—and not a child's.

Rarely had he witnessed, before the font, so many brilliant people. Were it an heir to the DunEden acres (instead of what it *was*) the ceremony could have hardly drawn together a more distinguished throng.

Monsignor Silex moved a finger from forehead to chin, and from ear to ear. The Duquesa DunEden's escapades, if continued, would certainly cost the Cardinal his hat.

'And ease my heart by splashing fountains.'

From the choir-loft a boy's young voice was evoking Heaven.

'His hat!' Monsignor Silex exclaimed aloud, blinking a little at the immemorial font of black Macæl marble that had provoked the screams of pale numberless babies.

Here Saints and Kings had been baptised, and royal Infantas, and sweet Poets, whose high names thrilled the heart.

Monsignor Silex crossed his breast. He must gather force to look about him. Frame a close report. The Pontiff, in far-off Italy, would expect precision.

Beneath the state baldequin, or Grand Xaymaca, his Eminence sat enthroned, ogled by the wives of a dozen grandees. The Altamissals, the Villarasas (their grandee-ships' approving glances, indeed, almost eclipsed their wives'), and Catherine, Countess of Constantine, the most talked-off beauty in the realm, looking like some wild limb of Astaroth in a little crushed 'toreador' hat round as an athlete's coif with hanging silken balls, while beside her a stout, dumpish dame, of enormous persuasion, was joggling, solicitously, an object that was of the liveliest interest to all.

Head archly bent, her fine arms divined through darkling laces, the Duquesa stood, clasping closely a week-old police-dog in the ripple of her gown.

'Mother's pet!' she cooed, as the imperious creature passed his tongue across the splendid uncertainty of her chin.

Monsignor Silex's large, livid face grew grim.

What,—disquieting doubt,—if it were her Grace's offspring after all? Praise heaven, he was ignorant enough regarding the schemes of nature, but in an old lutrin once he had read of a young woman engendering a missel-thrush through the channel of her nose. It had created a good deal of scandal to be sure at the time: the Holy Inquisition, indeed, had condemned the impudent baggage, in consequence, to the stake.

'That was the style to treat them,' he murmured, appraising the assembly with no kindly eye. The presence of Madame San Seymour surprised him; one habitually so set apart and devout! And Madame La Urench, too, gurgling away freely to the four-legged Father: 'No, my naughty Blessing; no, not now! . . . By and by, a *bone*.'

Words which brought the warm saliva to the expectant parent's mouth.

Tail away, sex apparent (to the affected slight confusion of the Infanta Eulalia-Irene), he crouched, his eyes fixed wistfully upon the nozzle of his son.

Ah, happy delirium of first parenthood! Adoring pride! Since times primæval by what masonry does it knit together those that have succeeded in establishing here, on earth, the vital bonds of a family's claim? Even the modest sacristan, at attention by the font, felt himself to be superior of parts to a certain unproductive chieftain of a princely House, who had lately undergone a course of asses' milk in the surrounding mountains—all in vain!

But, supported by the Prior of the Cartuja, the Cardinal had arisen for the act of Immersion.

Of unusual elegance, and with the remains, moreover, of perfect looks, he was as wooed and run after by the ladies as any *matador*.

'And thus being cleansed and purified, I do call thee "Crack"!' he addressed the Duquesa's captive burden.

Tail sheathed with legs 'in master's drawers,' ears cocked, tongue pendent. . . .

'Mother's mascot!'

'Oh, take care, dear; he's removing all your rouge!'

'*What?*'

'He's spoilt, I fear, your roses.' The Countess of Constantine tittered.

The Duquesa's grasp relaxed. To be seen by all the world at this disadvantage.

'Both?' she asked, distressed, disregarding the culprit, who sprang from her breast with a sharp, sportive bark.

What rapture, what freedom!

'Misericordia!' Monsignor Silex exclaimed, staring aghast at a leg poised, inconsequently, against the mural-tablet of the widowed duchess of Charona—a woman who, in her lifetime, had given over thirty million pezos to the poor!

Ave Maria purissima! What challenging snarls and measured mystery marked the elaborate recognition of father and son, and would no one then forbid their incestuous frolics?

In agitation Monsignor Silex sought fortitude from the storied windows overhead, aglow in the ambered light as some radiant missal.

It was Saint Eufraxia's Eve, she of Egypt, a frail unit numbered above among the train of the Eleven Thousand Virgins: an immaturish schoolgirl of a saint, unskilled, inexperienced in handling a prayer, lacking the vim and native astuteness of the incomparable Theresa.

Yes; divine interference, 'twixt father and son, was hardly to be looked for, and Eufraxia (she of Egypt) had failed too often before. . . .

Monsignor Silex started slightly, as, from the estrade beneath the dome, a choir-boy let fall a little white spit.

Dear child, as though *that* would part them!

'Things must be allowed to take their "natural" course,' he concluded, following the esoteric antics of the reunited pair.

Out into the open, over the Lapis Lazuli of the floor, they flashed, with stifled yelps, like things possessed.

'He'll tear my husband's drawers!' the Duquesa lamented.

'The duque's legs. Poor Decima.' The Infanta fell quietly to her knees.

'Fortify . . . asses . . .' the royal lips moved.

'Brave darling,' she murmured, gently rising.

But the Duquesa had withdrawn, it seemed, to repair her ravaged roses, and from the obscurity of an adjacent confessional-box was calling to order Crack.

'Come, Crack!'

And to the Mauro-Hispanic rafters the echo rose.

'Crack, Crack, Crack, Crack. . . .'

⊠⊠ *II* ⊠⊠

FROM the Calle de la Pasion, beneath the blue-tiled mirador of the garden wall, came the soft brooding sound of a seguidilla. It was a twilight planned for wooing, unbending, consent; many, before now, had come to grief on an evening such. 'It was the moon.'

Pacing a cloistered walk, laden with the odour of sun-tired flowers, the Cardinal could not but feel the insidious influences astir. The bells of the institutions of the *Encarnacion* and the Immaculate Conception, joined in confirming Angelus, had put on tones half-bridal, enough to create vague longings, or sudden tears, among the young patrician boarders.

'Their parents' daughters—convent-bred,' the Cardinal sighed.

At the Immaculate Conception, dubbed by the Queen, in irony, once 'The school for harlots,' the little Infanta Maria-Paz must be lusting for her Mamma and the Court, and the lilac carnage of the ring, while chafing also in the same loose captivity would be the roguish *niñas* of the pleasure-loving duchess of Sarmento, girls whose Hellenic ethics had given the good Abbess more than one attack of fullness.

Morality. Poise! For without temperance and equilibrium——
The Cardinal halted.

But in the shifting underlight about him the flushed camellias and the sweet night-jasmines suggested none; neither did the shape of a garden-Eros pointing radiantly the dusk.

'For unless we have balance——' the Cardinal murmured, distraught, admiring against the elusive nuances of the afterglow the cupid's voluptuous hams.

It was against these, once, in a tempestuous mood that his mistress had smashed her fan-sticks.

'Would that all liaisons would break as easily!' his Eminence framed the prayer: and musing on the appalling constancy of a certain type, he sauntered leisurely on. Yes, enveloping women like Luna Sainz, with their lachrymose, tactless 'mys,' how shake them off? 'My' Saviour, 'my' lover, 'my' parasol—and, even, 'my' virtue. . . .

'Poor dearie.'

The Cardinal smiled.

Yet once in a way, perhaps, he was not averse to being favoured by a glimpse of her: 'A little visit on a night like this.' Don Alvaro Narciso Hernando Pirelli, Cardinal-Archbishop of Clemenza, smiled again.

In the gloom there, among the high thickets of bay and flowering myrtle. . . . For, after all, bless her, one could not well deny she possessed the chief essentials: 'such, poor soul, as they are!' he reflected, turning about at the sound as of the neigh of a horse.

'Monseigneur. . . .'

Bearing a biretta and a silver shawl, Madame Poco, the venerable Superintendent-of-the-palace, looking, in the blue moonlight, like some whiskered skull, emerged, after inconceivable peepings, from among the leafy limbo of the trees.

'Ah, Don Alvaro, sir! Come here.'

'Pest!' His Eminence evinced a touch of asperity.

'Ah, Don, Don, . . .' and skimming forward with the grace of a Torero lassooing a bull, she slipped the scintillating fabric about the prelate's neck.

'Such nights breed fever, Don Alvaro, and there is mischief in the air.'

'Mischief?'

'In certain quarters of the city you would take it almost for some sortilege.'

'What next?'

'At the *Encarnacion* there's nothing, of late, but seediness. Sister Engracia with the chicken-pox, and Mother Claridad with the itch, while at the College of Noble Damosels, in the Calle Santa Fé, I hear a daughter of Don José Illescas, in a fit of caprice, has set a match to her coronet.'

'A match to her what?'

'And how explain, Don Alvaro of my heart, these constant shots in the Córtes? Ah, *sangre mio*, in what times we live!'

Ambling a few steps pensively side by side, they moved through the brilliant moonlight. It was the hour when the awakening fireflies are first seen like atoms of rosy flame floating from flower to flower.

'Singular times, sure enough,' the Cardinal answered, pausing to enjoy the transparent beauty of the white dripping water of a flowing fountain.

'And ease my heart by splashing—tum-tiddly-um-tum,' he hummed. 'I trust the choir-boys, Dame, are all in health?'

'Ah, Don Alvaro, no, sir!'

'Eh?'

'No, sir,' Madame Poco murmured, taking up a thousand golden poses.

'Why, how's that?'

'But few now seem keen on Leapfrog, or Bossage, and when a boy shows no wish for a game of Leap, sir, or Bossage——'

'Exactly,' his Eminence nodded.

'I'm told it's some time, young cubs, since they've played pranks on Tourists! Though only this afternoon little Ramón Ragatta came over queazy while demonstrating before foreigners the Dance of the Arc, which should teach him in future not to be so profane: and as to the acolytes, Don Alvaro, at least half of them are absent, confined to their cots, in the wards of the pistache Fathers!'

'To-morrow, all well, I'll take them some melons.'

'Ah, Don, Don!!'

'And, perhaps, a cucumber,' the Cardinal added, turning valedictionally away.

The tones of the seguidilla had deepened and from the remote recesses of the garden arose a bedlam of nightingales and frogs.

It was certainly incredible how he felt immured.

Yet to forsake the Palace for the Plaza he was obliged to stoop to creep.

With the Pirelli pride, with resourceful intimacy he communed with his heart: deception is a humiliation; but humiliation is a Virtue—a Cardinal, like myself, and one of the delicate violets of our Lady's crown. . . . Incontestably, too,—he had a flash of inconsequent insight, many a prod to a discourse, many a sapient thrust, delivered ex cathedrâ, amid the broken sobs of either sex, had been inspired, before now, by what prurient persons might term, perhaps, a 'frolic.' But away with all scruples! Once in the street in mufti, how foolish they became.

The dear street. The adorable Avenidas. The quickening stimulus of the crowd: truly it was exhilarating to mingle freely with the throng!

Disguised as a cabellero from the provinces or as a matron (disliking to forgo altogether the militant bravoura of a skirt), it became possible to combine philosophy, equally, with pleasure.

294

The promenade at the Trinidades seldom failed to be diverting, especially when the brown Bettita or the Ortiz danced! *Olé*, he swayed his shawl. The Argentina with Blanca Sanchez was amusing too; her ear-tickling little song 'Madrid is on the Manzanares,' trailing the ' 'ares' indefinitely, was ,ure, in due course, to reach the Cloisters.

Deliberating critically on the numerous actresses of his diocese, he traversed lightly a path all enclosed by pots of bergamot.

And how entrancing to perch on a bar-stool, over a glass of old golden sherry!

'Ah Jesus-Maria,' he addressed the dancing lightning in the sky.

Purring to himself, and frequently pausing, he made his way, by ecstatic degrees, towards the mirador on the garden wall.

Although a mortification, it was imperative to bear in mind the consequences of cutting a too dashing figure. Beware display. Vanity once had proved all but fatal: 'I remember it was the night I wore ringlets and was called "my queen." '

And with a fleeting smile, Don Alvaro Pirelli recalled the persistent officer who had had the effrontery to attempt to molest him: 'Stalked me the whole length of the Avenue Isadora!' It had been a lesson. 'Better to be on the drab side,' he reflected, turning the key of the garden tower.

Dating from the period of the Reformation of the Nunneries, it commanded the privacy of many a drowsy patio.

'I see the Infanta has begun her Tuesdays!' he serenely noted, sweeping the panorama with a glance.

It was a delightful prospect.

Like some great guitar the city lay engirdled ethereally by the snowy Sierras.

'Foolish featherhead,' he murmured, his glance falling upon a sunshade of sapphire chiffon, left by Luna: ' "my" parasol!' he twirled the crystal hilt.

'Everything she forgets, bless her,' he breathed, lifting his gaze towards the magnolia blossom cups that overtopped the tower, stained by the eternal treachery of the night to the azure of the Saint Virgin. Suspended in the miracle of the moonlight their elfin globes were at their zenith.

'Madrid is on the Manzan-ares,' he intoned.

But 'Clemenza,' of course, is in white Andalucia.

Concerning the Eccentricities

⊞ *III* ⊞

AFTER the tobacco-factory and the railway-station, quite the liveliest spot in all the city was the cathedral-sacristia. In the interim of an Office it would be besieged by the laity, often to the point of scrimmage: aristocrats and mendicants, relatives of acolytes —each had some truck or other in the long lofty room. Here the secretary of the chapter, a burly little man, a sound judge of women and bulls, might be consulted gratis, preferably before the supreme heat of day. Seated beneath a sombre study of the Magdalen way-laying our Lord (a work of wistful interest ascribed to Valdés Leal), he was, with tactful courtesy, at the disposal of anyone solicit-ing information as to 'vacant dates,' or 'hours available,' for some impromptu function. Indulgences, novenas, terms for special masses—with flowers and music? Or, just plain; the expense, it varied! Bookings for baptisms, it was certainly advisable to book well ahead; some mothers booked before the birth—; ah-hah, the little Juans and Juanas; the angelic babies! And arrangements for a corpse's lying-in-state: 'Leave it to me.' These, and such things, were in his province.

But the secretarial bureau was but merely a speck in the vast shuttered room. As a rule, it was by the old pagan sarcophaguses, outside the vestry-door, 'waiting for Father,' that *aficianados* of the cult liked best to foregather.

It was the morning of the Feast of San Antolin of Panticosa, a morning so sweet, and blue and luminous, and many were waiting.

'It's queer the time a man takes to slip on a frilly!' the laundress of the Basilica, Doña Consolacion, observed, through her fansticks, to Tomás the beadle.

'Got up as you get them. . . .'

'It's true, indeed, I've a knack with a rochet!'

'Temperament will out, Doña Consolacion; it cannot be hid.'

The laundress beamed.

'Mine's the French.'

'It's God's will *whatever* it is.'

'It's the French,' she lisped, considering the silver rings on her honey-brown hands. Of distinguished presence, with dark matted curls at either ear, she was the apotheosis of flesh triumphant.

But the entry from the vestry of a file of monsignori imposed a transient silence—a silence which was broken only by the murmur of passing mule bells along the street.

Tingaling, tingaling: evocative of grain and harvest the sylvan sound of mule bells came and went.

Doña Consolacion flapped her fan.

There was to be question directly of a Maiden Mass.

With his family all about him, the celebrant, a youth of the People, looking childishly happy in his first broidered cope, had bent, more than once, his good-natured head, to allow some small brothers and sisters to inspect his tonsure.

'Like a little, little star!'

'No. Like a *perra gorda*.'

'No, like a little star,' they fluted, while an irrepressible grand-mother, moved to tears and laughter, insisted on planting a kiss on the old 'Christian' symbol. 'He'll be a Pope some day, if he's spared!' she sobbed, transported.

'Not he, the big burly bull.' Mother Garcia of the Company of Jesus addressed Doña Consolacion with a mellifluent chuckle.

Holding a bouquet of sunflowers and a basket of eggs she had just looked in from Market.

'Who knows, my dear?' Doña Consolacion returned, fixing her gaze upon an Epitaph on a vault beneath her feet. ' "He was a boy and she dazzled him." Heigh-ho! Heysey-ho . . . ! Yes, as I was saying.'

'Pho: I'd like to see him in a Papal tiara.'

'It's mostly luck. I well recall his Eminence when he was nothing but a trumpery curate,' Doña Consolacion declared, turning to admire the jewelled studs in the ears of the President of the College of Noble Damosels.

'Faugh!' Mother Garcia spat.

'It's all luck.'

'There's luck and luck,' the beadle put in. Once he had confined by accident a lady in the souterrains of the cathedral, and only many days later had her bones and a diary, a diary documenting the most delicate phases of solitude and loneliness, *a woman's contri-bution to Science*, come to light; a piece of carelessness that had gone against the old man in his preferment.

'Some careers are less fortunate than others,' Mother Garcia exclaimed, appraising the sleek silhouette of Monsignor Silex, then precipitantly issuing from the Muniment-Room.

It was known he was not averse to a little stimulant in the bright middle of the morning.

'He has the evil Eye, dear, he has the evil Eye,' Doña Consolacion murmured, averting her head. Above her hung a sombre Ribera, in a frame of elaborate, blackened gilding.

'Ah, well, I do not fear it,' the Companion of Jesus answered, making way for a dark, heavy belle in a handkerchief and shawl.

'Has anyone seen Jositto, my little José?'

Mother Garcia waved with her bouquet towards an adjacent portal, surmounted, with cool sobriety, by a long, lavender marble cross. 'I expect he's through there.'

'In the cathedral?'

'How pretty you look, dear, and what a very gay shawl!'

'Pure silk.'

'I don't *doubt* it!'

Few women, however, are indifferent to the seduction of a Maiden Mass, and all in a second there was scarcely one to be found in the whole sacristia.

The secretary at his bureau looked about him: without the presence of *las mujares* the atmosphere seemed to weigh a little; still, being a Holiday of Obligation, a fair sprinkling of boys, youthful chapter hands whom he would sometimes designate as the 'lesser delights,' relieved the place of its austerity.

Through the heraldic windows, swathed in straw-mats to shut out the heat, the sun-rays entered, tattooing with piquant freckles the pampered faces of the choir.

A request for a permit to view the fabled Orangery in the cloisters interrupted his siestose fancies.

Like luxurious cygnets in their cloudy lawn, a score of young singing-boys were awaiting their cue: Low-masses, cheapness, and economy, how they despised them, and how they would laugh at 'Old Ends' who snuffed out the candles.

'Why should the Church charge *higher* for a short *Magnificat* than for a long *Miserere*?'

The question had just been put by the owner of a dawning moustache and a snub, though expressive, nose.

'Because happiness makes people generous, stupid, and often as not they'll squander, boom, but unhappiness makes them calculate. People grudge spending much on a snivel—even if it lasts an hour.'

'It's the choir that suffers.'

'This profiteering . . . The Chapter . . .' there was a confusion of voices.

'Order!' A slim lad, of an ambered paleness, raised a protesting hand. Indulged, and made-much-of by the hierarchy, he was Felix Ganay, known as Chief-dancing-choir-boy to the cathedral of Clemenza.

'Aren't they awful?' he addressed a child with a very finished small head. Fingering a score of music he had been taking lead in a mass of Palestrina, and had the vaguely distraught air of a kitten that had seen visions.

'After that, I've not a dry stitch on me,' he murmured, with a glance towards the secretary, who was making lost grimaces at the Magdalen's portrait.

A lively controversy (becoming increasingly more shrill) was dividing the acolytes and choir.

'Tiny and Tibi! Enough.' The intervention came from the full-voiced Christobal, a youngster of fifteen, with soft, peach-textured cheeks, and a tongue never far away. Considered an opportunist, he was one of the privileged six dancing-boys of the cathedral.

'Order!' Felix enjoined anew. Finely sensitive as to his prerogatives, the interference of his colleague was apt to vex him. He would be trying to clip an altar pose next. Indeed, it was a matter of scandal already, how he was attempting to attract attention, in influential places, by the unnecessary undulation of his loins, and by affecting strong scents and attars, such as Egyptian Tahetant, or Long flirt through the violet Hours. Himself, Felix, he was faithful to Royal Florida, or even to plain *eau-de-Cologne*, and to those slow Mozarabic movements which alone are seemly to the Church.

'You may mind your business, young Christobal,' Felix murmured, turning towards a big, serious, melancholy boy, who was describing a cigarette-case he had received as fee for singing 'Say it with Edelweiss' at a society wedding.

'Say it with what?' the cry came from an oncoming-looking child, with caressing liquid eyes, and a little tongue the colour of rasp-berry-cream—*so bright*. Friend of all sweets and dainties, he held San Antolin's day chiefly notable for the Saint's sweet biscuits, made of sugar and white-of-egg.

'And you, too, Chicklet. Mind your business, can't you?' Felix exclaimed, appraising in some dismay a big, bland woman, then descending upon the secretary at his desk, with a slow, but determined, waddle.

Amalia Bermudez, the fashionable Actress-manageress of the Teatro Victoria Eugenia, was becoming a source of terror to the chapter of Clemenza. Every morning, with fatal persistence, she would aboard the half-hypnotised secretary with the request that the Church should make 'a little christian' of her blue chow, for unless it could be done it seemed the poor thing wasn't *chic*. To be *chic* and among the foremost vanward; this, apart from the Theatre, meant all to her in life, and since the unorthodox affair of 'the Dun-Edens,' she had been quite upset by the chapter's evasive refusals.

'If a police-dog, then why not a chow?' she would ask. 'Why not my little Whisky? Little devil. Ah, believe me, Father, she has need of it; for she's supposed to have had a snake by my old dog Conqueror! . . . And yet you won't receive her? Oh, it's heartless. Men are cruel. . . .'

'There she is! Amalia—the Bermudez': the whisper spread, arresting the story of the black Bishop of Bechuanaland, just begun by the roguish Ramón.

And in the passing silence the treble voice of Tiny was left talking all alone.

'. . . frightened me like Father did, when he kissed me in the dark like a lion':—a remark that was greeted by an explosion of coughs.

But this morning the clear, light laugh of the comedienne rang out merrily. 'No, no, *hombre,*' she exclaimed (tapping the secretary upon the cheek archly with her fan), 'now don't, don't stare at me, and intimidate me like that! I desire only to offer a "Mass of Intention," fully choral, *that the Church may change her mind.*'

And when the cannon that told of Noon was fired from the white fortress by the river far away she was still considering programmes of music by Rossini and Cimarosa, and the colour of the chasubles which the clergy should wear.

⊠⊠ *IV* ⊠⊠

AT the season when the oleanders are in their full perfection, their choicest bloom, it was the Pontiff's innovation to install his American type-writing apparatus in the long Loggie of the Apostolic Palace that had been in disuse since the demise of Innocent XVI. Out-of-doorish, as Neapolitans usually are, Pope Tertius II was no exception to the rule, preferring blue skies to golden ceilings —a taste for which indeed many were inclined to blame him. A compromise between the state-saloons and the modest suite occupied by his Holiness from choice, these open Loggie, adorned with the radiant frescoes of Luca Signorelli, would be frequently the scene of some particular Audience, granted after the exacting press of official routine.

Late one afternoon the Pontiff after an eventful and arduous day was walking thoughtfully here alone. Participating no longer in the joys of the world, it was, however, charming to catch, from time to time, the distant sound of Rome—the fitful clamour of trams and cabs, and the plash of the great twin-fountains in the court of Saint Damascus.

Wrapped in grave absorption, with level gaze, the lips slightly pinched, Pope Tertius II paced to and fro, occasionally raising a well-formed (though hairy) hand, as though to dismiss his thoughts with a benediction. The nomination of two Vacant Hats, the marriage annulment of an ex-hereditary Grand Duchess, and the 'scandals of Clemenza,' were equally claiming his attention and ruffling his serenity.

He had the head of an elderly lady's-maid, and an expression concealed by layers of tactful caution.

'Why can't they all behave?' he asked himself plaintively, descrying Lucrezia, his prized white squirrel, sidling shyly towards him.

She was the gift of the Archbishop of Trebizond, who had found her in the region of the Coelian hill.

'Slyboots, slyboots,' Pope Tertius exclaimed, as she skipped from reach. It was incredible with what playful zest she would spring from statue to statue; and it would have amused the Vicar of Christ to watch her slip and slide, had it not suggested many a profound moral metaphor applicable to the Church. 'Gently, gently,' he enjoined; for once, in her struggles, she had robbed a fig-leaf off a 'Moses.'

'Yes, why can't they all behave?' he murmured, gazing up into the far pale-blueness.

He stood a brief moment transfixed, as if in prayer, oblivious of two whispering Chamberlains.

It was the turn-in-waiting of Baron Oschatz, a man of engaging

301

exquisite manners, and of Count Cuenca, an individual who seemed to be in perpetual consternation.

Depositing a few of the most recent camera portraits of the Pontiff requiring autograph in a spot where he could not fail but see them, they formally withdrew.

It had been a day distinguished by innumerable Audiences, several not uninteresting to recall. . . .

Certainly the increasing numbers of English were decidedly promising, and bore out the sibylline predictions of their late great and sagacious ruler—Queen Victoria.

'The dear *santissima* woman,' the Pontiff sighed, for he entertained a sincere, if brackish, enthusiasm for the lady who for so many years had corresponded with the Holy See under the signature of *the Countess of Lostwaters*.

'Anglicans . . . ? Heliolaters and sun-worshippers,' she had written in her most masterful hand, 'and your Holiness may believe us,' she had added, 'when we say especially our beloved Scotch.'

'I shouldn't wonder enormously if it were true,' the Pope exclaimed, catching through a half-shut door a glimpse of violet stockings.

Such a display of old, out-at-heel hose could but belong to Cardinal Robin.

There had been a meeting of the Board for Extraordinary Ecclesiastical Affairs, and when, shortly afterwards, the Cardinal was admitted he bore still about him some remote trace of faction.

He had the air of a cuttle-fish, and an enquiring voice. Inclined to gesture, how many miles must his hands have moved in the course of the sermons that he had preached!

Saluting the sovereign Pontiff with a deep obeisance, the Cardinal came directly to the point.

'These schisms in Spain . . .'

'They are ever before me,' His Holiness confessed.

'With priests like Pirelli, the Church is in peril!' the Cardinal declared, with a short, abysmal laugh.

'Does he suppose we are in the times of Baal and Moloch?' the Pope asked, pressing a harassed hand to his head. A Neapolitan of Naples (O Bay of Napoli! See Vesuvius, *and die*), he had curly hair that seemed to grow visibly; every few hours his tonsure would threaten to disappear.

The Cardinal sent up his brows a little.

302

'If I may tender the advice of the secret Consistory,' he said, 'your Holiness should Listen-in.'

'To what end?'

'A snarl, a growl, a bark, a yelp, coming from the font, would be quite enough to condemn . . .'

'Per Bacco. I should take it for a baby.'

' . . . condemn,' the Cardinal pursued, 'this Pirelli for a *maleficus pastor*. In which case, the earlier, the better, the unfrocking. . . .'

The Pontiff sighed.

The excellent Cardinal was as fatiguing as a mission from Salt Lake City.

'Evidently,' he murmured, detecting traces of rats among the papyrus plants in the long walk below.

'They come up from the Tiber!' he exclaimed, piloting the Cardinal dexterously towards a flight of footworn steps leading to the Court of Bramante.

'It's a bore there being no lift!' he commented (the remark was a Vatican cliché), dismissing the Cardinal with a benediction.

'A painful interview,' the Holy Father reflected, regarding the Western sky. An evening rose and radiant altogether. . . .

Turning sadly, he perceived Count Cuenca.

A nephew of the Dean of the Sacred College, it was rumoured that he was addicted, in his 'home' above Frascati, to the last excesses of the pre-Adamite Sultans.

'A dozen blessings, for a dozen Hymens—but only eleven were sent,' he was babbling distractedly to himself. He had been unstrung all day, 'just a mass of foolish nerves,' owing to a woman, an American, it seemed, coming for her Audience in a hat edged with white and yellow water-lilies. She had been repulsed successfully by the Papal Guard, but it had left an unpleasant impression.

'How's that?' the Vicar of Christ exclaimed: he enjoyed to tease his Chamberlains—especially Count Cuenca.

The Count turned pale.

'——,' he replied inaudibly, rolling eyes at Lucrezia.

Baron Oschatz had 'deserted' him; and what is one Chamberlain, alas, without another?

'The photographs of your Holiness are beside the bust of Bernini!' he stammered out, beating a diplomatic retreat.

Pope Tertius II addressed his squirrel.

'Little slyboots,' he said, 'I often laugh when I'm alone.'

Concerning the Eccentricities

❈ *V* ❈

BEFORE the white façade of the DunEden Palace, commanding the long, palm-shaded Paseo del Violón, an array of carriages and limousines was waiting; while, passing in brisk succession beneath the portico, like a swarm of brilliant butterflies, each instant was bringing more. Dating from the period of Don Pedro *el cruel*, the palace had been once the residence of the famous Princesse des Ursins, who had left behind something of her conviviality and glamour. But it is unlikely that the soirées of the exuberant and fanciful Princesse eclipsed those of the no less exuberant Duquesa DunEden. It was to be an evening (flavoured with rich heroics) in honour of the convalescence of several great ladies, from an attack of 'Boheara,' the new and fashionable epidemic, diagnosed by the medical faculty as 'hyperæsthesia with complications'; a welcoming back to the world in fact of several despotic dowagers, not one perhaps of whom, had she departed this life, would have been really much missed or mourned! And thus, in deference to the intimate nature of the occasion, it was felt by the solicitous hostess that a Tertúlia (that mutual exchange of familiar or intellectual ideas) would make less demand on arms and legs than would a ball; just the mind and lips . . . a skilful rounding-off here, developing there, chiselling, and putting-out feelers; an evening dedicated to the furtherance of intrigue, scandal, love, beneath the eager eyes of a few young girls, still at school, to whom a quiet party was permitted now and then.

Fingering a knotted scapular beneath a windy arch, Mother Saint-Mary-of-the-Angels was asking God His will. Should she wait for Gloria and Clyte (they might be some time) or return to the convent and come back again at twelve? 'The dear girls are with their mother,' she informed her Maker, inclining respectfully before the Princess Aurora of the Asturias, who had just arrived attended by two bearded gentlemen with tummies.

Hopeful of glimpsing perhaps a colleague, Mother Saint-Mary moved a few steps impulsively in their wake. It was known that Monseigneur the Cardinal-Archbishop himself was expected, and not infrequently one ecclesiastic will beget another.

The crimson saloon, with its scattered group of chairs, was waxing cheery.

Being the day it was, and the social round never but slightly varying, most of the guests had flocked earlier in the evening to the self-same place, i.e. the Circus, or *Arena Amanda,* where it was subscription night, and where, at present, there was an irresistibly comic clown.

'One has only to think of him to——!' the wife of the Minister of Public Instruction exclaimed, going off into a fit of wheezy laughter.

'What power, what genius, what——!' The young wife of the Inspector of Rivers and Forests was at a loss. Wedded to one of the handsomest though dullest of men, Marvilla de las Espinafre's perfervid and exalted nature kept her little circle in constant awe, and she would often be jealous of the Forests (chiefly scrub) which her husband, in his official capacity, was called upon to survey. 'Don't lie to me. I know it! You've been to the woods.' And after his inspection of the aromatic groves of Lograno, Phædra in full fury tearing her pillow with her teeth was nothing to Marvilla. 'Why, dear? Because you've been *among the Myrtles,*' was the explanation she chose to give for severing conjugal relations.

'Vittorio forbids the circus on account of germs,' the wife of the President of the National Society of Public Morals murmured momentously.

'Really, with this ghastly Boheara, I shall not be grieved when the time comes to set out for dear Santander!' a woman with dog-rose cheeks, and puffed, wrinkled eyes, exclaimed, focusing languishingly the Cardinal.

'He is delicious in handsomeness to-night!'

'A shade battered. But a lover's none the worse in my opinion for acquiring technique,' the Duchess of Sarmento declared.

'A lover; what? His Eminence . . . ? ?'

The duchess tittered.

'Why not? I expect he has a little woman to whom he takes off his clothes,' she murmured, turning to admire the wondrous *Madonna of the Mule-mill* attributed to Murillo.

On a wall-sofa just beneath, crowned with flowers and aigrettes, sat Conca, Marchioness of Macarnudo.

'*Que tal?*'

'My joie de vivre is finished; still, it's amazing how I go on!' the Marchioness answered, making a corner for the duchess. She had known her 'dearest Luiza' since the summer the sun melted the

church bells and their rakish, pleasure-loving, affectionate hearts
had dissolved together. But this had not been yesterday; no; for
the Marchioness was a *grandmother* now.

'Conca, Conca: one sees you're in love.'

'He's from *Avila,* dear—the footman.'

'What!'

'Nothing *classic*—but, *oh*!'

'Fresh and blond? I've seen him.'

'Such sep . . .'

'Santiago be praised!'

The Marchioness of Macarnudo plied her fan.

'Our hands first met at table . . . yes, dear; but what I always
say is, one spark explodes the mine!' And with a sigh she glanced
rhapsodically at her fingers, powdered and manicured and en-
crusted with rings. 'Our hands met first at table,' she repeated.

'And . . . and the rest?' the duchess gasped.

'I sometimes wish, though, I resembled my sister more, who cares
only for amorous, "delicate" men—the Claudes, so to speak. But
there it is! And, anyway, dear,' the Marchioness dropped her voice,
'he keeps me from thinking (ah perhaps more than I should) of my
little grandson. Imagine, Luiza . . . Fifteen, white and vivid rose,
and ink-black hair. . . .' And the Marchioness cast a long, pencilled
eye towards the world-famous Pietà above her head. 'Queen of
Heaven, defend a weak woman from *that*!' she besought.

Surprised, and considerably edified, by the sight of the dowager
in prayer, Mother Saint-Mary-of-the-Angels was emboldened to
advance: The lovely, self-willed donkey (or was it a mule?) that
Our Lady was prodding, one could almost stroke it, hear it bray. . . .

Mother Saint-Mary-of-the-Angels could have almost laughed.

But the recollection of the presence of royalty steadied her.

Behind pink lowered portières it had retired, escorted by the
mistress of the house. She wore a gown of ivory-black with heavy
golden roses and a few of her large diamonds of ceremony.

'I love your Englishy-Moorishy cosy comfort, Decima, and I
love——' the Princess Aurora had started to rave.

'An hyperæsthesia injection? . . . a beaten egg?' her hostess
solicitously asked.

'*Per caridad!*' the Princess fluted, stooping to examine a voluptuous
small *terre cuite,* depicting a pair of hermaphrodites amusing themselves.

306

She was looking like the ghost in the Ballet of Ghislaine, after an unusually sharp touch of Boheara; eight-and-forty hours in bed, and, scandal declared, not alone.

'A Cognac? . . . a crème de Chile? . . .'

'Nothing, nothing,' the Princess negligently answered, sweeping her long, primrose trailing skirts across the floor.

It was the boudoir of the Winterhalters and Isabeys, once the bright glory of the Radziwollowna collection, which, after several decades of disesteem, were returning to fashion and favour.

'And I love——' she broke off, nearly stumbling over an old blind spaniel, that resided in a basket behind the 'supposed original' of the *Lesbia of Lysippus*.

'Clapsey, Clapsey!' her mistress admonished. The gift of a dear and once intimate friend, the dog seemed inclined to outlive itself and become a nuisance.

Alas, poor, fawning Clapsey! Fond, toothless bitch. Return to your broken doze, and dream again of leafy days in leafy Parks, and comfy drives and escapades long ago. What sights you saw when you could see; fountains, and kneeling kings, and grim beggars at Church doors (those at San Eusebio were the worst). And sheltered spas by glittering seas: Santander! And dark adulteries and dim woods at night.

'And I love your Winterhalters!'

Beneath one of these, like a red geranium, was Cardinal Pirelli.

'Oh, your Eminence, the utter forlornness of Society! . . . Besides, (oh, my God!) to be the *one* Intellectual of a Town . . .' a wizened little woman, mistaken, not infrequently, for 'Bob Foy,' the jockey, was exclaiming plaintively.

'I suppose?' Monseigneur nodded. He was looking rather like Richelieu, draped in ermines and some old lace of a beautiful fineness.

'It's pathetic how entertaining is done now. Each year meaner. There was a time when the DunEdens gave balls, and one could count, as a rule, on supper. To-night, there's nothing but a miserable Buffet, with flies trimming themselves on the food; and the champagne that I tasted, well, I can assure your Eminence it was more like foul flower-water than Mumm.'

'Disgraceful,' the Cardinal murmured, surrendering with suave dignity his hand to the lips of a pale youth all mouchoir and waist.

307

These kisses of young men, ravished from greedy Royalty, had a delicate savour.

The One Intellectual smiled obliquely.

'Your eminence I notice has several devout salve-stains already,' she murmured, defending her face with her fan.

'Believe me, not all these imprints were left by men!'

The One Intellectual glanced away.

'The poor Princess! I ask you, has one the right to look *so* dying?'

'Probably not,' the Cardinal answered, following her ethereal transit.

It was the turn of the tide, and soon admittance to the boudoir had ceased causing 'heartburnings.'

Nevertheless some few late sirens were only arriving.

Conspicuous among these was Catherine (the ideal-questing, God-groping and insouciant), Countess of Constantine, the aristocratic heroine of the capital, looking half-charmed to be naked and alive. Possessing but indifferent powers of conversation—at Tertulias and dinners she seldom shone—it was yet she who had coined that felicitous phrase: *Some men's eyes are sweet to rest in.*

Limping a little, since she had sprained her foot, alas, while turning backward somersaults to a negro band in the black ballroom of the Infanta Eulalia-Irene, her reappearance after the misadventure was a triumph.

'Poor Kitty: it's a shame to ask her, if it's not a ball!' the Inspector of Rivers and Forests exclaimed, fondling the silvery branches of his moustache.

But, at least, a Muse, if not musicians, was at hand.

Clasping a large bouquet of American Beauty-roses, the Poetess Diana Beira Baixa was being besieged by admirers, to 'give them something; just something! *Anything* of her own.' Wedded, and proclaiming (*in vers libres*) her lawful love, it was whispered she had written a pæan to her husband's '. . . .' beginning *Thou glorious wonder!* which was altogether too conjugal and intimate for recitation in society.

'They say I utter the cry of sex throughout the Ages,' she murmured, resting her free hand idly on a table of gold and lilac lacquer beside her.

The Duchess-Dowager of Vizeu spread prudishly her fan.

'Since me maid set me muskito net afire, I'm just a bunch, me dear, of hysterics,'' she declared.

But requests for 'something; just something!' were becoming insistent, and indeed the Muse seemed about to comply when, overtaken by the first alarming symptoms of 'Boheara,' she fell with a long-drawn sigh to the floor.

⊞ *VI* ⊞

REPAIRING the vast armholes of a chasuble, Madame Poco, the venerable Superintendent-of-the-Palace, considered, as she worked, the social status of a Spy. It was not without a fleeting qualm that she had crossed the borderland that divides mere curiosity from professional vigilance, but having succumbed to the profitable proposals of certain monsignori, she had grown as keen on her quarry as a tigress on the track.

'It's a wearing life you're leading me, Don Alvaro; but I'll have you,' she murmured, singling out a thread.

For indeed the Higher-curiosity is inexorably exacting, encroaching, all too often, on the hours of slumber and rest.

'It's not the door-listening,' she decided, 'so much as the garden, and, when he goes awenching, the Calle Nabuchodonosor.'

She was seated by an open window, commanding the patio and the gate.

'*Vamos, vamos!*' Madame Poco sighed, her thoughts straying to the pontifical supremacy of Tertius II, for already she was the Pope's Poco, his devoted Phœbe, his own true girl: 'I'm true blue, dear. True blue.'

Forgetful of her needle, she peered interestedly on her image in a mirror on the neighbouring wall. It was a sensation of pleasant novelty to feel between her skull and her mantilla the notes of the first instalment of her bribe.

'Earned, every *perra gorda*, earned!' she exclaimed, rising and pirouetting in elation before the glass.

Since becoming the courted favourite of the chapter, she had taken to strutting-and-languishing in private before her mirror, improvising occult dance-steps, semi-sacred in character, modelled on those of Felix Ganay at White Easter, all in the flowery Spring. Ceremonial poses such as may be observed in storied-windows and olden *pietas* in churches (Dalilaesque, or Shulamitish, as the case might be) were her especial delight, and from these had been evolved an eerie 'Dance of Indictment.'

Finger rigid, she would advance ominously with slow, Salomé-like liftings of the knees upon a phantom Cardinal: 'And thus I accuse thee!' or 'I denounce thee, Don Alvaro, for,' etc.

'*Dalila!* You old sly gooseberry,' she chuckled, gloating on herself in the greenish-spotted depth of a tall, time-corroded glass.

Punch and late hours had left their mark.

'All this Porto and stuff to keep awake make a woman liverish,' she commented, examining critically her tongue.

It was a Sunday evening of *corrida*, towards the Feast of Corpus, and through the wide-open window came the near sound of bells.

Madame Poco crossed and recrossed her breast.

They were ringing 'Paula,' a bell which, tradition said, had fused into its metal one of the thirty pieces of silver received by the Iscariot for the betrayal of Christ.

'They seem to have asked small fees in those days,' she reflected, continuing her work.

It was her resolution to divide her reward between masses for herself and the repose and 'release' (from Purgatory) of her husband's soul, while anything over should be laid out on finery for a favourite niece, the little Leonora, away in the far Americas.

Madame Poco plied pensively her needle.

She was growing increasingly conscious of the physical demands made by the Higher-curiosity upon a constitution already considerably far-through, and the need of an auxiliary caused her to regret her niece. More than once, indeed, she had been near the point of asking Charlotte Chiemsee, the maid of the Duchess of Vizeu, to assist her. It was Charlotte who had set the duchess's bed-veils on fire while attempting to nip a romance.

But alone and unaided it was astonishing the evidence Madame Poco had gained, and she smiled, as she sewed, at the recollection of her latest capture—the handkerchief of Luna Sainz.

'These hennaed heifers that come to confess! . . .' she scoffed sceptically. For Madame Poco had some experience of men—those brown humbugs (so delicious in tenderness)—in her time. 'Poor soul! He had the prettiest teeth . . .' she murmured, visualising forlornly her husband's face. He had been coachman for many years to the sainted Countess of Triana, and he would tell the story of the pious countess and the vermin she had turned to flowers of flame while foraging one day among some sacks before a second-hand-clothes shop. It was she, too, who, on another occasion, had changed a handful of marsh-slush into fine slabs of chocolate, each slab engraved with the insignia of a Countess and the sign of the Cross.

'Still, she didn't change *him*, though!' Madame Poco reflected dryly, lifting the lid to her work-box.

Concealed among its contents was a copy of the gay and curious *Memoirs of Mlle. Emma Crunch,* so famous as 'Cora Pearl';—a confiscated bedside-book once belonging to the Cardinal-Archbishop.

'Ps! ps!' she purred, feeling amorously for her scissors beneath the sumptuous oddments of old church velvet and brocade that she loved to ruffle and ruck.

'Ps.'

She had been freshening a little the chasuble worn last by his Eminence at the baptism of the blue-eyed police-pup of the Duquesa DunEden, which bore still the primrose trace of an innocent insult.

'A disgraceful business altogether,' Madame Poco sighed.

Not everyone knew the dog was christened in *white menthe.* . . .

'Sticky stuff,' she brooded: 'and a liqueur I never cared for! It takes a lot to beat aniseed brandy; when it's old. Manzanilla runs it close; but it's odd how a glass or two turns me muzzy.'

She remained a moment lost in idle reverie before the brilliant embroideries in her basket. Bits of choice beflowered brocade, multi-tinted, inimitably faded silks of the epoca of Theresa de Ahumada, exquisite tatters, telling of the Basilica's noble past, it gladdened the eyes to gaze on. What garden of Granada could show a pink to match that rose, or what sky show a blue as tenderly serene as that azure of the Saint Virgin?

'*Vamos,*' she exclaimed, rising: 'it's time I took a toddle to know what he's about.'

She had last seen the Cardinal coming from the orange orchard with a dancing-boy and Father Fadrique, who had a mark on his cheek left by a woman's fan.

Her mind still dwelling on men (those divine humbugs), Madame Poco stepped outside.

Traversing a white-walled corridor, with the chasuble on her arm, her silhouette, illumined by the splendour of the evening sun, all but caused her to start.

311

It was in a wing built in the troublous reign of Alfonso the Androgyne that the vestments were kept. Whisking by a decayed and ancient painting, representing 'Beelzebub' at Home, she passed slowly through a little closet supposed to be frequented by the ghosts of evil persons long since dead. Just off it was the vestry, gay with blue azulejos tiles of an admirable lustre.

They were sounding Matteo now, a little bell with a passionate voice.

'The pet!' Madame Poco paused to listen. She had her 'favourites' among the bells, and Matteo was one of them. Passiaflora, too— but Anna, a light slithery bell, 'like a housemaid in hysterics,' offended her ear by lack of tone; Sebastian, a complaining, excitable bell, was scarcely better,—'a fretful lover!' She preferred old 'Wanda' the Death-bell, a trifle monotonous, and fanatical perhaps, but 'interesting,' and opening up vistas to varied thought and speculation.

Lifting a rosary from a linen-chest, Madame Poco laid the chasuble within. It was towards this season she would usually renew the bags of bergamot among the Primate's robes.

'This espionage sets a woman all behindhand,' she commented to Tobit, the vestry cat.

Black as the Evil One, perched upon a Confessional's ledge, cleansing its belly, the sleek thing sat.

It was the 'ledge of forgotten fans,' where privileged Penitents would bring their tales of vanity, infidelity and uncharitableness to the Cardinal once a week.

'Directing half-a-dozen duchesses must be frequently a strain!' Madame Poco deliberated, picking up a discarded mitre and trying it absently on.

With a plume at the side or a cluster of balls, it would make quite a striking toque, she decided, casting a fluttered glance on the male effigy of a pale-faced member of the Quesada family, hewn in marble by the door.

"*Caramba!* I thought it was the Cardinal; it gave me quite a turn,' she murmured, pursuing lightly her way.

Being a Sunday evening of corrida, it was probable the Cardinal had mounted to his aerie, to enjoy the glimpse of Beauty returning from the fight.

Oh, mandolines of the South, warm throats, and winged songs, winging . . .

Following a darkened corridor with lofty windows closely barred, Madame Poco gained an ambulatory, terminated by a fresco of Our Lady, ascending to heaven in a fury of paint.

'These damp flags'll be the death of me,' she complained, talking with herself, turning towards the garden.

Already the blue pushing shadows were beguiling from the shelter of the cloister eaves the rueful owls. A few flittermice, too, were revolving around the long apricot chimneys of the Palace, that, towards sunset, looked like the enchanted castle of some sleeping Princess.

'Bits of pests,' she crooned, taking a neglected alley of old bay-tree laurels, presided over by a plashing fountain comprised of a Cupid sneezing. Wary of mole-hills and treacherous roots, she roamed along, preceded by the floating whiteness of a Persian peacock, mistrustful of the intentions of a Goat-sucker owl. Rounding a sequestered garden seat, beneath an aged cypress, the bark all scented knots, Madame Poco halted.

Kneeling before an altar raised to the cult of Our Lady of Dew, Cardinal Pirelli was plunged in prayer.

'Salve. Salve Regina. . . .' Above the tree-tops a bird was singing.

⊞⊟ *VII* ⊞⊟

THE College of Noble Damosels in the Calle Santa Fé was in a whirl. It was 'Foundation' day, an event annually celebrated with considerable fanfaronade and social éclat. Founded during the internecine wars of the Middle Age, the College, according to early records, had suffered rapine on the first day of term. Hardly, it seemed, had the last scholar's box been carried upstairs than a troop of military had made its appearance at the Pension gate demanding, with 'male peremptoriness,' a billet. 'I, alone,' the Abbess ingenuously states, in relating the poignant affair in her unpublished diary: 'I alone did all I was able to keep them from them, for which they (the scholars) called me "greedy." ' Adding, not without a touch of modern socialism in disdain for titles, that she had preferred 'the staff-officers to the Field-Marshal,' while as to ensigns, in her estimation, why, 'one was worth the lot.'

Polishing urbanely her delicate nails, the actual President, a staid, pale woman with a peacock nose, recalled the chequered past. She hoped his Eminence when he addressed the girls, on handing them their prizes, would refer to the occasion with all the tactfulness required.

'When I think of the horrid jokes the old Marqués of Illescas made last year,' she murmured, bestowing a harrowed smile on a passing pupil.

She was ensconced in a ponderous fauteuil of figured velvet (intended for the plump posterior of Royalty) beneath the incomparable 'azulejos' ceiling of the Concert-room, awaiting the return of Madame Always Alemtejo, the English governess, from the printers, in the Plaza de Jesus, with the little silver-printed programmes (so like the paste-board cards of brides!), which, as usual, were late.

'Another year we'll type them,' she determined, awed by the ardent tones of a young girl rehearsing an aria from the new opera, *Leda*—'Gaze not on Swans.'

'Ah, gaze not so on Swan-zzz!...'

'Crisper, child. Distinction. Don't exaggerate,' the President enjoined, raising a hand to the diamonds on her heavy, lead-white cheeks.

Née an Arroyolo, and allied by marriage with the noble house of Salvaterra, the headmistress in private life was the Dowager-Marchioness of Pennisflores.

'*Nosotros,* you know, are not candidates for the stage! Bear in mind your moral,' she begged, with a lingering glance at her robe of grey georgette.

The word 'moral,' never long from the President's lips, seemed, with her, to take on an intimate tinge, a sensitiveness of its own. She would invest the word at times with an organic significance, a mysterious dignity, that resembled an avowal made usually only in solemn confidence to a doctor or a priest.

The severity of my moral. The prestige of my moral. The perfection of my moral. She has no dignity of moral. I fear a person of no positive moral. Nothing to injure the freshness of her moral. A difficulty of moral. The etiquette of my moral. The majesty of my moral, etc., etc.—as uttered by the President, became, psychologically, interesting *data*.

'Beware of a facile moral!' she added, for the benefit of the singer's accompanist, a young nun with a face like some strange white rock, who was inclined to give herself married airs, since she had been debauched, one otiose noon, by a demon.

'Ah, Madame Always.' The President swam to meet her.

British born, hailing from fairy Lisbon, Madame Always Alemtejo seemed resigned to live and die in a land of hitches.

'The delay is owing to the Printers' strike,' she announced. 'The Plaza's thronged: the Cigar factory girls, and all the rag-tag and bobtail, from the Alcazaba to the Puerta del Mar, are going out in sympathy, and——'

'The tarts?'

'The t's from Chamont are on the way.'

It was the President's custom to lay all vexations before Nostra Señora de los Remedios, the college's divine Protectress, with whose gracious image she was on the closest footing.

Consulting her now as to the concert-programmes, the President recalled that no remedy yet had been found for Señorita Violeta de las Cubas, who had thrown her engagement ring into a place of less dignity than convenience and refused to draw it out.

'Sapphires, my favourite stones,' the President reflected, wondering if she should ask 'la Inglese' to recover it with the asparagus-tongs.

But already a few *novios,* eager to behold their *novias* again, were in the Patio beneath the 'Heiresses' Wing,' exciting the connoisseurship of a bevy of early freshness.

'You can tell *that* by his eyebrows!' a girl of thirteen, and just beginning as a woman, remarked.

'*Que barbaridad.*'

'Last summer at Santander Maria-Manuela and I bathed with him, and one morning there was a tremendous sea, with *terrific* waves, and we noticed unmistakably.'

'I can't explain; but I adore all that mauvishness about him!'

'I prefer Manolito to Gonzalito, though neither thrill me like the Toreador Tancos.'

Assisted by Fräulein Pappenheim and Muley, the President's negress maid, they were putting the final touches to their vestal frocks.

'Men are my raging disgust,' a florid girl of stupendous beauty declared, saturating with a flacon of *Parfum cruel* her prematurely formed silhouette.

'Nsa, nsa, señorita,' Muley mumbled. 'Some know better dan dat!'

'To hell with them!'

'*Adios,* Carlo. *Adios,* Juan. Join you down dah in one minute.' The negress chuckled jauntily.

'Muley, Muley,' Fräulein chided.

'What wonder next I 'bout to hear?'

Delighting in the tender ferocities of Aphrodite, she was ever ready to unite the *novio* to the *novia.* For window-vigils (where all is hand play) few could contrive more ingeniously than she those fans of fresh decapitated flowers, tuberose punctuated with inebriating jasmine, so beloved in the East by the dark children of the sun. Beyond Cadiz the blue, the beautiful, in palm-girt Marrakesh, across the sea, she had learnt other arts besides. . . .

'Since seeing Peter Prettylips on the screen the Spanish type means nothing to me,' Señorita Soledad, a daughter of the first Marqués of Belluga, the greatest orange-king in the Peninsula, remarked.

'How low. She is not noble.'

'I *am* noble.'

'Oh no; you're not.'

'Cease wrangling,' Fräulein exclaimed, 'and enough of that,' she added sharply, addressing a *novio*less little girl looking altogether bewitching of naughtiness as she tried her ablest to seduce by her crude manœuvres the fiancé of a friend. Endowed with the lively temperament of her grandmother, Conca, Marchioness of Macarnudo, the impressionable, highly amative nature of the little Obdulia gave her governesses some grounds for alarm. At the Post Office one day she had watched a young man lick a stamp. His rosy tongue had vanquished her. In fact, at present, she and a class-chum, Milagros, were 'collecting petals' together—and much to the bewilderment of those about them, they might be heard on occasion to exclaim, at Mass, or in the street: 'Quick, did you see it?' 'No.' 'Santissima! *I* did!'

'Shrimp. As if Gerardo would look at her!' his *novia* scoffed. 'But let me tell you, young woman,' she turned upon the shrinking Obdulia, 'that social ostracism, and even, in certain cases' (she slapped and pinched her), '*assassination* attends those that thieve or tamper with another's lover! And Fräulein will correct me if I exaggerate.'

Fräulein Pappenheim was a little woman already drifting towards

the sad far shores of forty, with no experience of the pains of
Aphrodite caused by men; only at times she would complain of
stomach aches in the head.

'Dat is so,' Muley struck in sententiously for her. 'Dair was once
a young lady ob Fez——'

But from the Patio the college chaplain, Father Damien Forment,
known as 'Shiny-nose,' was beckoning to the heiresses to join their
relatives in the reception-hall below.

Since that sanguinary period of Christianity, synchronising with
the foundation of the institution of learning in the Calle Santa Fé,
what changes in skirts and trousers the world has seen. Alone
unchanging are women's ambitions and men's desires.

'Dear child. . . . She accepts him . . . but a little à contre-cœur,'
the President was saying to the Marchioness of las Cubas, an im-
poverished society belle, who went often without bread in order to
buy lip-sticks and rouge.

'With Violeta off my hands . . . Ah, President, if only Cecilio
could be suitably *casada.*'

'In my little garden I sometimes work a brother. The heiresses'
windows are all opening to the flowers and trees. . . . The boy should
be in polo kit. A uniform interests girls,' the President murmured,
turning with an urbane smile to welcome the Duquesa DunEden.

She had a frock of black kasha, signed Paul Orna, with a cluster of
brown-and-pink orchids, like sheep's-kidneys, and a huge feather hat.

'I'm here for my God-girl, Gloria,' she murmured, glancing
mildly round.

Incongruous that this robust, rich woman should have brought
to the light of heaven no heir, while the unfortunate Marchioness,
needy, and frail of physique, a wraith, did not know what to do with
them!

The President dropped a sigh.

She was prepared to take a dog of the daughterless Duquesa.
A bitch, of course. . . . But let it be Police, or Poodle! It would
lodge with the girls. A cubicle to itself in the heiresses' wing; and
since there would be no extra class-charge for dancing or drawing,
no course *in belli arti*, some reduction of fees might be arranged. . . .
'We would turn her out a creature of breeding. . . . An eloquent
tail-wave, a disciplined moral, and with a reverence moreover for
house-mats and carpets.' The President decided to draw up the
particulars of the prospectus by and by.

'Your Goddaughter is quite one of our most promising exhibitioners,' she exclaimed, indicating with her fan some water-colour studies exposed upon the walls.

'She comes of a mother with a mania for painting,' the Duquesa declared, raising a lorgnon, critically, before the portrait of a Lesbian, with dying, fabulous eyes.

'Really?'

'A positive passion,' the Duquesa answered, with a swift, discerning glance at an evasive 'nude,' showing the posterior poudrederizé of a Saint.

'I had no idea,' the President purred, drawing attention to a silvery streetscape.

'It's the Rambla from the back of Our Lady of the Pillar! It was rare fun doing it, on account of the *pirapos* of the passers-by,' the artist, joining them, explained.

'Dear child, I predict for her a great deal of admiration very soon,' the President murmured, with a look of reproach at a youthful pupil as she plied her boy-Father with embarrassing questions: 'Who are the chief society women in the moon? What are their names? Have they got motor-cars there? Is there an Opera-House? Are there bulls?'

The leering aspect of a lady in a costume of blonde Guadalmedina lace and a hat wreathed with clipped black cocks' feathers arrested her.

Illusion-proof, with a long and undismayed service in Love's House (sorry brutes, all the same, though, these men, with their selfishness, fickleness and lies!) the Marchioness of Macarnudo with her mysterious 'legend' (unscrupulous minxes, all the same, though, these women, with their pettiness, vanity and . . . !), was too temperamentally intriguing a type to be ignored.

'Isn't that little Marie Dorothy with the rosebuds stuck all over her?' she asked her granddaughter, who was teasing her brother on his moustache.

'To improve the growth, the massage of a *novia's* hand,' she fluted, provoking the marchioness to an involuntary nervous gesture. Exasperated by resistance, struggling against an impossible infatuation, her Spanish ladyship was becoming increasingly subject to passing starts. Indeed only in excitement and dissipation could her unsatisfied longings find relief. Sometimes she would run out in her car to where the men bathe at Ponte Delgado, and one morning, after a ball, she had been seen standing on the main road to Cadiz in a cabochon tiara, watching the antics of some nude muleteers: *Black as young Indians*—she had described them later.

'My sweet butterfly! What next?' she exclaimed, ogling Obdulia, whose elusive resemblance to her brother was really curiously disturbing.

Averting a filmy eye, she recognised Marvilla de las Espinafre, airing anti-patriotic views on birth control, her arms about an adopted daughter. 'Certainly not; most decidedly *no*! I should scream!' she was saying as from the Concert-room the overture began thinning the crowd.

'It's nothing else than a national disaster,' the marchioness declared to her grandson, 'how many women nowadays seem to shirk their duty!'

'Well, the de las Cubas hasn't, anyway,' he demurred.

'Poor thing. They say she jobs her mules,' the marchioness murmured, exchanging a nod with the passing President.

Something, manifestly, had occurred to disturb the equilibrium of her moral.

'Such a disappointment, *Nostra Señora*!' she exclaimed. 'Monseigneur, it seems, has thrown me over.'

'Indeed; how awkward!'

'I fear though even more so for his chapter.'

'He is not ill?'

'*Cardinal Pirelli has fled the capital!*'

❂❂ *VIII* ❂❂

STANDING amid gardens made for suffering and delight is the disestablished and, *sic transit,* slowly decaying monastery of the Desierto. Lovely as Paradise, oppressive perhaps as Eden, it had been since the days of the mystic Luigi of Granada a site well suited to meditation and retreat. Here, in the stilly cypress-court, beneath the snowy sierras of Santa Maria la Blanca, Theresa of Avila, worn and ill, though sublime in laughter, exquisite in beatitude, had composed a part of the *Way of Perfection,* and, here, in these same realms of peace, dominating the distant city of Clemenza and the fertile plains of Andalucia, Cardinal Pirelli, one blue mid-day towards the close of summer, was idly considering his Defence. '*Apologia*, no; merely a defence,' he mused: 'merely,' he flicked the ash-tip of a cigar, 'a defence! I defend myself, that's all! . . . '

A sigh escaped him.

Divided by tranquil vineyards and orange-gardens from the malice and vindictiveness of men it was difficult to experience emotions other than of forgiveness and love.

'Come, dears, and kiss me,' he murmured, closing consentingly his eyes.

It was the forgetful hour of noon, when Hesperus from his heavens confers on his pet Peninsula the boon of sleep.

'A nice nap he's having, poor old gentleman.' Madame Poco surveyed her master.

Ill at ease and lonely in the austere dismantled house, she would keep an eye on him at present almost as much for company as for gain.

As handsome and as elegant as ever, his physiognomy in repose revealed a thousand strange fine lines, suggestive subtleties, intermingled with less ambiguous signs, denoting stress and care.

'He's growing almost huntedish,' she observed, casting a brief glance at the literature beside him—The Trial of Don Fernando de la Cerde, Bishop of Barcelona, defrocked for putting young men to improper uses; a treatise on The Value of Smiles; an old volume of Songs, by Sà de Miranda; The Lives of Five Negro Saints, from which escaped a bookmark of a dancer in a manton.

'Everything but his Breviary,' she commented, perceiving a soutaned form through the old flowered ironwork of the courtyard gateway.

Regretting her better gown of hooped watered-silk, set aside while in retreat (for economy's sake), Madame Poco fled to put it on, leaving the visitor to announce himself.

The padre of Our Lady of the Valley, the poor padre of Our Lady, would the Primate know? Oh, every bird, every rose, could have told him that: the padre of Our Lady bringing a blue trout for his Eminence's supper from the limpid waters of Lake Orense.

Respecting the Primate's rest Father Felicitas, for so, also, was he named, sat down discreetly to await his awakening.

It was a rare sweetness to have the Cardinal to himself thus intimately. Mostly, in the city, he would be closely surrounded. Not that Father Felicitas went very much to town; no; he disliked the confusion of the streets, and even the glories of the blessed basilicas made him scarcely amends for the quiet shelter of his hills.

The blessed basilicas, you could see them well from here. The giralda of Saint Xarifa, and the august twin towers of the cathedral, and the azulejos dome of Saint Eusebio, that was once a pagan mosque; while of Santissima Marias, Maria del Carmen, Maria del Rosario, Maria de la Soledad, Maria del Dolores, Maria de las Nieves, few cities in all the wide world could show as many.

'To be sure, to be sure,' he exclaimed absently, lifting his eyes to a cloudlet leisurely pointing above the lofty spur of the Pico del Mediodia. 'To be sure,' he added, seeking to descry the flower-like bellcot of Our Lady of the Valley just beneath.

But before he had discovered it, half concealed by trees, he was reminded by the sound of a long-drawn, love-sick wail, issuing out of the very entrails of the singer, of the lad left in charge of his rod by the gate.

                    'On the Bridge to Alcantara.'

With its protracted cadences and doleful, vain-yearning reaches, the voice, submerged in all the anguish of a Malagueña, troubled, nostalgically, the stillness.

God's will be done. It was enough to awaken the Primate. Not everyone relished a Malagueña, a dirgeful form of melody introduced, tradition said, and made popular in the land, long, long ago, beneath the occupation of the Moors.

Father Felicitas could almost feel the sin of envy as he thought of the flawless choir and noble triumphal organ of the cathedral yonder.

Possessed of no other instrument, Our Lady of the Valley depended at present on a humble guitar. Not that the blessed guitar, with its capacity for emotion, is unworthy to please God's listening ear, but Pepe, the lad appointed to play it, would fall all too easily into those Jotas, Tangos, and Cuban Habaneiras, learnt in wayside fondas and fairs. Some day, Father Felicitas did not doubt, Our Lady would have an organ, an organ with pipes. He had prayed for it so often; oh, so often; and once, quite in the late of twilight while coming through the church, he had seen her, it seemed, standing just where it should be. It had been as though a blinding whiteness.

'A blinding whiteness,' he murmured, trembling a little at the recollection of the radiant vision.

Across the tranquil court a rose-red butterfly pursued a blue. 'I believe the world is all love, only no one understands,' he meditated, contemplating the resplendent harvest plains steeped in the warm sweet sunlight.

'My infinite contrition!' The Cardinal spoke.

A rare occurrence in these days was a visitor, and now with authority ebbing, or in the balance at least, it was singular how he felt a new interest in the concerns of the diocese. The birth-rate and the death-rate and the super-rate, which it was to be feared that the Córtes——

Sailing down the courtyard in her watered-silken gown, Madame Poco approached with Xeres and Manzanilla, fresh from the shuttered snowery or nieveria.

'And I've just buried a bottle of champagne, in case your Eminence should want it,' she announced as she inviolably withdrew.

'As devoted a soul as ever there was, and loyal to all my interests,' the Primate exclaimed, touched.

'God be praised!'

'An excellent creature,' the Cardinal added, focusing on the grey high road beyond the gate two youths on assback, seated close.

'Andalucians, though of another parish.'

'I should like much to visit my diocese again; it's some while since I did,' the Cardinal observed, filling the Padre's glass.

'You'd find up at Sodré a good many changes.'

'Have they still the same little maid at the Posada de la Melodia?'

'Carmencita?'

'A dainty thing.'

'She went Therewards about the month of Mary.'

'America? It's where they all go.'

'She made a ravishing corpse.'

'Ahi.'

And Doña Beatriz too had died; either in March or May. It was she who would bake the old Greek Sun-bread, and although her heirs had sought high and low no one could find the receipt.

The Cardinal expressed satisfaction.

'Bestemmia,' he breathed; 'and I trust they never may; for on the Feast of the Circumcision she invariably caused to be laid before the high-altar of the cathedral a peculiarly shaped loaf to the confusion of all who saw it.'

And the Alcalde of Ayamonte, Don Deniz, had died on the eve

of the bachelors' party he usually gave when he took off his winter beard.

'Ahi; this death . . .'

Ah, yes, and since the delicacies ordered by the corpse could not well be countermanded they had been divided among Christ's poor.

Left to himself once more Cardinal Pirelli returned reluctantly to his Defence.

Half the diocese it seemed had gone 'Therewards,' while the rest were at Biarritz or Santander. . . .

'A nice cheery time this is!' he murmured, oppressed by the silent cypress-court. Among the blue, pointing shadows, a few frail oleanders in their blood-rose ruby invoked warm brief life and earth's desires.

'A nice cheery time,' he repeated, rising and going within.

The forsaken splendour of the vast closed cloisters seemed almost to augur the waning of a cult. Likewise the decline of Apollo, Diana, Isis, with the gradual downfall of their temples, had been heralded, in past times, by the dispersal of their priests. It looked as though Mother Church, like Venus or Diana, was making way in due turn for the beliefs that should follow: 'and we shall begin again with intolerance, martyrdom and converts,' the Cardinal ruminated, pausing before an ancient fresco depicting the eleven thousand virgins, or as many as there was room for.

Playing a lonely ball game against them was the disrespectful Chicklet.

'Young vandal,' the Cardinal chided, caressing the little acolyte's lustrous locks.

'Monseigneur? . . .'

'There: run along; and say a fragrant prayer for me, Child.'

Flinging back a shutter drawn fast against the sun, the boundless prospect from the balcony of his cell recalled the royal Escorial. The white scattered terraces of villas set in dark deeps of trees, tall palms, and parasol-pines so shady, and, almost indistinguishable, the white outline of the sea, made insensibly for company.

Changing into a creation of dull scarlet crêpe, a cobweb dubbed 'summer-exile,' Cardinal Pirelli felt decidedly less oppressed. 'Madrid is on the Manzanares,' he vociferated, catching sight of the diligence from Sodré. Frequently it would bring Frasquito, the postman—a big tawny boy, overgiven to passing the day in the woods with his gun and his guitar.

'The mail bag is most irregular,' he complained, fastening a few dark red, almost black, roses to his cincture. It was Cardinal Pirelli's fancy while in retreat to assume his triple-Abraham, or mitre, and with staff in hand to roam abroad as in the militant Springtide of the Church.

'When kings were cardinals,' he murmured quietly as he left the room.

It was around the Moorish water-garden towards shut of day he liked most to wander, seeking like some Adept to interpret in the still deep pools the mirrored music of the sky.

All, was it vanity? These pointing stars and spectral leaning towers, this mitre, this jewelled ring, these trembling hands, these sweet reflected colours, white of daffodil and golden rose. All, was it vanity?

Circling the tortuous paths like some hectic wingless bird, he was called to the refectory by the tintinnabulation of a bell.

In the deep gloominous room despoiled of all splendour but for a dozen old Zurbarans flapping in their frames, a board, set out with manifest care, was prepared for the evening meal.

Serving both at Mass and table, it was the impish Chicklet who, with a zealous napkin-flick (modelled on the *mozos* of the little café-cum-restaurant 'As in Ancient Andalucia' patronised by rising toreadors and *aficionados* of the Ring), showed the Primate to his chair.

Having promised José the chef a handsome indulgence, absolved him from bigamy, and raised his wages, Cardinal Pirelli, in gastronomy nothing if not fastidious, had succeeded in inducing him to brave the ghostly basements of the monastery on the mount.

Perhaps of the many charges brought against the Primate by his traducers, that of making the sign of the cross with his left foot at meals was the most utterly unfounded—looking for a foot-cushion would have been nearer the truth.

Addressing the table briefly in the harmonious Latin tongue, his Eminence sat down with an impenetrable sigh.

With vine-sprays clinging languorously to the candle-stands, rising from a bed of nespoles, tulips, and a species of wild orchid known as Devil's-balls, the Chicklet, to judge from his floral caprices, possessed a little brain of some ambition, not incapable of excess.

'I thought you were tired of jasmine, sir, and th'orange bloom's getting on,' he chirruped, coming forward with a cup of cold, clear consommé, containing hearts, coronets and most of the alphabet in vermicelli.

'I'm tired, true, child; but not of jasmine,' the Primate returned, following the little contretemps of a marqués' crown, sinking amid a frolicsome bevy of *O's*.

'I hope it's right, sir?'

'Particularly excellent, child—tell José so.'

'Will I bring the trout, sir?'

'Go, boy,' the Cardinal bade him, opening a volume by the menu-stand formed of a satyr sentimentalising over a wood-nymph's breasts.

While in retreat it was his fancy, while supping, to pursue some standard work of devotion, such as Orthodoxy so often encourages or allows: it was with just such a golden fairy-tale as this that he had once won a convert: Poor woman. What had become of her? Her enthusiasm, had it lasted? She had been very ardent. Perfervid! 'Instruction' would quite wear it out of them. Saint Xarifa's at fall of day; . . . an Autumn affair! Chrysanthemums; big bronze frizzlies. A Mrs. Mandarin Dove. American. Ninety million sterling. Social pride and religious humility, how can I reconcile? The women in Chicago. My God! ! ! My little step-daughter. . . . Her Father, fortunately. . . . Yes, your Eminence, he's dead. And, oh, I'm *glad*. Is it naughty? And then her photograph à la Mary of Magdala, her hair unbound, décolletée, with a dozen long strands of pearls. 'Ever penitently yours, Stella Mandarin Dove.'

'I'd rather have had the blonde Ambassadress to the Court of St. James', he reflected, toying with the fine table-glass of an old rich glamour. A fluted bell cup sadly chipped provoked a criticism and a citation from Cassiodorus on the 'rude' ways of boys.

Revolving around an austere piece of furniture that resembled a Coffin-upon-six-legs, the Chicklet appeared absorbed.

'I hear it's the Hebrew in heaven, sir. Spanish is seldom spoken,' he exclaimed seraphically.

'Tut, dear child. Who says so?' the Primate wondered, his eyes wandering in melancholy towards the whitest of moons illumining elusively the room—illumining a long, sexless face with large, mauve, heroic lips in a falling frame, and an 'apachey,' blue-cheeked Christ, the Cardinal noticed.

'Who, sir? Why, a gentleman I was guide to once!'

The Cardinal chuckled comprehensively.

'I should surmise, dear child, there was little to show.'

'What, not the crypt, sir? Or the tomb of the beautiful Princess Eboli, the beloved of Philip the Second, sir?'

'Jewel boy. Yum-yum.' The Cardinal raised his glass.

'And the bells, sir? Last night, I'll tell you, sir, I thought I heard old "Wanda" on the wind.'

'Old Wanda, boy?'

'She rings for deaths, sir.'

'Nonsense, child; your little ears could never hear as far,' the Cardinal answered, deliberating if a lad of such alertness and perception might be entrusted to give him a henna shampoo: it was easy enough to remove the towels before it got too red. The difficulty was to apply the henna; evenly everywhere; fair play all round; no favouring the right side more than the left, but golden Justice for each grey hair. Impartiality: proportion! 'Fatal, otherwise,' the Primate reasoned.

'Are you ready for your Quail, sir?'

'Quail, quail? Bring on the *dulces*, boy,' his Eminence murmured, regarding absently through the window the flickering arc-lights of Clemenza far away. Dear beckoning lamps, dear calling lamps; lamps of theatres, cinemas, cabarets, bars and dancings; lamps of railway-termini, and excessively lit hotels, *olé* to you, enchantress lights!

'And, after all, dears, if I did,' the Cardinal breathed, tracing a caricature of his Holiness upon the table-cloth lightly with a dessert-fork. ('Which I certainly deny' . . .), he brooded, disregarding the dissolving Orange ice *à la* Marchioness of Macarnudo.

'Had you anything in the Lottery, sir?'

'Mind your business, boy, and remove this ballroom nastiness,' the Primate snapped.

It was while lingering, after dinner, over some choice vintage, that he oftenest would develop the outline of his Defence. To escape the irate horns of the Pontiff's bull (Die, dull beast) he proposed pressing the 'Pauline Privilege,' unassailable, and confirmed *A.D. 1590* by Pope Sixtus V, home to the battered beauty of the Renaissance hilt. 'With the elegance and science,' he murmured, 'of a *matador*.'

'I have the honour to wish you, sir, a good and pleasant night.'

'Thanks, boy.'

'And if you should want me, sir' . . . the youthful acolyte possessed the power to convey the unuttered.

'If?? . . . And say a fragrant prayer for me, child,' the Cardinal enjoined.

Resting an elbow among the nespoles and tulips (dawn-pink and scarlet, awakening sensitively in the candle-glow), he refilled reflectively his glass.

'God's providence is over all,' he told himself, considering dreamfully a cornucopia heaped with fruit. Being just then the gracious Autumn, a sweet golden-plum called 'Don Jaime of Castile' was in great perfection. It had been for the Southern orchards a singularly fertile year. Never were seen such gaily rouged peaches, such sleek, violet cherries, such immensest white grapes. Nestling delectably amid its long, deeply-lobed leaves, a pomegranate (fruit of joy) attracted the Cardinal's hand.

Its seeds, round and firm as castanets, evoked the Ortiz 'Ah, Jesus-Maria. The evening she waved her breasts at me!' he sighed, attempting to locate the distant lights of the Teatro Trinidades. Interpreting God's world, with her roguish limbs and voice, how witching the child had been but lately in *The Cestus of Venus*. Her valse-refrain 'Green Fairy Absinthe' (with a full chorus in tights) had been certainly, theatrically (if, perhaps, not socially), the hit of the season.

'The oleanders come between us,' he deliberated, oppressed by the amative complaint of some sweet-throated, summer night-bird.

'It's queer, dears, how I'm lonely!' he exclaimed, addressing the ancient Zurbarans flapping austerely in their frames.

The Archbishop of Archidona, for all his air of pomposity, looked not unsympathetic, neither, indeed, did a little lady with a nimbus, casting melting glances through the spokes of a mystic wheel.

'It's queer—; you'd be surprised!' he murmured, rising and setting an oval moon-backed chair beside his own.

As usual the fanciful watch-dogs in the hills had begun their disquieting barking.

'The evenings are suicide,' he ruminated, idly replenishing his glass.

Sometimes, after the fifth or sixth bumper, the great Theresa herself would flit in from the garden. Long had her radiant spirit 'walked' the Desierto, seeking, it was supposed, a lost sheet of the manuscript of her *Way of Perfection*. It may have been following on the seventh or even the eighth bumper that the Primate remarked he was not alone.

She was standing by the window in the fluttered moonshine, holding a knot of whitish heliotropes.

'Mother?'

Saint John of the Cross could scarcely have pronounced the name with more wistful ecstasy.

Worn and ill, though sublime in laughter, exquisite in tenderness she came towards him.

'. . . Child?'

'Teach me, oh, teach me, dear Mother, the Way of Perfection.'

⊞⊞ *IX* ⊞⊞

VERIFYING private dates, revising here and there the cathedral list of charges, Don Moscosco, the secretary of the chapter, seated before his usual bureau, was at the disposal of the public. A ministerial crisis had brought scattered Fashion home to town with a rush, and the pressure of work was enormous. 'Business' indeed had seldom been livelier, and chapels for Masses of special intention were being booked in advance as eagerly as opera-boxes for a première, or seaside-villas in the season.

'If the boys are brisk we might work in Joseph,' he mused, consulting with closely buttoned lips his Tarifa and plan; 'although I'd rather not risk a clash.'

Unknown to double-let like his compères on occasion outside, the swarthy little man was a master organiser, never forgetting that the chapter's welfare and prestige were inseparable from his own. Before allotting a chapel for a mass of Intent, it was his rule to analyse and classify the 'purity' of the intention (adding five per cent. where it seemed not altogether to be chaste, or where the purpose was 'obscure').

'I see no inconvenience,' he murmured, gauging delicately the motif of a couple of great ladies of the bluest blood in Spain who were commissioning masses for the safety of a favourite toreador in an approaching *corrida*.

'Five hundred flambeaux, at least, between them,' the secretary, negligently, spat.

It was the twenty-first day of September (which is the Feast of Saint Firmin), and the sacrista, thronged with mantons and monsignori, resembled some vast shifting parterre of garden-flowers. Having a little altercation together, Mother Mary of the Holy Face and Mother Garcia of the Company of Jesus, alone, seemed stable. In honour of Saint Firmin the door of Pardon (closed half the year) had just been thrown open, bringing from the basilica an odour of burning incense and the strains of a nuptial march.

How many of the bridal guests knew of the coffin installed in the next chapel but one? the little man wondered, rising gallantly to receive a client.

She wore no hat, but a loose veil of gold and purple enveloped her hair and face.

'I fear for him!'

'There, there. What is it?'

'I fear for him'—a man and the stars, nights of sweet love, oleander flowers were in her voice.

By her immense hooped earrings, as large as armlets, he knew her for the Adonira, the mistress of the toreador Tancos.

'Come to me after the Friday miserere,' the official objected: 'let me entreat an appointment.'

'No. Now.'

'Well.'

'I want a Mass.'

'The intention being ... ?' The secretary sent up his brows a little.

'His safety.'

'Whose?'

'My lover's.'

'But, señorita, it's all done! It's all *done,* dear lady,' the words were on Don Moscosco's lips. Still, being the pink of chivalry with *las mujares* and a man of business, he murmured: 'With what quantity of lights?'

'Two. Just for him and me.'

'Tell me how you would prefer them,' he exclaimed, glancing whimsically towards the canvas of the Magdalen waylaying our Lord.

'How I would——' she stammered, opening and closing the fansticks in her painted, love-tired hands.

'You would like them long and, I dare say, gross?'

'The best,' she breathed, almost fainting as though from some fleeting delicious vision in the air.

'Leave it to me,' Don Moscosco said, and dropping expressively his voice he added: 'Come, señorita; won't you make a date with me?'

'A date with you?'

'Ah-hah, the little Juans and Juanas; the charming cherubs!' the secretary archly laughed.

Returning however no answer, she moved distractedly away.

'Two tapers! *Two*. As many only as the animal's horns. It's amazing how some women stint,' he reflected, faintly nettled.

The marriage ceremony was over. From the summit of the giralda, volley on volley, the vibrant bells proclaimed the consummation.

'It was all so quick; I hope it's valid?' Madame la Horra, the mother of the 'Bride,' looked in to say. With a rose mole here and a strawberry mole there, men (those adorable monsters) accounted her entirely attractive.

'As *though* we should hurry, as *though* we should clip!'

'Ah?'

'As though we were San Eusebio, or the Pilar!'

'Forgive me, I came only to—I, . . . I, . . . I, . . . I think I cried. The first spring flowers looked so beautiful.'

A mother's love, and contrition, perhaps, for her own short-comings, the secretary brooded. 'I shall knock her off five per cent.'

Lost in bland speculation Don Moscosco considered the assembly collected outside the curtained *camarin* of the Virgin, where the gowns of the Image were dusted and changed.

For Firmin she usually wore an osprey or two and perfumed ball-gloves of Cordoba, and carried a spread fan of gold Guadalmedina lace. Among devotees of the sacrista it was a perpetual wonder to observe how her costumes altered her. Sometimes she would appear quite small, dainty and French, at others she would recall the sumptuous women of the Argentine and the New World, and aficionados would lament their fairy isle of Cuba in the far-off Caribbean Sea.

Traversing imperiously the throng, Don Moscosco beheld the Duquesa DunEden.

Despite the optimism of the gazettes it looked as though the Government must indeed be tottering, since the Duquesa too was up from her country quinta.

'I have a request to make,' she began, sinking gratefully to a chair.

'And charmed, in advance, to grant it.'

'I suppose you will have forgotten my old spaniel, Clapsey?'

'Ah, no more dogs!'

'She is passing-out, poor darling; and if the Church could spare her some trifling favour——'

'Impossible.'

'She is the first toy tail for my little cemetery!'

'Quite impossible.'

'Poor pet,' the Duquesa exclaimed undaunted: 'she has shared in her time my most intimate secrets: she stands for early memories; what rambles we'd go together, she and I, at Santander long ago! I remember Santander, Don Moscosco (imagine), when there was not even an hotel! A little fishing-village, so quiet, so quiet; ah, it was nicer, far, and more exclusive then. . . .'

'I dare say.'

'You know my old, blind and devoted friend was a gift from the king; and this morning I said to her: "Clapsey! Clapsey!" I said: "where's Carlos? Car-los . . . ?" And I'll take my oath she rallied.'

Don Moscosco unbent a shade: 'A token, is she, of royalty?'

'He also gave me "Flirt"!'

'Perhaps a brief mass . . .'

'Poor dearest: you'll keep it quiet and black?'

'We say all but the Black.'

'Oh?'

'One must draw the line somewhere!' Don Moscosco declared, his eye roving towards a sacristan piloting a party of travel-stained tourists, anxious to inspect the casket containing a feather from the Archangel Gabriel's wing.

'I know your creative taste! I rely on you,' the Duquesa rose remarking.

Nevertheless, beneath the routine of the sacristia the air was surcharged with tension. Rival groups, pro- or anti-Pirellian, formed almost irreconcilable camps, and partisanship ran high. Not a few among the cathedral staff had remained true to his Eminence, and Mother Sunlight, a charwoman (who sometimes performed odd jobs at the Palace), had taught her infant in arms to cry: 'Long live Spain and Cardinal Pirelli!'

Enough, according to some extreme anti-Pirellians, to be detrimental to her milk.

'I'm told the Pope has sent for him at last,' the laundress of the Basilica, Doña Consolacion, remarked to Sister June of the Way Dolorous.

'Indeed, indeed; it scarcely does to think!'

'Does anyone call to mind a bit of a girl (from Bilbao she was) that came once to stop as his niece?'

'Inclined to a moustache! Perfectly.'

'Phœbe Poco protests she wasn't.'

'Ah, well; a little *Don Juanism* is good,' the laundress said, and sighed.

'She declares . . .'

'She tells the truest lies, dear, of anyone I know!'

'Be that as it may it's certain he's getting increasingly eccentric But Sunday last, entertaining his solicitor, it seems he ordered coffee after the merienda to be served in two chamber-pots.'

'Shameful—and he in his sunset years!' Mother Mary of the Holy Face commented, coming up with Tomás the beadle.

'It wouldn't surprise me,' he declared, drowsily shaking a heavy bouquet of keys, 'if the thread of his life was about to break.'

'*Hombre* . . .' The laundress expressed alarm.

'Often now, towards Angelus, as I climb the tower, I hear the bell Herod talking with old Wanda in the loft. Eeeeeeee! Eeeeeeee! Horrible things they keep saying. Horrible things they keep saying.'

'Nonsense,' Doña Consolacion exclaimed, bestowing a smile on Monsignor Cuxa. Old, and did-did-doddery, how frail he seemed beside Father Fadrique, the splendid swagger of whose chasuble every woman must admire.

'Sent for to Rome; ah, *sangre mio*, I wish someone would send for me,' a girl, with a rose in the hair beautifully placed, sighed romantically.

'Be satisfied with Spain, my dear, and remember that no other country can compare with it!' Doña Generosa, an Aunt of one of the cathedral dancing-boys (who drew a small pension as the widow of the late Leader of applause at the Opera-house), remonstrated.

'I've never travelled,' Doña Consolacion blandly confessed: 'but I dare say, dear, you can't judge of Egypt by *Aïda*.'

'Oh, can't I, though?' Doña Generosa sniffed, as the Father of an acolyte raised his voice.

'Spain!' he exclaimed, exalted, throwing a lover's kiss to the air, 'Spain! The most glorious country in God's universe, His admitted masterpiece, His gem, His——' He broke off, his eloquence dashed by the sad music of Monsignor Cuxa's hæmorrhage.

An office in the Chapel of the Crucifix was about to begin, recalling to their duties the scattered employees of the staff.

Hovering by the collection-box for the Souls in Hades, the Moorish maid from the College of Noble Damosels, bound on an errand of trust as ancient as the world, was growing weary of watching the people come and go.

'I must have missed him beneath the trees of the Market Place,' she ruminated, straightening on her head a turban wreathed in blossoms.

It was the matter of a message from Obdulia and Milagros to the radiant youth whose lips they were so idyllically (if perhaps somewhat licentiously) sharing.

'Fo' sh'o dis goin' to put dose heiresses in a quandry,' she deliberated, oppressed by her surroundings.

Eastern in origin like the Mesquita of Cordoba, it was impossible to forget that the great basilica of Clemenza was a Mosque profaned.

Designed for the cult of Islam, it made her African's warm heart bleed to behold it now. Would it were reconverted to its virginal state, and the cry of the muezzin be heard again summoning men to Muhammad's house! Yes, the restitution of the cathedral to Allah was Muley's cherished dream, and it consoled her, on certain days when she was homesick, to stand before the desecrated mihrab in worship, her face turned towards Africa, and palm-girt Marrakesh across the sea.

'I almost inclined to slip across to de Café Goya,' she breathed, moving aside for a shuffling acolyte, bearing a crucifix on a salver.

Led by the pious sisters of the noble order of the Flaming-Hood, the Virgin was returning to her niche.

She was arrayed as though bound for the Bull-ring, in a robe of peacock silk, and a mantilla of black lace.

'*Santissima!* . . .'

'*Elegantissima!*' Devotees dropped adoring to the floor.

Alone, the African remained erect.

'Muhammad mine, how long?' she sighed, turning entreating eyes to the cabbalistic letters and Saracenic tracings of the azulejos arabesques.

Concerning the Eccentricities

❊❊ *X* ❊❊

MIDNIGHT had ceased chiming from the Belfry tower, and the last seguidilla had died away. Looking fresh as a rose, and incredibly juvenile in his pyjamas of silver-grey and scarlet (the racing colours of Vittoria, Duchess of Vizeu), the Cardinal seemed disinclined for bed.

Surveying in detachment the preparatives for his journey (set out beneath an El Greco Christ, with outspread, delicate hands), he was in the mood to dawdle.

'These for the Frontier. Those for the train,' he exclaimed aloud, addressing a phantom porter.

Among the personalia was a passport, the likeness of identity showing him in a mitre, cute to tears, though, essentially, orthodox; a flask of Napoleon brandy, to be 'declared' if not consumed before leaving the Peninsula; and a novel, *Self-Essence*, on the Index, or about to be.

'A coin, child, and put them for me on the rack,' he enjoined the wraith, regarding through the window the large and radiant stars.

The rhythmic murmur of a weeping fountain filled momentously the night.

Its lament evoked the Chicklet's sobs.

'Did I so wrong, my God, to punish him? Was I too hasty?' the Primate asked, repairing towards an ivory crucifix by Cano; 'yet, Thou knowest, I adore the boy!'

He paused a moment astonished by the revelation of his heart.

'It must have been love that made me do it,' he smiled, considering the incident in his mind. Assuredly the rebuff was unpremeditated, springing directly from the boy's behaviour, spoiling what might have been a ceremony of something more than ordinary poignance.

It had come about so.

There had been held previously during the evening, after the Basilica's scheduled closing hour, a service of 'Departure,' fastidiously private, in the presence only of the little Ostensoir-swinger 'Chicklet,' who, missing all the responses, had rushed about the cathedral after mice; for which the Cardinal, his sensitiveness hurt

334

by the lad's disdain and frivolity, had afterwards confined him alone with them in the dark.

'Had it been Miguilito or Joaquin, I should not have cared a straw for their interest in the mice! But somehow this one——' the Cardinal sighed.

Adjusting in capricious abstraction his cincture, he turned towards the window.

It was a night like most.

Uranus, Venus, Saturn showed overhead their wonted lights, while in the sun-weary cloisters, brightly blue-drenched by the moon, the oleanders in all their wonder—(how swiftly fleeting is terrestrial life)—were over, and the bougainvillæas reigned instead.

'It must have been that,' he murmured, smiling up at the cathedral towers.

Poor little Don Wilful. The chapter-mice, were they something so amusing to pursue? 'I've a mind, do you know, to join you, boy; I declare I feel quite rompish!' he told himself, gathering up, with a jocund pounce, a heavy mantle of violet cloth-of-gold.

'Tu-whit, tu-whoo.'

Two ominous owls answered one another across the troubled garden.

'I declare I feel——' his hand sought vaguely his heart: it went pit-a-pat for almost nothing now! 'The strain of the diocese,' he breathed, consulting a pier-glass of the period of Queen Isabella 'the Ironical.'

'The Court may favour Paul Orna, but in my opinion no one can rival Joey Paquin's "line"; I should like to see him "tailor" our Madonna; one of the worst and most expensively dressed little saints in the world,' his Eminence commented, folding toga-wise the obedient tissues about his slender form.

An aspect so correctly classic evoked the golden Rome of the Imperial Caesars rather than the so tedious Popes.

Repeating a sonorous line from Macrobius, the Cardinal measured himself a liqueur-glass of brandy.

Poor little Don Bright-eyes, alone in the obscurity. It was said a black dervish 'walked' the Coro—one of the old habitués of the Mosque.

'Jewel-boy. Yum-yum,' he murmured, setting a mitre like a wondrous mustard-pot upon his head. *Omnia vanitas;* it was intended for Saint Peter's.

'Tu-whit, tu-whoo!'

Grasping a Bishop's stave, remotely shepherdessy, his Eminence opened softly the door.

Olé, the Styx!

Lit by Uranus, Venus and Saturn only, the consummate tapestries on the stairs recording the Annunciation, Conception, Nativity, Presentation, Visitation, Purification and Ascension of the Virgin made welcome milestones.

' . . . Visitation, Purification.' The Primate paused on the penultimate step.

On a turn of the stair by the 'Conception,' a sensitive panel, chiefly white, he had the impression of a wavering shadow, as of someone following close behind.

Continuing, preoccupied, his descent, he gained a postern door. A few deal cases, stoutly corded for departure, were heaped about it. 'His Holiness, I venture to predict, will appreciate the excellence of our home-grown oranges, not to be surpassed by those of any land,' the Primate purred, sailing forth into the garden.

Oh, the lovely night! Oh, the lovely night! He stood, leaning on his wand, lost in contemplation of the miracle of it.

'Kek, kek, kex.'

In the old lead aqua-butt, by the Chapter-house, the gossiping bull-frogs were discussing their great horned and hoofed relations. . . .

'There was never yet one that didn't bellow!'

'Kek, kek, kex.'

'*Los toros,* forsooth!'

'A blessed climate. . . .' The Primate pursued his way.

It was in the face of a little door like the door of a tomb in the cathedral's bare façade (troubled only by the fanciful shadows of the trees) that he presently slipped his key.

Olé, the Styx!

He could distinguish nothing clearly at first beyond the pale forked fugitive lightning through the triple titanic windows of the chancel.

'Sunny-locks, Don Sunny-locks?' the Cardinal cooed, advancing diffidently, as though mistrustful of meeting some charwoman's pail.

Life had prepared him for these surprises.

Traversing on his crozier a spectral aisle, he emerged upon the nave.

Flanked by the chapels of the Crucifix, of the Virgin, of the Eldest Son of God, and of divers others, it was here as bright as day.

Presumably Don April-showers was too self-abashed to answer, perhaps too much afraid. . . . 'If I recollect, the last time I preached was on the theme of Flagellation,' the Primate mused, considering where it caught the moon the face of a fakir in ecstasy carved amid the corbels.

'A sermon I propose to publish,' he resolved, peering into the chapel of Santa Lucia. It was prepared, it seemed, in anticipation of a wedding, for stately palms and branches of waxen peach-bloom stood all about. 'Making circulation perilous,' the Primate mused, arrested by the determined sound of a tenacious mouse gnawing at a taper-box.

'An admirable example in perseverance!' he mentally told himself, blinking at the flickering mauve flowers of light in the sanctuary lamps.

Philosophising, he penetrated the engrailed silver doors connecting the chapel of the Magdalen.

The chapel was but seldom without a coffin, and it was not without one now.

Since the obsequies of the brilliant Princess Eboli it had enjoyed an unbroken vogue.

Besides the triumphal monument of the beloved of Philip II, the happy (though, perhaps, not the happiest) achievement of Jacinto Bisquert, there were also mural tablets to the Duchesses of Pampeluna (*née* Mattosinhos), Polonio (*née* Charona), and Sarmento (*née* Tizzi-Azza), while the urn and ashes of the Marchioness of Orcasitas (*née* Ivy Harris) were to be found here too, far from the race and turmoil of her native New York.

'Misericordia! Are you there, boy?' the Cardinal asked, eyeing abstractedly the twin hooded caryatides that bore the fragile casket white as frozen snow containing the remains of the all-amiable princess.

Folded in dainty sleep below, he perceived the lad.

Witching as Eros, in his loose-flowing alb, it seemed profane to wake him!

'. . . And lead us not into temptation,' the Primate murmured, stooping to gaze on him.

Age of bloom and fleeting folly: Don Apple-cheeks!

Hovering in benison he had almost a mind to adopt the boy, enter him for Salamanca, or, remoter, Oxford, and perhaps (by some bombshell codicil) even make him his heir.

'How would you like my Velasquez, boy? . . .' His Eminence's hand framed an airy caress. 'Eh, child? Or my Cano Crucifix? . . . I know of more than one bottle-nosed dowager who thinks she'll get it! . . . You know my Venetian-glass, Don Endymion, is among the choicest in Spain. . . .'

There was a spell of singing silence, while the dove-grey mystic lightning waxed and waned.

Aroused as much by it as the Primate's hand, the boy started up with a scream of terror.

'Ouch, sir!'

'Olé, boy?'

The panic appeared to be mutual.

'Oufarella! . . .' With the bound of a young faun the lad was enskied amid the urns and friezes.

The heart in painful riot, the Primate dropped to a chair.

Ouching, Oléing and Oufarellaing it, would they never have done? Paternostering Phœbe Poco (shadowing her master) believed they never would. 'Old ogre: why can't he be brisk about it and let a woman back to bed?' she wondered.

Thus will egotism, upon occasion, eclipse morality outright.

'And always be obedient, dear child,' the Cardinal was saying; 'it is one of the five things in Life that matter most.'

'Which are the others, sir?'

'What others, boy?'

'Why, the other four!'

'Never mind now. Come here.'

'Oh, tral-a-la, sir.' Laughing like some wild spirit, the lad leapt (Don Venturesome, Don Venturesome, his Eminence trembled) from the ledge of A Virtuous Wife and Mother (Sarmento, *née* Tizzi-Azza) to the urn of Ivy, the American marchioness.

'You'd not do that if you were fond of me, boy!' The Cardinal's cheek had paled.

'But I *am* fond of you, sir! Very. Caring without caring: don't you know?'

'So you do care something, child?'

'I care a lot!...'

Astride the urn of Ivy—poised in air—the Chicklet pellucidly laughed.

'Tell me so again,' the Cardinal begged, as some convent-bell near by commenced sounding for office before aurora.

For behind the big windows the stars were fading.

'It's to-day they draw the Lottery, sir.'

'Ah; well, I had nothing in it....'

'ooo50—that's me!'

The Cardinal fetched a breath.

'Whose is it, boy?' He pointed towards the bier.

'A Poet, sir.'

'A Poet?'

'The name, though, he had escapes me....'

'No matter then.'

'Where would his soul be now, sir?'

'Never mind, boy; come here.'

'In the next world I should like to meet the Cid, and Christopher Columbus!'

'Break your neck, lad, and so you will.'

'Pablo Pedraza too....'

'Who's that, boy?'

'He was once the flower of the ring, sir; superior even to Tancos; you may recollect he was tossed and ruptured at Ronda; the press at the time was full of it.'

'Our press, dear youth, our press!!!...' the Primate was about to lament, but an apologetic sneeze from a chapel somewhere in the neighbourhood of the Eldest Son of God arrested him.

It seemed almost to confirm the legend of old, Mosque-sick 'Suliman,' said to stalk the temple aisles.

The Cardinal twirled challengingly his stave—*Bible* v. *Koran*; a family case; cousins; Eastern, equally, each; hardy old perennials, no less equivocal and extravagant, often, than the ever-adorable *Arabian Nights*! 'If only Oriental literature *sprawled* less, was more concise! It should concentrate its roses,' he told himself, glancing out, enquiringly, into the nave.

Profoundly soft and effaced, it was a place full of strange suggestion. Intersecting avenues of pillared arches, upbearing waving banners, seemed to beckon towards the Infinite.

'Will you be obliged to change, sir; or shall you go straight through?'

'Straight through, boy.'

'I suppose, as you cross the border, they'll want to know what you have to declare.'

'I have nothing, child, but myself.'

'If ooo5o is fortunate, sir, I hope to travel, too—India, Persia, Peru! !... Ah, it's El Dorado, then.'

'El Dorado, boy?' The Cardinal risked an incautious gesture.

'Oh, tral-a-la, sir.' Quick as Cupid the lad eluded him on the evasive wings of a laugh; an unsparing little laugh, sharp and mocking, that aroused the Primate like the thong of a lash.

Of a long warrior line, he had always regarded disobedience (in others) as an inexcusable offence. What would have happened before the ramparts of Zaragoza, Valladolid, Leon, Burgos, had the men commanded by Ipolito Pirelli in the Peninsular War refused to obey? To be set at defiance by a youngster, a mere cock-robin, kindled elementary ancestral instincts in the Primate's veins.

'Don't provoke me, child, again.'

From pillared ambush Don Prudent saw well, however, to effect a bargain.

'You'd do the handsome by me, sir; you'd not be mean?'

'Eh? . . .'

'The Fathers only give us texts; you'd be surprised, your Greatness, at the stinginess of some!'

' . . .?'

'You'd run to something better, sir; you'd give me something more substantial?'

'I'll give you my slipper, child, if you don't come here!' his Eminence warned him.

'Oufarella. . . .'

Sarabandish and semi-mythic was the dance that ensued. Leading by a dozen derisive steps Don Light-of-Limb took the nave. In the dusk of the dawn it seemed to await the quickening blush of day like a white-veiled negress.

'Olé, your Purpleship!'

Men (eternal hunters, novelty seekers, insatiable beings), men in their natural lives, pursue the concrete no less than the ideal— qualities not seldom found combined in fairy childhood.

'Olé.'

Oblivious of sliding mantle the Primate swooped.

Up and down, in and out, round and round 'the Virgin,' over the worn tombed paving, through Saint Joseph, beneath the cobweb banners from Barocco to purest Moorish, by early Philip, back to Turân-Shâh—'Don't exasperate me, boy'—along the raised tribunes of the choristers and the echoing coro—the great fane (after all) was nothing but a cage; God's cage; the cage of God! . . .

Through the chancel windows the day was newly breaking as the oleanders will in spring.

Dispossessed of everything but his fabulous mitre, the Primate was nude and elementary now as Adam himself.

'As you can perfectly see, I have nothing but myself to declare,' he addressed some phantom image in the air.

With advancing day Don Skylark *alias* Bright-eyes *alias* Don Temptation it seemed had contrived an exit, for the cathedral was become a place of tranquillity and stillness.

'Only myself.' He had dropped before a painting of old Dominic Theotocópuli, the Greek, showing the splendour of Christ's martyrdom.

Peering expectantly from the silken parted curtains of a confessional, paternostering Phœbe Poco caught her breath.

Confused not a little at the sight before her, her equilibrium was only maintained by the recollection of her status: 'I'm an honest widow; so I know what men are, bless them!' And stirred to romantic memories she added: 'Poor soul, he had the prettiest teeth. . . .'

Fired by fundamental curiosity, the dame, by degrees, was emboldened to advance. All over was it, with him, then? It looked as though his Eminence was far beyond Rome already.

'May God show His pity on you, Don Alvaro of my heart.'

She remained a short while lost in mingled conjecture. It was certain no morning bell would wake him.

'So.' She stopped to coil her brier-wood chaplet about him in order that he might be less uncovered. 'It's wonderful what us bits of women do with a string of beads, but they don't go far with a gentleman.'

Now that the ache of life, with its fevers, passions, doubts, its routine, vulgarity, and boredom, was over, his serene, unclouded face was a marvelment to behold. Very great distinction and sweetness was visible there, together with much nobility, and love, all magnified and commingled.

'*Adios*, Don Alvaro of my heart,' she sighed, turning away towards the little garden door ajar.

Through the triple windows of the chancel the sky was clear and blue—a blue like the blue of lupins. Above him stirred the wind-blown banners in the Nave.

Printed in the United States
85495LV00001B/9/A